PURGED IN FIRE

SARAH HEGGER

COPYRIGHT

Copyright © 2021 by Sarah Hegger
All rights reserved.
No part of this book may be reproduced in any form or by any electronic or mechanical means, including information storage and retrieval systems, without written permission from the author, except for the use of brief quotations in a book review.

Cover: Deranged Doctor Design

ISBN: 9798750675128

❀ Created with Vellum

DEDICATION

Vir Ronel

Baie dankie vir al die ondersteuning.
Dit beteken soveel, en hierdie een is vir jou.

ACKNOWLEDGMENTS

This book has taken a while to make it to publications Both personally and professionally, it's been a hard year for me, and it would be remiss not to acknowledge the people who have gotten me through.

To Chris Kennedy, for always being you and for knowing what's bothering me before I do (and also for never saying *I told you so*.) Your friendship means more than I can express.

To Tara Cromer, who has been a constant and unwavering source of professional knowledge and support. For the friendship that we've forged that has meant so much.

To Penny Barber, for always working her editing magic, and giving me her time and wisdom.

To my family, who are my everything. One day at a time, sometimes one breath at a time, we made it through.

And to my readers, who so patiently—and yes, you really were patient—waited for this book and greeted its arrival with unmitigated delight. Many of you have walked this journey with me for a while now, and you're the reason I got myself back in front of a keyboard.

1

Niamh's fur ruffled in a freshening breeze, and beneath her paws, the earth pressed cool and damp. She raised her face to the cold full moon, distant and so achingly beautiful. The moon called to her, reaching silvery remote rays within Niamh and illuminating the dark barren center of her.

Persistent danger pressed past the gnawing isolation, and she scented for the source. Air quickened across her nostrils and brought the night's olfactory bouquet—brine, tree sap, humus, bark, a vole, older rabbit droppings, and the lingering scent markings of a deer. That last made her heart pump thick with the thrill of the hunt, but she wasn't hungry.

Life, abundant and busy, was happening all about her, yet she stood alone beneath the temptress moon. She had no litter; she had no pack; she had no mate. Surrounded by all creatures irrevocably drawn to her magic, she stood. Alone.

From within her, solitude pressed out, stretching her skin as if it could no longer be contained. Niamh threw back her head and howled. She howled to the moon who had forsaken her. She howled the ache of her loneliness.

From the west, the wind brought a faint answering howl.

He comes.

Niamh woke with a start and sat up. "Shit!"

Her neck had stiffened from falling asleep on the desk. She'd drooled on the six-hundred-year-old journal she'd been reading, and she carefully dabbed at the spot with the sleeve of her wooly jumper.

"He comes?" Her voice echoed in the cavernous library.

A fox poked her head around the large leather sofa and blinked at her.

"Yup." Niamh stopped dabbing. "Not a clue either."

The fox sat and tucked her tail around her forepaws. Cocking her head, she fixed bright topaz eyes on Niamh.

"You've got a point," she said to the fox. "I could be desperate for that special someone." She felt like a twit for even thinking as much.

A skinny tortoiseshell cat leaped sure and soft pawed onto the manuscript and butted Niamh's chin with her head. Her straggly tail tickled Niamh's nose.

Obediently, Niamh stroked the cat's spine. "Yes, I always have you lot."

It helped. Her animals anchored her as life at Baile flash-changed what felt like daily. Sometimes Niamh wanted to flip the pages back, back to when life had seemed so much simpler, back to when they'd all been blissfully unaware of the peril gathering around them.

The cat dropped to her side next to some long-dead cré-witch's diary that Niamh had been plodding through. The blunt tip of the cat's tail twitched as she tried to outstare the fox.

Niamh had volunteered to do research, and the rest of the coven had snatched up her offer. Movement drew her gaze to the large vellum map on the wall above the hearth. A weasel scurried across the mantel, stopped in the center, and stared up at the map.

More questions. Niamh sighed. "I know."

The weasel started and froze. The fox stood and scented the air. Even the cat bestirred herself to widen her eyes. That map meant something. She sensed it, as did her furry companions.

"I feel it too," Niamh said. "There's something there." But what? Reading through pages and pages of dead witches' journals and notes had unearthed nothing.

"Oops." Her drool had smudged a few words of the long - dead Siobhan's neatly penned recipe for bramble jam. It was now anyone's guess how many cups of sugar would be needed. "Sorry about that, but it's not like it's the only one in here."

Siobhan's innermost secrets, or rather lack of secrets, were the reason she'd dropped off in the first place. Nothing but recipes— with a puzzling obsession with bramble jam—household tips and useless bits of gossip that made no sense to Niamh out of context.

Exhibit A: *Mary is up to her nonsense again.* Or even more confounding: *P and S still not speaking to L. If only they knew what I know.* What had L done to earn not being spoken to and what salacious secret had Siobhan been hiding about the three of them? Goddess, Niamh wished Siobhan had written down the good stuff. Bookshelves towered above her on three sides. All that knowledge and no answers.

The coven was relying on her to find something, anything, that could help them locate the cardinal power point for the fire element. And all she'd found was how to make bramble jam, several ways.

"Goddess, this could all be a waste of time." She poked the manuscript away from her.

The cat gave the manuscript a languid paw pat.

Like in her dream, Niamh wanted to throw back her head, open her throat and howl to the moon outside the window.

Tonight's dream left her even more confused and on edge. Who was coming and why? Also, that howl still echoed in her mind. A wolf's howl, which was impossible because wild wolves had been extinct in England since the sixteen-hundreds. Her power did not link her with mythical beings, only the living and breathing variety. She wished Baile had another guardian who she could ask. All she had was Roz, and although technically a guardian, Roz was...well...not all there.

So many questions, not enough answers, and time continued whipping past.

Only six witches left, where once there had been hundreds, and the task ahead of them pressed down like a poised stampede. For all those hundreds and hundreds of years the coven had been at full strength and functioning, every witch had been trained and worked her blessing with all four cardinal elemental points providing the power. Witches of old had reached for their power like she would flip a light switch. Also like electricity, they had taken that power for granted so much that nobody had considered where the power came from. Certainly, nobody had bothered to record the locations of the cardinal points.

A couple months ago, Bronwyn had activated the water point, right here in the caverns beneath Baile. Right away she, Mags, Sinead, and Alannah, had all looked for their cardinal points, but nothing doing. Fire, air, and earth points were not within Baile's wards. Which point they should find and activate next had been hotly contested. However, both Niamh and Maeve called fire, and that had been the clincher. Now the search was on for fire, and they needed to get there before Rhiannon found it, because she would destroy it and they'd lose fire magic forever.

Beyond the tranquility of the moonlit night, Niamh sensed the ever-present animals around her. Like her, they were restless tonight, tapping at the outer edges of her consciousness and trying to get her attention.

Propping her chin on her hand, Niamh took a deep breath and stared into the blaze nestled in the great hearth. A warm night made the fire superfluous, but having her element around comforted her.

She'd definitely howled with a wolf in her dream. Believing the impossible had become habit the last few weeks at Baile. Maybe, somehow, a wolf had survived here, protected by the wards. The idea lit her up inside with tiny fireflies of excitement. She let her awareness spread like creeping mist. Sights, sounds, and scents all assaulted her as the closest animals shared their perceptions with her. The cat was bored, the fox alert, and the weasel wanted to return to the forest. She expanded her search outside the walls of Baile and into the land beyond. A tsunami of senses rushed her and made her tummy lurch.

She breathed to steady herself and pulled fire. Her magic reached for her with hungry, happy tendrils, dancing and gamboling and teasing her with the more she couldn't access yet. Flames in the hearth flared higher, pushing out a blast of heat, as she drew deeper on her element. The sweet tangy earth tones of basil and strawberry surrounded her.

Her magic, her *precious*.

Thomas popped into sight in front of the table. "Guardian?" He raised an eyebrow in silent warning. "Too much."

Goddess! So bloody frustrating. She pulled a face at Thomas and reduced her magic to a thin ribbon.

With a pop, the flames subsided to gently flickering.

"Better." Thomas perched a hip against her desk, looking so corporeal his thigh seemed to conform to the harder wood surface. His jeans even bunched and pleated as if he were flesh and blood. Thomas had updated his garb since Roderick had taken up modern clothing. He cocked his head. "They're rest-less tonight."

Niamh sifted through the sensory overload still battering her mind. The diurnal animals were tucked into their dens and burrows, so she blocked their input and concentrated on the nocturnals venturing into the night on the business of survival. She quested to the outside of her perception. Fresh wind carried the scents of the village of Greater Littleton, exhaust fumes, dinners being cooked, humans and their offspring.

Strong apex energy pressed at her mind and drifted away. She glanced at Thomas. "What was that?"

"An old friend." He winked, an enigmatic smirk lighting his handsome face. Bloody ghosts with their cryptic statements.

Thomas grinned as if he'd read her mind, and said, "There have to be some advantages to my current state."

"How about the whole invisibility thing?" She shoved the edge of a large tome at his thigh. The book passed right through the illusion of his body.

"What do they want, Guardian?" He waved a hand about them. "What's got the animals all excited?"

"Not sure yet." Niamh turned her attention inward. Straw-berries and basil scented the air as she used her magic. The animals were disturbed, no...excited, expectant.

A face flashed into her mind. Hard, angular lines, pale blue eyes, cropped hair. The face vanished.

Niamh gasped and sat back. She couldn't have seen a face. Her blessing didn't work like that. She could ride along in an animal's awareness and see the world from their minds, but they didn't send her visions. They bloody well never sent her images of strange men, at least not ones floating along in a vacuum, and they also never howled at the moon when they didn't exist anymore.

Thomas studied her face. "What?"

She shook her head, not knowing how to make sense of it. "They showed me a person."

"What was this person doing?" Thomas leaned closer.

"Nothing." If Thomas laughed, she'd...well, she didn't know what she'd do because he'd poof out of there if she tried anything. "It wasn't someone they were watching; it was just a face."

Thomas raised one of his dark, sculpted brows. "They don't do that."

"I know that." Thanks to Thomas for stating the glaringly obvious. "But they did this time."

"Hmm." Thomas stood and paced to the hearth. "A man?"

"Yes." She got the sense he was saying less than he knew. "You know what that means, don't you?"

Face inscrutable, he stared into the fire. "There's another of us coming."

"Ghosts?" Niamh rather thought one of those was enough. Especially if they were all like Thomas.

"No." He chuckled. "Another brother."

Excitement fluttered through her chest. "You mean another coimhdeacht?"

"Hmm." Thomas shrugged. "I had this sense..." He took a breath. "I should speak to Roderick first. As leader of the coimhdeacht, he might be feeling the new one as well."

Another coimhdeacht. Another warrior guardian headed for Baile, which meant he would bond with a witch. *He comes.* Could that be what her dream wolf had been telling her? "Who's he coming for?"

Please say me, please say me. She almost couldn't allow herself to hope. A person for her, and not one compelled by her guardian magic to like her.

"Only he knows that." Thomas grinned. "The warrior finds the witch, remember."

Niamh let what she thought of that show on her face. "I

don't see why it's got to be that way around. It's probably some sexist hangover from your time."

"If you don't like it, take it up with Goddess." Thomas's grin widened. "I need to speak with Roderick."

Poof.

"Nice chatting." Niamh called to the empty spot by the hearth. "Bye now. Enjoy the rest of your night."

Roz stuck her head around the library door and blinked at Niamh. *Whoo-ah-whoo.*

A familiar tightening clenched Niamh's gut. Her aunt, but not her aunt. The animals' disturbance would have affected Roz. Niamh reached for Roz's mind and found the confusion of owl and human, both were hungry. Motioning her aunt closer, she rattled a container of cheese, nuts and fruit. "Come on then. Dinner time."

Roz cocked her head and locked eyes on the container.

Click, vrrrt, click. She skittered closer and hopped onto the desk.

Wood protested the weight of an adult woman perched on its edge. Built sturdy to accommodate men of Roderick's size, the desk blessedly didn't tip.

The cat hissed, leaped off the desk and flounced away. The fox disappeared back behind the couch.

"Here." Niamh held up a grape, and Roz ate it from her hand.

Roz swallowed and turned her head a sickening two hundred and seventy degrees before coming back and bobbing her head at Niamh.

Niamh held up a walnut and cheddar combo. If she let Roz feed from the container, food would fly across the library. Despite her being stuck in the awareness of a barn owl, Roz's human mouth didn't peck and pick up food like a beak would.

"What's the plan for tonight?" Niamh couldn't even remember what Roz's human voice sounded like anymore.

She'd been an owl for so many years now. Her aunt had always been strange, but Roz had helped Niamh explore her guardian gift when she was a child. Roz had held the pieces of her together after Niamh's mother had died.

Click, click, click. Roz bobbed her head for more food. *Vrrt.*

"More mouse chasing?" She gave her another grape, followed by a block of cheese. "Just remember no eating them."

Whohooo-ah. Roz lifted and dropped her shoulders.

Goddess, that had been disgusting when she'd found Roz slurping down a half-chewed rat carcass. Not an experience she'd care to have again in a hurry. Also, why she made sure to feed Roz.

She never knew how much of Roz was left inside the owl. There were times when Roz veered close enough to human that she communicated. Those were the worst times, because it was too easy to hope Roz would come back to her. As it was, Roz was her living, breathing cautionary tale, the reason Thomas warned her against using too much magic. When she activated the fire cardinal point and could bond her magic to Goddess, she could use the full extent of her gift, safe in the knowledge it was grounded through Goddess and would never consume her as it had Roz.

As she ate, Roz peered over her shoulder at Siobhan's journal.

"I don't think we need to bother with starching your pinafores. I have a hard enough time keeping you in clean knickers and nightshirts." She gave Roz more cheese. With the owl's preference for an all-meat diet, balancing Roz's diet was a challenge. "Any ideas where to look next?"

Roz did her icky head twist and shimmied like she was settling feathers.

"Me neither." Niamh sighed. Wasted time niggled at her. "And if we can't find the bugger, we can't activate it, which is bad news for me and even worse news for you."

Click vrrrt whooo-ha-ha. Roz looked almost apologetic.

If Niamh could access her full gift, she might be able to reach Roz and bring her back to them. As coven healer, and the only witch able to have the use of her full blessing thus far, Bronwyn had offered to look into it as well. "We'll find the answer, Roz."

Roz lifted her shoulders and shuddered.

"Did you see the man?" She gave Roz the last grape. "The one in my mind."

Roz cocked her head and bobbed. She met Niamh's stare.

Strong jaw, high cheekbones, beaky nose, and those penetrating eyes staring at her as if they could see her.

"You did." Niamh leaned closer, barely daring to breathe. "You saw him too?"

2

CRÉ-WITCH CHRONICLES

W arren hunched over, leaned his elbows on his knees and kept his gaze focused on the brown and gray checked floor beneath his boots. He followed a crack in the linoleum to a set of platter-sized boots to his left. He shouldn't have come to group today but faced with group or pacing the confines of his shitty flat he'd gone with the meeting. That and the court order demanding he make time for Gary and their band of misfits. Debra certainly didn't need any more ammunition against him handed to her.

The minute hand on the clock over the double doors at the far end of the church hall hesitated and then dropped to twenty-three past, another thirty-seven minutes before he could make his escape. Most meetings he got something out of, but not today. Today he just wanted to pass unnoticed.

Making yourself small could be challenging when you were six foot four and weighed somewhere in the region of two-fifty. Still, Warren kept trying to be inconspicuous enough not to be noticed by Gary of the everything's-going-to-come-up-daisies smile and desperate need for Warren to share his feelings.

Warren's feelings boiled and stewed beneath his skin. If he opened his mouth, they would vomit from him, fueled by rage at his impotence against his ex's latest decree.

The thing was, Gary would look at him with those wounded puppy eyes, and Warren wanted to tell him something, anything, to make him feel better. It didn't take much. Gary ran their anger management slash inmates getting reintroduced to society support group, and he'd settle for anything that wasn't unbridled aggression or homicidal rage.

Gary was shit out of luck on both counts with Warren. He'd overtaken both unbridled aggression and homicidal rage on his way to bullet-chewing fury. Not that his fury would do him any good. Debra had decided to keep Taylor from him, and there was fuck all he could do about it. His own past actions had given her enough fuel to win care and custody of their daughter, and Debra's brutal thirst for revenge made her wield the only weapon she had that could still draw his blood, his little girl, the sodding light of his fucking life.

"The bitch is on my back all day long." Patrick had held the talking stick for the past ten minutes. "Nagging at me about getting a bloody job. On my case when I want a rest. I need to rest. I got health issues."

Patrick would have larger health issues soon if he didn't shut it.

Warren could do with a scapegoat, and Patrick's familiar gripe and high-pitched nasal whine volunteered him for the position. Either that, or Warren could snatch the talking stick and stab his own ears so he wouldn't have to listen to any more of this.

"Thank you, Patrick." Gary's ever-hopeful voice cut into Patrick's tirade about his wife. "Does anybody want to respond to Patrick?"

Big mistake, Gary. Big.

Halfway through Patrick's narrative, Warren had sensed

Jack's building need to respond to Patrick. The big bastard sitting next to Warren was also known as Slick Jack, Jack the Sicko, and Psycho Jack. Not particularly original nicknames, but straight to the heart of Jack's ruling MO. Jack's Street rep included fists, boots and/or biting. Unless he liked you, and then all that aggression sat firmly at your back. He and Jack had sized each other up on Warren's first day at group and reached detente by a chin jerk of agreement that it would hurt too much to go any other way. By week three, he and Jack had been sharing a pint after group.

Warren had a brief fantasy about going full Jack, but that's what had landed him for a brief stint behind bars, followed by group. According to the law, and Debra, his temper made him a danger to society, and now Taylor.

Aching desperation gnawed at him at the idea of days without Taylor in them. Fuck knew how long Debra could keep this up.

"Yeah." Jack's voice came out poured over hot gravel. "I got a response."

"Lovely," Gary chirped, finally sounding wary. "Would you...um...like to share?"

Jack shifted his shoulders. "I—"

"Sorry, Jack." Gary grimaced and sat up straighter. "I would like to take this opportunity to remind everyone that this is a neutral space." The corners of his mouth jerked up in his wince-smile. "An accepting space in which there is no right or wrong, only feelings." Pleading smile in Jack's general direction. "Carry on, Jack."

"Right." Jack sniffed and shifted his weight. "Respectfully then, Patrick. You're a sniveling, whining piece of shit and your old lady should toss you out on your fucking ear."

Speak it, mate. For the first time that day, Warren wanted to laugh.

"Hey!" Patrick kept the protest low-key. Smart lad and

proving that not only did Patrick have the personality of a cockroach, but their survival instincts as well.

"You got yourself sent down when she was pregnant with your fourth kid." At least Jack was still using his words. "Left her a single mum." Group gossip murmured that Jack was the son of a single mother and had a huge soft spot for them. "What's the fucking matter with you? Get off your lazy arse and get yourself a job. You ain't too good for honest work." Jack sniffed. "And buy some fucking condoms. Your missus don't need another kid."

"Um...Jack." Gary swallowed. "With respect. Neutral space." Gary made tight circles with his forefingers. "Feelings." He blinked. "No right or wrong."

"What a load of bollocks." Jack crossed his tree-trunk arms over his barrel chest and glowered at Gary. "Taking care of your missus and the kids is the right thing to do."

Gary, who couldn't weigh more than one-twenty soaking wet, managed to hold Jack's stare. It was classic David and Goliath stuff. In this case David wilted back in his chair and looked ready to cry.

"Anybody else like to share?" Puppy dog eyes swung in his direction. The ever-fervent hope shining bright in Gary. "Warren?"

Ah, shit and bollocks! All gazes snapped his way, including Jack's. A question lingered in Jack's eyes.

"Later," he murmured.

Jack nodded

"I'm fine." He squeezed the words out to the larger group. "Fine."

Gary deflated.

"Fine is not an answer," Fergus—aka the angry Scot, infamous for his whisky-fueled berserker-type rages— rumbled. "It's a deflection."

So true, and there went his opportunity to slide out of sharing. He took a deep breath. "Er..." Their attention crawled like ants over his skin. He just wanted to put in the hours and for Gary to sign his attendance register. He didn't want to talk about Debra and Taylor. The flash of Taylor's smile through his mind nearly brought him to his knees. He went with a truth, if not the whole truth. "Well, I'm having trouble sleeping."

"Really?" Gary lit up from within. His opportunity to do good hovered before him in a blinding vision of pure intentions. "Tell us about that."

"I get this...kind of...restless feeling when I'm in bed."

Jack stretched his long legs into the center of the sharing circle and sank his chin to his chest. Yeah, Jack wasn't buying it, and Warren saw a pint and interrogation session in his immediate future.

Leaning far enough forward to endanger his balance, Gary locked eyes on him. "You've been with us for how many months now? Five?"

"Four." Warren hated talking about himself. Mum Betty, his favorite and only worthwhile foster parent, had always told him if you didn't have anything good to say, don't say anything at all.

"Well, Warren." Gary gave him the smile of good cheer and sunny skies. "Many of our members find this period of self-reflection and reevaluation challenging."

"Progress not perfection," Fergus muttered.

"Precisely." Enthusiasm swelled Gary's voice. "Learning new behaviors takes time, and we need to be patient with ourselves."

"That's what I meant." Patrick sat bolt up in his chair. "That's what I try and tell that—" He shot a quick glance at Jack. "That's what I tell my wife, but she don't understand."

Warren saw the gap and bolted for it. "Maybe you should try telling her in a different way."

"We'll circle round to Patrick." Gary made forefinger air circles. "Patrick, could you hand the talking stick to Warren?"

With one last fond look at the talking stick, Patrick handed it to his neighbor.

Carried hand to hand, the talking stick headed for him, a live wire he didn't want anything to do with. And then Jack was handing it to him, and he took it. The stick felt heavy with the weight of everyone's expectations. "I really don't have that much to say."

"You don't have to say a lot." Gary glowed at him. "Speak to the not sleeping."

Actually, talking might not be that bad. "Like I said, I get this restless sense at night. Like I'm not where I should be."

"Uh-huh." Gary nodded his encouragement.

"There's this nagging sense like I've forgotten something or left something undone."

"Yes, Warren." Gary squirmed in his seat. "This is all valid stuff. Keep going."

Warren didn't want to meet anyone's eye and he trained his gaze over the left shoulder of the man sitting opposite him in the circle. "It didn't bother me at first. Like you've said, there's always a period of adjustment. But I think it's getting worse."

"Worse?" Gary blinked at him. "Worse how?"

Fergus shifted in his chair and made it squeak. Probably whisky withdrawal setting in. The man stank like a distillery.

On a huff, Patrick dropped his head back and stared at the ceiling, not interested now that someone else had the talking stick.

"I struggle to get to sleep. I keep wanting to get up and go somewhere."

Gary nodded. "Where?"

"I don't know, and I feel like I should know." He might as well tell them the final piece. Maybe Gary had it right, and someone here could help him. "Then there's the dreams."

"I got a lot of dreams. Really vivid ones," said a gangly man from three seats to his right. Warren thought his name might be Curtly. "They used to wake me up yelling. Me missus didn't know what to do with me."

"Yes." Someone got him. Warren didn't have a missus, but the dreams woke him up. The relief at being understood eased some of the pressure in his chest. A chat with Jack later would help with the rest. The big bastard had a way of putting crap into perspective.

"I used to see my former cell mate." Curtly gave him a gap-tooth grin. "Only he were a lot bigger and more of a bastard than he really was. And always I could hear that sound. That clang of the doors opening and closing."

"Many former inmates suffer from a form of PTSD. Vivid and terrifying dreams are quite common." Gary glowed, having the best sharing circle of his life. "Can you speak to what you see in your dreams?"

"Nah." Heat crawled up Warren's neck. "It's nothing. Stupid."

"Neutral space." Fergus gave him a nod of encouragement. "No wrong or right here, just feelings."

Warren's dreams rose fresh in his mind. Actually, dream, as in one and the same one every night. "No, I don't see anything like that. I see a girl, a woman really."

Jack shifted and stared at him. "How old?"

"Twenties."

"Pretty?" Fergus pursed his lips.

"I suppose so." Pretty, nah, that didn't describe the girl in his dreams. Magnetic, compelling, tantalizing, and Warren didn't even have to close his eyes to see her. "She's got a lot of red hair. Kind of curly and shiny and long, like a redheaded Bardot. But it's her eyes that get me. Dark brown, and she looks over her shoulder at me. She's laughing and then she calls me to her, and I know I have to go to her."

Silence greeted him.

Then Patrick broke into a guffaw. "You haven't got PTSD, mate." He winked and nudged the man beside him. "You're just horny."

3

CRÉ-WITCH CHRONICLES

Halfway across the great hall the next morning, a black and white cat hissed and shot up the stairs, warning Niamh that Sinead was on the warpath. Niamh had slept fitfully—what with extinct wolves howling and strange coimhdeacht who may or may not be coming to Baile and may or may not be coming for her. Before Roderick had defrosted out of the statue on the village green with Maeve, she'd strongly suspected coimhdeacht belonged in the same category as King Arthur or Aragorn. Nice fantasy but not a reality. Goddess, but what a fantasy it was.

Last night's full moon had stirred the animals up even more, and they'd been in a sharing is caring frame of mind. Outside the castle, summer had creatures busy making babies, and filling Niamh with unfortunate urges. When she had been younger, Niamh had found a convenient outlet in the village boys, but she'd learned her lesson the hard way. Village boys got drawn into her magic, and hearts got wounded.

"You know how I feel about these bloody wands." Sinead's voice reached her as a ferret slunk out of the kitchen tossing Niamh a long-suffering look.

Alannah replied, her tone conciliatory and soothing. "I know that, but they always sell so well at the market."

"It's not right," Sinead said, followed by a thump, which was probably her fist on the table. Since Sinead had launched Arcane Activists, the Harry Potter wand objections had gathered impetus. "We're dealing with the dilution of magical lore through juvenile literature."

The twins had discovered it was ridiculously easy to imbue the wands with a sprinkle of earth magic. Waving the wand created an aura of green sparkles that lasted about as long as a standard battery.

"But they're such great books," Alannah said.

"What books? Who is Harry Potter?" Roderick asked, so he must be in the kitchen as well.

A murmur followed as someone explained to their resident medieval knight another missing piece of what had happened in his six-hundred-year or so nap.

"A boy wizard?" Roderick sounded incredulous. "Regardless, there will be no going to market until it is safe to do so."

"No going to the market?" Alannah said. "But we need to sell our stuff. My fuel of the future, the wands. How will we make money?"

"No market. No going anywhere," Roderick said. "Rhiannon lurks outside our wards, waiting for an opportunity to strike."

"Now listen up, big man." Sinead's tone carried a stiletto edge. "You can't keep us locked up in this castle forever."

"I can if it keeps you safe." Roderick said.

Niamh stopped in the kitchen doorway and gathered herself.

Sinead caught sight of her and stopped the launch of her tirade against Roderick. "Morning."

Also there, and looking his normal tall, dark and devastatingly handsome, was Alexander. Even in jeans and a T-shirt, he managed to look runway ready. The bloody man probably had the most perfect bone structure known to humanity. He gave her a knee trembler of a smile, his dark eyes deadly and inviting. "Niamh, my morning just got better."

Roderick snorted and threw Alexander the stink eye. Those two probably would never learn to play nicely. The whole deadly enemies for centuries thing took a lot of getting over.

"You're such a creep," she said as she kissed Alexander's cheek. He smelled the sort of heavenly that made a girl want to roll around in him. Fortunately, she was as immune to Alexander's charm as he was to her magical lure. "Where's your better half?"

"Still in bed." Alexander gave her his trademark lazy grin. She'd seen him reduce rooms full of women to gawking emotional rubble with that one. "She's feeling a bit under the weather this morning."

"Probably from the company she keeps." Roderick smirked.

Alexander chuckled and leaned his chair back on two legs. "I don't see Maeve up and about this morning either." He was also a devil at finding Roderick's sore spot and kicking it. "Except, she doesn't share a bed with you, does she?"

Roderick glared.

Alexander sneered.

"Shuddup, you two." Sinead dropped the box of wands on the floor with a clatter. "You're boring the crap out of the rest of us with your bickering."

"Imagine how I feel." Thomas appeared close to where Alannah stood beside the stove. "I have to listen to their bitching all the time."

"Good morning." Willowy, elegant with high cheekbones, sleek auburn hair all the way to her waist and intimidatingly beautiful, Alannah got even lovelier as she looked at Thomas. She lit up from within whenever Thomas was around, and Thomas was around Alannah a lot.

Her twin and exact mirror in looks, as much as she was

Alannah's opposite in personality, Sinead frowned at the couple.

Thomas had his mouth close enough to Alannah's ear that only she could hear what he said.

Niamh shared Sinead's dislike of the situation. A ghost and a mortal witch didn't have happily ever after scrawled all over their future.

"Maybe our two bickering beauties will join forces against the new one," Thomas said to the room at large and sauntered closer to the table. Watching him walk jarred her. All the motions looked right, but his feet never contacted the ground.

"That's coimhdeacht business," Roderick snapped.

Thomas winked at her. "Oops, but Niamh already knew."

"Knew what?" Sinead's penetrating green gaze landed on her. "What's coimhdeacht business? What new one?"

Folding his arms over his chest, Roderick dropped his chin and glared at Thomas.

"We think there's a new coimhdeacht on the way," Thomas said.

"What!" Alannah and Sinead gaped at him and then each other.

Mags wandered into the kitchen, her tie-dye caftan sliding off her bony shoulders. She had always been slim but these days she looked like a stiff wind would carry her away. "Oh good." With a beaming smile at the room, she sat beside Alexander. "I'm glad you told them about the new coimhdeacht. I was going to do it." She leaned forward and snagged the teapot and peered inside. "Any more tea?"

"I didn't tell them, sweetheart." Alexander tucked a strand of Mag's wayward ginger hair behind her ear. "Thomas let the cat out the bag, and Roderick is weally, weally cwoss with him."

"You'll like this coimhdeacht." Mags wrinkled her nose at Roderick. "I believe he's distantly related to you."

Black eyes glinting, Alexander dropped his chair back on all fours and leaned closer to Mags. "Do tells us more, oh mighty Seer. Is this some wayward seed of Roderick's planting many centuries ago?"

"Ew." Mags blushed, almost the exact color of her hair.

Niamh had to laugh. Able to see into the future and the past, Mags was fey and unworldly in all other aspects of her life, and a total prude.

"According to the journals I've read." Niamh couldn't resist tweaking Roderick. "Sir Roderick the Ready spread his seed ably upon the land."

Mags looked like she might throw up. "Double, triple eww."

"You." Roderick jabbed a thick forefinger in her direction, but his pale blue eyes hadn't gone that deadly cold of a hunting great white, so she knew he wasn't offended. Only Alexander had the power to really get beneath his skin. "Should mind your manners when speaking to your elders." He raised an eyebrow. "I will have you know I was called Roderick the Ready due to my constant state of battle readiness."

Alexander got there before her. "Oh, we're sure of that. We've heard all about the readiness of your sword."

"Argh!" Mags leaped to her feet with the teapot. "Tea!"

Alannah took it from her and gave her a quick side hug. "Never mind, Mags, they'll give it a rest now." She glanced at Thomas as she turned to fill the teapot. "Tell us about the new mystery man."

"He's blond," Niamh said. The image of the man's face was still clear to her this morning. That had to mean something, right? And only she had seen him. She was getting ahead of herself. "Blue eyes, actually a lot like Roderick's."

All gazes swung her way.

Mags frowned harder. "How did you know that?"

"You've seen him?" Roderick frowned.

"I'm really not sure." And she wished she could be sure because with all that had changed in the last couple of months

—Bronwyn joining them from America, Maeve and Roderick coming to life from the village statue, learning about Rhiannon, finding out Alexander was her son, temporarily defeating Rhiannon—she was done with surprises. "My gift has never shown me a face before. The animals were restless last night, and I checked in with them. They showed me him." She almost mentioned the howling but decided against it.

Roderick glanced at Alexander and Thomas.

Thomas shook his head.

"I've never known anything like it either." Alexander shrugged. "But things are changing. Magic is changing. Rhiannon shouldn't be able to do what she does. I shouldn't be sitting in this kitchen—"

"Bloody right!" Roderick snorted.

"—but I am. It's not entirely out of the realm of possibility that magic grows and evolves."

"Great!" Sinead scowled. "We haven't even learned to use what we should have, and now you're suggesting it might be changing."

"Did you see anything else?" Alannah put a fresh pot of tea down and added a loaf of homemade bread and a crock of Sinead's butter. Her smile gentled. "And if you saw him, it must mean he's coming for you."

Niamh's heart gave a hopeful bound. She tried to tamp it down. Sensing her emotion, a terrier trotted into the kitchen and hopped onto her lap. It blinked patient brown eyes at her, sending her calm and peace. "We don't know that for certain."

A coimhdeacht. She barely dared hope. A warrior guardian bonded to her for life. A companion who shared her thoughts, emotions and spirit. A soul grafted so closely to hers it was an even greater bond than a lover. It hurt too much to even hope he might be hers.

"Oh, he's Niamh's all right." Mags slathered butter and honey on a hunk of bread.

Niamh had no idea how she stayed so sodding skinny with the way she ate, but Mags had said the new coimhdeacht was hers. She could even forgive her that amazing metabolism.

Roderick nodded. "It makes sense." He smiled at her as if he sensed her need and wanted to reassure her. "You have a task to perform and it's a vital one. It makes perfect sense for Goddess to send you help."

They were still learning all that their coven had forgotten over the hundreds of years since Rhiannon had nearly destroyed them. "What if he doesn't like me? If he doesn't have a choice about this whole business, then he might not be happy about it."

Thomas and Roderick exchanged a knowing look.

"Some of us resent the calling at first," Thomas said. "I certainly had no plans to be the protector of a witch for the rest of my days."

Roderick snorted. "I sort of tripped into it."

Neither of their responses gave her the warm fuzzies. Times had changed and some poor sod was getting a cosmic wakeup call from a deity he'd, in all likelihood, never heard of.

"But I have no regrets," Roderick said.

Thomas smiled. "Nor I."

And that was saying something, considering both men had lost all their coimhdeacht brothers, and Thomas his witch, the day Rhiannon had nearly destroyed the cré-witches forever.

"Morning." Bronwyn stumbled into the kitchen wearing Ren and Stimpy pajamas with her copper hair caught up in an untidy bun. She looked like a rumpled cherub.

The smile on Alexander's face made Niamh's breath catch in her throat.

The terrier pushed his head against her chest.

Just once she'd love to have a man look at her the way Alexander looked at Bronwyn. Not like he wanted to possess

her, or own her, but like his world had righted when she staggered into the room.

He held out an arm and Bronwyn tripped toward him and
dropped on to his lap. She immediately burrowed into him and
tucked her knees up to her chest.

"Are you feeling better?" Alexander kissed the top of her
head.

"Uh-huh." Bronwyn nodded and tucked her hands under
her chin. "I'm hungry now."

"We can fix that." He wrapped his arms around her.
"Bread?"

"Anything." Bronwyn covered her mouth and yawned. "My
stomach is feeling like my throat has been cut."

Alexander chuckled. "Well, we can't have that."

The way he held Bronwyn so tenderly also wacked Niamh
right in the feelings. He bloody, sodding well *cradled* her. Niamh
was pea-green jealous. She wanted to be cradled. She wanted
someone to look at her as if she was some kind of daily miracle
he'd gotten lucky enough to hitch along with. She wanted a
man to go all warm and tender when he looked at her.

Alannah looked wistful. Then she turned and added eggs
and bacon to a frying pan.

Sinead was also staring at Alexander and Bronwyn, but
more of a searchlight than the longing of her twin. "What are
you two now? A couple? Friends with benefits?"

Bronwyn raised her head slightly and smiled at Alexander.

He smiled back. "Absolutely nothing."

THE KNIFE BIT into Rhiannon's palm. Blood, viscous and warm,
slid over her hand into the water bowl.

One, two, three drops. Like crimson jellyfish, they formed
and sank, leaving dissipating tentacles behind them. She closed

her hand and squeezed. Drops quickened into a stream, spreading through the pinkening water.

Rhiannon swelled the magic within her and pulled it forth. "Show me."

Like spikes of shattering pain, magic defied her mastery. Not today. Not any day. It would obey her. She wrenched it to her command. The dull-knife pain sharpened into an axe cut, blunt but deep. A pain she knew well. Every time, magic fought her, trying to separate itself from the taint of blood magic. Lately, magic had intensified, stronger than Rhiannon had felt it in eons. Water was active again.

After centuries of silence, Goddess had stepped onto the battlefield. Too late. Goddess had squandered her chance to shape the world. Now it was Rhiannon's time. Like a faint pulse to the south, Rhiannon sensed her, a slow spreading stain on her horizon. Let the bitch come. Rhiannon had used the endless stretch of years to grow stronger, unassailable. She would mold life to her hand and craft a better creation than Goddess had ever conceived.

In Baile, they thought they had won a major victory in taking Rhiannon's son. If it weren't so convenient, she would have shown them the error in underestimating her. The spawn would breed with that water witch of his and fulfill the prophecy. If the witch wasn't whelping already, she would be soon. Prophecies had a way of making sure they happened.

The ungrateful shit she'd brought into this world had thought to foil her with his betrayal. She'd birthed him without a healer, the old-fashioned way, like humans did it, for secrecy. She'd had him to fulfil the prophecy and the child it spoke of, the one yet to be born, was hers. Alexander cowered behind Baile's wards and continued to defy her. But even now, his weakness worked against him. Unless she mistook matters, he loved his water witch, and a man in love could always be counted on to act on his baser nature.

Pain in her palm anchored her, and Rhiannon tightened her fist. Blood poured into the water, staining away the clear. "Show me."

Subsiding to a gnawing torture, the magic allowed her passage. A hazy image swirled and stabilized in the bloody water.

Two babies hovered through the red streaks, a boy and a girl. So much power that Rhiannon shivered. It pulsed through the vision. Never in the long march of her life had Rhiannon sensed anything like it. Not yet born, their presence, potent and imminent, thrilled her.

"Mine." With that much power, she would be unassailable for eternity. It fizzed through her like champagne bubbles, the craving for that infant power. "I will take what is mine."

She wouldn't be second anymore, repeatedly thrown over for lesser witches.

Goddess would rue how she had dismissed her. Years spent in groveling servitude only to be overlooked time and time again. Her, Rhiannon, the most talented and powerful of the first four and always second to Tahra or Deidre. They would all bend to her.

4

CRÉ-WITCH CHRONICLES

W arren stopped his bike on the shoulder. Removing his helmet, he stared at the castle. Baile Castle, built in the 1100s by Sir Roderick of Cray, and still privately owned. He might be a bit of a technophobe and had a theory on how much fucking information they could get on you through cell phones, but even he could google.

What his search hadn't told him was how beautiful Baile was and how she radiated ageless peace. It was like she'd always been there, and long after the rest of them were fertilizing the soil, she'd still be there. Like a graceful gray bird, she perched on the edge of her cliff, which rose straight out of the sea. She loomed over the village clustered at her feet like a sentry. He was being fanciful, but the castle's beauty hit him in the belly.

Here.

His chest tightened. His nape prickled. He'd never been here before, but the roiling inside him stilled, and he knew he was in the right place, which left him stymied. Knocking on the door and letting the good folk of the castle know he'd arrived and where he felt himself meant to be wasn't an option. Well, not the sort of option that would get him invited in for tea and cakes anyway.

Leaving was impossible. Even the idea brought the restlessness churning back. Like Baile, he was here, and here he aimed to stay.

Beneath him, the steady purr of the powerful engine and the heat it put out anchored him. A briny sea breeze cooled the sweat on his forehead.

As a kid, he'd always loved the sea. Holidays with Mum Betty at Bamburgh, filled with coconut scented sunblock and ice cream. Hot, sticky, sand-encrusted days that stretched into the endless summer twilight. And Rudy. Thinking about Rudy always scraped like sandpaper in his chest, so he slammed the memories shut.

His stomach growled, demanding he do something about having not eaten since a slice of toast at first sparrow's fart. He'd head to the village below the castle, find a pub and get a meal and a room. A shower wouldn't hurt any either.

A big dog shot out of the thick trees to the left of the drawbridge. It stopped in front of him and barked.

Warren liked dogs, and he held out his hand. "Hello"—quick check of the dog's undercarriage—"boy. Where did you come from?"

The dog took a step closer and increased the pitch and pace of its barking.

So, not about making friends.

Warren eased his bike forward.

The dog snarled and came right at him. It snapped at his ankle and withdrew to the front of his bike, its teeth almost polishing his front tire.

He revved his engine, hoping to make the animal move.

Its hackles came up, lips curled on a low, meaning-business growl.

"Get out of it!" He made his voice low and menacing.

So did the dog, only the dog was much better at it.

As much as he liked dogs, this one needed a lesson in manners, and the owner should know that.

Trying to ease forward again, he got the same response. He didn't want to risk running over the dog, but the bloody thing wouldn't let him go. At least not without a fight, and there was enough German shepherd in his opponent to give Warren second thoughts.

"Hello." A woman emerged from the same direction the dog had. Surrounded by more dogs—no, one of those dogs was a cat and one a...fox?—she moved up the short path to the roadway like she belonged to the earth beneath her bare feet. Long, toned legs, the milk white of a true redhead, ended in a pair of khaki shorts. Her untucked T-shirt was smudged with dirt and told him Driver Picks the Music.

Breath left his lungs like he'd been kicked in the chest. She was more than beautiful. Beautiful was too insipid a word for the earthy sensuality shimmering around her. He was staring like a starstruck git with his gob hanging open. He cleared his throat. "Is that your dog?"

"My dog?" She cocked her head, a gesture mirrored by a big retriever at her side. "How can any one soul own another?"

Oookay! The German shepherd joined the pack around her and wagged its tail. "He certainly seems to think he's yours."

"I told you—"

"Yeah—" He was too tired and hungry for more drivel from her. He felt off balance, wrong-footed. "I don't want to be this guy, but your dog nearly attacked me."

Her dark brown eyes saw right through his skin. Wind ruffled her gleaming red hair, and he swore he could smell strawberries and basil. "Then don't." She shrugged.

"Don't what?" Warren couldn't tear his gaze away from hers. Unease churned inside him, and he didn't like it.

"Be that guy," she said. She stroked the German shepherd's head. "And he wasn't about to attack you." She smiled down at the dog.

It grinned back at her as if the two of them were sharing a laugh. At his expense.

"Whatever." He gave vent to how much enough he'd had of this conversation. "But if you're going to own a dangerous animal, you should take care it doesn't attack people."

She laughed. "He didn't attack you."

"Yes—"

"He was only giving me a hand."

She'd said what now? Warren struggled against the rising swell of irritation and lost. "You set that dog on people?"

"No." She rolled her eyes. "He was making sure you didn't go anywhere before I got here."

Fresh breath rushed into his starved lungs. She might be touched in the head. "Eh?"

"We've been waiting for you." She looked up from the German shepherd and smiled over her shoulder at him.

Recognition slammed into him. He gawped at her. Turbulent emotion swirled through him, and his tone grew brusque. "Who the hell are you?"

"I'm Niamh." She looked taken aback, as if that should have meant something to him.

"Who?"

"Niamh." She blinked at him and frowned.

"I heard you the first time." He gritted his teeth against the urge to yell. "But who are you and why—" He didn't know where to go from there. Asking her what the fuck she'd been doing in his dreams would only make him look like a nutter. "Never mind."

She stared at him expectantly.

Warren didn't understand, and he gaped back, his mind

blank and his chest tight like a giant fist was playing squeeze ball with his lungs.

She cleared her throat. "It's a lovely evening, isn't? Nice and warm. Sunshiny."

Warren's hold on the situation snapped. He turned his bike and gunned it down the hill.

"Sunshiny?" Niamh made eye contact with the fox.

The fox tried to look encouraging and failed.

"Argh!" She covered her face with her hands. "I sounded like a complete idiot."

The German shepherd whined.

Niamh wanted to whine too.

"I'm sorry." she said, patting his head. "And after you did such a good job keeping him here for me."

The German shepherd radiated smug satisfaction that he'd made the man nervous.

Probably not the best introduction then, but his surliness had taken her off guard. She didn't know what she'd expected the new coimhdeacht to be like, but grumpy hadn't once occurred to her. Goddess, what a beautiful man.

"So, that's him." Niamh patted a silky head pressed against her thigh. When she'd first seen him from the forest, perched on his bike and staring at Baile, she'd tripped over a tree root and hit the ground. Pity the fall hadn't jolted her back to sense.

Her brief flashes of his face hadn't carried his magnetism, or the hardness in those cold blue eyes. Her gift had sensed the turmoil in him and the deep wells of pain he kept carefully buried. Something in her had wanted to reach inside those abysses and bring him out again.

Sunlight flashed off metal as he left. The bike grumbled in

the quiet as he wound his way away from her, down the hill toward Greater Littleton.

"Do you think he'll be back?"

The cat sat and tucked her tail to the side of her paws. She blinked at Niamh with knowing yellow eyes.

"I know." Niamh pulled a face at it. Cats were always so certain. It could be maddening. "The whole coimhdeacht deal and all that. Goddess calls, and he is compelled to answer."

The cat straightened a back leg and commenced grooming.

The retriever nudged Niamh's inert hand.

Niamh obeyed instruction and stroked as the new coimhdeacht disappeared from sight. "Well, I suppose we should let Roderick know his new friend has arrived."

HALF AN HOUR LATER, Warren strode into a pub on what appeared to be Greater Littleton's main drag, cutely called the Hag's Head. Hag not nag, he got it, and if the thigh slapper was still too subtle for you, the sign outside sporting the crone with the warty chin clued you in further.

The Hag's Head was a nice surprise for a southern pub. From the quaint, touristy quality of the rest of the village, he'd been well afraid this would turn out to be one of those sodding gastropubs.

Jesus give him strength. Gastropubs. Not everything had improved since he'd been deployed. Gastropubs had been around before, but now they littered the country like zits on a teenager's arse. Some things you didn't mess with, solid pub grub being one of them—fish and chips, pie and chips, and steak, egg and chips. Also mushy peas. A man needed to rely on some things staying the same.

For midafternoon, the pub was surprisingly full. A couple of gazes swung his way, and Warren stiffened.

The encounter at the castle still had him edgy and on guard. That woman had blown his tiny mind. In person, she was...

He didn't have the right words.

Forcing himself to relax, he took a deep breath of the yeasty, familiar smell of the pub. An olfactory past-blast of beer, stale cigarettes, old carpets and varnished wood.

Taking up most of the right-hand wall, a massive smoke-stained inglenook fireplace dated the pub as late sixteenth century. The solid wooden beam holding up the roof hinted at the pub's origins being much earlier. Poky windows at the far end from the door played peep at an incredible view of the sea.

Brass brackets held row upon row of glasses suspended above the bar counter. An older woman in a bright pink T-shirt scrutinized him as he approached. She leaned her elbows on the bar top and gave him eyeballs full of crinkly cleavage.

"Hello, darling." She grinned, flashing her crooked, smoke-stained teeth. "What can I do for you?"

She assessed him, looking for his weakness, ready to pounce and exploit whatever chink she found in his armor. Predatory women came in all shapes and sizes, some of them so exciting a man ignored the obvious and let her lead him dick-first into life's-a-crapper.

"A pint of bitter, please." He turned sideways to keep most of the room in sight. The brain-scrambling redhead from his dreams existed, and she'd set her dog on him. Oh, excuse him, she'd set the dog she hung out with on him.

Not that he gave a crap. He'd obeyed whatever twisted instinct had brought him to Greater Littleton. The redhead had been a kick to the balls he hadn't needed.

Putting his pint in front of him, the bartender gave him more teeth. "I'm Bonnie, and I can sort you out for whatever you need."

Piss poor planning promotes piss poor performance, and if

he wanted to get to the bottom of what he was doing here, he could do with some tangible intel. "You live in Greater Littleton, Bonnie?"

"All my life." She gave him another cleavage shot, pushing her boobs together and sending flesh teetering on the edge of her T-shirt. "That's how I know I've never seen you around."

Her mental undressing set his teeth on edge, but he sipped his pint and forced a smile. "No, just arrived. Went to look at the castle first."

"Right, Baile." Bonnie straightened and glanced out the window with a view of the castle. "That's what brings most folks to our little village." She sighed. "Quite something isn't she? Even though I grew up looking at her, she still makes an impression."

"Hmm." The bitter was good, and Bonnie looked in the mood to chat. "Is it true she's still privately owned?"

"Oh, yes." Bonnie brought her attention back to him, a slight tension to her shoulders. "Been in the same family since the year dot. The Crays."

"The Crays?" He eased off. "Never heard of them. Do you have any rooms available?"

Bonnie gave him a feral grin. He made a mental note to lock his door. "For the likes of you, darling, always."

"Thank you. I'm not sure how long I'll be staying." He tried to look coy but probably ended up looking more constipated.

It didn't bother Bonnie, who eyed him head to toe. "You stay as long as you like. You couldn't overstay your welcome. Not you."

"Right you are." He fished around for his one and only credit card. He also had a theory about those fucking plastic squares of we're-watching-you. "I'll start with three nights?"

"Three nights it is." Bonnie shifted over to her bar top computer and pressed on the screen. She pushed a piece of paper and a pen his way. "I'll get you to fill your bits and bobs in there."

Everybody wanted to know everything about you all the time. Warren filled in his name, phone number and the address of the shithole he'd most recently vacated. Jack had argued long and hard to stop him from coming here, and Warren had agreed with every one of his points. With Debra withholding custody of Taylor, his mandatory group sessions, his inability to find better work than the odd construction job, he didn't have time for messing about chasing dreams.

"From up north, are you?" Bonnie read his information off the sheet. "I've heard good things about Northern lads."

He didn't want to hear what Bonnie had heard, so he went back to what he really wanted to know. "I bet the Crays come in here all the time."

"Why would you think that?" Mouth pursed, Bonnie got all squinty eyed.

Her anger took him by surprise, and he scrambled to recover. "Just making conversation is all."

"Huh!" Bonnie jabbed her thumb at his pint. "You gonna have another of those?"

Apparently, he was off Bonnie's menu. "Er...yes, please."

"Want anything to eat?" All business, she slapped a menu on the bar in front of him.

"I could have a look." He'd been riding all day and hadn't eaten since the toast. He didn't like his chances of Bonnie not spitting in his food though.

"I'd go with the burger." A blonde slid on the bar stool next to him, and for the second time that day, he gaped at a woman. "It's safer."

Then she smiled, and he had to tighten his jaw to stop it from dropping open. "Safer?"

Christ! The blonde was fit. Nope, she was a fucking knock-out. She leaned closer and her voice dropped to a husky whisper. "The food here is not great."

"Thanks for the warning."

"Edana." Bonnie slid a coaster in front of the blonde and tenderly placed a glass of red on the coaster. She edged both to within reach of Edana's hand. "It's from one of the special bottles."

"Thank you." Edana leaned closer, her cloying perfume a touch strong. She winked at him. "I come here often."

Bonnie's attitude had morphed into an obsequious smile with Edana's arrival. Forget come here often; she must own shares in the place. "Have you decided what you'd like to eat?"

"The burger?" He glanced at Edana for confirmation and got a nod. "The burger, with chips."

"Very good, sir." Bonnie scampered off to place his order.

Edana eyed him over her wineglass. Her eyes were the color of tobacco. "You're not from here."

"And you have massive powers of observation."

She laughed and touched his forearm. "I think it has a lot more to do with the chronic shortage of men in the village."

"Ah." He almost felt sorry for Bonnie now. Every pot needed to find its lid.

"So...Warren Masters." Edana had slid his registration form her way from where Bonnie had left it beside the till. "What brings you to Greater Littleton?"

Edana clearly didn't rate privacy highly, but she was still talking to him, and Bonnie had shut him down. "Guess."

Her eyes warmed, and her smile felt like a stroke on his skin. Sensuality oozed from her. "Oooh! A game. I'm good at games."

Bonnie reappeared with his new pint and added a bowl of peanuts and pretzels. "On the house."

Before he could thank her, Bonnie fled.

"People come to Greater Littleton for all sorts of reasons.

Let me see." Edana tapped her full red mouth with the tip of her shiny red forefinger. "Over there." She jerked her head at the shadowy corner to the right of the inglenook fireplace. "We have the hard-core Wiccans, and I'm guessing you're not one of them."

Four women and one man sat hunched over their glasses, talking intently to each other.

"Note the little hex bags around their necks," Edana said. "They look like they're getting a head start on Halloween. They stick to themselves mostly, except for the brunette, and she is not shy, if you know what I mean." Edana gave a husky laugh and touched his knee. "Of course, you know what I mean."

Warren was intrigued despite himself, and her attention was flattering. "Why do the Wiccans come here?"

"Magic." Edana widened her eyes and laughed. "They sense the force and come to dwell in its power."

"Uh-huh." She made him laugh too. "Who else have we got?"

Edana scanned the pub. "Now on the opposite side of the room, as far from the Wiccans as possible, we have your hard-core Druids." Edana leaned closer and lightly grasped his knee as she whispered, "At first glance, one group could be mistaken for the other." She held up one forefinger. "Until you notice nearly all of the Druids are wearing the triquetra in one way or another."

Not really understanding what the hell Edana was talking about, Warren still found himself staring at the second group. Her hand on his knee wasn't unbearable. She might be coming on to him. "Triquetra?"

"Little triangle thingy made up of interconnecting lines." Edana laced her fingers in a triangular shape. "The hard-core Wiccans and the hard-core Druids do not speak to each other. But the other group, the third one, closest to the door, now they are made up of a mixture of both, and they're lovely to chat to."

"That's a lot of Wiccans and Druids."

"Mmm." She purred and sipped her wine. A man could get incinerated by the heat in those eyes, and unless he totally missed his guess, Edana was definitely coming on to him.

He toyed with whether to take her up on her offer as he kept the conversation going. Close to one of the sea-facing windows, two middle aged couples shared a meal. Warren gestured to them. "What's their story? What brings them here?"

"Tourists," Edana said. "Baile dates back to eleven fifty-three. Up until earlier this year, it was open to the public. But now..." She shrugged. "But that doesn't stop them from coming anyway. Hoping they'll get a look in anyway."

"I could be a tourist." Warren shifted so he could see the castle from where he sat. Square stone towers marked it as Norman in origin, but several smaller buildings from different periods sprawled around it.

"I think not." Edana shook her head slowly. Her silky curtain of hair swished and caught the light. "I suspect a far more interesting story."

"You could be setting yourself up for disappointment." He couldn't put his finger on it, but he sensed so much beneath her picture-perfect surface.

Edana pulled a face. "Maybe." She laughed, soft and sultry. "But if you're here, then maybe you know what they say about Greater Littleton."

Not a clue, but he made a noncommittal noise and sipped his beer.

"They say we're all witches." Edana winked and sipped her wine.

Warren laughed with her. He didn't know about witches, but between the woman at the castle and Edana, there must be something in the water creating these good-looking women. "You gonna put a spell on me?" He nearly put a fist in his own mouth. What part of him thought that line was a good idea?

Edana smirked. "Would you like me to?"

He wasn't ready to answer that, and he took the distraction and pointed at her glass. "Another?"

Bonnie delivered his burger with a flourish and some cutlery and a napkin. She saved Edana the bother of answering him and refilled her glass.

"It looks good." He motioned his burger.

Edana picked up her fresh glass. "Go ahead. You must be hungry, big boy like you."

Okay, that made him feel a lot better about his corny line. Apparently, somebody had passed Edana the cheese. But she was right about the burger, it was good, as were the chips.

"So." Edana leaned forward and stole one of his chips.

Where the hell did women get the idea men liked that? If you wanted chips, order your own.

"Let's circle back to the mystery of you." She swirled his chip in his ketchup and popped it between her perfectly painted red lips. "You're neither Wiccan nor Druid, and you don't look like a history buff."

He inched his plate closer to him. "What does a history buff look like?"

"Good question." She wrinkled her nose. "Why don't you put me out of my misery and tell me what you're doing here."

"Nothing particular." He managed to hit the right off-hand note. "I'm a sort of tourist. Going wherever the mood takes me."

"A man of mystery then." She licked red wine off her top lip. "I can work with that."

5

CRÉ·WITCH CHRONICLES

For two men who couldn't be in the same room without sniping at each other, Roderick and Alexander looked like mirror images tonight. Arms crossed, legs akimbo, chins to chests, they stood in united opposition against her. She'd gone back and forth with herself all day about her inter- action with the new coimhdeacht. It hadn't gone well, and she wanted a chance to meet him under better circumstances, maybe get to know him better. Definitely get to know him better. She drew teeny-weeny comfort from the suspicion that men who looked like that were probably used to women making idiots of themselves.

"But he's here for me. You said so." Niamh suppressed the urge to stamp her foot. Giving in to her inner toddler wouldn't help get her own way.

"He's probably here for you. The coimhdeacht bonds the witch, not the other way around," number one stubborn prat answered. Number one because as far as she could tell Roderick was the marginally older of the two of them. "Which is irrelevant, because you're not to leave Baile. It isn't safe."

"Go nowhere?" She loaded as much derision into the words

as she could. Goddess, they couldn't stay cooped up in the castle forever, however large it was.

Number two stubborn prat raised one perfectly sculpted brow with rapier precision and said, "For as long as Rhiannon is out there looking for a way to destroy this coven, you will all stay put, where we can keep you safe."

Niamh had heard it all before. She knew all about Rhiannon. How Rhiannon had kidnapped Bronwyn and locked her in a room with Alexander. She also knew Rhiannon had nearly willed Alexander to rape Bronwyn, and make that bloody prophecy come true. She really didn't fancy tangling with the evil bitch, but she needed to know more about Mr. Tall, Blond and Crotchety. "He came to Baile. I saw him. I spoke to him." *Made a twit of myself.* "I want to get to know him."

"He'll be back." Roderick sounded so sure of himself.

Niamh didn't share Roderick's optimism. He could decide the whole summoning thing was not for him and turn around and disappear on his bike again. "You don't know that."

"Yes, he does," Alexander said.

Niamh gaped. Alexander agreeing with something Roderick said needed to be written down. Maeve would swallow her tongue. "How?"

"It's a coimhdeacht thing," Roderick said.

Niamh folded her arms. She set her legs apart and waggled her head to let them know what she thought of their magic boy's club. "How very convenient for you, but I don't have your faith."

"It matters not." Roderick went medieval knight when contradicted. "You shall remain within Baile."

"I'll sneak out."

Thomas popped into view and made himself stubborn prat number three when he smirked and said, "You could try."

Three of them lined up like hens on a perch with all their feathers ruffled up. Well, she had moves they could do nothing about, and she was going to see her coimhdeacht. Goddess might have—probably had—sent him for her. So, she was only doing what Goddess would want her to do.

Right? Right!

"We need to sort this out." They'd get suspicious if she gave in too easily. "Because we can't stay locked up here forever."

"It will be sorted." Alexander eased up on the heavy and gave her charm. "As soon as I rid us of Rhiannon."

"As soon as *I* rid us of Rhiannon." Roderick growled.

Alexander glared.

Roderick glowered back.

Business as usual. Niamh made her escape.

She passed Mags on the stairs, and Mags looked at her and winked. "Happy travels."

"Thanks." Love Mags as she did, it got downright creepy and inconvenient to live with a seer who knew what you were about to do before you did it.

She reached her bedroom and locked the door. A dog immediately scratched at the door, so she opened it again and let today's pack in—three dogs, a fox, two ferrets and a lemur. She had no idea where the lemur had come from, but some wanker who felt the need for an exotic pet had probably brought the poor thing to England and then grown tired of him.

Getting comfortable on the window seat, she addressed her audience. "Right, you lot, I'm going to need some peace and quiet in here."

As the pack settled around her room, she lit a candle. Lighting the hearth fire might tweak Thomas's curiosity, and he'd tattle for certain. She'd taken one of the rooms in the east tower for its view over Baile's land and because it was far enough away from her coven sisters to alleviate their complaints about her menagerie.

Lying on her bed, Niamh focused on the familiar toile

pattern of cavorting milkmaids and cast her awareness out in thin tendrils. Not too much or nosy Thomas would pop in and ruin everything.

An owl sat in the oak outside the kitchen. He searched the dark yard for prey. Owls made her think of Roz, and she veered away.

She spread herself under the oak and into the damp leafy carpet at its feet.

Another possibility, a mouse foraging through the dead leaves.

Hating to interrupt dinnertime she moved on. Niamh skimmed over the sleeping chickens and cast wider. Chickens had limited use as hosts. They tended to get distracted too quickly.

The fox slipped suddenly through the undergrowth, and Niamh slid into her mind. She went through a momentary disorientation as her eyesight sharpened, her sense of smell grew thousands of times more acute, and her hearing range increased.

The fox moved fast, leaping ditches, slipping under hedgerows, as she took Niamh to the edge of Greater Littleton.

Too long away from her kits, the fox balked at going into the village, so Niamh left her and caught a ride with a rat. Rat brains processed a lot more information than most animals, and their interpretation of that information was surprisingly sophisticated.

Being with a rat again reminded her of the friend Rhiannon had killed when they'd been trying to find Bronwyn. She'd get even with Rhiannon for that one day. Rat had only been helping her, and he had paid the ultimate price.

A gentle push persuaded her current rat to give up the interesting stench in the Gardners' rubbish and move on to the pub. Fortunately, the pub had even more pungent rubbish, and Niamh left him gnawing on a pork chop bone. A younger rat skulked away, and she caught a ride and nudged him to the kitchen door. He got distracted by a crate of spoiled vegetables.

A sleepy dormouse woke to the touch of her mind and took her up the stairs. His fear leaked into her, and Niamh sent warm reassuring thoughts of sunlight and ripening grain through his mind. For a moment, he almost turned about and went to look for those things, so she pulled back a little and reminded him how tired he was and that upstairs, in the guest rooms, were the best places to sleep. The house cat very rarely made an appearance up there.

Small creatures took real finesse, and Niamh could feel the pull on her fire-based power. She drew on the candle flame beside her bed. Strawberry and basil perfumed the room. Instinct guided her past two guest rooms, and then she stopped. He was behind the next door.

From the direction of Baile, a wolf howled.

At the hint of an apex predator, the dormouse stopped dead, quivering and scenting. Niamh nearly lost control of the dormouse. Somewhere in Baile, there was a wolf, and it was not her imagination.

Getting back to the task at hand, she slid her dormouse under the lit doorway and scampered beneath a chest of drawers and waited. Warm darkness beneath the furniture soothed the dormouse and Niamh let her little friend calm and finally drop off to sleep. From here, she could rest lightly in the very top of his mind. She eased up on the power. Without her friend's instincts bleeding into her perception, she could look around the room more like a person would.

Blood magic stench lingered in the room, and she tensed. Her heart pounded. That smell meant Rhiannon or one of her minions was nearby. If Roderick or Alexander found that tidbit out about her excursion, she'd never hear the end of it. She'd never hear the end of it if they found out she'd dropped by anyway.

From the bathroom, came the sound of running water. He must be taking a shower. A duffle bag lay on the bed, a pair of jeans folded over it. Beside the bed, a pair of large boots sat neatly positioned side by side.

The shower snapped off, and the pipes groaned. Her dormouse startled at the sound, and Niamh soothed him back to sleep.

Large male feet padded out of the bathroom. From her position Niamh could see nothing more than his tanned, hairy calves. Bugger it! She wanted to find out more about him.

He had the sort of muscular calves that meant he probably worked out. From what she remembered about his broad shoulders, they belonged with those calves.

Keeping the lightest grasp on the dormouse, she brushed across the top of the man's mind. She could read the awareness of all animals; it wasn't considered polite to do so with other humans.

Still, this one might soon share her every thought and emotion anyway, so it wasn't like she was snooping. Much.

Nothing. She could read nothing from him, not even catch the faintest stir of emotion. Niamh probed a bit deeper. It felt like running headlong into a wall and she withdrew sharply.

He snatched up the remote and the TV flickered on.

The dormouse woke and wasn't happy about its proximity to the man. She could compel the tiny creature to stay, but that didn't seem fair, and the fatigue of using her gift for this length of time without being able to draw extra power from fire was beginning to tell on her.

The potential coimhdeacht remained a mystery. There didn't appear to be any sign of who or what had left the blood magic stench. Blood magic carried an unmistakable sickly-sweet odor of decay and death. It wasn't a smell Niamh cared to catch again, but she risked staying a smidge longer.

He sat on the edge of the bed and her view slid up to his knees.

As his thighs dropped open, his towel gaped.

Holy Hell!

Snake! The dormouse bolted for the door, taking Niamh with him. Tiny heart hammering, he scampered down the hallway, down the stairs, through the kitchen and out into the yard. Only when he'd reached the safety of his tiny bolt-hole did Niamh have the chance to touch his awareness again. Laughing, she searched the empty driveway for her lift home.

A large awareness brushed hers. *Come. Run.*

The cool touch of night flooded her mind. Moist sea air brushed her senses, carrying thousands of night scents. Wind ruffled her fur, and power surged through her muscles. Blood pumped, and her heart pounded in her chest.

Come. Run.

Exhilaration filled her, and Niamh slid away from the dormouse. The wolf caught her, and with a joyful bound, he turned and powered into the night.

6

"We should go for a stroll." Mags stood in Niamh's bedroom door and blinked at her. Her eyes had the jade film over them, which as well as making them look oddly opaque and quite frankly creepy, also meant Mags was having one of her thingies.

The cat on Niamh's lap dug her claws in, sure that a walk was a horrible idea on such a dreary day. Niamh didn't fancy the fine drizzle and gray clouds herself, but Mags was never wrong about her thingies. "Should we?"

"Oh, yes." Mags nodded and her eyes returned to their normal emerald green. "You're expected."

"Expected?" Niamh gently moved the cat to the window seat cushion and stood, disturbing an overweight rabbit at her feet. The rabbit could definitely do with a walk.

Mags flapped her hands and clattered her armful of bracelets, charms and bangles. "It's not easy to explain, but it will make sense when we get there."

"Okay." Niamh reached for her raincoat and slipped it over her shoulders. If the weather got worse, she wanted to be prepared.

Her current crop of animals stayed where they were.

A dog snoozing on the bed sat up, his expression almost apologetic.

"Nobody is coming with me?" Niamh couldn't remember the last time she'd gone anywhere without a creature of some kind following her.

The dog blinked and lay down again with a groan.

"We need to go." In a swirl of green and magenta chiffon maxi skirt, Mags turned and left.

Niamh followed her, stopping only long enough in the kitchen to put her wellies on.

"You off somewhere? In this?" Maeve sat at the kitchen table eating a hunk of Alannah's homemade bread, butter and honey dripping off the sides.

Niamh eyed the misting rain and wrinkled her nose. "Apparently I'm expected."

"She is." Mags settled an enormous army poncho over her shoulders.

Maeve shrugged and wrinkled her nose. "Rather you than me."

"Where's Roderick?" It was rare to see Maeve without her coimhdeacht looming over her and scowling at anyone who breathed too harshly in Maeve's direction.

Sweetly pretty with big, blue eyes and a swathe of vanilla hair, Maeve looked like she needed protecting. Until you got to know her, and then you knew she definitely needed protecting. Maeve had a way of innocently bumbling where angels feared to tread. Roderick had his work cut out for him.

"He went off with Alexander." Maeve licked dripping butter off her hand.

"Voluntarily?" That bread and honey looked so much better than going out in the drizzle. A cup of tea to go with it—

"You need to come." Mags nudged her.

"They both looked happy to trundle off together." Maeve

shrugged and bit into her bread. "I think they've gone to see the new coimhdeacht."

"Ah." For some reason Niamh hadn't gotten around to telling them about the blood magic stink she'd detected in the new one's room. Some reason was a bit of a stretch. She hadn't told them about the blood magic because then she'd have to explain what she'd been doing in his room, and they would not be happy. She looked at Mags. "Maybe that's who's expecting me."

"No." Mags shook her head. "And you need to come. Now."

Well, that settled that, and she followed Mags into the gloomy afternoon.

Mags's long legs made short work of the distance. She led them out of the bailey and over the drawbridge. Leaving the road, she followed a small dirt track into the forest.

The forest was strangely subdued in the rain, just the dripping of raindrops through the canopy and the squelch of their feet through the mud. Niamh could sense animals about, but they were lying low. She picked up something else...an anticipation.

Mags tromped to the northern edge of the forest to where it thinned into a sweep of sodden meadow, the grasses all hanging low and heavy with moisture.

"Not much longer," Mags called over her shoulder.

The meadow sloped upward and became rockier as they approached the crags that marked the northern boundary of Baile's demesne. According to Roderick and Maeve, the wards had gotten weaker over the years. They'd shrunk in on themselves, and now covered only a third of the land they should. With Roderick being back among the breathing again, the wards had started strengthening and expanding.

Roderick thought that once they got Alannah and Sinead to activate earth, they could push the wards back to where they should be. He didn't have an answer for what would happen when the wards reached the housing development further along the coast.

Of course, none of that would happen until she found the fire point and activated it. She should be spending her afternoon doing research in the library, not tramping through the damp. "Is this going to be much longer?"

"Nope." Mags stopped and cocked her head. Then she turned to Niamh with a grin. "They're on their way. And I need to go."

With a cheery grin, she picked up her long, soaked skirts and trotted back the way they'd come.

"Mags!" Niamh nearly turned and followed her.

Waving a hand above her head, Mags called, "They're not comfortable with people yet."

"What do you mean, not comfortable with people." Niamh had to raise her voice to reach the scurrying Mags. "I'm a people."

An awareness brushed Niamh's mind. Strong, predatory and demanding her attention. The same presence had playfully run with her after her spying expedition. Niamh's breath caught in her throat. The rain and the gloom didn't bother her anymore.

A howl floated plaintively through the murk. A real one, not inside her mind. Goddess, she hoped that meant what she thought it did.

Her nape prickled, and she turned to the carelessly littered boulders breaking up the rising slope.

A lone gray wolf stood beside a large boulder, his fur near enough the same color as the rock. With steady amber eyes, he watched her.

Niamh quested for him.

His hackles rose and he showed her his teeth in a gentle warning. The sort of warning he would give a puppy to mind its manners.

She stopped and awaited permission.

His mind reached out to her, and Niamh dug her nails into her palms to keep the connection.

She'd never been in the mind of such a powerful apex predator before. Not fully, anyway. The other night, when she had run with him, he had only let her see his perceptions of the world around him, and now, he let her fully within.

His determination of purpose, the single-minded focus of the predator frightened her, and she had to breathe deep. But the raw force of his nature thrilled her.

Head lowered, the wolf padded closer, his powerful body moving effortlessly and gracefully.

Niamh felt the surge of blood through his muscles. Sensed the latent potential for strength he had. His aggression thrummed through her and found an answering rhythm within her.

More wolves appeared from between the boulders. They stood back as the alpha approached her, wary but curious.

Alpha stopped with only three feet separating them and sat down.

Niamh crouched until she was slightly below his eye level.

About six other wolves stood between the boulders, and she looked at each in turn. A heavily pregnant female stood to the back, flanked by two younger males.

She saw them all through the connection with the alpha. Learned their names, which were not names as humans understood them, but rather a collection of sense memories associated with a particular wolf.

Through Alpha she learned that like the coven, pack had suffered and withered in the years since the coven had fallen. Alpha was young and strong, and he wanted more for pack.

They had been waiting for her. The revelation didn't make sense, so Niamh tucked it away to think about later. Alongside the incredible reality that she had connected with a pack of wolves. In England.

Apparently not nearly as extinct as everyone thought.

Pack had always been here, silent and unseen as they bided their time. Until her.

She would help pack. Together they would grow in power.

She *was* pack.

THERE WAS A DAMNED good reason Warren had been sentenced to anger management workshops, but the surge of primal hostility currently thrumming through him was unlike anything he'd felt before.

It scared the crap out of him.

The prat next to him deserved a smackdown for the way he spoke to the girl with him, but the kind of unadulterated fury gripping Warren was more of the taking him apart limb by limb variety.

He breathed deep and sipped his pint.

Since his hook up with Edana, Bonnie just had to glance his way to have his pint poured and waiting. Fortunately, he hadn't seen Edana since that night. He shouldn't have taken her up on her offer, but in the end, the beer, her persistence, and the desire to forget his shit for a moment had ambled him straight down thinking-with-my-cock boulevard, and he'd taken her back to his room.

Memories got a bit hazy after his door had shut, and he preferred it that way.

"Don't be so fucking stupid." Dead Man Walking stuck his face into his girl's and hissed at her.

Fuck him up! Maim! Kill!

Warren's blood rose fiercer and hotter, and he gripped his

pint so hard he was afraid the glass would crack, but it was that or murder.

Nearly Dead had one of those boy band hairdos that probably took longer than his girlfriend's to perfect. Sickly sweet aftershave waft blanketed Warren's side of the pub, and that alone was reason enough to take him apart.

Some dimly yelling part of Warren's brain tried to let him know that Houston most definitely did have a problem. But the pounding in his blood and the rise of aggression drowned nearly everything else out.

Walking Corpse's girlfriend lowered her head and tried defending herself. "I'm not stupid, Ricky. Don't call me stupid."

"I'll call you what I fucking well want." Dead Ricky stuck his chin out and squared his shoulders. "And you'll take it. You know why?"

Eyes huge and staring, she shook her head.

Warren leaned closer to catch Dead Ricky's last words on this planet.

"Because you're a worthless cunt." Dead Ricky smirked. "In every way. You're not even a halfway decent shag. Nothing but a stupid, worthless cunt."

Warren stood and grabbed Dead Ricky's shoulder.

Still full of bravado, Dead Ricky turned and fronted. "What the fuck—"

He looked up and up some more and met Warren's gaze. Then he turned paler than his crisply pressed white shirt and swallowed.

"Outside." Through the pounding fury, Warren had enough presence of mind not to commit murder in a crowded pub.

Dead Ricky shook his head. "I don't got no quarrel with you, mate."

"You do now." Warren hauled him to his feet. Dead Ricky must work out but gym-boy pretty muscle didn't stack up against the kind you paid for in blood. "The minute you opened your fucking mouth and disrespected your girl, you earned yourself my attention."

A tall man with dark hair appeared behind Dead Ricky. Another dark-haired man stood beside him. They looked like brothers, kind of. There was something about them...

"Good evening." The first one spoke in a deep voice that must have come from way, way down inside his barnlike chest. He looked right at Warren and paid no attention to Dead Ricky.

Dead Ricky tried to squirm away, but the second man blocked him. "Horribly bad idea," he drawled in an accent so posh it made Warren's teeth ache. "My friend is already a tad excited, and you don't want to rev him up more."

Friend? Warren raised his eyebrow at the prick and called bullshit.

The prat was good looking enough for even him to notice. He raised his eyebrow and chuckled at Warren.

Both men were the same height as him. The first one might even be an inch or two taller. He was, for sure, an inch or two wider than Warren. The term built like a brick shithouse fit him.

"Sit down." Brick Shithouse scowled at Dead Ricky.

Dead Ricky sat. "I didn't do nothing," he sniveled.

"Dear God." Pretty Boy flinched. "I should kill you for crimes against the English language." He turned to Dead Ricky's girlfriend and smiled. "And how are you?"

"Fine." Agape, she blinked at him like she'd just seen God. "Ricky didn't mean nothing by it."

Pretty Boy flinched again. "Anything," he said. "Ricky didn't mean anything by it, and if he didn't mean anything by it, he shouldn't have said it." He leaned closer to her, and she flushed and watched him as if hypnotized. "And if I may say so, a lovely woman such as yourself deserves so much better."

"Are you fucking wenching?" Brick Shithouse turned on Pretty Boy. "Now?"

"I never wench." Pretty Boy smirked. "I don't need to. But I am merely letting the young woman know she is worth more than this piece of shit."

"Hey," whispered Dead Ricky, but very, very softly.

Brick Shithouse snorted and turned back to Warren. "What you're feeling now. The battle fury." He shook his head. "Not you." Then he frowned. "Well, not entirely you."

Warren could only stare at the guy. He had no idea how he'd known that. "Huh?"

"Words are not Roderick's strong suit." Pretty Boy stepped in with a translation. "You're feeling abnormally bellicose. More than you normally do. Are we right?"

Before he could think of a response, his head beat him to it and nodded.

"Granted, that is an annoying little prick." He jerked his head at Dead Ricky. "And you'd step in anyway, but right now you'd like to kill him."

Dead Ricky fumbled for his phone. "I'm calling the coppers."

"Shut your hole." Roderick crowded Dead Ricky against the bar. He grabbed his phone and crushed it in one meaty fist.

Warren winced. Those iPhones did not come cheap.

Dead Ricky whimpered as Roderick dropped the bits of iPhone to the floor. "You can't do that."

"He's a barbarian." Pretty Boy smirked. "You have no idea what he's capable of."

Warren believed him.

Roderick glared at Pretty Boy.

Pretty Boy chuckled.

Warren managed his first coherent sentence since their arrival. "Who are you?"

"We'll get to that," Pretty Boy said, and then leaned closer to Dead Ricky. "Run away now."

Dead Ricky legged it.

His girlfriend stood and stared at Pretty Boy.

Pretty Boy took her hand and led her away from the bar. "Let me get you an Uber."

Roderick eyed Warren's pint then reached over and grabbed it. He downed it in one drink and slammed it back on the bar.

Eyeing his empty glass, Warren had to chuckle. "Would you like a drink?"

Roderick chuckled. "It looked really tasty."

"Was it?"

"Aye." His smile looked rusty, like he didn't use it often. "I came here for you."

Bonnie was nowhere in sight all of a sudden as Warren looked for her to order another pint. He should be getting twitchy about some random huge fucker stating he had come looking for him, and then finishing his pint, but he wasn't even slightly bothered. The bloke felt familiar in a strange way, but Warren knew he'd never met him before.

"You've been having dreams," Roderick said. "You came here because of those dreams." He chuckled and Warren wanted to laugh with him, but he resisted. "Truth be told, you could not stop yourself from coming here, and now you are wondering why."

Roderick couldn't have sucker punched him more with one of those massive hammer fists. "Eh?"

"You've been dreaming of a woman, and she's calling you. There's also a redhead in the same dreams, and you saw her the other day at Baile as well." Tense and alert, Roderick scanned the pub constantly. "But here is not the place to speak of this."

"Where then?" He needed to know how this guy knew as much as he did. He wanted fucking answers. His earlier aggro had dissipated, however, and that baffled him right along with the rest of this weird interaction.

Roderick nodded. "Baile. Come to Baile tomorrow, and we'll answer all your questions."

"And if I don't?" He had to voice a token protest about them thinking they could fuck with him.

"Then you don't get your answers." Roderick shrugged. "But you will come."

The arrogance could go as well. "You're sure of that?"

"Aye." Roderick leaned closer. "Because you're one of us." He pounded Warren on the shoulder. "You are coimhdeacht, and you have been called." He turned and called over his shoulder. "Baile. Tomorrow."

Niamh woke the next morning to the smell of bacon and eggs cooking. It took her a moment to realize that she could smell them from all the way in her tower. She'd only left the wolves when night forced her back home yesterday, but a greater sense of smell seemed to have stayed with her.

It gave her a new appreciation for the dogs who always surrounded her.

Tummy rumblingly hungry for one of Alannah's breakfasts, she got dressed and left her room. She wanted to know what had happened when Alexander and Roderick had gone to the Hag's Head to speak with the new one. She'd like to put a name to his face, and soon.

Vrrrt! Woo-hoo-haha. Arms stretched straight out behind her, Roz skittered toward her. She circled Niamh, and then stopped in front of her and bobbed.

"Good morning, Roz." She always spoke as if her aunt still understood. "I'm on my way to the kitchen if you'd like some breakfast."

Roz bobbed and cooed and then dropped into place

beside her.

That was new. Roz normally ran ahead of her.

"Did you sleep well?"

Roz had made a nest in a small corner of the great hall, dragged bits of paper and fabric into a pile. Chances were, if a bill or a letter went missing, Roz was using it as bedding.

Roz ignored the question and clicked. More than the normal amount of clicking, and Niamh studied her closer. With pink cheeks and sparkling eyes, Roz wore an air of suppressed excitement.

Niamh stopped. "What is it?"

Woo-hoo-ha. Click. Click. Click.

One of these days, she or Bronwyn would find out how to get through to Roz and communicate with her more effectively.

Roz ran ahead, stood there bobbing, and then ran back.

"You want me to hurry?" And Niamh's increased sense of smell let her know that Roz was due a bath soon, a fun procedure involving cajoling, threats and bodily force.

Roz bobbed and clicked, so Niamh took that as a yes and hurried after her.

From the way Roz behaved, it didn't feel like a bad surprise waiting.

In the kitchen, most of Baile's inhabitants had beaten her to breakfast.

Maeve sat beside Roderick, who had his arm draped over the back of her chair. Sheltering Maeve within his physical presence was second nature to Roderick.

"Good morning, Niamh." Maeve gave her a sweet smile.

"Hi." Niamh liked Maeve, and she fit into their coven as if she'd always been there, which she kind of had, only as a statue for almost five hundred years. It made her head hurt thinking about it too much. "Nice outfit."

"I'm fly." Maeve grinned back. She wore a floaty boho top and jeans this morning and had painted each of her fingernails a different color. Maeve had adjusted to some parts of this century with great gusto. She'd experimented with dying her blond hair, but it always went right back to its natural color by the next morning.

Sinead looked over from where she was buttering toast and jerked her chin. "You were out late last night."

"Yes." Niamh didn't know why, but she wanted to hug the discovery of the wolves to herself for a while. She still didn't quite believe it, and talking about it, and seeing her coven sister's doubts would sour the sweetness of the secret. "It was a great night."

Roderick snorted. "If you're a duck."

"Quack, quack!" She lightly punched the top of his shoulder as she went past. It would take a jackhammer to make a dent in that shoulder.

Alannah turned to her from the stove, her face pink from the heat of cooking. Spatula in one hand, she cocked her head and studied Niamh. "You look different this morning."

"I slept well." Niamh took her seat beside Alexander and winked at him. "Hey, handsome. Looking particularly tasty this morning."

"Right back at you." He winked back and gave her his knee-trembling smile.

Sinead pulled a face. "Ugh! You two are nauseating."

"But in a good way, right?" Alexander grinned at Sinead.

And even hard arse Sinead wasn't immune to all that male charm aimed at her.

"We met your coimhdeacht," Alexander said.

"They are not bonded yet," Roderick grumbled. "He is not her coimhdeacht until he accepts the calling and bonds his witch."

"My bad." Alexander rolled his eyes. "We met your potential coimhdeacht last night."

Roderick huffed. "You cannot call him coimhdeacht until he accepts the calling."

"Where is that written?" Alexander turned and stuck his chin out at Roderick.

"I am the first coimhdeacht." Roderick jabbed a thumb at his chest. "I don't need to see it written somewhere in order to know that a thing is true."

"Jesus. Can any of us forget that?"

Maeve touched Roderick's forearm and looked at Alexander. "It's true though. He is the first, and he has been doing this for a very long time."

Always a sucker for Maeve, Alexander simmered right down again. "You're right, sweeting. But you know he and I cannot resist a fight."

"Can you tell me more about him?" Niamh couldn't believe how far off topic they'd gotten.

"We could." Roderick nodded.

Maeve elbowed him in the ribs.

"He is of a height with Alexander and me," Roderick said. "Closer to my build than that piece of thistledown over there."

"Don't hate me because I'm beautiful." Alexander batted his eyelashes at Roderick.

Niamh wanted to bang their bloody heads together. "I know what he looks like, I saw him. What was he like?"

Roderick and Alexander looked bemused and then glanced at each other.

"I think Niamh wants to know more about his personality." Alannah put a platter of sausages and bacon on the table. "Was he nice? Did he have a sense of humor?"

Roderick gaped at her. "We only met him for a few minutes."

"And frankly, for all of those he was about ready to take some prat's head off his shoulders," Alexander said.

Niamh's heart sank. "He's a thug?"

"No." Alexander stilled. "Well, I don't think so at any rate. After Roderick, Goddess stayed away from the brainless louts."

"He was in the grip of a protective rage." Roderick piled sausages and bacon on his plate. "You're near and his calling is urging him to protect you. You must have been doing something that his calling registered as not safe."

"I wasn't." Even she knew she'd spoken a tad too fast. The fact that everybody was now staring at her confirmed her suspicion. "I mean, I was walking outside, but I was still within the wards, and thus perfectly safe."

Alpha flit through her awareness, and she thought he might be amused by the conversation.

Pack.

Thomas popped into sight beside Alannah, making Sinead jump.

"Sodding hell!" She nearly tipped her plate of toast on the floor. "Could you hang a bell around your neck or something? The way you do that is bloody creepy."

Thomas shrugged. "Creepy is part of the whole ghost thing."

"It's dumb." Sinead slammed the toast on the table and took her seat.

Thomas leaned over Alannah's shoulder. "That looks good enough to make me wish I could eat it."

She smiled back at him and blushed, then brought a large bowl of scrambled eggs to the table and put it down. She sat beside Sinead, and Thomas hovered behind her.

He looked right at Niamh and mouthed the word pack.

After breakfast she was definitely getting him alone and asking him how much he knew about the wolves. His first bond had been with a guardian, like her, and it stood to reason Lavina would have known about the wolves. They might not even have been extinct when Lavina was alive.

"We will know more today," Roderick said, adding a mountain of eggs to his plate. "We invited him to Baile."

Really? They couldn't have told her that first?

Maeve shook her head at Roderick. "You should have said that first."

"And ruin the suspense?" He gave Maeve the sweet half smile he saved only for her.

"He might come today." Alexander shrugged.

Roderick dug into his breakfast. "He'll come."

"Maybe."

"Definitely."

"When?" Niamh cut in before they could get started again.

Both men shrugged.

Before she could get after them, Bronwyn stumbled into the kitchen looking pale and exhausted. She took one look at the bacon and grimaced. "Ugh!"

Alexander pushed his chair back and held out his hand.

Like they had it choreographed, Bronwyn took his hand and slid onto his lap.

He kissed her temple. "Feeling any better?"

"Not really." Bronwyn pulled a face. "But I thought I could try some tea and toast."

Something smelled different. Niamh stopped eating and isolated the scent. She sifted through the food smells and one by one eliminated the people, until she came to Bronwyn. The new smell came from Bronwyn, and it wasn't chemical, it came from inside her.

Alpha perked up in her awareness and concentrated on the smell. What the smell meant popped into her head as an image and she sat up straight.

"Bronwyn you're—"

"Tired." Alexander's stare bored into her. He spoke deliberately and slowly. "Bronwyn is tired and not feeling great."

Niamh wanted to argue with him, but the way he looked at her issued a clear warning to be quiet. She didn't get it.

Bronwyn was pregnant. She knew it, and she suspected Alexander knew it as well. Alpha had confirmed it.

She sent Alexander a look that told him she would keep her mouth shut. For now. But he better have a damn good reason.

He gave her a subtle nod and turned his full attention back to Bronwyn dozing against his chest.

Mags peeked at Bronwyn, her eyes sparkling with a delightful secret. She looked at Niamh and winked.

Sinead, Alannah and Maeve seemed blissfully ignorant, but Roderick studied Bronwyn with a speculative gleam, and the look he threw Alexander said he knew exactly who was to blame for what he suspected.

Breakfast passed quickly as nobody had much to say. Bronwyn left halfway through, looking a pale shade of green as she did.

"I know." Alexander held up his hand to forestall Niamh before she could demand an explanation. "And I will tell her."

"Tell me I am misunderstanding." Roderick looked ready to behead someone. You only needed one guess to know who.

Alexander spread his hands and looked apologetic. "You know as well as I that there is no preventing a prophecy. We did all we could to avoid this."

"Prophecy?" Sinead perked up. "What prophecy? I only know of one prophecy and that was about Alexander and Bronwyn getting together and...oh!" She snapped her mouth shut.

Alannah leaned forward and whispered, "Bronwyn is pregnant?"

"Oh, yes." Mags beamed. "But she's ignoring it."

"Why?" Maeve frowned. "Children are such a blessing."

"She's a healer." Alexander leaned back in his chair. "She knows better than any of us the signs, and if she's not acknowledging the reality, then it means she's not ready to. She's had a lot to deal with since she arrived in England, and I'm not going to rush her into getting comfortable something this big."

"But—" And Niamh's argument died in her throat, because it was kind of sweet. Bronwyn's life had been turned on its head since she'd come here from America. Being the mother to a child from an ancient prophecy would make anyone edgy. "What are you going to do?"

"Wait for her to tell me," Alexander said. "And pretend like hell I had no idea."

8

W arren stood at his bedroom window and stared. "It's just a fucking castle on a fucking hill."

But he was, at best, only half convinced and repeating it did nothing but tighten the knot in his gut. If he wanted answers, he had to go up there and talk to Roderick and his pretty friend. After meeting them, he didn't think they were brothers anymore, but there was a definite resemblance. It could be the way they held themselves.

He had been standing staring at Baile for the better part of an hour. "All dressed up and too scared to go," he whispered, and then checked the room behind him as if he suddenly expected someone to be standing there—having somehow gotten through the locked door without him being aware.

Maybe it was the age of the place, but the Hag's Head unsettled him. He found himself checking behind him constantly. There had never been anyone there, but that feeling of being watched persisted.

"I bet you can't tell me why that is," he said to the silent castle. "For all your claims that you have the answers I'm looking for."

But was he really looking for answers?

Mum Betty had always told him never to ask questions he didn't really want to hear the answers to, and this situation dovetailed neatly with that piece of advice.

He had a strange woman calling him in his dreams to a place he'd not known before. It still boggled his brain that he was actually here. Then there was the stunning redhead at the castle and the overwhelming sense of connection he'd felt with her. Finally, Roderick and company showing up last night as he was about to pound the hell out of Dead Ricky.

He had shit back home that needed sorting. Big crap, like getting Debra to let him see Taylor again. Debra would be mollified if he could get a better job, meaning one that paid better, than the construction work he had been doing. Turns out people didn't like hiring large men with anger management issues. True story.

Tired of his procrastinating, he picked up his phone and dialed Jack.

"What the hell's going on?" Jack answered.

Warren picked his words carefully. "Funny story."

"I'm always up for a laugh."

"Remember the place I told you about? The one in my dreams." He wasn't quite sure how to carry on without shooting himself in the foot.

Jack took a deep breath. "The one I told you not to go to?"

"I'm there." The truth was out there now, and Jack knew.

"Why?"

That was an even harder question to answer. "I've explained it to you before."

"Give it another go."

So, he did. Words were horribly inadequate to describe the strength of the compulsion he felt to be here, his reaction to the castle, the sense of being exactly where he should be...even the redhead. He wound down with his encounter last night with Roderick and company.

"Now, I'm standing in my room pissing about as to whether to go to the castle or not."

Jack went silent for a long moment. "You might as well." He sighed. "You've gone all that way on a woman talking to you in a dream. Dropping by for tea and a chat with two blokes who might be able to clear some of this up hardly seems a stretch."

Jack had a handy knack for putting things in perspective. "I suppose. What about the redhead?"

"What about her?"

"I think she lives there. At least, I saw her up there."

"Let's leave the woman out of this." Jack chuckled. "Don't take this the wrong way, mate, but you have horrible luck with women."

Ouch! "I'll give you Debra, but that's it."

"The waitress at the Raven," Jack said.

"Okay, but I didn't know she had a boyfriend."

Jack laughed harder. "Who happened to be part of a biker gang."

"All right." He knew when he was beat. "I'll give you those two."

"The girl with—"

"Shut up, Jack. Nobody likes a fucking know-it-all."

Jack's guffawed and Warren had to hold the phone away from his ear out of respect for his eardrums.

Eventually Jack sobered. "Go for the answers and leave the woman alone. You pick the needy ones," he said. "The ones who want to bleed you dry."

As much as he'd like to argue—Debra. Another true story. "So, you're thinking I should go to the castle?"

"I'd be disappointed if you didn't."

"Right then." Outside his window, Baile napped in a gentle

midday sun. The sea slunk around the beach at her feet. "I'm off to a fucking castle on a fucking hill."

HE WASN'T the bloody fanciful sort, but as Warren rode slowly up the one winding road to Baile, it felt like the sodding castle beckoned him.

His surprise holiday into Club Crazy had taken one step further. He was going to ask those smug fuckers for the answers they'd promised. Only, he'd ask politely because even Pretty Boy was a formidably big bastard, and maybe he wouldn't call them fuckers either—at least not to their faces.

Baile loomed closer. Impressive and timeless in a way that modern buildings dreamed they'd grow up to be. It must be a bugger to keep something that big clean, and he didn't even want to think of their heating bill. Seemed to him like keeping it open to the public and taking money for tours would have been a no brainer. He'd add that to his list of questions, but he already had a bunch that all started with *what the fuck*.

He passed the point where he had stopped on the shoulder last time and cursed himself for scanning for the redhead.

His brief encounter with the redhead had burrowed into his brain the way a night with Edana hadn't. He still hadn't run into her again, which was odd, considering Bonnie had treated her like a difficult to please regular. Not that he wanted to run into her again. The night he'd spent with her had been a mistake and yanked him back to a time when nights like that had been one on a shopping list of bad decisions and mistakes.

The itch swept over him suddenly, tiny pinpricks beneath his skin. It centered on his left arm and then disappeared as suddenly as it had come.

Warren stopped his bike and shrugged out of his jacket to check his arm.

"What the fuck?" Apparently, he did have another WTF for the list. Umber swirling patterns decorated his forearm, and then faded. He stared at his arm, waiting for the marks to come back, but his skin looked the same way it always did. It must be this place getting to him.

He rode slowly over the drawbridge, beneath the gatehouse and into the bailey.

Home.

"I beg your pardon." He stopped his bike again and removed his helmet. There was nobody there, but he'd already known that, and still the voice had sounded as real as if someone had whispered in his ear.

Gray stone interspersed with windows surrounded the bailey. Sharp gull shrieks undercut the murmur of the sea.

The top half of a stable door opened directly opposite from where he sat, and Pretty Boy leaned his forearms against the bottom ledge. "Is that as far as you're coming?"

"Maybe." And in that moment, he was sorely tempted to turn his bike around and forget he'd ever seen this place. An odd sense of inevitability nagged at him.

A door to his right opened, and a cute redhead stepped into the bailey and gave him a smile. She was petite but still managed to curve in all the right places. "Hi, I'm Bronwyn, and all this must feel overwhelming."

"Hi." He took the hand she offered. She was American.

Pretty Boy beelined it for Bronwyn and slid his arm around her. "Hey, little witch."

Witch? Strangely enough, not the weirdest thing he had to contend with since that bloody voice had started whispering to him.

Alexander's gaze met Warren's over her head, and the message was clear—mine, all mine.

Warren edged his bike to a spot near the wall and parked it.

He stepped off and hung his helmet on the handlebars. "You said you had answers."

"We also have tea." Bronwyn was pretty enough, but that big, open smile of hers took her into beautiful territory. "Or something stronger, if you'd prefer. I'd stay away from Sinead's elderberry cordial if I were you."

"No cordial." He nodded and slipped his leather jacket off his shoulders. With no wind to dissipate the heat, the sun baked down and made him sweat.

Alexander motioned him through the door. "After you."

Warren wasn't sure what he'd expected on the other side of the door, but a large, comfortable kitchen wasn't it. A solid wooden table sat in the center with seating for at least twelve people. A huge range oven occupied what must have once been the cooking hearth. From the ceiling, drying plants and copper pots dangled. The modern fridge and dishwasher stuck out like dog's balls in what might have been a time warp into a bygone century.

"Oh, you're here." Another redhead appeared through the dark arch leading into the rest of the castle. Tall and reed slim, her hair reached past her waist. Her face was quietly pretty but for her compelling green eyes. Those eyes made him feel stripped to his essence, all his sins exposed before her. She wore a white cotton muumuu type thing, and her bare feet peeped out from the hem. She held out a bracelet-bedecked arm to him. "I'm Mags, and you're Warren Masters."

"Eh?" His hackles came up. "You know my name?"

She shrugged and wrinkled her nose. "Sorry, but I know stuff. It's what I do."

"Have a seat." Pretty Boy clapped him on the shoulder. "Roderick will be along as soon as I get the cork out of the whisky."

Bronwyn walked past Warren and put her hand on his shoulder. "I know." Her smile held him transfixed for a moment. "It's all a lot to take in. I've only been here a couple of months, and I still struggle with all of it."

"All of what?"

Bronwyn left him with another sweet smile.

"We'll get to that." Pretty Boy slid a whisky glass his way and held out his hand. "In all the excitement, I haven't introduced myself. Alexander."

"Warren." He took the proffered hand and glanced at Mags. "Masters. Warren Masters."

She gave him a nod of approval like he was in nursery school and had managed to color inside the lines. "I'll see you later, Warren. You're going to be fine, and I know this because I know stuff."

"Thanks, Magsie." Alexander put his arm around her shoulder, and unlike the gesture with Bronwyn, this one was purely platonic. "Roderick and I will take it from here. Maybe you can let Niamh know Warren is here?"

"She's with her wolv—she's out." Mags wrinkled her nose. "But they can sense him, which means she will to."

Whatever that meant. Warren sipped his whisky. He stopped and sniffed. He would hardly call himself a whisky connoisseur, but he knew enough to know he was sipping the sort of single malt he'd have to sell his bike to drink again.

"Ah!" Roderick strode into the kitchen from outside.

A gorgeous blonde trailed him into the kitchen and stood there and grinned at him. "Oh, hello. Aren't you a handsome one? Niamh is a very lucky girl."

Roderick raised an eyebrow and stared at her.

The blonde giggled and made a face at Roderick. "He's got a mirror."

"And his own witch."

She slid her arm through Roderick's and turned her laughing face up to him. "And I have you."

Warren wouldn't say Roderick softened. His big, hard body

and harsh face could never gentle, but it was like something inside his cold blue eyes melted. "I'll be busy for a while. Stay out of trouble."

"Maybe." She nudged Roderick with her shoulder and winked at Warren. "You are a most welcome addition to Baile."

He nearly stopped her to tell her he wasn't anyone's addition, but she'd get the idea soon enough anyway.

"Right." Roderick rubbed his hands together and looked at Alexander. "Barracks, I think."

"Lead the way." Alexander stood.

Roderick strode for the same doorway the blonde had walked through. "Come along then." He glanced over his shoulder and jabbed a thumb at the whisky bottle. "And bring that."

The arched doorway led to a stairwell. Roderick in front, Alexander bringing up the rear and him in the middle—the idiot sandwich.

The stairwell opened onto a great hall. Easily a hundred meters long, it was half that wide. Stone pillars marched in regular intervals down both sides of the hall, with a good four modern stories above, and arched wooden beams formed an intricate lattice of support. That way of supporting a ceiling was called something. He'd learned about it when he was in school.

"Stone vaulted ceiling," Alexander murmured. "History buffs cream themselves about it."

Their footsteps echoed through the empty hall. Strangely, the hall didn't carry that atmosphere of an abandoned place. It merely seemed to be... waiting. Waiting for its people to come and fill it again.

How many people would it take to make a space like this feel full? And was he supposed to be one of them?

Large fabric banners hung at intervals between the pillars. He glimpsed symbols that he promised himself he would come back and examine in more detail later. Colors still bright, the banners showed no signs of age, as he'd expect in a castle this old, and Warren got the uneasy feeling they were genuine.

At the far end of the hall, sunlight streamed through a stained-glass window and made colored mosaics on the stone floor.

Warren stopped and stared. Something about the image set his teeth on edge. Three women stood beside a pool under a large spreading tree. Beside the last woman—surprise, surprise, a redhead—there was negative space that looked as if it needed filling.

"The first three." Roderick stopped and came to stand beside him. "Deidre, Tahra and Brenna." He pointed at the women in turn. "Healer, guardian and seer, and also three of the first four witches called into service to Goddess."

The men in this place threw the W-word around. "Goddess?"

"Aye." Roderick's voice deepened and his face filled with awe. "The creator of all that is life, power and joy. Mother to all of us, and the one who has been whispering into your dreams."

"Not the redhead?" Of all the things he could have said, he picked that one. Jesus, he was a stupid prat.

Roderick grinned, and it made him semi approachable. "You mean Niamh?"

"We have a plethora of redheads." Alexander flanked him. "But of course you mean Niamh."

"Why of course?" It wasn't often that he stood shoulder to shoulder with other men.

"Because she's your witch," Roderick said. "But we'll get to that."

"There were four witches called originally." Alexander stared at the stained-glass window, green and pink light playing over his face. "One for each element: air, fire, water and earth."

"And one for each of the original blessings," Roderick said. "Healer, seer, guardian and warden."

Warren gestured the window. "You're missing someone."

"She got tired of playing second fiddle to Goddess." Roderick's face hardened and Warren suppressed the desire to take a life-preserving step away from him. "She tried to take over from Goddess, lost, and was cast out of the coven and cut off from the magic."

Witches and covens, and now they were tossing in goddesses and magic. "So, she's dead?"

"Unfortunately, not." Alexander grimaced. "She popped up about three hundred years after they tossed her out and tried to overrun the coven."

Three hundred—

"Enough." Roderick's voice grew as cold as his expression. "We have time for history lessons later, but for now, all you need to know is her name is Rhiannon. She is ancient, she is powerful, and she is Alexander's mother." He spun and strode away. "Also, you are now on her list of people she would like to kill."

"Eh?" He stood there like someone had planted him and tried to sort all he'd heard into sense.

Alexander gave him a sympathetic grimace. "All true. Now, come along."

Feeling like a toddler on a nightmare trip to the zoo, he trailed the other men to a massive arched wooden door bristling with metal reinforcement. "I guess you don't want anyone going in there without an invitation."

Roderick grunted and pushed the door open. "Fortunately, you received your invitation via dream."

Beyond the door, light streamed into a corridor lined with windows along one side. The whole of Greater Littleton spread before him, but Roderick and Alexander weren't stopping to admire the view, which meant neither was he. Stone floors gleamed in the sun, and wooden wainscoting ran along the opposite side to the windows.

Above the wainscoting, massive tapestries displayed battle scenes in vivid, and often gory, detail. It was like a reenactors wet dream, with a dragon thrown in for good measure. One figure caught his eye and he stopped. "Hey." He pointed to a huge, dark-haired man swinging a battle axe. "He looks like you," he said to Roderick. "Ancestor?"

Roderick grunted and kept walking.

The corridor ended in six wide stone steps leading down to an arched double door. There was more metal on this one than the previous door. "Did Baile get attacked a lot?"

"Only once." Roderick pushed the doors open and strode through.

"Welcome."

"You are returned."

"Enter."

"You are of us."

Barely discernible male voices came from within him and gave him the most complete sense of peace he'd ever experienced.

He walked farther into the wide-open space and stopped.

The place was an armory. The walls were lined with weapons and armor. Swords of varying sizes and shapes, daggers of every kind. Then there were pikes, lances, battle axes, maces, longbows, crossbows, war hammers and flails. His low whistle broke the silence. "Expecting trouble?"

"A coimhdeacht always expects trouble," Roderick said. "This is our armory."

He'd guessed that already. Unable to resist, the little boy in him demanding to be appeased, he reached out and touched the edge of the gleaming six feet of sword.

Blood bloomed on his finger moments before he realized he'd cut himself. "Motherfucker."

"Regard that as your first lesson." Alexander clapped him

on the shoulder. "Swords are sharp, because if they're not sharp, they're not much good to you."

Roderick huffed and kept walking. He passed to the right of a wooden table with benches. Another three tables kept it company in the center of the room. Through an open archway, Roderick led them into an even bigger, oval-shaped room.

"The practice yard." Roderick gestured around them. "You will need to master the sword."

Baile's people made a truckload of assumptions about him and what he would and wouldn't do.

More weapons hung on the walls, but these were more businesslike and looked well used. The far wall of windows provided a bird's-eye view to all land approaches to Baile.

The last thing Roderick had said registered with him. "What the hell am I going to do with a sword?"

"Protect Niamh." Roderick looked at him as if he was short a fuse or two in the brainbox.

It pissed Warren off enough to say, "Pretty sure I can do that already, and much better with a semi-automatic."

"Even a handgun." Alexander smirked. "But you should learn the sword anyway."

He thought they'd lost their minds, but he'd play along for now. "Why?"

"It's a sword." Alexander grinned. "Is there a boy alive who doesn't want to know how to use one?"

He opened his mouth to argue, and then shut it again. Because fair point. Forget about only boys wanting to play with swords, his Taylor would give her eye-teeth to know how to sword fight.

"We sleep through there." Roderick gestured another doorway and passage. "There are currently only two rooms occupied, so you can pick which one you want."

"I'm not staying here." Several doors opened off the corridor, and Warren guessed they each went to a room.

Male laughter sounded around him, but neither Alexander nor Roderick joined in. They stared at him incredulously. The hair on his nape stood on end. "Who's laughing?"

"Your brothers," Roderick said, as if it were the most logical explanation in the world. "The souls of our lost brothers can choose to remain at Baile. They already know the battle you wage within yourself, because each one of them waged it. And lost."

"Did you?" He was starting to feel hemmed in, and he didn't fucking like it.

Roderick smiled. "Indeed, I did." He spread his arms. "But as you can see, I also lost."

Warren turned to Alexander. "I guess the same goes for you."

"No." Alexander shook his head. "I am not coimhdeacht."

"What now?" Warren had heard that word in his dream it sounded like kweev and duct but it made no sense to him.

"It's an ancient word meaning guardian and escort," Alexander said. "Roderick was the first."

"But that's impossible." They must be having him on. The first of these kweev-whatevers must go back to those tapestries he'd seen on the way here. "He doesn't look a day over thirty-five."

Alexander chuckled. "Oh, he's many days past thirty-five, but he gets grumpy if we remind him of his age."

With a scowl tossed at Alexander, Roderick came to stand behind him. "You have been called to a higher purpose, Warren Masters. You have been chosen by Goddess to join an ancient and noble brotherhood."

Alexander scoffed. "Laying it on a bit thick, old man."

"If you accept your calling, you will bond your life to that of a witch, and your life's purpose will be to guard and protect her, and Goddess will shower blessings upon you, one of her chosen, for your service."

Warren tried not to feel special about the whole chosen one thing, because a lot of what they bandied about didn't sit right with him. "Why would anyone want to do that?"

"To be part of something greater than themselves. To make their life meaningful. To be an agent of change for the better," Alexander said. He motioned for Warren to turn. "See. Your brothers in arms join you."

Warren turned and froze.

Shadowy figures appeared and vanished. Men, all dressed like warriors, and they stood in the practice yard and looked at him.

"For hundreds of years, we have served." Roderick put his fist on his chest and bowed.

Ghost warriors bowed with him.

"But these guys are all dead." Part of his brain keep nattering on about him looking at a room full of ghosts. That same brain part also insisted that the ghosts looking back should scare the balls off him.

Instead, he felt...serene. At home. "These guys have all died?"

"Aye." Roderick cleared his throat. "It is the warrior's way."

Years as a soldier had taught Warren as much. It was part and parcel when you signed up for the job. "Tell me again what this means for me."

One of the ghosts stepped forward, and if Warren hadn't seen the bugger blink into existence, he would have believed him flesh and blood.

"I am called Thomas," he said. "And I was the last coimhdeacht called before...well, before you." Thomas grinned.

Warren wanted to hear the thing Thomas hadn't said. The mysteries were doing his head in. "When was that?"

"Before you were born," Thomas said. "Like you, I was unprepared for what it meant and not sure I wanted it."

Warren nodded. Then the nag in his brain stepped up. *We're agreeing with a ghost.*

"You have been called to protect Niamh," Thomas said. "In the earlier days, when the witches numbered many, it was harder to work out who your witch was. Except when you met her, you knew."

Roderick nodded and folded his arms.

"As her coimhdeacht, you will bond with Niamh."

It didn't sound like a sexual thing, but he needed to clarify. "What does this bond entail?"

"It's a merging of two minds, hearts and spirits," Roderick said. "You will feel what she feels, experience what she experiences and know her thoughts as she has them."

"Fuck." He really didn't like the sound of that. "That's a bit intrusive, isn't it?" And then the problematic flip side to that last revelation reared its head. "If I can know all this about her, then she can know the same about me."

"In theory." Thomas winked. "But we have ways of keeping the witches out of our minds."

"Then they must have ways of keeping you out of theirs."

"Not so much." Roderick chuckled. "We are less effective if we cannot be with them all the time."

Warren let the information filter through his brain fog. Less than two months ago, he'd been a retired soldier, father of one incredible daughter, working a dead-end construction job and keeping up with his anger management classes. "And this woman...Goddess, she chose me to do this protection thing for Niamh?"

Roderick nodded. "Aye."

"Are you sure?" He wasn't the heroic or noble type.

Alexander laughed. "You're here, aren't you?"

"Fuck."

Alexander held up the bottle of single malt. "Drink?"

"Yes."

9

CRÉ-WITCH CHRONICLES

"He's here?" Niamh slid to a halt inside the kitchen door and tried to catch her breath. She'd run straight for the castle the moment Alpha had shared the image of the new coimhdeacht entering Baile. "How long has he been here?"

"A while." Blinking at her, Alannah sounded apologetic. "You were out, and Roderick and Alexander took him to the barracks."

"But he is here now?" Alpha wouldn't have shown her a false image, but she was so thrilled he was here. The little girl part of her couldn't help but need to hear the information verified.

"As far as we know." Sinead shrugged and helped Alannah take muffins out of the baking tin. "He hasn't come this way, so he must still be here."

"Right!" She took the stairs two at a time. Her coimhdeacht, *hers*, was in the castle. Seems Roderick had been right that he would be back. She forced herself to stop and breathe at the door to the barracks. Her second chance to make a first impression had presented itself and she needed not to blow it by charging around like a sugared-up toddler.

"Breathe," she whispered to herself. Her heart deleted the memo and thumped in her chest. Goddess, but along with wolf packs, meeting her coimhdeacht was quite possibly one of the most exciting things to ever happen to her. Maybe her coimhdeacht. She kept forgetting that part.

Barely stopping herself from running, she located them sitting around a table sharing a bottle of scotch.

Warren had both elbows on the table and his blond head lowered over his glass.

Looking up at her, Roderick said, "Blessed."

"Coimhdeacht." Warren looked upset. Maybe the explanation part hadn't gone that well. Even Thomas looked grave. Unfortunate choice of words on her part, given Thomas was dead. She needed to stop with the mental babbling.

Then Warren looked up and their gazes met. And locked. She forgot to breathe.

He had the palest blue eyes, and they seemed to see right through her. "Hi."

"Hello again." She didn't know the right thing to say in the circumstances. Thanks for coming seemed flippant. Her spying trip lingered embarrassingly in the back of her mind.

Warren was a complete stranger to her. They knew nothing about each other, yet he was at Baile to enter into a bond with her that would make them more intimate than lovers. Might be about to enter a bond with her. The coimhdeacht chose the witch. Then again, Mags had said he was hers, and Mags was never wrong. More bloody mental babbling.

"I'm Niamh," she said when the silence had stretched to the screaming point. "I didn't introduce myself the other night. On the road I mean."

"How's the dog?"

"Fine."

He nodded. "My name is Warren. Warren Masters." He had a northern accent, and his voice was deep and raspy. Laugh lines grooved the sides of his mouth and fanned out from his eye corners.

"We were attempting to answer some of Warren's questions." Alexander slid smoothly into the leaden silence. "As you can imagine, he has many."

"Yes." She couldn't look away from Warren.

As children, they'd all heard stories of the mighty warrior guardians, the coimhdeacht. Before she'd met Roderick, she'd thought them a fairy tale, but that hadn't stopped her girlish heart from wishing she could have one. A guardian devoted entirely to you. A person for whom you were simply the most important being in their lives. For a girl who'd grown up as a coven orphan, there was something so achingly desirable about being so valued by one person that they'd forfeit their lives for you. "I'm sure this is all a bit of a shock." She made a silly waving motion to encompass the castle and all of them in it. "All of this."

He rubbed his nape. "I'm not sure I believe it, to be honest."

"I grew up here." She took a few steps forward. "And even I struggle with it."

Roderick slid the bench out for her. "Join us, Blessed." He grinned and poured her a shot of whisky.

Warren sat opposite her, closer than he'd been the other night. A small scar rested high on one cheekbone, and pale scruff matched the cropped blond hair on his head. He smelled like leather and soap and gave off palpable body heat. He also didn't gaze at her like he'd been ensnared by her magic.

"I see you have more dogs." Warren indicated her three-dog escort. "Are they all yours?"

"They follow me." She sipped her whisky. "They are my companions. I don't believe any creature owns another."

"Right." Warren narrowed his eyes. "But if they follow you; that would make you responsible for them and their actions."

Going that conversational route hadn't ended well at their first meeting. They had more important things to discuss, and she wanted to get to those. "I'm a guardian witch. Animals are my thing. I am linked to them."

"And that means?" Challenge hung in the air between them.

It caught her off guard. People didn't generally bristle around her. For the first time, ever, she kind of wished he had been caught in her lure. No, she didn't. What the bloody hell was she thinking?

Roderick, Alexander and Thomas rubbernecked like spectators at Wimbledon.

"It means I respect their nature as animals," she said. "I don't own them and I'm not some sort of weird overlord." She tried to keep her shrug light. "But I'm as much a part of the natural kingdom as they are."

"As a guardian witch, Niamh shares a bond with all animals." Roderick said. "She can share their senses and their awareness. She is here to protect and care for them."

"Not own them," Niamh said.

"Right." Warren nodded in a way that made it clear he didn't believe a word she said.

Niamh didn't think she'd said anything peculiar.

"What about the witch part?" Warren frowned. "Does that mean you have...magical powers." A hint of derision colored his tone. "Could you turn someone into a toad or something?"

"No." Unease trickled through her sternum.

Alexander glanced at her and then frowned at Warren. "We understand what we're telling you is all new to you."

"Yeah. So far today, we have castles, and ghosts, and Goddesses." Warren sat back with a supercilious grin and crossed his arms. "But witches? Come on, mate. You must be having me on." He indicated Niamh. "She doesn't look like any witch I've met."

"And you've met enough to say for sure?" Niamh didn't like his attitude one iota. Was he being confrontational with her? She was definitely picking up fight reflex. Even the dogs sensed an aggressive undertone coming from him.

Warren grimaced. "Fair enough, but witches are from a kid's story."

Accepting witches was only the beginning of their supposed future relationship. Needing to get them on more amicable footing, she smiled and tried to make a joke. "It doesn't work like that. I don't crinkle my nose or click my heels together either."

"No flying on broomsticks then?" He scoffed and downed his whisky. "God, this shit is messing with my head."

"By this shit, do you mean you being called?" Sweeping her arm, she encompassed the room. She wasn't handling this well, but her ability to soothe even the most difficult animal had momentarily deserted her.

Roderick regarded Warren through narrowed eyes.

"Baile? Them?" Niamh pointed to their avid male audience. "The existence of magic?" She'd spent her life as one of those "odd Cray women from the castle." Warren joining the ranks of her critics stung. Lump in her throat, she asked the question that would smart the most. "Or is it me?"

"It's been a lot of stuff coming at him." Alexander caught her hand and squeezed it. "I think Warren was merely expressing—"

"And I think Warren is doing a bang-up job expressing exactly what he thinks." Niamh turned back to Warren. She wanted to hear it from him.

Warren dropped her gaze. "I didn't mean it like that."

"Of course you didn't." Roderick refilled his glass.

"I meant this is all new to me. I'm having a hard time

believing any of this is real, believing that any of this is happening to me." He met her gaze. The direct look daring her to contradict him.

Niamh tried to see the situation from his point of view. All the new information flying his way had to be confusing. "I may have grown up with this, but I didn't have a choice either. I was born into a coven, and I've spent my whole life in that coven. But you coming here." She tried to organize her thoughts. "Perhaps to bond with me." She gestured between them. "That is all new."

He raised an eyebrow at her. "Really?"

"Yes, really." His antagonism felt personal. "I understand how all of this must sound to you. How you must feel—"

"I doubt that." He snorted.

Niamh ran out of words. Her previous excitement sat in a grizzled lump in her throat.

He stared at her with his arctic eyes, like she was the cause of his discontent.

It hurt, and Niamh wanted to go somewhere, anywhere he wasn't and sort through her jumbled thoughts and emotions. She finished her whisky and stood. "I'll leave you with Roderick and Alexander."

Maybe they could do a better job than she had of explaining things to him.

Warren, Alexander and Roderick stood with her.

"You're leaving?" Roderick frowned at her like she'd erred in some way.

"Yes. I have to..." She tried to pull herself together. She had always been good with people. Except for now when she had needed that ability most. "Things. I have things I need to do."

"Niamh?" Alexander's expression softened, and his sympathy threatened her composure further.

"Nice to meet you," Warren said.

The look on his face belied his statement. Why did we all

say things we didn't mean? She'd take animals over people every time. You always got the truth with animals. Warren Masters had not been pleased to meet her at all. Not one tiny bit.

THE REDHEAD HAD A NAME, Niamh, and it suited her. Wild, free and beautiful, she'd lost none of her impact since the first time he'd met her. He was sinking fast, and he needed to find his footing. Putting his glass down, he stood. "I think I'll go back to the pub."

Alexander and Roderick stood with him.

Roderick frowned and looked set to argue, but Alexander put a hand on his arm. "Look, we get it. There is so much to take in, and you need time to process."

"Process?" Roderick snorted. "What the hell does that mean?"

Alexander shook his head at Roderick and said to Warren, "He's a little old fashioned. Comes from a time when men were men and sheep were frightened."

Roderick looked ready to thump Alexander. Actually, it would be a fight worth watching. Both men looked like they could look after themselves. Bone weariness slunk through Warren. He needed a pint, another of those excellent burgers and space to think. Process. Christ, now he sounded like Debra.

He left the barracks and the other two men tailed him through the great hall and down into the kitchen.

A pair of drop-dead gorgeous redhead twins looked up from something they were busy making at the kitchen table.

"Sup." The one dressed in camo pants and a T-shirt that said *Arcane Activists, Shhh! It's a kind of magic* jerked her chin at him. "You the new one?"

"No," he said at the same time Alexander and Roderick said yes.

She raised her eyebrows.

"Maybe." Warren wasn't sure what he was, and he didn't want Alexander and Roderick thinking they could push and shove him into their world. "I'm still working it out."

She nodded. "I get you." Sticking out her hand she said, "I'm Sinead, and in case you can't tell, this is my twin Alannah."

"Hi." Alannah gave him a gentle smile. She wore a pretty summer dress with flowers on it that clung to her long, lithe body.

Warren did his best not to stare, but the twins were...nope, he didn't have the right words. It was like being in the presence of a movie star. Not that he ever had, but if he imagined how it might feel, then meeting these two would come close. "Hi." He jerked his thumb over his shoulder. "I was on my way back to the village."

Sinead stilled and glanced at Roderick. "Is that safe?"

"No." Roderick folded his arms. "But he's a big strong lad."

"He certainly is." Alannah's big purply blue eyes twinkled at him.

He'd never seen eyes that color, like Mum Betty's favorite irises. Heat crawled up his cheeks, and he knew he was blushing like a schoolboy. He tried to think of a flash exit line and came up emptyheaded.

"But the lovely Alannah does raise a pertinent point," Alexander said, sauntering to peer over her shoulder at what she was making.

Roderick sneered. "Which is?"

"Why don't you call me the lovely Sinead?" Sinead stuck her chin out at Alexander.

He laughed. "Because you'd remove my balls with a rusty spoon."

Sinead nodded. "You have a point."

"Can we get back to the point Alannah made?" Roderick took a deep breath. "About Warren's safety."

"Right." Alexander stuck his finger in whatever Alannah was stirring and licked it. "Basically, you're not safe, brother."

Fucking hell! The day was getting better and better. "Define not safe."

"Rhiannon. The missing fourth witch." Alexander went for another finger dip and got his hand smacked. "She's going to want to make sure you don't protect Niamh."

"I think I can hold my own against an elderly woman." Or he'd toss in his man card forever.

Alexander laughed.

Sinead and Alannah stared at him for a second, and then they laughed.

Even Roderick cracked a smile. Then he said, "Rhiannon is neither old nor merely a woman. She's an extremely powerful blood magic witch who could strip the flesh off your bones without even trying."

"I don't believe in bloody witches." The words burst from him, bubbling up from way deep inside him. None of this could be real. Gathering momentum yanked him this way and that and he wanted it to stop.

He sensed her behind him before Niamh said, "Then that would make protecting one particularly difficult."

BONNIE SLID a full pint across the polished bar top to him and he nodded his thanks.

After Niamh had spoken, he'd bumbled and burbled an apology out the door and driven straight to the Hag's Head.

"Need anything to eat?" Bonnie wiped the counter around him and nudged a bowl of peanuts closer.

Warren nodded. "Burger, please."

"Coming right up." She adjusted his glass. "And if you need anything in the meantime, you whistle."

"Will do." Right now, he needed silence and his pint.

Bitter slid down his throat smooth as butter.

The look on Alannah and Sinead's faces at his outburst had been bad enough, but the wounded expression on Niamh's had sliced him to the bone. Another thing that made no sense. He'd met her twice. If he added up total time in her company, he'd be hard put to get to five minutes.

Bonnie stacked glasses in the metal racks over the bar, and he decided to pump her for information.

"Bonnie?"

She glanced over at him and stopped. "Is there anything you need?"

"You've lived here your entire life?"

"In Greater Littleton?"

"Yes."

Bonnie nodded and sidled closer. "Yes, I have. Why?"

"The women on the hill. The ones in the castle. You know them?"

Eying him warily, Bonnie stopped and crossed her arms. "I've seen them about. I don't think anybody really knows them. They stick to themselves." She sniffed. "Home schooling and all that lark."

"Right." Bonnie might not like the topic, but he forged on. "Can you tell me about them?"

She narrowed her eyes. "Why?"

"I met one of them." He improvised. "Today. I met one of them today. Her name was Niamh." He feigned a careless shrug. "At least that's what I think she said."

"Niamh!" Bonnie near enough spat the name. "I wouldn't go near that one."

"Why not?"

Bonnie shook her head and snorted. "I can see I'm already

too late. One look and every straight man around can't get enough of bloody Niamh."

He couldn't leave it there. "I don't know about that, but I was riding up near the castle and I met her. You seem to know everyone and everything that happens around here, so I thought I'd ask." A bit of flattery never hurt.

"They're odd, all of them." Bonnie glared out the window at Baile. "Hardly deign to come out of their bloody castle to mix with the rest of us, and we're grateful for it too."

Bonnie looked like she was on a tear, so he sipped his pint and let the silence work for him.

"That Niamh is the worst of the lot." Bonnie leaned closer to him. "I'm not one to slut shame another woman. God knows I've had my adventures. But that Niamh is a fucking tart."

Her vehemence almost made him rear back.

"Isn't a man in this village she hasn't tried it on with." Bonnie's mouth pursed. "She goes from one to the other of them, using them up and then dropping them. She doesn't care what families and marriages she breaks up; all she cares about is the man. And then once she has him." She snapped her fingers. "She turns around, drops him and moves on to the next." Getting almost in his face, she jabbed the bar top with her finger. "You'll stay away from that one. If you know what's good for you."

Warren had heard enough. Nausea swirled in his belly. He knew women exactly like the one Bonnie described. Niamh sounded like another Debra. Just his fucking luck.

10

CRÉ-WITCH CHRONICLES

Niamh didn't watch his bike disappear down the hill to the village this time. Again, that had not gone as she wanted it to. What had she expected? That he would be as thrilled about the idea of being her coimhdeacht as she was about having one.

Stupid! She'd done the very thing she didn't want to do, and got swept away in the excitement.

She crossed the bailey to the arched wooden door in the wall that guarded the seaward side of the bailey.

She took the steep stairs down as they hugged the cliff all the way to the entrance to the caverns. There, in the caverns, was the only sort of comfort she needed right now. She needed to come into the presence of Goddess and remind herself that Goddess didn't make mistakes. If Warren Masters was here for her, and was her coimhdeacht, then Goddess had willed it so and she must have an excellent reason.

Her eyes adjusted to the dimness of the caverns. Small rodents scurried throughout the series of joined caves and she could sense them all around her. They let her know that Maeve was in the caverns as well.

Shells, crystals and bits of bone and rock, laid in intricate patterns, lined the walls and ceiling of the caverns. They formed the story of cré-magic. When a witch passed on, the coven spirit walker used the shells and crystals to lay the pattern of that witch's magic and life on the walls. The sigils formed a portal for the spirit walker between the world of the living and the world of the dead. She could activate the sigils and enter the sacred grove to speak with any witch who had come before.

Until Maeve had reanimated out of the statue of her and Roderick, they'd not had a spirit walker. Maeve said it was because there could only ever be one per coven and she had not been technically dead.

As Niamh moved from one cavern to another, deeper into the mountain, the peace of the place surrounded her. Niamh walked amidst the witches past, her sisters in magic.

Since the water point had been activated, the sigils of the past water witches glowed brighter than the rest.

Niamh went through the arched passage and into the central chamber. Maeve stood frowning at the cavern wall.

"Hi." The sandy floor cushioned Niamh's feet. "What are you doing?"

Maeve turned to her and made a face. "I'm trying to open the sacred grove, but without my magic, all I can get is echoes and resonances."

Like her, Maeve drew fire. Another reason they'd all voted to activate the fire point next. Once Maeve could commune with the dead again, they had access to the accumulated knowledge and wisdom of every witch who had gone before. "We'll find the cardinal point and give you all your power back."

"We must." It couldn't happen soon enough for Maeve. Unlike the rest of them, Maeve had known what it was to use her full power. She'd grown up at Baile when the coven had been more than ninety witches strong, all of them using their blessings and able to pull their elements.

"I saw your coimhdeacht earlier." Maeve picked up a large wicker basket and went to sit beside Goddess Pool. "He's a handsome one."

Good looking on the outside. "I suppose."

"You didn't like him?" Maeve patted the ground beside her.

Today the pool, the source of the water cardinal point, which nestled in the middle of the central cavern glowed a gentle pink. The pool was also their easiest way to connect with Goddess, and its presence brought serenity.

"He doesn't believe in any of this." Niamh sat beside her as Maeve opened the basket. Alannah didn't like anyone to skip a meal and she packed these for Maeve when Maeve planned to spend time in the caverns. Alannah even packed them for Bronwyn when she went to the healer's hall.

Maeve pulled out a chicken sandwich and handed half to Niamh. "Uh-oh. Well, he is about to discover how wrong he is."

"He isn't happy about anything we told him." Niamh bit into her sandwich.

"Oh, dear." Maeve shook her head. "That will not do at all."

Having a sympathetic audience helped soothe her stirred up emotions. "No, it won't." She chewed and swallowed before she voiced one of her larger fears. "And I don't think he liked me."

Maeve chuckled. "Everybody likes you, Niamh darling. You're a guardian witch."

"Right." She'd never spoken of this to any of her coven sisters before. "But they like me because I'm a guardian. Not because I'm me."

Shaking her head, Maeve gave her a gentle smile. "That may be part of why they are drawn to you." She nudged Niamh's shoulder with her own. "But there are other, much stronger, reasons people like you."

Niamh shrugged, but she did like hearing what Maeve said.

"It's true." Maeve laughed. "You're sweet and kind and funny. People sense your warmth and your generous heart." Maeve lowered her voice. "And you're hot AF."

Niamh laughed. Maeve had a way of trotting out modernisms that was dead cute. "Somebody should tell Warren Masters that."

"He knows." Maeve winked at her. "Or he will do soon enough."

If only she could believe that. Niamh finished her half sandwich before she asked, "Is it possible, or has it ever happened, that Goddess made a mistake when she paired up a witch and a coimhdeacht?"

Maeve blinked at her over her sandwich and then chuckled. "Oh, Niamh." She put her sandwich on a napkin and took Niamh's hand. "I asked exactly the same thing when Roderick first bonded me. In fact, I was so sure it was Edana he was going to bond that they virtually had to push me into the bonding ceremony."

"Really?" Maeve and Roderick seemed to work like a well-oiled machine, granted with a few creaks in the gears. Still, they had an ease around each other she envied.

"Oh, yes." Nodding, Maeve picked up her sandwich. "And no, Goddess doesn't make mistakes. Instead, it sometimes takes us a while to see her true purpose."

Balls, but Niamh hoped Maeve was right. Then admitted what she had barely even fully formulated. "I'm not sure I liked him either."

"No?" Maeve wrinkled her nose. "I thought Roderick was an overbearing arse, and I was completely intimidated by him."

Niamh laughed. "Roderick is an overbearing arse."

"So true." Maeve sighed and finished her sandwich. "He's right most of the time as well, which makes it even more difficult to swallow."

Not hungry, Niamh shook her head when Maeve offered her another half. "But you guys overcame that, right?"

"We did." Maeve rummaged in the basket and found an apple. "But I wouldn't say we're there yet. Not the way I used to see bonded couples around me back when we were in the other time. We're new and still learning to work with each other."

"How does it feel?" Niamh tucked her knees up to her chest. She wanted to believe she and Warren could form a working bond, value and respect each other. The loneliness in her needed to believe they could. "To have him in your head all the time?"

"Odd, at first." Maeve bit into her apple. "I resented it and how much he knew about me without me having to say a word. It took any mystery away. I couldn't have any secrets from him." She shrugged. "Now, it would be hard to imagine me without him."

"And you two get on?" She couldn't imagine Warren even wanting access to her most private thoughts, much less how she would trust him with that ability.

"Now...we find our way together." Maeve heaved a huge sigh and bit into her apple. She looked sad and lonely.

"What's the sigh about?" Niamh nudged Maeve's shoulder with hers.

Staring into Goddess Pool, Maeve chewed and swallowed. "Have you noticed the way Alexander looks at Bronwyn?"

"Yep." Who could miss how Alexander looked at Bronwyn as if his universe centered on her? "Roderick looks at you like that."

"Sometimes." Maeve made a face. "He looks at me like that sometimes."

"And the problem with that is?"

Maeve took a deep breath. "Because that's as far as it goes, looking and maybe saying things."

"But you know how he feels about you," Niamh kept her

tone casual. Maeve didn't share often. "You can feel it through the bond."

"I can." Maeve chewed her apple morosely. "In a way that makes it worse. I know what we should be to each other. I know what we both want. But we aren't...that."

Oh, crud, but they were drifting into some rather personal territory here. "You mean you and Roderick haven't..." She raised her eyebrows.

"Not even close." Maeve tossed her half-eaten apple into the basket and scowled at it. "And I watch the way Alexander is with Bronwyn and it makes me want to scratch their eyes out."

Niamh laughed. She knew the feeling.

For all she looked like a classic Disney princess, Maeve had an edge. "You're jealous."

"So jealous." Maeve sighed.

"Me too." She'd so wanted an Alexander of her own. "I want someone to look at me like that."

Maeve snorted. "Every person you meet looks at you like that."

"Not like that." Niamh's spirits dipped further. "The way people look at me and are with me is about my blessing. They can't help themselves. Alexander sees Bronwyn. The good and the bad, and he still adores her."

Maeve made a sympathetic grimace and then giggled. "At least you're not officially the oldest virgin in the world."

With Maeve over five hundred years old, Niamh had to give her that one. "Have you thought maybe of finding someone else?"

"No." Maeve growled. "Because I don't want anyone else. I want Roderick and he wants me. But he hasn't even kissed me. Not properly anyway."

Niamh wasn't sure she was the best person to give relationship advice, but she was the best Maeve had in the moment. "Then, what's the problem?"

"I don't know." Maeve thrust her hands into her hair. "He gives me these smoldering looks, and then he says things like us being a couple is inevitable. I can feel that he means it through the bond as well, but something always holds him back."

"There's nothing stopping you," Niamh said. Sharing head-space with animals colored her view of intimacy with animal pragmatism. If animals had an itch, they scratched.

Maeve went pinker than the Goddess Pool water. "What?"

"If Roderick is dragging his heels, then you make the first move."

"No." Maeve sat back and gaped at her as if Niamh has suggested she steal the crown jewels. "I couldn't."

Niamh didn't see it that way. Women had needs and wants too, and they didn't need to sit back and wait for those to come to them. "Of course, you can. You know he wants you. There's no harm in giving the man a nudge."

Maeve shook her head slowly. "I couldn't do that."

"Yes, you could." Maeve was so adorable Niamh gave in to the urge and hugged her. "There's nothing to it. Give him a good, solid nudge and let nature take its course."

Maeve giggled and blushed harder. "You modern women are so much braver."

"Nah." Maeve had more courage than the rest of them put together. She and Roderick had faced Rhiannon and all the traitorous witches the night they'd tried to capture Baile. That same night Maeve had allowed her coven sisters to throw her into stasis toward an uncertain future so cré-magic could be preserved for witches still to be born. Maeve had courage to spare. "We're more sexually emancipated."

"Huh." Maeve frowned and mulled. "I think I would like to be sexually emancipated."

"Atta girl!" Niamh held her hand up for the high five.

Maeve blinked at it.

Reaching over, Niamh took Maeve's hand and slapped her own. "Go get him, sister."

She stayed a bit longer, and then left Maeve trying to reach her dead. Outside the caverns, the day had turned overcast. It matched her mood and Niamh quested Alpha.

Pack hovered close to the castle, and she could feel Alpha's strong presence. She stopped in the bailey and let it wash over her. Pack rested in an old grove, and they'd not long since fed. Their bellies were full, and most were dozing. A couple of juveniles were playing to Alpha's right, and he kept a vague eye on them, in case anything got out of hand. The black juvenile had the scent of a future alpha and needed reminding from time to time that he did not lead the pack.

Alpha sensed her disquiet and prodded at it.

Niamh opened her thoughts and senses to him. Let him see Warren, let him experience her disappointment.

His calm assurance centered her. *Pack is pack, and pack is always best.*

11

CRÉ-WITCH CHRONICLES

The next day, needing a break from Bonnie and burgers, Warren sat in the Copper Cauldron trying to force down a dry ham and cheese sandwich. He'd had a shit night's sleep, not all of which he could blame on the foreign couple banging each other's brains out in the room next to his.

He didn't know what to do. Logic, reason, good sense, all those worthy attributes insisted he get on his bike and go home. His life was already on the skids, and Debra was trying to grease it along the tracks even further. He needed to talk to his ex and try to get his right to see Taylor sorted. If talking to Debra didn't work, he'd have to get himself a lawyer.

Taylor was his everything. When the PTSD had been at its worst, the only reason he'd gotten up some mornings was because Taylor didn't deserve to grow up without a dad. Of course, if Debra got her way, Taylor would grow up that way anyway.

Debra's anger at him showed no sign of lessening. He'd failed to be the husband she wanted, and she was determined to punish him for the rest of his life. The husband she had wanted would have given her a big house in the sort of development where being a neighbor was a competitive sport, a holiday to Spain or Greece every year, posh dinners out once a week, and karats to demonstrate his love. Mostly, though, she had wanted a man who brought it home to her every night.

He had never been that man. He'd stayed in the army long past when she felt he should take retirement, and then gone places he couldn't tell her, to do stuff he didn't want her knowing about.

At first, she'd been hurt, then angry and now bitterness had set into her marrow. He could understand her for that, even forgive her, but using Taylor as a weapon disgusted him.

Mum Betty had never liked Debra and warned him to watch himself. Of course, he'd been in lust and letting his dick do the talking. When Debra had fallen pregnant a year into their relationship, getting married had seemed the logical next step. Whatever he felt for Debra, however, Taylor had been a miracle, and it had been to secure her future that he'd taken those high paying missions. He'd been too young and stupid to think those same missions could have taken Taylor's father away from her. A fit, young, highly trained twenty-something, he'd half imagined he was immortal.

"Hello." A middle-aged woman with her hair in a jaunty ponytail stood beside his table. She held out her hand and gave him a grin that made him wonder what she was selling. "I'm Hermione."

"Hi." For all he knew she was going to tell him she was the older version of Hermione Granger and Hogwarts was real. That's pretty much how his week had been going. True story.

She gripped the top of the chair opposite his, her knuckles going white. "I'm the Greater Littleton tour guide."

"Ah." That would explain the cute cartoon bus logo on the breast pocket of her crisply ironed pale blue shirt. "I'm not really into tours."

"Really?" She cocked her head and set her ponytail bouncing. "Tours are the best way to see a historic landmark. Sometimes one doesn't know what one is missing until an informed person points it out."

"Right." He pushed his sandwich away. The bread was stale and the ham like cement.

"Anyway, that's not what I'm here about." Hermione motioned the chair. "If you have a moment, I'd love to sit and explain."

Warren did have a minute, although he was far from sure he wanted to give those minutes to Hermione, but he caught her edge of desperation. Call him a sap, but he motioned her to take the seat.

"Thank you." She beamed and her ponytail jerked. Chair legs scraped on the floor as she took her seat. "Greater Littleton is a small town, a village really, so word gets around."

Warren waited.

"As I said before, I am the local tour guide, and part of my tour used to be Baile." She stared out the window at the castle nestled above the village and sighed. "But the family has decided to end all tours."

"I heard that in the pub," he said.

"Yes." She heaved an even bigger sigh and focused back on him. "But I heard you visited the castle. Yesterday. And were allowed in. And stayed for a long time."

It sounded like she had an entire intel setup in Greater Littleton. "I did."

"And I was wondering if the family letting you in meant they planned to open the castle to tours again soon." She pursed her lips. "Also, I feel emboldened to tell you that if you're from a competing firm, the council will not take kindly to an interloper. We are the only tour company granted a mandate for the village."

Hermione looked a bit crazed, and Warren moved his utensils out of her reach. "I'm not in the tourist industry."

"Good." And her perky smile reappeared. "As to my other question?"

"I don't know." Warren went with the bald truth. "I'm an... acquaintance of the family, and they allowed me inside for a meeting."

Shoulder's drooping, Hermione stared back at Baile. "Well, at least you're not a competitor."

"No." And then Warren's brain kicked in. A tour guide would know all about the history of the village and the castle and be able to fill in blanks for him without him having to wonder if the truth was being manipulated. "But I have some questions about the village and the castle. Perhaps I can buy you a cup of tea and pick your brain?"

"Oh." Hermione straightened and blinked at him. She checked her watch. "Well, I have a village green tour in half an hour, but that's enough time for a cup of tea."

He motioned the waitress and ordered two teas.

"What's on the village green?" Warren could see the green from where they sat, and it looked fairly unremarkable to him. A mostly rectangular swathe of clipped green grass with a stone church on one side and a couple of huge oaks providing shade.

Hermione leaned forward. "Well, I can tell you what was on the village green up until very recently."

He'd bite. "What?"

"A statue." Hermione sat back and let him absorb her words.

He must be missing something. "Did someone take it down?"

"No." She giggled. "It disappeared." She clicked her fingers. "One day *The Lovers* were at the end of the green near the church." She pointed to a large gray plinth. "And the next day —gone!"

It couldn't have been a very big statue for someone to have made off with it. "Someone stole your statue?"

"That's what the police say." She lowered her voice and did a quick scan about before leaning in closer. "But they have no idea how someone could have made off with a solid stone, life-size statue of two people in the middle of the night and nobody saw or heard a thing." Her voice thickened with mystery. "No fingerprints or any sign of how they managed it."

The waitress scuffed over to their table and plopped two mugs of tea on the table. Tea slopped over the sides of their mugs.

With a grimace at the waitress's back, Hermione produced a packet of wet wipes from her bag and mopped up the tea, then wiped the bottom of their mugs. She made an apologetic face. "Mel is new."

A week ago, if Hermione had told him the statue story, he'd have thought her round the twist, but he'd heard and seen things in the last few days.

"The statue has always been a bit of mystery." Hermione bent and dug in her handbag. "Hang on a tick, I've got so many photos of the thing." She found a smartphone and started thumbing through it. "We've never known exactly who erected the statue in the first place, or who it's of. Most historians believe the male figure is the knight who built Baile, Sir Roderick."

Warren's hackles stirred. All Alexander's snide asides about Roderick's age pricked at his mind.

"Here we go." Hermione beamed and held her phone out to him. "That one is as good as any photo you'll find in a guidebook."

And his hackles leaped to attention. That was fucking Roderick. In the statue, he had a woman tucked against him and you couldn't see her face, but the way Roderick sheltered her was one hundred percent protective.

Words failed him. Fortunately, Hermione had no problem filling the silence.

"Of course, now people come to see the site of the disappearing statue, and it would be lovely if we could arrange a way to get them into the castle." She blinked at him hopefully.

He felt like a right shit lying to her, but he suddenly needed to know everything she knew. "I'll have a word." He held up a hand when her face lit up. "I can't promise anything, but I'll see what I can do."

"Thank you." Tears sprang into her eyes. She added milk to her tea and sipped. "I appreciate you trying."

"Tell me about the magic." He pointed to the Copper Cauldron's sign outside. "There seems to be a theme."

"Oh, there is." Hermione looked much brighter now, and he was a dickhead for leading her on. He didn't see Alexander or Roderick being in any way happy about castle tours. "It all centers round Baile." Hermione sipped her tea. "Legend has it that Baile was built on an ancient pagan holy site. And that the castle has been home to a coven of witches ever since." Hermione tittered. "Now, I know what you're thinking. Superstitious nonsense, right?"

Not even close to what he was thinking. He was thinking he might owe Niamh and the other women at Baile the benefit of the doubt. For now, he stirred milk and sugar into his tea.

Hermione sat back with a pensive look. "There have always been rumors of strange happenings around that castle, and the family themselves have always been a touch...eccentric." She cleared her throat. "And then of course, there were the witch hunts."

Warren sipped his tea and waited. Somebody had to teach southerners how to make a decent cup of tea. The swill in his mug tasted like tepid dishwater. Or it could be the growing taste of humble pie souring his palate.

"In 1645, a nasty individual by the name of Mathew Hopkins

declared himself Witchfinder General and got a real bee in his bonnet about the alleged coven at Baile."

"Alleged?"

"Well, nothing had ever been proven. There were rumors of course, and the women of the castle did do an awful lot of handing out herbal remedies and attending births. There were also stories about certain castle inhabitants having a way with animals. Other of them being able to tell your fortune." She waved her hand. "Harmless nonsense, all perfectly easy to find a logical explanation for."

"I take it this Hopkins came to Baile." He pushed his mug away.

"Indeed, he did." Hermione's expression dimmed. "At the time there was also a terrible plague that hit the village and people were getting sick and dying all over the place. Regardless, this next bit doesn't reflect very well on our village, but he also persuaded the villagers that the women of Baile were witches who had caused the plague. The only way to cure the village was to get rid of the witches."

"He had them executed?" The empty passages and spaces of Baile echoed in his mind. "How many women?"

"Over ninety." Hermione fiddled with her mug handle. "Hopkins led the villagers to invade Baile and kill all the occupants. There were some men living there as well. They fought to the last man to help those women, but between the villagers and Hopkin's huge band of followers..." She shrugged.

Warren felt sick. The shadowy figures he'd seen in the barracks suddenly became unbearably real to him. Thomas had spoken of that night. He had been there and lost his life fighting to defend his witch.

"They all died?" It didn't feel like Hermione was talking about long dead strangers or vague historical figures. If Roderick was to be believed, those had been his brothers in arms, and the sadness and anger balled in Warren's chest and made his breathing labored.

"Most of them. It was a horrible tragedy." Hermione had gone back to staring at the castle. "And since then, the village and the women of Baile have lived in an uncomfortable sort of tolerance."

"But some women must have survived." His mind caught up with the conversation. "Because their descendants are still living there."

"A few did." Hermione nodded. "I'm proud to say that my family was one of the few who managed to hide a witch and get them to safety. They drifted back to Baile once the furor had all died down again."

"There are good people even in the worst of times." It was a trite platitude, but Warren reeled under the impact of Hermione's story.

"Our family legend goes that a mysterious stranger appeared with a witch at our door and we hid her. Apparently, we saved a healer," Hermione said. "I'm sure it's not true, but the healer is said to have laid hands on the youngest son in the family who was deathly ill with the plague. Family legend tells that she cured him, just like that."

Roderick and Alexander had told him that Bronwyn was a healer. "Imagine how that would be if it could happen," he said.

"Yes." Hermione's eyes filled with tears, and she ducked her head. "I'm sorry. So silly of me, but my daughter is not well. And then you said what you said, and it got me thinking how useful it would be if miracles were real."

"I have a daughter." He wanted to reach out to her parent to parent. "She's twelve."

"Oh, that's how old Gemma is." Hermione patted at her eyes with a tissue. "I only have the one."

"Me too." He didn't want to pry into what was wrong with her daughter.

Hermione sat up straighter and put her tissue away. "Anyway, there are always rumors about the Cray family. I'm sure most of the village ignore them now."

"Not everyone in the village ignores them," he said. "I've heard a few things."

"From Bonnie?" Hermione's eyes narrowed. "Tell me that dreadful old gossip didn't bend your ear."

"Umm..." He didn't want to start a village feud. "She doesn't have much time for Niamh."

"That woman." Hermione rolled her eyes. "Her useless son has got such a thing for Niamh. Niamh is charming. Everyone likes her. Especially the men around here. Anyway, Bonnie's got this useless shit—" She flushed. "I beg your pardon."

Warren had to smile. "Tell me about the useless shit."

"Peter. And he's always been trouble." Hermione sniffed. "He panted after Niamh and made a right nuisance of himself. Even ended up leaving his wife for Niamh."

"He had an affair with Niamh?"

"No." Hermione shoved her phone and wet wipes in her handbag and zipped it shut. "As far as I could see, Niamh wanted nothing to do with him. Peter wouldn't take no for an answer."

A surge of protectiveness shot through him. "I hope he didn't do anything untoward." Or Peter was dead.

"Oh, he would follow her around, make a nuisance of himself. There was the one time at the local shop when he grabbed her and wouldn't let go, but a couple of our heftier lads sorted him." Hermione checked her watch. "Well, this has been quite a chat."

"Yes, it has." And he would have a word with the castle folk about the tours. "I hope your daughter gets better."

Hermione's face softened as she stood. "Thank you. And I hope you enjoy the rest of your stay in our village."

Warren paid the bill and wandered down the street, closer

to the cliff Baile sat atop. Sheer rockface rose above the water. The tide bubbled and streamed over the base of the cliff. There didn't appear to be any access to the castle from the sea. About halfway up the cliff face, the dark opening of a cave drew his eyes.

That cave...

The prickling sensation started along his arm again and he rubbed it. He needed to go to that cave. He needed to get in there.

He walked to the edge of a small stone pier. Tourists thronged around him, buying fish and chips, shopping for espadrilles and knickknacks in the stores lining the pier, but he kept his eyes on that cave.

Acting on an instinct he hadn't even identified he reached out to the voice he'd heard. *Are you in that cave?*

Coimhdeacht. You are called.

12

CRÉ-WITCH CHRONICLES

Bronwyn slammed shut another useless ancient tome. Had her mood been any less volcanic, she would have been appalled to treat such an old book that way. The real reason for her mood had nothing to do with the poor book, and she gave the cover an apologetic stroke. Rapid-fire emotions roiled inside as she plopped on her stool and put her elbows on the huge rectory table in the healer's hall.

Anger masked fear, which would officially classify her as terrified.

Through the bank of west facing windows, the sun had streaked vivid pink across the clouds. Since she'd started using the healer's hall, she'd filled the window boxes with herbs and healing plants. Alannah and Sinead came along every now and again and whispered to the plants—or whatever the hell they did—and created a verdant green jungle.

"There's nothing there," she said to her plants. She needed to keep her mind busy and away from the real issue.

The plants dipped their heads in the evening breeze and carried on being plants.

Lately she'd become obsessed with Roz and helping her.

Niamh said her aunt was trapped in the awareness of an owl. That being the case, there had to be some way to reverse that. If her blessing allowed her to examine a person from the inside out, there had to be some way to rewire Roz.

"All these collections of recipes and spells and not one thing that will help." She motioned the pile of books, scrolls and manuscripts she'd stacked neatly on the scrubbed wooden table. The meticulously labeled shelves of dried herbs behind the table seemed sympathetic, but who could tell. "Of course, I might be able to use them more if I was actually allowed to leave this castle and heal."

Shoving her anger toward her enforced isolation in Baile, kept the panic at arm's length.

Maeve had told her that during the time of the coven massacre, a deadly plague had raged through the village. Fiona, who had been coven leader then, had forbidden the healers from going to the village to help. Maeve had snuck them into the village anyway. The story hadn't ended well. Rhiannon had been expecting the healers to do just that and had been waiting for them. At the time, Alexander had been on Team Super Murderous Bitch and had led the villagers in an attempt to capture the healers. Roderick had saved Maeve and the healers, but he'd had to fight Alexander to get them free.

Alexander claimed victory for that fight, but Roderick maintained he'd cheated.

She didn't know about cheating or who had won, but she was beginning to understand what had compelled the healers to go against Fiona and go to the village anyway. Later they'd discovered Fiona and her bestie, Edana, had been working with Rhiannon all along. Both women were still alive and kicking and still with Rhiannon. Bronwyn had experienced the distinct displeasure of meeting them both.

A huge yawn almost split her jaw in two. The large leather couch she'd installed to the left of the door looked mighty inviting. She'd put it there mostly so Alexander could come and hang out with her while she worked. Damn, Alexander was part of the problem. He and Roderick kept her locked up in the castle like something from a Greek tragedy.

Fatigue crept through her, and the couch made another bid for her patronage.

"No." She hauled another book closer and refused to let her mind wander. "I need an answer, and there has to be one in here somewhere."

Panic overtook her as *that*—the thing she refused to think about—tapped at her awareness. She wouldn't have it. It wasn't true anyway.

"Hey, little witch." Alexander stood with one shoulder braced on the doorjamb. He held up a plate. "Alannah sent you something to eat."

"I don't want that." The words whipped out of her. "Why is she always feeding people?"

Alexander strolled closer and put the food beside her. He kissed the top of her head and put one large, warm hand in the small of her back. "Because she cares about you, and she shows her love by feeding people."

Bronwyn knew that, and she loved Alannah, but her surge of anger shoved all that away. "What are you doing here?"

"I missed you." He found the exact spot in the small of her back that needed rubbing. "I thought I'd come and see what you were doing."

He knew.

She could see it in his eyes he knew about *that,* but he wasn't going to say anything. Well, fuck it then. If he was keeping it on the DL, then so was she. "I need to heal, Alexander." She pounded her fist against the table so hard it smarted. "I need to heal people. It's my gift. It's what I do." Her anger built as she spoke. A tiny part of her knew she was being irrational, but the rest of her didn't give a crap. "What's the point in having activated water and having all this power and I can't do anything with it."

Picking up the hand she'd hit the table with, he smoothed out her fingers and kissed the part that still throbbed. "You know why you can't leave Baile. You more than any other witch."

Her anger whipped free, and she snatched her hand back. "That's bullshit! It's all fucking bullshit. Some stupid prophecy is not going to rule my life. It isn't even true."

"Really?" He brushed her cheek with the backs of his fingers. "Don't cry, little witch. I'm with you."

"I'm not crying." But she was. Angry, frightened, overwhelmed tears outed her anger as the paper-thin camouflage it was and demanded she acknowledge the truth. She couldn't do it. "I'm going to find a cure for Roz."

"If anyone can, it would be you." He tugged her from the stool.

"I can get inside her and find where things are going wrong." If she stuck to words about healing, *that* stayed unacknowledged between them. "It's how the healing works, you know."

"Hmm." He wrapped both arms around her and surrounded her in the unique sandalwood and smoke scent of him.

"I push my gift into people, and it allows me to find out what's wrong. Like some kind of nano bot, or something. They have those now, you know." If she kept talking about other stuff, she could make it through another day of not facing *that*. "Did you ever see that old movie *Inner Space*?"

"Little witch—"

"Stop calling me little. It's insulting and demeaning, and sexist."

"No, it's not," he said, and his calm made her want to hit

him. "You know it's my way of telling you how much I love you."

Goddess! How did you get mad at a man who said shit like that? "Couldn't you call me something else?"

"Mighty witch?"

"Shuddup."

"Bronwyn." His tone was IRS serious. "We need to talk about this."

She tried to push free. "There's nothing to talk about. You don't know anything. You're guessing."

He looked at her.

"It's impossible," she yelled. "I'm on the pill, and you always use condoms. It can't be."

"But it is." He slid a hand beneath her hair and cupped her nape. "The son of death shall bear the torch that lights the path. And the daughter of life shall bring forth water nascent and call it onto the path of light. Then they will bear fruit. And this fruit will be the magick. The greatest of magick and the final magick."

"It can't be." She shook her head.

"But it is." He kissed her softly. "Prophecies have a way of making sure they come true, and that one has been around for hundreds of years. The moment we met, the ball started rolling, and it will keep rolling until it comes to pass."

Sagging against him, she finally opened her mouth and *that* came out. "I'm pregnant."

"I know," he said. "And this is a happy thing, a blessed thing."

"But I'm not ready." She pressed her forehead into his warm, smooth neck. "I'm not ready to be a mother."

"Were you ready to discover you were a cré-witch?"

"Not really."

"And that you belonged here at Baile?"

"That was unexpected."

"And that you and I were destined to be?"

She encircled his waist and clung to the back of his shirt. He had become her anchor. "I wasn't really expecting any of it. I mean, I came here for answers." Her chuckle didn't convince either of them. "And boy did I get them."

"But you're not alone anymore," he said. "You have me."

She did have him. The connection between them they both refused to put a name to because nothing seemed right, was new but potent. He wasn't her coimhdeacht, but she could feel him, know what he was thinking. And like the warrior guardians, he would protect her, stand at her back and fight for her.

"I'm scared," she whispered the fear she hated acknowledging. "I'm scared to be a mother. I'm not sure I'll be any good at it. And how do you mother the apocryphal kid anyway? How do you put a kid like that in timeout?"

Alexander chuckled. "We'll do it one day at a time. And we have an entire coven to help us if we falter."

"Six witches in this coven." Their vulnerability filled her with dread. Even more so now that she had a child to consider. "Only I have my full power, and I'm not sure how much good I'll be in a fight if it came to that."

"When it comes to fighting, we surprise ourselves." Inching away from her, he put his big, battle-scarred hand on her belly. "Especially when we are fighting for what matters most to us."

Her pregnancy wasn't showing yet, but the warmth from his hand seeped beneath her skin. She liked to imagine that her baby felt his touch and drew comfort from it like she did.

"I'm all tangled up inside." She placed her hand over this, to hold him closer to them. "I keep thinking about my mother and how young she was when she died. I don't want this baby to know what losing their mother feels like."

"Our baby won't lose their mother." Alexander's voice took on a cold, formal tone. "This I vow to you, and I vow to our unborn child. You will be there to watch them grow and guide and nurture them into adulthood."

Nobody could make those sorts of promises for sure, but she knew he would do anything to keep his vow. "She's going to want the baby."

Bronwyn refused to use Rhiannon's name aloud. Superstition had convinced her that like Voldemort, that bitch would come when named. She hadn't said the name aloud since Rhiannon had had her kidnapped and kept her prisoner. All Rhiannon lived for now was getting control of this child. The child nestled and growing in Bronwyn's belly.

"She can't have our baby." The fierce surge of protectiveness found a home deep inside her. "We won't let her."

"No, we won't." Alexander kissed her. "And neither will Roderick, or Maeve or any of the others. This baby is all of our futures."

"No pressure." She snorted.

Alexander ducked and his gaze met hers. "Hey, little witch, guess what?"

"What?" She'd play, and that sparkle in his eye always got her.

"We're having a baby," he said and grinned. "And I love you."

13

CRÉ-WITCH CHRONICLES

They gathered for dinner that evening, and they should have been cheerful because Alannah had made her world-famous fish pie. Well, it should have been world famous, but Alannah never cooked for anyone outside the castle.

Four castle cats wound around Niamh's ankles as she sat at the table and waited for her dinner.

A dog whined and she put her hand on his head to comfort him. Poor bugger could sense the tension in the air. Hell! They could all sense the tension in the air.

Roderick sat like he had a lance shoved up his arse.

Looking sulky, Maeve kept inching her chair away from his.

Sinead divided her scowls between Thomas hovering around Alannah and Roderick looking all stoic and uptight.

"Oh, fish pie." Mags tripped over her curry-yellow caftan as she scurried into the kitchen. She had black charcoal marks on her cheeks and paint-stained hands.

Alannah intercepted one of those fingers heading for the fluffy mound of mashed potatoes topping her pie. "Wash those first."

"Right." Mags looked at her hands as if she'd seen them for the first time. "I've been drawing."

"More vision drawings?" Alannah put the pie on the table and turned back for the second one. With Roderick around, she always made extra.

"Mmm." Mags had her head cocked and her eyes had gone opaque. "I can't...nope, gone!"

"Have you tried focusing your gift on the location of the fire point?" Roderick served Maeve first and then himself.

Sinead glared at his plate. "We are still waiting for Alexander and Bronwyn."

"Alexander needs to shift his arse then." Roderick took a heaping plateful and looked at it mournfully.

Alannah laughed and nudged him. "Go ahead and start; there's plenty for everyone."

"I have been looking for the fire point." Mags served herself a full plate and then sat and stared at it. When she got lost in a vision or a seeing, Mags would forget to eat. Even if the food was right in front of her. "But it's all fuzzy and misty. It's like looking through a pane of glass with water running down it."

Maeve wrinkled her nose. "I get something similar when I try to contact the past witches."

"Could she be blocking us somehow." Alannah never used Rhiannon's name out loud either.

Roderick shoveled, chewed the barest minimum and swallowed. "It's possible."

He'd made huge gastronomic strides from his almost strictly meat and potatoes diet when he'd first awoken. Mind you, Alannah's cooking would do that to anyone.

"Frankly, we don't know much about what she's capable of anymore," Roderick said. "She could have learned much over the years she has been alive."

The back door opened, bringing in damp, warm air.

Alexander had his arm around Bronwyn, who was red eyed and blotchy faced. Over her head, he shook his to prevent any questions and seated her at the table. "Good evening."

"You're late." Roderick grunted.

"And you eat like your dinner is going to make an escape." Sinead pinned Roderick with a stare. "We've spoken about table manners."

"You spoke, I ignored you." Roderick barely raised his head from his dinner. "Typical woman, talking like she can never hear enough of her own voice."

Everyone sucked in a collective breath.

Roderick was in for another feminism lecture.

Putting her fork down carefully by her plate, Sinead steepled her fingers in front of her face. "Now you know you only said that to piss me off."

"You have a foul mouth. For a woman." Roderick glared back.

"And your brain has shrunk under all that brawn and the complete onslaught of testosterone." Sinead sneered at him. "Frankly it's a good thing you've got Maeve, because you'd be shit out of luck in the romance line otherwise."

Maeve snorted and ate her pie.

"What?" Roderick turned to her.

Maeve kept eating and shrugged. "Nothing."

Oh boy! Every woman there knew what that nothing meant.

Then Maeve followed it up with the clincher. "I'm fine."

Niamh almost fled the room, but Alannah's fish pie kept her arse in her chair.

"Clearly you're not fine." Roderick shook his head. "I can feel what you feel, Maeve."

"Clearly not." She scowled at him. "Otherwise, you wouldn't be such a dumb ox."

Sinead thumped the table. "Tell him, sister."

"Matters between my witch and myself do not concern you." Roderick barely glanced at her. His entire focus was Maeve. Niamh could almost feel the ton of information passing back and forth through their bond.

"Then give her the respect she deserves." Sinead picked up her fork and ate. "And tonight, you're being an extra special horse's arse." She studied him. "What's bothering you, big guy?"

"He's frustrated," Alexander said. "And as much as it galls me to agree with the dumb ox, I share his frustration. Rhiannon is out there, planning her next move, and we can be damn sure we factor largely in that move. The only thing preventing her from getting what she wants is Goddess, and we're between her and Goddess."

Alannah sighed. "What is it that she wants?"

"To be Goddess." Alexander stretched his arm across Bronwyn's chair back. "She wants to supplant Goddess and take her place." He yawned. "Your bog-standard world domination."

"Wow!" Sinead rolled her eyes. "You can't say she lacks ambition."

"It's an obsession," Alexander said. "Rhiannon was the most powerful of the four first witches. I think Goddess always sensed in her that she had this dark side, and so, according to the creepy finger and thumb, she favored the other witches over her."

"She wanted to lead the first four," Roderick said. "Rhiannon was never content to be part of something. She needed to be all of that thing."

"Having only as much power as Goddess would grant her, she found humiliating. I think, for her, it was like looking through the shop window at all the pretty things inside." Alexander shrugged. "Having all that power is her entire driving force."

Niamh didn't like bringing up Rhiannon with Alexander. It

felt a bit like rubbing salt in a fresh wound, but if he was feeling chatty about her, then she was going to take advantage. "We were wondering if Rhiannon could be blocking our magic somehow. Is that possible?"

Alexander thought it over. "As far as I know, she cannot penetrate the wards. Even though she created them. They recognize her when she comes near them and repel her."

Mags sighed. "Well, that's a relief."

"But she'll try." Sinead looked grim. "The wards feel...not right."

Roderick stopped eating and stared at her. His eyes lost focus. "They feel fine to me."

"And they are." Alannah joined the conversation. "On the surface, but it's when Sinead and I try to delve deeper into them. It's like there is some sort of distortion inside them."

"Bugger." Roderick started eating again. "Rhiannon is an experienced enough campaigner not to attack only on one front. She could be trying to dismantle the wards."

"Oh, I can bloody well guarantee that," Alexander said as he nudged Bronwyn's plate closer to her. "Because she first created them, she sees them as hers to do with as she chooses."

"Bitch." Sinead scowled at the table. "And we were that close to killing her."

When they'd rescued Bronwyn, Roderick had been about to turn back into the house and finish the job with Rhiannon, but her minions had arrived. Roderick had decided that getting Bronwyn to safety was their priority.

"I will not miss my chance a second time," Roderick said.

Maeve snorted. "I've heard that before."

He gaped at her as Maeve delicately ate her fish pie and ignored him.

Niamh hoped Maeve took her advice soon, because on top of everything else they were dealing with, they didn't need Roderick and Maeve flaying each other with sexual tension.

Not all coimhdeacht and witch pairings were romantic. When he'd been alive, Thomas had served Lavina, a guardian witch. Lavina had been several years older than Thomas and more than happy to let him whore his way around Baile.

Another black mark against Thomas in her book. The way he flirted with Alannah gave no indication that particular leopard had changed his spots.

Thomas had adored Lavina and still did. His greatest sadness was that Lavina and fourteen other Blessed who had sent Maeve and Roderick into stasis had paid the ultimate price for using blood magic. They'd sacrificed their lives for enough power to work the stasis spell. Goddess forbade blood magic, particularly for her cré-witches. Even though they'd only done the spell to save cré-magic forever, it made no difference. Lavina and the thirteen witches and one apprentice were trapped in the moment of their death for eternity. They could never move on, and they would never reincarnate. Their souls remained earthbound forever.

Thomas, who could still feel resonances of what Lavina felt, was desperate to free them.

They were all hoping when Maeve got her full power, she could help them, which brought Niamh all the way back to that bloody fire cardinal point. They needed to find it, and they didn't have time to fanny about. "I've worked my way through most of the old journals," she said. "There's no mention of it, because no witch who wrote those journals had ever lived in a time when all cardinal points weren't active."

Maeve nodded. "The elements were always there."

"We need to find the remaining three cardinal points," Roderick said. "And we need to do so before Rhiannon does. If we're searching, we can be sure she is as well."

"I can confirm." Alexander looked grim. "And I know there is enough pressure on this already, but it's become doubly important."

All eyes swung his way.

Pregnancy smell on Bronwyn was even stronger now. Strangely enough, and Niamh hadn't noticed before her connection with the wolf pack, but Alexander and Roderick shared several scent markers.

Bronwyn looked at Alexander and then the table. "I'm pregnant."

"Fuck!" Roderick scowled at Alexander. "You knew this would happen, and still you—"

"This is not his fault." Bronwyn shoved herself to standing and stared Roderick down. "There were two consenting adults involved in what happened between me and Alexander."

"Consent." Sinead nudged Roderick. "Remember that clip I showed you, the one with the cups of tea?"

Roderick threw her an exasperated glance and went right back to Alexander. "He, more than anyone, knows the danger being with child places you in."

"And so do I." Bronwyn squared her shoulders. "I know this pregnancy puts a great big target on my back, and that bitch is going to go rabid when she finds out."

"I—"

"Not done yet." Bronwyn put her hand on her belly. "But this is a baby, not a curse." She took Alexander's hand. "It's our baby, and prophecy or no prophecy, we're going to have this baby—boy or girl—and love it and raise it right." She met every eye at the table. "And we're asking for your help. But we'll do it without you if we need to. This baby will not be treated like anything other than a welcome and cherished gift." She zeroed in on Roderick. "Do I make myself clear?"

"Perfectly." He nodded. "Cherished and beloved, and I declare I will do everything within my power to help you in whatever way you require."

Sinead punched his shoulder. "Good recovery, big guy."

"I like babies." Roderick blushed.

"Rumor has it you certainly made enough of them." Maeve sniffed and then smiled at Bronwyn. "I'm very happy for you, and you know you don't even have to ask. You are coven, which means your child is coven."

"Children." Mags glanced up from shoveling fish pie. "She's having two. Boy and a girl. Twins."

14

No way in hell Niamh could sleep. After Mags's less than tactful revelation, there'd been more tears from Bronwyn and a load of adorable from Alexander. Finally, he'd made Bronwyn smile, and then giggle.

The way he had cradled her while she cried had made Niamh feel more isolated than ever. She always coped, it's what she did, a bone-deep lifetime habit. It meant that people assumed she would always cope and be fine. She didn't necessarily have an issue with being a coper, because it was largely true, but sometimes she wanted to be cradled and nurtured.

Niamh flopped to her back, careful not to kick any of her furry bedmates. The open window allowed the gentle susurration of the sea into her bedroom. Shadows flit across her bed canopy.

Like her, poor Maeve had watched Alexander with Bronwyn tonight and looked devastated. Normal relationships had enough challenges, but add magic and bonding, and you got a nasty snarl of emotions, personalities and agendas.

A dog grumbled and shifted in his sleep.

Niamh had known Alexander for years. She couldn't even

remember when she'd first met him, but he'd been there since she, Mags, and the twins had been children. Of course, until a few months ago, she'd attributed the fact that he never seemed to visibly age to excellent genes. Now she knew the truth about his longevity. Alexander was almost as old as Roderick. He wasn't immortal. He could be killed, but his injuries would have to work faster than his body's ability to heal. Given that he was several hundred years old and steeped in magic, his body could heal astoundingly fast.

Rhiannon was much older and even more powerful. One would literally have to decapitate her to kill her.

Juxtaposed against the tenderness between Alexander and Bronwyn that evening, had been Maeve bitching at Roderick and Roderick manfully ignoring. The more he'd ignored, the bitchier Maeve had gotten until they'd all fled as soon as dinner was over. No lingering over fish pie, helping themselves to a little bit more.

Niamh sighed and disentangled her legs from the two dogs, cat, and rabbit cuddling her. Through her window, the lights of Greater Littleton twinkled up at her. She located the Hag's Head, where Warren was.

Was he sleeping?

Maybe, like her, he couldn't still his thoughts and was struggling to wrestle all the new information he'd received into an acceptable logic.

Through the still night, she quested for pack.

Alpha slid into her awareness, the connection light and tenuous. He was hunting, and it took most of his attention. Through him she experienced hunger and the thrill of the hunt. He had the scent of a wounded deer and was tracking it.

In the silence of the sleeping castle, she couldn't deceive herself as easily as in daylight. Her loneliness and fear of rejection had made her hedgehog prickly with Warren. In her mind, she'd built him up to be the superhero answer to all her problems. Nobody could have lived up to her impossible expectations.

Warren had a life, and she hadn't even asked him about how the calling would impact him. He might even have a special person he wanted to get back to.

Watching Roderick and Maeve's mostly silent battle had driven the point home about how complicated the witch and coimhdeacht relationship could be. Even Thomas with his gnawing worry and grief about Lavina's spirit carried a lesson. Warren accepting the bond, magic, her, was only the first step in a treacherous journey.

Real danger lay outside Baile's wards, and they didn't have time for head butting. She had a vital job to do, and that would mean leaving Baile. Wherever the fire point was, she was going to have to go there and activate it. She needed a coimhdeacht with her. If she allowed their bond to be strained, it would make working together tough.

It didn't matter if she liked Warren Masters or not. It didn't even matter if he liked her. They would be bonded. What needed to happen would happen. Alexander and Bronwyn being pregnant had made that clear. Larger happenings were being played out through all of them.

Pack was strongest when it worked as a unit.

Niamh reached for her jeans and hauled them on. Hopefully her two guardians would be busy tucked up in bed with their respective others. She invited the Labrador and his best buddy an older German shepherd to join her. They would provide some protection, and she could use their senses to heighten her own.

She needed to talk to Warren, just her and him, and it needed to happen before any more shots to the head hit the coven.

Wearing her trainers and a hoodie she and her two-dog

escort slipped out of the castle. They reached the caverns with nobody being any the wiser.

As she reached the rock outcropping hiding the entrance to the underground tunnel, Thomas materialized. "Blessed."

"Thomas." A ghost she could handle. Especially as he didn't have his backup team of glowering mates with him.

Thomas folded his arms. It was uncanny how corporeal he appeared. "What are you doing here?"

"I think you know the answer to that." Maeve had taught her the incantation to open the secret passage to the village, and she could be down it and out the other side before Thomas had dobbed on her to Roderick.

"And I think you know what I'm going to say." Thomas superciliously raised an eyebrow.

She'd like to Superglue that eyebrow to his head. All Thomas could do was say stuff, however; he couldn't physically stop her. Still, she tried to reason with him. "I need to speak to him."

"Then wait until morning, and Roderick will fetch him here." Thomas knew exactly who she was talking about.

"I don't want to do that." His bond with Lavina had started out rocky. There was an outside chance Thomas would understand why she needed to do this. "I want to speak to him without anybody else about. Just him and me."

Thomas cocked his head. "Why?"

"It's all so new to both of us," she said, trying to organize her thoughts as she spoke. "When you were bonded, you had the chance to come here and see the coven and the other coimhdeacht. You were able to spend time with Roderick and the others and get to know them, and also get to know the witches." A lot of what she said was guesswork, but Thomas was still listening. "You also lived in a time when magic was not such a strange concept. Your lives were not so dominated by science and technology. Warren and I don't have time, and we live in an age of skepticism."

"I understand, Blessed." Thomas's expression softened. "But for your safety, I cannot let you pass."

"I need to." She got closer to Thomas. "I need to find out more about him, and for him to feel like he knows more about me. We're about to enter this intimate relationship, and we're both circling each other like stray cats. It doesn't auger well for our future." As Thomas thought that through, she pressed home. "I don't want this to take Warren and me by surprise like it did with Bronwyn. I want us to be ready, and more comfortable with all the changes that are going to come." Changes coming at them at warp speed. "We don't have time for a protracted period of Warren and I dancing around each other and getting comfortable. We have to hit the ground running."

Thomas pursed his lips and stared past her shoulder. "Lavina did not like me when we first bonded."

"And I'm not sure I like Warren."

He chuckled. "She thought I was too free with my favors amongst her coven sisters and far too young for her."

"What happened?"

Thomas shrugged. "We found a way to coexist."

"But I'll bet that took time." Niamh held her breath until he replied.

Shaking his head, Thomas put his hand on the wall and muttered the incantation. "If I were not already dead, Roderick would kill me for this."

"But as you are dead, there's not much he can do," Niamh said.

Rock groaned and a tunnel appeared. Soft ambient light guided her way as Niamh stepped into the tunnel.

Thomas slid in behind her and shut the opening. "You keep the dogs with you at all times and rely on their senses to watch for you."

"I promise." She really didn't want a run in with Rhiannon and the twisted twosome, Edana and Fiona. "In fact, I plan to get him out of the Hag's Head and take a walk with me."

"Follow me." Thomas strode ahead of her.

Niamh had to trot to keep up with him. "It's low tide, so I thought I could take him to the beach, get both of us behind the wards."

"Good idea." Thomas nodded. "But I will still have to let Roderick know where you are."

The stubbornness of men brought Niamh to a halt. "But why?"

"Because he leads the coimhdeacht." Thomas kept on moving. "And we do not lie to each other."

Bugger it! Roderick would tell Alexander and both of them would come storming down to haul her back to Baile. "How long have I got before you tell them?"

"Not long." They reached the end of the tunnel, and Thomas put his hand on the rock and muttered the incantation. "I've already sent a message to Roderick."

"How—" It didn't really matter, and Niamh stepped into the crypt below the village church. She let the dogs go ahead of her, scenting the air through them, listening to the night sounds.

They crept up the lichen and moss encrusted steps to the churchyard, and the dogs wound through the tumble of gravestones littering the thick grass. They kept scenting the air, tense and alert, but not finding any danger.

Niamh stopped where the wards did and took a deep breath. Both dogs trotted over the wards and stopped to look at her. Neither of them showed any concern.

She looked behind, but Thomas had gone already. "Third time's a charm."

∾

WARREN SLEPT BADLY. Every time he closed his eyes. Niamh crept into his mind. The knock on his door was so soft he almost missed it. Before he opened, he knew it was her.

"Hi." Niamh stood in the dark hallway, a hoodie hiding her face. Looking around, she whispered, "Could you come for a walk?"

"At this time?" He'd only pulled on a pair of jeans to answer the door. "You could come in?"

"Umm..." She eyed his bare chest and flushed. "Actually, I shouldn't, but if you come for a walk, I'll explain everything."

More explanations of shit he didn't understand. Fucking smashing!

But she was here, at his door, and a huge part of him wanted to take a walk with her or invite her into his room. They could share a beer. She could get out of her oversized hoodie, and—

A walk it was. "Let me grab a shirt."

"Okay." Relief brought a flush to her creamy skin. "It's not really safe for me to be here."

Her safety kneed him into action, and he slipped into a pair of trainers and grabbed a T-shirt.

As he closed his room door, two dogs stood from either side of it and gave him big, goofy grins. He recognized the German shepherd from their first encounter.

Wagging his tail, the dog gave him a tongue loll. A retriever sniffed at his legs and wagged a greeting

"With you?" He petted both dogs.

She wrinkled her nose. "My early warning system."

"Cool." The dogs led the way as he followed her into the hallway and down the stairs. Both dogs scented the air as they moved.

"What's the danger?" he whispered because it seemed like the thing to do.

She motioned him to silence. "I'll tell you in a bit." Peering around a corner first, she quick timed it to an exit door. "Once we're at the beach."

A midnight stroll on the beach. Could be romantic. Probably not. And he had no reason to be disappointed about that.

Outside the pub, Niamh's shoulders dropped away from her ears, and she took a deep breath. Her early warning system continued their vigilance, but their hackles smoothed, and their ears relaxed.

Warren bided his time. The more he got told about shit here in Greater Littleton, the more he realized how little he knew. Their steps matched as they walked down the esplanade toward the beach. All the stores were shut for the night, and they could be the only two souls out and about. A full moon flirted with streaky clouds above them, and a light onshore breeze drifted damp and cool over his face.

Stopping where the pavement gave way to sand, Niamh slipped off her shoes and rolled the cuffs of her jeans. Warren did the same.

The dogs trotted ahead of them, tails waving like feathery banners, noses working the air gleefully.

"Is it safe now?" Inexplicably, tension drained from him as well. Their hands brushed and Warren felt the impact spark along his nerve endings.

Niamh made a face. "Almost. The wards start a little further along the beach, but we're close enough, and we can see anyone coming."

"Who would be coming?"

"We have dangerous enemies." She peered up at him. "Didn't Roderick and Alexander tell you?"

"You mean that Rhiannon person?"

Niamh started and glanced behind her. She caught herself and gave a sheepish laugh. "Sorry, in my head, she's going to pull a Voldemort."

"Do Roderick and Alexander know you're here?"

"Thomas does." She wrinkled her nose.

"That's a no, then?"

She frowned and nodded. "That's a no."

"Then why are you here?" And he was suddenly pissed off with her for putting herself in danger.

Answering irritation sparked in her eyes, but she took a deep breath. "No." She shook her head. "I didn't come here to fight with you."

He waited for her to answer the obvious question.

"I thought we should have a chat." She got right to the point. "A getting to know you sort of chat." She had quickened her pace slightly and he couldn't see her face from where she walked a pace ahead of him. She cleared her throat. "A lot has happened. For both of us. All of this is new for me, and I'm floundering a bit. Tonight, it occurred to me that you might be floundering too."

He could front bravado, but her honesty deserved better. "Yeah. I don't really know what to make of any of this."

"Me neither." She dangled her shoes from her fingers. "I mean, I grew up in Baile, surrounded by legends of witches and old stories about who we were and what we were." Stopping, she stared up at the castle. Moonlight found the delicate hollows of her face. "But that's all I thought they were, legends and stories. I had abilities, for certain. My way with animals wasn't a figment of my imagination, but it also wasn't...this."

She looked fragile, lost, and Warren stepped closer to her. He wanted to reassure her but had no clue why. He wanted to hold her tight until the vulnerability disappeared. "What is this?"

"All the new information we're dealing with. All that's changing around us." She huffed a wry laugh. "I'm not sure about anything anymore. It's an evolving situation, and we're finding out as we go along." She raised her hands as if reaching for the moon. "Who knows what I'll be able to do if I ever activate the fire point."

Warren didn't know how to respond, but intrinsically he understood her. His assumption he was being drawn into a world she was familiar with had been off base. Like him, she was inching her way forward in the blinding dark, trying to make decisions about her life with only fragments of information to guide her. "I feel adrift."

"Yeah." She sighed. "Bewitched, bothered and bewildered."

He laughed. "Couldn't have said it better."

Niamh's unfettered smile felt like a blessing. Her smile was borne mainly in her dark, velvety eyes and came from the rawest most elemental part of her.

She'd made the first move and he wanted—no needed—her to know he was reaching back. "I'm sorry about all the witch cracks." Apologizing had never come easy to him but having Niamh upset with him felt worse. "I found out some stuff today, about the witches and their history." He didn't want to dredge up a past that must be painful. "I didn't know."

"How could you know any of it?" She shrugged. "Especially as we do our best to keep things quiet."

They stood there, staring at each other. The moonlight did mind-emptying things to her lovely face, gleaming off the delicate jut of her cheekbones and turning her eyes deep and mysterious. He wanted to touch the pale glow of her porcelain skin and see if it felt as smooth and cool as it looked. Temptation won and he brushed his fingers over her cheek. Pure silk. "So, you're a witch?"

"So they tell me." A half smile played over her full, soft mouth. Her eyes darkened.

He shifted closer and slid his fingers into her hair. "Good to know."

"And you're coimhdeacht?" Mischief tilted her mouth into a gentle smile.

Such a sweet looking mouth. He wanted to taste. "So they tell me."

"Good to know," she whispered.

Being with her stilled the churning of his mind and filled him with peace. There was nowhere he'd rather be than right here with her. Unless it was in a bedroom with her. "I'm glad you came to chat," he said.

"Me too."

The dogs growled and stood.

Footsteps crunched behind them, and a man said, "Me three."

Both dogs stiffened, hackles raised.

Adrenalin shot through Warren, and he turned.

Three men had followed them onto the beach. Shorter than the other two, the one in the front spread his hands. "Look, we don't got no worries with you, mate. It's the witch we want."

Blood pounded through his veins, pumping into his muscle, beating a primal bass beneath his skin. "That's my witch."

15

Niamh whirled as Warren lunged toward the three strangers. "Warren!" She grabbed his arm. There were three of them, and the wards were only a few meters away. "Come with me."

"My witch!" Warren roared. He shook off her grip and put himself between the men and her.

"Warren!"

The dogs surged forward with him, teeth bared, out for blood.

Protect! Protect! Protect!

It pounded through her, but it was not coming from her. The dogs and Warren radiated rage as they attacked the men.

Alpha's primal duty to guard pack joined Warren and the dogs' and pulsed beneath her skin. They were beyond listening to her, and somehow dogs, wolves and man fed into each other in a chain so crackling and alive with instinct that it dragged her along in its wake.

The dogs kept one man pinned to the rock wall while Warren had another man by the throat, dangling from his hand as Warren shook him like a rat.

A third man circled them. A knife gleamed in his hand.

"Warren!" She screamed. "He has a knife."

"A pound says he gets nicked by the knife." Alexander appeared beside her.

Roderick shook his hand. "Done! He breaks the bastard's arm before the knife gets close."

Warren tossed his captive, whirled and grabbed the man with the knife by the wrist. The cracking of bone sounded above the dogs snarling and the screaming man they had pinned.

"Get these fucking dogs off me. I'll call the police."

"Peter?" Niamh got a good look at the man captive against the rocks. "Is that you?"

"Bloody hell, Niamh." Peter stared wild-eyed at the dogs. "Get these fucking dogs away from me."

"Niamh." Alexander inclined his head toward Peter. "Your call, but they'll rip his throat out if you don't do something."

The German shepherd sunk his teeth into Peter's arm and hung on grimly. The Labrador had him by the ankle. Niamh called them off.

Both dogs tried to ignore her, but she repeated the compulsion and they eased away, teeth bared and growling a warning that it wouldn't take much to renew their attack.

"You should go before they kill you," Niamh said to Peter.

"If Warren doesn't do it first." Roderick folded his arms and watched the fight. "He has good form."

Peter turned and ran from the beach.

Alexander watched Warren fight.

His opponent attempted to fight back, but even with her lack of experience in these matters, Niamh could see Warren had him outclassed.

"Definitely military training. Oh!" Alexander looked impressed. "Martial arts as well. You could learn from this one."

Roderick snorted but he watched Warren more closely.

The man with the broken wrist crouched on the sand cradling his arm and whimpering.

Warren closed on his opponent.

"Aren't you going to help Warren?" Niamh thumped Alexander on the arm.

Alexander looked wounded. "Does he look like he needs help?"

Warren delivered a tremendous kick to his opponent and sent him sailing twenty meters back in the sand. That shouldn't have been possible.

Not wanting to wait around for more, the man scrambled to his feet and made like Peter and ran for it.

Warren rounded on the one with the broken wrist. His face an intent frightening mask of violence.

"But I will help him." Alexander stepped between the injured man and Warren. "Hang on there, Superman." He put a hand in the center of Warren's chest. "We don't do the ripping limb from limb thing, tempting as that is at times."

"I make an exception to that rule for Rhiannon." Roderick hauled the injured man up and gave him a shove. "I'd run if I were you. He's still in a protective haze and I can't guarantee your safety." He made a regretful face. "Truth be told, I'm not sure I want to either."

"Get out of my way." Warren bared his teeth at Alexander.

"Going to have to say no to that," Alexander said. "Not ever advisable to litter the place with dead bodies."

"Breathe!" Roderick clapped his hand on Warren's shoulder. "Niamh is safe. She's standing right over there."

Warren's gaze locked on her, so fierce in its intensity she took a step back.

"You are well?" He stepped toward her.

He looked like his entire being hung on her answer, and Niamh closed the distance between them and took his hand. "I'm fine. They never got a chance to come near me."

"Which brings up a point." Alexander stared at her and raised his eyebrow. "That point being, what the hell you think you're doing here in the first place."

Warren growled at him. "Don't speak to her like that."

"We'll talk about it later." Roderick nodded to Niamh as he stepped closer to Warren and pushed back the sleeve of Warren's sweatshirt.

The same markings Roderick carried over his right arm, shoulder and most of his back and torso flickered across Warren's skin. "There are your coimhdeacht marks," Roderick said. "Once you accept your fate, they will become permanent and tell the story of your journey as coimhdeacht."

Warren stared at the shadowy marks on his forearm and then glanced at her. The tension drained from him, and his shoulders slumped. Pushing a hand through his hair, he said, "I picked a man up with one arm."

"Yes, you did." Alexander nodded.

"A grown man." Warren flinched. "I shouldn't be able to do that."

"Normal men can't," Roderick said. "And you also threw one like a haunch of venison."

"I shouldn't be able to do that either." Chest heaving, Warren stared at his arm. "But I did it." He squeezed his eyes shut. "I wanted to kill them."

"You were protecting me." Niamh wanted to ease the torment in his face, and she took one of his big, rough hands in hers. She soothed the cracked, slightly bloody knuckles with her fingers then raised it to her cheek. "You did protect me. They didn't get close to me."

"It was like that time in the pub." Warren looked at Roderick. "When you first met me."

"And it will be like that again." Roderick shrugged. "Until you make a decision."

Warren shook his head and sighed. "You're saying I have a choice. I can walk away now?"

"Can you?" Roderick cocked his head.

"No." Warren swallowed. His gaze met hers, unflinching and steadfast. Clear in a way that told her this was not her blessing he was responding to. "I will never be able to walk away from you."

And she never wanted him to walk away from her.

"Right!" Alexander clapped his hands. "Being on this beach is giving me the shits. The ovaries of evil could appear at any second, and I'd like to get our fire witch all safely tucked up behind the wards." He looked at Warren. "Any more questions?"

Warren raised his chin. "I'll pack my bags and meet you at Baile."

ALEXANDER LET Niamh precede him across the tidal beach and up the stairs to the caverns. The beach was only ever available at low tide with the wards concealing the stairs from everyone who Baile didn't welcome.

Wards drifted like cobwebs over his skin as they crossed them, and he allowed himself a breath of relief. When Thomas had first told them where Niamh had gone, he'd nearly lost it. Roderick had lost it, and he would be repairing tables for a couple days.

Thomas flickered into being beside him. "That worked out well."

Alexander scrabbled for his patience and breathed deep. "You took a huge risk letting her go to him."

"But he's not hesitating anymore." Thomas looked smug.

Alexander needed to ask Roderick how one punched a ghost. "But you didn't know the outcome when you let her go. If that had been Rhiannon or even Fiona and Edana, the outcome could have been catastrophically different."

"I came to find you as soon as she'd gone." Thomas looked wounded. "It's not like I intended to let her wander around the village without protection."

"How good of you." Alexander glared at him. "If that had been Lavina, and I'd let her go traipsing into Greater Littleton, what would you do?"

Thomas's expression darkened. "I'd rip your head from your neck."

Alexander stared pointedly at Thomas's neck. "Precisely, and you had better hope Warren doesn't feel the same."

RHIANNON LOOKED at the three quivering lumps of men Fiona had brought to her and tried to comprehend what they'd done. They looked like Warren had beaten them thoroughly and that almost mollified her anger.

"Why?" Especially since she'd given explicit instructions that Warren Masters was not to be approached or touched in any way. She hadn't been vague about it either, because she never was.

"Forgive us, lady." Peter bowed nose to knee. "We happened to be passing and we saw Niamh on the beach. We know you want the witches."

She wanted them all right. Dead. Every last one of them, but first she needed them to help her find what she needed. "She was with the coimhdeacht."

Warren had been unsure, hesitating as to what to do, like any modern man would have done in his position. Now these idiots had driven him straight into Baile, which she'd wanted anyway. Therefore, she'd be lenient. Plans within plans coming to fruition, but disobedience demanded a response.

"There was only one of him," Peter whined.

The other two shrunk away from Peter, happy to let him take the brunt of her anger. They would still pay for their cowardice and stupidity. "What did I say about Warren Masters?"

"He was not to be touched," Peter mumbled.

"Which does not explain to me why you touched him."

The balding one cradled his arm to his chest and appeared to be in some pain. He would be in a lot more before the night was done.

"Up until tonight, Warren Masters had no idea what being a coimhdeacht really meant. He doubted what Roderick and my traitorous spawn were telling him. He was not sure of either his powers or the threat I presented."

Fiona approached the trio from behind. "Now he doubts none of that, and he is on his way to bonding with his witch."

Rhiannon would tolerate Fiona's participation for now. The woman had brought these miscreants to her, after all. Her plan had been simple. Let Warren come here and discover his fate. Let him join them at Baile, but in the absence of any corroborating evidence, let him also doubt all that he heard was true.

Doubt, like a maggot, ate away at the healthy flesh of certainty and purpose, and it served her to lull the new coimhdeacht into a false sense of security. Besides she had the matter of Warren Masters well in hand. Her plan already hummed to completion while Roderick and his spawn looked elsewhere.

She motioned Fiona for the athame. It was one of the last things Alexander had procured for her before his defection. Even in the privacy of her mind, she could not speak his name without the peculiar sensation in the center of her chest. She hated that sensation; it made her feel weak and she tolerated no weakness. No weakness in her followers, and no weakness in herself.

"Choose," she said to the three men.

Peter gulped. "Lady?"

"One of you dies, choose." Her constant attempts at scrying chewed through her store of blood magic and already it needed replenishing. Alexander would commend her for her expediency. If he were here. The ache in her chest intensified and she shoved it away. He was not here to speak with her, even make her laugh on occasion. She would forget him, as if he had never existed.

The three idiots gaped at her.

"Very well, Fiona will choose for you." She glanced at Fiona.

Fiona nodded to the one cradling his arm. "That one is half broken already."

"Lady." He paled and sputtered. "It's only broken. Just a break. I'll be fit again in—"

Rhiannon plunged the dagger into his carotid artery. Blood sprayed and hit her face, warm and viscous, and she licked it.

The man collapsed to his knees, trying to stem the flow of his life with his hands.

Frozen in fear, his cohorts stared on in horror. They wouldn't forget this moment, and neither should they. They were all expendable to her.

Blood pumped in spurts from his neck and soaked his shirt and trousers. Blood pooled on the wooden floor, spreading across it.

Rhiannon sank to her knees in the blood puddle, reaching her hands into it and spreading her fingers.

"Yes." The life force contained within blood pulsed through her. His life faded fast, and she would have to be quick. She called to the north and to earth.

Fiona sprinkled soil into the growing blood.

Earth magic lashed at her control. Like a dull, relentless blade, it hacked at her connection through the man's waning lifeforce and tried to break it. But Rhiannon had been mastering the magic for hundreds of years and she drew on the blood, beating back the force of earth. It was strong, and it fought her, flooding her senses with the taste and feel of the earth, ripping through her body.

Rhiannon held it. With their cardinal points still dormant, earth, air and fire lacked their true potency. Water grew in power, and the traitor would tell his water witch how using her power would make the elemental stronger.

Earth gave up the battle with a backward lurch and Rhiannon fell face forward into the blood. It soaked her face and her growing hair, filled her nostrils and coated her tongue with its coppery tang.

The man gurgled his last breath, and his eyes dulled. The surge of his life into her was sweet in its agony, and she drew deep, cutting him off forever from the cycle of death and rebirth. Blood magic killed not only the physical life but ended a soul, and that was what she needed to sustain her blood magic. She, the most powerful cré-witch of all time, having to resort to stealing magic through death, to fighting agonizing battle after agonizing battle merely to access the magic of her birthright.

That bitch Goddess had cut her from magic, excised it from her and left her raw and wounded. For that, she would pay, like she would pay and pay and keep paying in blood and souls for daring to underestimate the force that was Rhiannon.

16

From the elevated position of the sun outside his window, Warren could tell he'd slept late the next morning. It wasn't like him, but he tucked his arms behind his head and lay there a while longer.

Now that he'd decided to join this crazy carnival, the knot of tension that had ridden along in his torso for weeks unraveled and dissipated. He would have to find a solution to Taylor and Debra, but now that he was here, he might see if anyone in the castle could help him. As far as he could tell, they could manage all kinds of outlandish crap.

Clash of steel against steel interrupted his study of the cloud formations drifting by the castle. He got up, the stone floor surprisingly warm under his bare feet, and hauled on a pair of track pants.

He followed the sound into the training yard.

Both stripped down to drawstring workout pants and armed with long, deadly looking swords, Roderick and Alexander faced each other in the middle of the yard.

Alexander lunged and Roderick parried. Eyes intent, they circled, muscles loose but ready, weight balanced and steady.

"Well hello, Warren." Bronwyn sat on a bench to the side of the practice space and grinned at him. She gave his bare chest a comically obvious ogle. "Aren't you better than a strong espresso in the morning."

Beside her, Maeve had turned and watched him as well. She flushed and waggled her fingers at him. "Hello."

He nearly went back for a shirt, but Alexander and Roderick hadn't bothered, so neither did he. Obeying Bronwyn's pat of the bench beside her, he took a seat. "You're in for a treat," she said. "I love it when they spar."

Steel crashed into steel as Roderick attacked. And it was on.

The two men moved like a graceful ballet in a fiendishly fast game of attack and retreat.

Roderick was the heavier set of the two, but Alexander was wickedly quick and had a slight reach advantage.

Warren felt like a schoolboy watching the ultimate little boy fantasy. And sweet Jesus, if that was how all knights had fought with swords, he was very glad he hadn't been in the army back then.

Impossibly, the dance sped up. Swords blurred through the air, showering sparks whenever they connected. Both men sweat freely but neither was the slightest bit winded.

It took him back to last night on the beach and what he shouldn't have been able to do. "It's not humanly possible."

He only realized he'd spoken aloud when Maeve said, "No, it isn't, but it's a gift from the Goddess to her favored sons."

"Sword fighting?" He tried to lighten the mood, but apprehension snuck up on him. What if he had no control of his new abilities? That night in the pub, he'd almost killed a man for being rude to his girlfriend, and last night Alexander and Roderick had stepped in before he could do what his blood demanded he do.

Maeve giggled and nudged him. "No, silly. You'll have to learn to do that."

"Great." Neither Roderick nor Alexander held back, the force and ferocity of their blows obvious to any watcher. "They could kill each other."

"A few weeks ago, both of them would have liked nothing more." Bronwyn snorted. "Now they deal with their mutual aggression this way."

Alexander managed to sneak a blow against Roderick's ribs that had to have broken something.

"Oops." Maeve made a face. "That's going to make him grumpy."

That had to hurt like crap. "Isn't he hurt?"

The injury didn't slow Roderick. If anything, he moved even faster.

"Superhuman pain threshold and ability to heal," Bronwyn said. "Another rather useful gift."

All the strength without the threat of consequences made him nervous. If he had less fear of getting hurt, there wasn't much that could stop a man. A man like that was like an armed nuclear warhead. "That much power without control could be dangerous."

"That's why you're here." Thomas materialized beside Maeve. "We'll teach you how to manage your aggression and channel it appropriately."

The sword fight kept going strong. It looked like they could do that for hours and hours.

"What if you can't teach me control?" Months of anger management classes hadn't managed that much. "What if I lose it and hurt someone?" His next words came from a fear he hadn't even realized he harbored. "What if I hurt someone here, like Niamh?"

Maeve and Thomas laughed.

"Niamh is the last person you could or would hurt," Maeve said. "Especially once you and she are bonded."

Their laughter annoyed him. "You can't be sure of that. You

know barely anything about me." And those things they didn't know weren't pretty.

"But I know the bond." Maeve patted his knee. "I know how it works with Roderick. He is incapable of hurting me."

Warren had an entire lifetime of experience that proved her wrong. "People are capable of all kinds of things."

"Not coimhdeacht." Maeve stuck her chin out.

He didn't want to fight with Maeve, she was cute and likable, but her naiveté scared him. "Accidents happen."

"Not with coimhdeacht," Maeve all but growled at him. Then she did growl and hopped to her feet. "I'll show you."

Bronwyn stood. "Maeve, what are you doing?"

Maeve strode into the practice yard and straight for the fighting men.

Warren leaped to his feet to stop her, but she was too quick.

"Shit." Bronwyn gasped.

Faster than the eye could follow, Roderick's sword flew toward Maeve's neck.

"Maeve!" Alexander bellowed.

The air blurred at Roderick's sword tip, and everything froze.

Chest heaving, eyes wide, Roderick stared at his sword edge resting against Maeve's neck.

"See." Undeterred and either ignoring or blissfully unaware of the building storm of male rage behind her, Maeve grinned and looked at him. "Roderick could never hurt me."

The grumble came from a primal place inside Roderick. "Maeve."

Warren didn't blame him. What Maeve had done was foolish beyond belief and so dangerous it gave him the fucking shakes.

Staring at his sword with a strange look on his face, Alexander took a step back. He dropped his sword and shrugged at Bronwyn.

She went to him immediately and spoke softly.

Alexander shook his head with a rueful smile.

Cupping Maeve's elbow, Roderick tossed the words over his shoulder as he near enough carried Maeve out the room. "You will excuse us."

That didn't look like a friendly chat about to happen over tea and cakes. Warren considered interfering.

"He won't hurt her." Thomas joined him and watched Roderick and Maeve disappear into Roderick's chamber. "But he's going to bellow for certain."

The slam of Roderick's door echoed through the barracks.

Thomas and Alexander winced.

"Right." Warren still couldn't believe what he'd seen. The speed those men had been fighting, their focus on each other, Maeve could have been sushi.

"She is right, however," Thomas said. "You will never hurt Niamh. You are incapable of doing so. Even in his fury now, Roderick could not and would not ever do harm to Maeve."

Roderick's closed door tempted him. Maybe he should knock and check on Maeve.

"Don't do it." Thomas shrugged. "Let them work it out for themselves. There's a lot of emotional baggage they need to unpack. It's like that with many bonded pairs." His smile held traces of sadness. "Two individuals bond, but it can take time for them to work as one. It was thus with Lavina and me. It is why I let Niamh take the risk of coming to speak with you last night." Then he grinned. "And also, there is nothing that makes a coimhdeacht accept his purpose faster than a real-life demonstration."

Thomas was a shit stirrer, and when Warren knew him better, he'd tell him so. "You knew about those men?"

"No." Thomas shook his head. "But with the way Rhiannon has packed her spies into the village, there was a fairly good chance something would happen." He glanced at Warren. "You know the Hag's Head belongs to her?"

"Rhiannon?" Cold slithered down his spine.

"It used to belong to Alexander, but since his defection she's taken over most of his assets." Thomas sighed. "Which is a real pity because he'd amassed an impressive liquor collection over the years."

Warren didn't know what to say to that. In the back of his mind, a voice whispered about how he was conversing with a ghost and he should be freaking out.

"Lavina was a guardian like Niamh." Thomas chuckled. "Each blessing creates particular challenges for her coimhdeacht to manage."

"Blessing?"

"Gift," Thomas said. "Magic ability. Guardians are linked to animals, able to communicate with them. Their purpose is to guard and protect those same animals."

Warren already knew that about guardians, but the other part of what Thomas had said was an open invitation. "So, what's the challenge of bonding a guardian?"

Thomas winked. "Wait until Spring and mating season kicks in."

ADMITTEDLY, Bronwyn hadn't been involved with Alexander for long, but the man needed to understand that just because they both had chosen not to define their relationship, it didn't mean he could try to lie to her.

Not that he'd outright lied, but more a lie by omission, and she'd waited until they were alone in his room before she spoke to him. He didn't spend much time in his room, and with its large-post bed and clothing chest, it had a monastic vibe. Most nights, Alexander spent with her in her bedroom.

"What was that?" Bronwyn crossed her arms and gave him a look that meant business.

It was almost comical watching him consider and then discard the idea of keeping his coverup going. Not being bonded didn't mean she couldn't tell what he was thinking.

He stared at his hands as if he was seeing them for the first time. "Buggered if I know."

"But I'm getting the feeling this is not the first time something like that has happened." She knew her man.

Alexander sighed. "No, it's not. The first time I noticed something was after you healed me in Goddess Pool."

"What happened?" He'd said nothing to her at the time.

"I have this power." He flexed his long fingers. "It's not blood magic, but it's definitely magic of some kind."

She took a seat on the bed beside him and took one of his hands in hers. Callouses from weapons practice and whatever else he and Roderick did to each other thickened along the pads of his fingers. "You never said anything."

"To be honest, I didn't know what to say. I had this power like an electric current running through my hands, but it went away." He balled his hand into a fist. "Until today."

According to the entire coven, cré-magic had only ever manifested in women. "Is it from Goddess or...her?"

"Goddess." Alexander took her hand and threaded their fingers together. "I can't feel her behind the wards, but I know there's still a connection to her." He touched their twined hands to his chest. "No, this is definitely from Goddess."

"And you said nothing because of Roderick?" It was a guess on her part.

He nodded. "He already doesn't trust me—and with good reason given our history. Can you imagine how he'd react if he knew I had magic."

"Not well." The secret settled like a dead weight in her middle.

Roderick was looking for a reason to get rid of Alexander. The two of them had been bitter adversaries for centuries, and Roderick wasn't letting go without a fight.

"I'll have to say something eventually," Alexander said. "But I'd like to understand what the hell I'm dealing with first."

"What we're dealing with." Bronwyn squeezed his hand. "We're in this together, oh son of death."

He chuckled. "Fated lovers."

"As long as we keep the ill away from fated, we're good." She still woke in the night and watched him sleep. That awful woman was not done with Alexander, and Bronwyn didn't need Mags's foresight to know there was still a reckoning to come between herself, him and Rhiannon. She would find out about their pregnancy for sure, and then the game would be on with a vengeance.

As if he'd read her thoughts, Alexander pressed his free hand over her belly. "We may have been prophesied for each other, but from here we can make our own path."

"Yes." Dear Goddess, she hoped so. "Can you describe what happened with Maeve just now?"

He shook his head. "I can't believe she did that."

"I can." Sweet as she looked, Maeve had a crazy side to her that was making itself known to all of them.

"Roderick's sword was heading for her, and I stopped it." He cleared his throat. "I formed the intention to stop it and it stopped. Like the current left my hands and made a cushion in time." He shook his head. "And then it was over, and Roderick was looking at me suspiciously."

"Then he knows." Like Alexander, she would've liked more answers before they revealed this wrinkle in the way things had always been.

"He suspects," Alexander said. "He's been around magic for so long, even though he can't wield it, he can sense it. Especially if it's cré-magic."

No way Roderick would let Alexander's new abilities go. Fortunately, he had elected to deal with Maeve first. Bronwyn snuggled closer to him, letting the feel of him seep into her and comfort her. "Looks like we're breaking all the rules again."

17

Heart pounding in her ears, Maeve faced down a livid Roderick. As per her demonstration, she knew he would never hurt her, but an angry Roderick was a formidable being. The new witches hadn't grown up in a coven where Roderick held a position of reverence and respect. As the oldest coimhdeacht, he'd been head rooster in the henhouse of the coven in their former time.

Old habits die hard, and she forced herself to meet the lash of his pale blue gaze.

A muscle ticked in his jaw, and he flexed his fists. He appeared to be having trouble producing words.

Not one to wait meekly for the cart to run over her, Maeve jumped in. "I knew I would be safe."

"You...I..." He spun away from her and stalked to the window. Hand braced against the wall he stared out, his shoulders rising and falling with each deep inhalation he took.

It had been an impulsive thing to do, but with Warren looking like he did not believe a word she said, Maeve had taken the opportunity to make a memorable point. Also, and being entirely honest with herself, it didn't hurt that her actions had shaken Roderick from his calm, assured complacency around her. Since her conversation with Niamh, Maeve had been searching for ways to ruffle the calm waters of Roderick's certainty.

On a large breath, he turned. Breathing hadn't done much good, because his eyes shot sparks of fury at her. "I could have cleaved you in two." He pushed a shaky hand through his hair. "Alexander could have separated your head from your body."

"You cannot hurt me." She'd staked her life on that not five minutes ago. "And neither would you allow Alexander's sword near me."

He gaped at her. "In all my considerable years as coimhdeacht, I have never seen a witch do something so foolhardy, so risky, so...so..." His temper got away from him and he bellowed the last part. "Fucking idiotic."

Remorse nipped at her. She'd really frightened him with her tiny exploit. "I understand why you would think that." She went for a reasonable tone, hoping to calm him down. "Although, I have to disagree. It was not f-fucking idiotic. It was perfectly logical." She didn't curse much and very rarely used that word. In this time, however, women seemed to have far fewer restrictions on their behavior.

His mouth opened and shut as he tried to form words.

"You are called by Goddess to take care of me. It would be impossible for you to hurt me," she said. Perhaps her impulsive action might have been a touch foolhardy.

From the incredulous scowl she received, she surmised he remained on team fucking idiotic. Then he said, "And Alexander? He has no such calling."

Well, she hadn't been relying on Alexander's calling. "You are driven to stop any hurt from reaching me. He could not hurt me when you are about."

His gaze bored into her as he sputtered and then tightened

his jaw. He took another couple of turns about the room. "I cannot argue about this with you. Not now."

Not ever if she had any say in the matter, but she wisely kept that to herself. "I know you are upset with me, and I understand why, but I am perfectly well." She raised her arms at her sides. "As you can see."

"Maeve." He sawed in a massive breath. "What if you were not fine? Did you think about the consequences if something had happened to you?"

Not at all. Thinking had not formed a large part of her actions. "Of course, I did, but I knew nothing would happen to me."

"Where would these new witches be without you?" He waved his hand to indicate the rest of the coven. "Thirteen witches and an apprentice died so that you could survive, and the knowledge of the cré-witches with you. Playing with your life is not worthy of their sacrifice."

The low blow hit home, and she flinched. "I was never in any danger. Never."

"But you cannot know that, Maeve." He approached her slowly and stopped in front of her. His expression changed and became tender. "And me, Maeve? Where would I be without you?" He'd done it again, looked at her as if he meant to act. But he wouldn't act. He already had the look in his eyes akin to regret that would have him backing away again.

"Where would you be without me?" She was so tired of it. "You would be fine, Roderick. You would carry on being Roderick, like you always do."

"Maeve." He knew what she was thinking because she hadn't concealed her thoughts from him. He knew what she was feeling because she also hadn't concealed her emotions from him. "You are so young. You do not understand."

"To you, everyone is young." She threw up her hands in frustration because as excuses went, his left much to be desired.

He owed her a decent explanation, not more vague platitudes. "Being young does not stop me from seeing things, wanting things."

He cupped her chin and gazed down at her. "I want the same things, Maeve. You only need to look through the bond to know that, but I..."

She waited a moment for him to finish and then stamped her foot. "You what?"

"I've been lying to you." His unflinching, honest blue gaze made her suddenly nervous. Now that they came to it, she didn't know if she was ready for the truth.

"I've been lying to you from almost the first moment I discovered you were my next witch," he said.

Maeve's heart beat so erratically that she feared it would jump right out of her chest. She could hardly formulate thought, let alone words. "Why?"

"Because I am a coward." Self-mockery tinged Roderick's smile. "You have such power over me it terrifies me."

Power over him? Surely, he had that the wrong way around. Older, wiser, and more experienced, he made her feel like a mere infant. She shook her head. "No."

"Aye, Maeve." He stroked his thumb over her cheek. "But you are young, and you do not fully understand what you are asking for."

That hurt and hadn't been what she expected. "I do know what I want." She lifted her chin out of his grasp. "I want what Alexander and Bronwyn have. I want the intimacy they share. I want you to deliver on what I sense you feel for me."

"You want that we should be lovers." Roderick pressed his forehead to hers. "And you know well I want that too, but being lovers is not so simple for us."

"Why?" He was a man, and she was a woman, and they shared so much of each other as it was.

He straightened away from her, and his expression shuttered. "We are bonded, and decisions we make today are decisions we will need to live with for Goddess alone knows how many years to come."

"Or we could both die tomorrow." He was going to leave her wanting again, and her frustration bubbled up like spring water. "Not even you could have foreseen how many years of our lives we wasted in stasis. What if that happens again? What if worse happens and we never acted on what is between us?"

He shook his head. "Maeve—"

Rising to her toes, she pressed her lips to his. She had never been kissed, had almost no idea how, apart from kisses she had seen on those shows the new witches had shown her. She knew only that what she wanted began with kisses, deep, passionate kisses that led to other things, things she desired with every part of her.

Roderick froze, his lips still beneath hers.

She was doing this all wrong, but she had no other ideas, so she kissed him again, pressing her lips to his. "Please."

On a soft groan, he grabbed her hips and brought them flush with his. He took over the kiss, slanting his lips across hers. "Is this what you seek?"

"Yes."

His eyes blazed. One hand tangled in the hair at her nape and positioned her head as he wanted it. He sought entry to her mouth with his tongue and Maeve gave willingly.

Sensation coursed through her and down their bond.

Roderick's answering desire swept like an inferno through her.

It was almost too much, the passion of their kiss coming at her from both of them. It surrounded her and uncoiled within her. Everything he felt, she felt, and the same for him. She lit up from within, her body responding to their mutual need and clamoring for more.

Maeve grew dizzy and clung to him for balance.

He tasted tart and smoky as he explored her mouth, encouraging her to do the same to him.

His chest pressed hard against her breasts, but Maeve sought an even greater closeness. She wanted to be part of him in the most elemental way.

She almost screamed when she recognized him drawing back, pulling back control of the situation. "No." She whimpered and swayed toward him.

"Maeve." He panted her name, his breath hot on her damp lips. "Listen to me."

"No." She tipped her mouth toward him. She didn't want more stupid words.

Roderick put more distance between their mouths. His gaze flickered hot and needy to her lips and then met her eyes. "Tahra was my first witch, and I was bonded to her for nigh on two hundred years."

"Tahra?" Maeve did not want to speak of other witches he had bonded. She wanted more kissing. She wanted him to lay her down on his bed and make her his.

"Listen." He took her by the shoulders. "I loved her, Maeve. I loved Tahra with everything in me. She was my everything."

His words hurt and penetrated her lust fog.

"But Tahra was weary. She was already ancient when she bonded me, and she had no desire to stay on this plane. She wanted to move on. I loved her and wanted to make her stay, but in the end, I had to let her go."

His grief seeped through the bond and brought tears to her eyes.

"And she loved me too. She stayed far longer than she wanted because of me. I knew that." His fingers dug into her shoulders. "In the end, I had to love her enough to let her go. Do you understand what I am telling you?"

"That you will always love her?" Saying the words felt like scraping her heart raw.

"Yes, I will always love her." Roderick made an impatient noise in his throat. "But much time has passed since Tahra, and time heals. I loved her and I lost her. But you..." He shook his head. "You, Maeve, have the power to undo me."

Coven gossip had insisted Roderick had been in love with Tahra, but Maeve had never had the courage to ask him about it. Sometimes knowledge was a mixed blessing.

"I loved Tahra." Roderick stepped back. "I loved her so much that after she died, I swore I would never love another witch again." He shrugged his shoulders. "And I never have. Until I met you, and knew that you would be my next witch, and knew that I could love you like I loved her."

Maeve's head spun and she sat down hard on her bed.

"Regardless of what happens between us, Maeve, we will be together a long time. Whether we act on our feelings or not, we are bound together." He took a seat beside her. "What we are to each other will change many times over the course of our journey together. If one of us ends up heartbroken, we will still be bonded. If one of us falls out of love, we will still be bonded." He shrugged and spread his hands before him. "I have been around long enough to know how I feel and what that means for me. You are the one for me, Maeve, and that will not change."

Maeve found her voice at last. "I feel the same."

"I know you believe that, and I can also feel what you feel." He touched the center of his chest. "But before we leap off the precipice together, Maeve, I would like you to be certain. Do me the favor of considering thoroughly if you want to be mine." Picking up her hand, he threaded their fingers together and kissed her knuckles. "Because when you are mine, I will not be able to let you go. I let Tahra go because I could no longer claim to love her and keep her with me, but you I will not let go. Once you are mine, you are mine forever."

Words deserted her, and Maeve sat there staring at their

joined hands. Her mind crowded with what ifs that she didn't want to acknowledge. What if they did have a passionate affair and it went badly? They would still be joined together in the most intimate of bonds. The stasis spell had frightened her to the core of her being. All that time wasted had made her panic and not want to waste another moment, but she couldn't ignore Roderick's words.

They were not just a man and a woman who met, fell in love and acted on that. Had they been a normal couple, at worst, their commitment would have lasted the course of a normal marriage, forty or fifty years if they were lucky. But both she and Roderick had already lived for hundreds of years, and if they defeated Rhiannon, they would have many more hundreds before them.

"I've taken you by surprise." He stood and walked to the door. With his hand on the latch, he stopped. "Give me until autumn solstice, Maeve. That is not so long for either of us to wait. If by autumn solstice you decide the price of being with me is too great, I will step back, and we need never speak of this. I cannot promise you I will be immediately accepting should you take another man, but over time, one can learn to live with a great many things."

Doubt and hope warred in her mind, and she nodded. "Until the autumn solstice then."

18

Alexander sensed Roderick enter the kitchen behind him, but he kept his gaze on the bailey outside. He'd been expecting Roderick to confront him since their aborted sparring session yesterday. The cowardly part of him had been hoping Maeve could divert Roderick's attention. But Roderick the steady, the ever ready, the relentless, hadn't earned those monikers for nothing.

"Care to explain?" Roderick spoke from behind him, and it wasn't a question.

"Not particularly." Playing for time, he sipped his coffee and faced Roderick.

The rest of the coven had breakfasted and left the kitchen already,

Roderick glowered and took a purposeful step toward him. "I sensed it."

"I know." Alexander admitted as much of the truth as he could. "And I can't explain, because I don't have the answers."

Tension vibrated from Roderick, and his gaze grew deadly. "If you wield blood magic again—"

"It isn't blood magic." Since the night he'd taken part in the coven massacre, he hadn't touched his mother's foul brand of magic. "I know that much."

Roderick snarled. "You can't be sure of that."

"Yes, I can." He held Roderick's stare. "I don't know what it is, but I do know the source of whatever I have isn't blood magic."

"Give me a reason." Roderick stepped into him, chest to chest. "The slightest reason will do, and I will gladly end you."

Longtime habit had him responding with a smirk. "You can try."

A car engine purred and gravel crunched beneath tires behind him.

Roderick's gaze moved to the window, and fresh tension emanated from him. "Who the hell is that?"

"And how did they get past the wards?" Alexander finished Roderick's thought.

A compact SUV stopped, and a woman climbed out. She blinked at the kitchen door and hesitated.

"It's Hermione." Alexander recognized her. "The woman who used to run the castle tours."

The tours remained a touchy spot with Roderick, and he growled at Alexander. "We'll finish this later."

Oh, what joy! Alexander stepped around him and out the kitchen door. "Hermione?"

"Lord Donn?" She blinked at him. Her knuckles turned white where she gripped the top of her open car door.

Hermione had lost weight, and an air of fragility clung to her. Dark circles beneath her eyes suggested many sleepless nights.

"Good morning." Alexander tried to put her at ease with a smile.

She frowned and her eyes flitted past him. "Good morning."

"And to you." Roderick filled the kitchen doorway and stared down at Hermione.

An odd protective urge filled Alexander. Roderick needn't loom and intimidate all the time. Other than an annoying tendency to fawn over him, Alexander liked Hermione.

"I'm Hermione." She cocked her head and studied Roderick intently.

He nodded. "Roderick."

"Oh." She gave a self-conscious laugh. "I thought I knew you from somewhere, but you must be related to the Cray family. It must be the resemblance—"

"Yes." Roderick folded his arms. "Is there a reason you are here?"

Now, that was rude and inhospitable. Alexander made up for Roderick by gesturing the kitchen. "Can we offer you a cup of tea or coffee?"

"Yes, please." Hermione swallowed and nodded, not letting go of her car door.

"Inside?" Alexander prompted gently.

"Right." She gave a shallow laugh. "Yes. Inside."

Sidling past Roderick, she slipped into the kitchen and stood inside the door. She stared around her as if she'd never seen it before, which he knew wasn't the truth. Although Hermione had kept her tours to the public rooms of the castle, she must have been in the kitchen before.

"Hermione?" Alannah walked into the kitchen. She held her hands out to the other woman and kissed her on both cheeks in greeting. "How lovely to see you."

Hermione's shoulders relaxed an inch, and she took a small step toward a chair.

"Tea or coffee?" Alannah bustled over to the range.

"Coffee, please." Hermione's eyes went wide as Roderick moved closer and took a chair at the kitchen table.

Roderick motioned the chair opposite him. "Sit."

"Please." Holding the chair out for her, Alexander glared at Roderick over her head. The rude bastard could tone down the hostility.

Uncomfortable silence reigned as Alannah bustled about with cups and saucers.

"How have you been?" Alannah said as she put a pot of coffee on the range. "I see you're still doing your green tours."

"Yes." Hermione's gaze fixed on Roderick. "They're more popular than ever since the statue disappeared."

Alannah laughed. "I can imagine. Nothing like a bit of mystery to sell tickets."

Cocking her head, she said to Roderick, "Are you sure we haven't met?"

"He has that kind of face. Common as muck." Alexander took the seat beside her.

"How is your daughter?" Alannah put a plate of cookies on the table. "Gemma, isn't it?"

Pain twisted Hermione's features and she blinked rapidly. "She's..." She cleared her throat. "Actually, she's not well. She's...ill. Very ill."

"I'm sorry to hear that." Alannah squeezed her shoulder, her beautiful face soft and genuine. "I had heard something about her not being well, but I'd hoped she was getting better."

"She won't." Hermione's voice grew hard and brittle. "She won't get better, that is." Hermione's hands shook, and she clenched her fingers and rested them on the kitchen table. "She has an inoperable tumor, I'm afraid. In her brain, and the doctors—" Her voice caught on a sob, and she lowered her head, breathing hard.

Alannah took the seat on her other side and put a hand over Hermione's. "I'm so very sorry."

Alexander ached for Hermione. Her grief poured from her in stifling waves. Nobody deserved to lose a child. He wasn't a father yet, but already he could feel an inkling of what Hermione must be dealing with.

Roderick leaned on his elbows, and his tone was tender as he asked, "Is that why you're here?"

A jolt of understanding seared Alexander. He would never have guessed the reason for Hermione's visit, but it made sense.

Hermione started and gaped at Roderick. "I'm not sure...yes."

Alannah glanced at Alexander uneasily and stood to fetch the coffee.

"My family..." Hermione twisted her fingers until her knuckles whitened. "This is going to sound insane, but when you're desperate, when it's your daughter..."

Alexander got it.

"We have this family story, a legend really." Pale, her eyes stark and bright, Hermione took a breath. "That the night all the witches died here in the coven, that a couple of them escaped and we sheltered one of them. She was a healer." Hermione stared at him defiantly, as if daring him to laugh at her. "They say she healed a family member out of gratitude before she disappeared."

The pitiful handful of witches left today would not have existed if Rhiannon's plans had come to full fruition that awful night.

"There are many stories about the coven," Roderick said, his face gentle. "But that's all they are."

Alannah's head jerked up and she stared at Roderick. "They're not—"

"Stories." Roderick insisted, keeping his gaze on Hermione. "I am sorrier than I can say for your terrible tragedy, but what you speak of is nothing more than village gossip."

Hermione sagged as if her last glimmer of hope had died. She gave a brittle little laugh. "I know that." She shrugged and pulled her mouth into a painful parody of a smile. "Of course, I know that. Legends, myths, just stories."

Alannah put the coffeepot on the table with a thump and glowered at Roderick. "Surely, there is some—"

"Nothing." He met her stare with an implacable look. "There is nothing we can do."

He didn't want to agree with Roderick, but Alexander did. To help Hermione would expose the coven at a time when danger pressed from all sides. More specifically, they would expose Bronwyn, a pregnant Bronwyn. The last time the coven had helped heal the villagers it had nearly destroyed them. Coimhdeacht and witches had been slaughtered that fateful day. Rhiannon had created that plague, and Gemma's tumor could be her doing as well. Even if it wasn't, the risk to Bronwyn was unacceptable.

"No," Bronwyn spoke from the doorway, her cheeks flushed with angry color, and her eyes bright and determined. "There is something we can do."

All heads snapped in her direction.

Roderick stood. "Blessed—"

"I'm not sure I can make any difference." Bronwyn softened her tone as she spoke to Hermione. "But I can see her." She crouched beside Hermione. "It won't hurt for me to meet her and see if I can help."

ALEXANDER REACHED for his waning patience. "You, more than anyone, know why not."

They'd been having this argument since Hermione had left, and Bronwyn showed no sign of giving way. Goddess had known what she was doing when she chose women to be her Blessed. Give a magic-gifted woman a blessing and you created an unstoppable force.

"I know that." She growled at him. "I was the one your bitch of an incubator kidnapped, and I still think it's worth the risk."

Nothing, ever, was worth the risk of Bronwyn or their baby —correction, babies—getting hurt. "I don't."

"I'm a healer." Strained patience filled her voice. "That means I was created to heal. Not to sit here in this castle and hide away."

"You're pregnant." He couldn't believe he had to point that out to her. "Rhiannon wants those babies more than anything. Ergo, you will remain behind the wards, where all three of you are safe."

"Urgh!" She stamped her foot. "You are the one who told me magic grows stronger the more I use it."

She had him there, but he couldn't let her take the risk. "Here." He pointed to a bruise on his arm, courtesy of Roderick and a lance. "Heal that."

Grabbing his arm, she covered it with her hand. "Done."

He'd barely felt a tingle. Her power was growing.

"I need more. The world needs what I can do." Her big eyes implored him. "I can help Hermione's daughter. I know it."

"You don't know that." Alexander tried a different tack. "Gemma has cancer." He stressed the word. "Cancer. I'm not even sure you can do anything about cancer. It would be cruel to give Hermione hope and then snatch it away."

Gemma was too ill to move, and it meant taking Bronwyn into Greater Littleton to see the girl.

"There are plenty of sick people in this world, little witch." He took her in his arms. "You were given your blessing for a reason. When the danger has passed there will be plenty of time and opportunities for you to heal people."

She wriggled out of his hold, her chin stubbornly set. "And when will the danger pass? A month from now? A year? Longer. That child is mine to heal. I know it." She tapped her chest. "I know it." And then she said the thing that terrified him. "And I'm going to heal that child. The only thing you get to decide is whether you come with me and protect me or not."

"That's not going to happen." If he had to lock her in a tower.

"You can't stop me." She crossed her arms. "Unless you're prepared to lock me up."

Bloody woman must be reading his mind. "If I must."

"Don't you fucking dare." She went flinty eyed and a bit scary on him. "You can't open my gift to me and then tell me I can't use it."

According to Roderick, the first healer, Brenna, had been as determined and stubborn. If there was a nick, graze, broken limb or deadly disease within her scope, she had to heal it. It was the curse and the miracle of all cré-healers; their blessing was an imperative. When Rhiannon had lured the healers out of Baile in the 1600s, she had known that all she had to do was present them with a bunch of sick villagers. Nothing would stop them from going, and from the look on his little witch's face, nothing was going to stop Bronwyn either.

Her gaze met his and didn't waver. Determination set her shoulders in an unrelenting line.

Alexander swallowed the bitter draft of defeat. She would go, with or without his agreement. He needed to do damage control. "Let me talk to Roderick."

"And tell him I'm going." She crossed her arms as she pressed her point home.

Beneath her crossed arms, rested their babies, and it was his job to keep all three of them safe and away from Rhiannon. His sigh came from the center of his being as he twisted between a rock and a hard place. "I'll explain to him we are going and what we're going to do. He and I will discuss the timing and how to mitigate the risk." Once Roderick finished bellowing like an enraged bull. Alexander gave her belly a pointed stare. "Because there is more than just you and I to think of now."

"I know that." She touched her belly. "And I'm not going to risk our babies, but I can't not do this."

Another sigh rattled through him, because he knew it was thus. "I know."

"Soon," she yelled at his retreating back. "Make sure he knows I'm going soon."

Stomping through the great hall to the barracks, he voiced his discontent, "Fucking hell." His voice echoed through the cavernous space.

"Problem?" Thomas materialized with a smirk.

"Yup." Maybe locking her in a tower wasn't such a bad idea. She'd forgive him eventually. Two, three hundred years, she'd be over it, the babes would be born and already doing their final magick thing. And then Bronwyn would march right out of the tower he'd locked her in and go and heal the first sick person she could sense. "Fucking hell!"

"I'm guessing Bronwyn." Thomas drifted along beside him.

Ghosts were pretty useless for the most part, but they always knew where to find somebody. "Do you know where Roderick is?"

"In the yard." Thomas jerked his head toward the barracks. "Maeve is working in the caverns, and he's hiding from her."

That took his mind off his problem and made him feel marginally better. He wasn't the only man having woman trouble. "What is going on with them anyway?"

"Sex." Thomas sighed. "Goddess, but I miss sex."

"Stay away from Alannah."

Thomas looked affronted. "I say I miss sex and that's where your head goes."

"Are you denying you hover around her like a horny bumble bee?"

"I...what...bumblebee?" Thomas glowered at him. "Firstly, I

will have you know that I am an apparition, a specter, a wraith, a spirit. Pick one. I am not a bumblebee."

"Right." Alexander let his derision color his tone. "But you're still not denying that you hover around her like a randy wraith."

Thomas deflated. "Alannah and I are...it's complicated."

"Really." He burst out laughing. "That's what you're going with? It's complicated?"

"Well, it is." Thomas vanished, probably to sulk somewhere before he went back to hovering.

Roderick had a table in the center of the yard, and on it he had gathered a collection of firearms, which he was scowling at.

Alexander knew better than to ask where they'd come from, so he joined Roderick in staring at them. "What are we doing?"

"What I am doing." Roderick sneered. "This has naught to do with you."

"It does if you're thinking of using one of those." Roderick was wickedly accurate with a crossbow and a longbow, but guns were another matter. "Have you ever fired a gun?"

"I have not." A muscle worked in Roderick's jaw. "Have you?"

"Absolutely." It didn't give him as much satisfaction as he would have thought it would to be able to do something the big lout couldn't. "But I still don't like them. They take the fun out of a good fight. They're too immediate."

"Aye." Roderick poked a Glock. "But our enemy is proficient, and it strikes me I should learn to be too. Edana would never have gotten away with Bronwyn had I been able to shoot back."

The night Bronwyn had been kidnapped, Edana had emptied five bullets into Roderick at close range to stop him. She had stopped him and gotten away with Bronwyn. It had taken Roderick precious days to heal enough to go after them.

"It certainly gave her an unfair advantage." Alexander

picked up an ancient looking Colt. "I think we can skip this one and go straight to modern handguns."

"Hello." Looking refreshed and less stressed than Alexander had seen him thus far, Warren strode into the yard. There was something very familiar about Warren, and it nagged at him. He knew he hadn't met the man before, but it was in the way he moved and held himself. Of course, it wasn't a far stretch to believe him to be descended from one of the earlier coimhdeacht. The gift, as with witches, was hereditary.

Warren stopped at the table and chuckled. "Wow! You went all out on the procurement front."

"I knew not what kind was best." Roderick must have ground a molar to powder to admit he didn't know something, especially weapons related.

"Right, then!" Warren picked through the selection. "Before I teach you to handle a weapon, we're going to cover gun safety." He palmed a Smith & Wesson. "First rule, you always keep your weapon's muzzle pointed in a safe direction. If people didn't point at things they didn't intend to shoot, there would be no accidental shootings. Got it?"

Roderick nodded and picked up the Glock and pointed the muzzle to the ground. "Got it."

"Before you get started, I need to tell you something." Alexander didn't need to be here for this, and Roderick would probably prefer him not seeing him try to master a new skill. The bastard was a born warrior, however, and Alexander had no doubt firearms would present very few challenges to Roderick. "Bronwyn is determined to go to the village."

Roderick turned and glared at him. "No."

"First off, you don't get to decide anything for my witch or myself." Alexander tamped down on his irritation. "And secondly, and more relevantly, I don't want her to go either, but I don't think we can stop her. She heard Hermione and that was it for her."

Pulling his shoulders back, Roderick shook his head. "She can't leave the wards. You of all people know exactly why not."

"I do." And wouldn't it be brilliant if for once Roderick could give him the bloody benefit of the doubt. "But Bronwyn is a healer and a powerful one. You can sense it as much as I can. She can't help herself. She's going to heal people."

"She can do that?" Warren looked like he wasn't certain he wanted the answer to his question.

"She can." He spared a brief sympathetic thought for how much Warren had to grasp in a short time. "But more importantly, healers are the biggest pains in the arse of all Blessed. Not only are they able to heal nearly anything, but you can't stop them from doing it. It's bigger than they are."

"Aye." Roderick looked grim. "We tried to stop them from going to the village when it was beset by plague."

Warren glanced between them. "I'm guessing it didn't go so well."

"No." Roderick went on the explain, but kept it brief, leaving Maeve's part in the story out.

"Who does she want to heal?" Warren asked.

"Hermione's daughter," Alexander said. "She came here earlier today, and Bronwyn heard her."

Warren frowned. "I met Hermione. She seems like a good woman."

"That's irrelevant." Roderick sighed. "If it were not this child, it would be another. Healers are like that."

Warren cleared his throat. "What happened last time? When the healers went to help with the plague?"

"Would you like to answer that?" Roderick turned to him with a malicious gleam in his eye.

Yup, the smarmy bastard was loving this. He'd never believe the other role Alexander had played that night. Not that Alexander would ever tell him. "I had a mob of frenzied witch-hating villagers waiting for them."

"Ouch." Warren looked like he regretted bringing the subject up.

"Maeve snuck out with them." Roderick took over the story.

Alexander felt duty bound to point out. "I never knew Maeve would be with them."

"Would it have changed anything?" Roderick sneered.

"No."

Warren stepped between them. "I'm sensing more to this story."

"Then Roderick came to Maeve's rescue. Although I wouldn't have let them drown Maeve." Alexander couldn't resist rubbing the lout's nose in it at times. "I liked Maeve, and I probably would have kept her for myself."

Roderick growled.

Sighing, Warren looked at Alexander "Seriously?"

"All right." Warren didn't deserve to play peacekeeper. "Suffice to say I was still Rhiannon's minion then. Roderick came to rescue Maeve. We fought. I won, and then the other coimhdeacht rescued him and the witches."

"You won because it was you and a mob." Roderick sneered. "Otherwise, I would have wiped the ground with your pompous, weak—"

"All right!" Warren shook his head at them. "You're like schoolboys, you know that, right?"

"One of us is." Alexander went for the obvious dig and felt marginally ashamed of himself. Only marginally because the irritation pouring off Roderick was worth the childish shot. "However." Time to grow the fuck up. "The point to the story is that if healers have decided they want to heal a person, there is nothing we can do to stop them."

"We could lock her up," Roderick said.

"I've already thought of that." Despise each other as they did, their minds often ran along the same track.

"I'm going to have to veto that one, lads." Warren folded his arms. "You can't go around locking modern women up. They don't stand for it, neither does the law, and neither will I."

Roderick raised a brow. "Even if it's for their own good?"

"Right." Warren sniffed. "We gave up deciding what was for women's good a while ago. Now we acknowledge they can do it for themselves."

Given the circumstances, Alexander felt as happy about that as Roderick's doubtful expression telegraphed. "All things considered, I really believe it's best if I take her and make sure she gets back safely." Alexander pressed his advantage into the silence. "I can sense Rhiannon from miles away and she won't get near me or Bronwyn. Also, she won't be expecting us to do this."

"She won't be expecting it because it's an insane risk," Roderick said. "Particularly in Bronwyn's condition."

Alexander did not disagree with him. "But if she's going to do it, and believe me she is, then we can at least control the outcome."

"I've got a daughter," Warren said and glanced away. "I'd do anything if Taylor was sick. Anything." His jaw set in an uncompromising line. "I'll take Bronwyn if neither of you will."

Roderick grunted and balled his fist. "You have no under-standing of the risk."

"And you have no idea what being a parent is like." Warren didn't flinch under Roderick's glare.

"I'm taking her." Alexander gave way to the inevitable, because Warren spoke true. If that were his child, he'd stop at nothing, take any risk, to save her.

"Stay in contact via mobile," Warren suggested.

"Baile messes with mobile phones." Alexander would love it if she didn't. "They don't work here." He grabbed a Ruger. "But this and Warren coming with me should tip the odds in our favor."

Warren picked up a box of bullets. "The three of us will at any rate."

Roderick looked confused. "Three of us? I am coming?"

"Nah, we don't want to commit our entire force on one sortie." Warren showed him the handgun. He grinned like a naughty child as he said, "It's me and Smith and Wesson."

19

On the short drive from Baile to the village, Alexander's hatred of her leaving the protection of the wards radiated off him. Bronwyn wished she could reassure him that everything would be fine, but he was too smart for that. Besides, she was taking a huge risk, and everyone in the Landy knew it.

Including her.

However, even having experienced the danger firsthand, it wasn't enough to stop her from needing to go. The compulsion to make things right, to put Gemma out of pain, to win one back from death gnawed at her, and she couldn't ignore it.

The only person who might agree with her decision would be Deidre, her grandmother. They'd been twin souls, her and Deidre, bound together by the family's gifts and forged in the furnace of the amount of death and loss they'd both suffered. Deidre had believed if someone needed your help, you helped them. They didn't need to be worthy of that help or even deserve it.

She still remembered when Deidre had helped a woman in their hometown of Saw Tooth, Maine, to ease her hot flashes.

The woman had been a bitch to Deidre and her for years, always spreading malicious gossip about the strange Beaty women. She'd also been the person responsible for the rumor that Deidre had killed her own daughters, Bronwyn's mother and aunt. But Deidre had helped her regardless.

"Our gifts are our blessings," Deidre had said when Bronwyn had asked her why. "We don't judge who is worthy of receiving their benefits. After all, we didn't do anything worthy to get our gifts. They were given to us when we were born."

Once her hot flashes had disappeared, the same woman had renewed her attack on Deidre and Bronwyn with the energy not consumed by menopause, but it hadn't mattered to Deidre. "We can't change how they see us; we can only control the way we behave."

While not nearly as resigned as Deidre, Bronwyn did share her grandmother's need to help people, and it had been magnified since she'd wakened water and unleashed the full potential of her power. Without an older healer to guide her, however, most of what she did was self-taught, and all those stupid books in the healer's hall made massive assumptions about what she should already know.

"This is the house." Alexander pulled up beside a cheery red door on a small, winding village street. White, terraced houses marched in an orderly row on both sides of the street, more modest and affordable than those homes built near the ocean.

"Stay put." Warren hopped out of the back. "Let me take a quick gander."

He prowled down the street, tense and alert, head moving left to right in slow, steady sweeps.

"Was it really necessary to bring him?" Bronwyn knew the answer before it came, but she needed a distraction from her galloping apprehension. What if, after insisting they bring her here, she could do nothing for Gemma? She'd never attempted a healing anywhere near as large as cancer.

Similarly tense, Alexander scrutinized the street. "Yup."

She didn't want to make this harder on him, and she motioned the door. "Shouldn't I get moving? You know, sooner done, sooner back to Baile."

Alexander grunted, watching Warren as he passed them and moved to give the road behind the Landy as thorough a perusal.

"All clear." Warren tapped on the roof. "I'll stay out here. Keep an eye."

Nodding, Alexander climbed out the Landy, came around to her side and opened the door. "Come on, little witch. Let's get this over with."

Not exactly vibrating with enthusiasm, but she knew he was worried. Bronwyn lifted the fox head door knocker and rapped.

"She's not home." Alexander sounded relieved. "Let's go—"

The door opened, and Hermione stood there and blinked at her. "You're here?"

"Yes." Bronwyn smoothed her damp palms over her jeans. Goddess, please let her be able to do something for Gemma.

"Good morning, Hermione." Alexander poured on the charm as he stepped into Hermione's line of sight. "How are you?"

Hermione opened and shut her mouth. "Fine. I'm fine." She stared at Warren. "Oh, it's you. From the Copper Cauldron."

"Hello again." Warren nodded

Alexander gestured the interior of the house. "May we come in?"

"Of course." Hermione flushed as she stepped back and let them into her cottage.

Honey colored wood floors gleamed beneath their feet. Beeswax and a faint medicinal astringent smell filled the air. A stairway ran along the whitewashed wall to their right.

Shutting the door behind them, Alexander glanced at her before taking charge. "Would you like to take us to Gemma?"

"Um..." Hermione snapped her mouth shut and frowned. "I know I came to you for help, but I've been thinking. Actually, I don't know what I was thinking. I was desperate, and I'd just come from the doctor." She straightened her shoulders. "It's just that Gemma has already been through so much. All the tests and the treatments. All the pointless hope."

"I understand." Alexander took Hermione's hand between his. "And we can't make you any promises. Let Bronwyn take a look."

Bronwyn's heart ached for both Hermione and Gemma. "I won't make her any promises I can't keep."

Hermione stiffened and then nodded. "Okay, then. I must seem stupid to you, begging you to help and then questioning you when you get here."

"I get it." Bronwyn would bleed her gift dry before she left Hermione and Gemma to their fate. "You can trust me."

Hope, doubt, nerves, and anger all crossed Hermione's face as she stared at Bronwyn.

"Mum?" A young girl stood at the top of the stairs. Lank brown hair hung on either side of her thin face, her eyes and skin dull with exhaustion and pain. "She says she can help."

"Gemma." Hermione positioned herself at the bottom of the stairs, between them and her daughter. "You should be resting."

Even with her pregnancy being so new, Bronwyn understood that primal desire to protect. "Let me try," Bronwyn said. Gemma needed her; it sang through her blood and pounded through every cell of her body. "Let me try."

"Let her, Mum." Gemma plopped down on the top step as if her legs had run out of hold. "She can't make anything worse."

"Don't say that." Hermione's tone grew brittle with forced

cheer. "You're going to fight this thing. We're going to fight this and get you back on your feet again."

"Mum." Gemma's young voice held the ghastly wisdom of death. "We both know that's not true."

Resolve growing, Bronwyn slipped past Hermione and climbed toward Gemma. She held out her hand. "I'm Bronwyn."

"I'm dying." Gemma grinned.

Hermione sobbed and choked on inarticulate words.

"Let's make some tea." Alexander put his arm around Hermione's shoulders. "I think we're all going to need a cup."

"I don't—" Hermione let him lead her away, but she kept looking over her shoulder.

"She's trying to protect me," Gemma said. "She doesn't want me to know how bad it is."

"But you do know, don't you?" Bronwyn sat on the step beside her. Gemma twisted her heart like a soggy rag.

Gemma nodded. "I worry about her. When I'm gone."

"You're not gone yet," Bronwyn said. Goddess, please be with her now and give her all the power of her blessing. Cancer couldn't take this round.

Gemma studied her. "Everybody around here says the Cray women are witches, are you one of them?"

"I am." Bronwyn nodded. "As near as we can work out, my ancestor made it over to America. I came back to trace my roots." She leaned in and whispered, "You should see me on Halloween."

"Right." Gemma nodded as if witches were a commonplace event in her day. "So, what is it you can do exactly?"

"I'm not sure." Bronwyn went with stark honesty. "I'm new to all of this. I only know I need to be here to help you."

Gemma laughed, and glimmers of the child she was without her illness peeked through at Bronwyn in her mischievous glance. "Real life trick or treat."

"Something like that." Bronwyn had to do this. She must do this. She would do this. "You ready?"

"For what?" Gemma eyed her suspiciously.

"Not sure." Bronwyn stood and motioned the hallway. "But it would be a safer bet to do this lying down."

Standing, Gemma nodded. "It can't hurt."

Goddess, please grant that be the truth.

Gemma led her through the first open door and into her bedroom. Bright yellow and pink butterflies on the curtains and counterpane melded with signs of a girl on the edge of her teens. Photographs of Gemma and two other girls plastered on the mirror of a dressing table littered with makeup. A large, battered teddy shared the bed with a sparkly pillow that announced itself *Queen of effing everything.*

"Shall I lie or sit?" Gemma motioned the bed.

"Get comfortable," Bronwyn said. "Can I get a bowl of water?"

"Water?" Gemma frowned. "To drink?"

"Not really." Bronwyn winked at her. "You'll see in a minute."

Gemma frowned. "You're not going to pour it over me, or dunk my head in it or anything are you?"

"No." Bronwyn held her hand up. "I solemnly swear the water will not touch you."

"Okay." Gemma looked only half convinced. "There's a bucket in the bathroom, will that do?"

"Perfectly." Bronwyn followed Gemma's pointed finger to a bathroom across the hall. The bucket sat beside the toilet, and she filled it to the brim before going back to the bedroom.

Gemma stretched out on her bed. She motioned a crammed bookshelf beside the door. "I have all my scans, and my blood tests, Mum has—"

"Those are meaningless to me." Bronwyn placed the water

beside the bed and sat next to Gemma. "I'm not a medical doctor."

"Oh." Gemma sighed. "Well, I've seen plenty of those anyway."

"Would you give me your hand?" Bronwyn held out hers. "Then you sit here, and I do the rest."

"No needles?" Gemma looked skeptical. "No sitting as still as I can?"

"You can if you want." Bronwyn took her hand. "But don't bother on my account."

Bronwyn reached for her magic. Water rose joyfully to her bidding in the twinned scents of honey and sage. The more magic she used, the more responsive it grew. She quested gently through their held hands and into Gemma, checking if her defenses were up. Honey and sage flowed freely into Gemma. "That's good," she said. "You're not resisting me."

"Whatever you're doing, it tickles." Gemma giggled.

Bronwyn pulled more water and let her Blessing work. Honey and sage anchored itself firmly and went hunting for the problem. It hooked on to Gemma's nervous system and shot up her spinal cord to her brainstem. They found the tumor instantly, nestled into the tissue surrounding her brainstem, a hostile invader stealing the life of its host.

Honey and sage surrounded the invader. Bronwyn drew harder on water. She'd never used this much power before, and it flowed like lava through her and into Gemma.

The invader tried to break free.

Bronwyn dragged more power from water and reinforced the walls of honey and sage. The tumor tried to repel them, but Bronwyn braced and pulled even more power.

Water surged into the gap and fed her magic's voracious need. She pulled on the water in the bucket, found water in the pipes in the old building, and it responded to her instantaneously.

An internal warning system blinked at her, trying to make her aware of the danger of pulling too much power too fast. She would not be able to hold the magic for long at this intensity, and the backlash would hit her and Gemma.

The tumor writhed under her onslaught, driven by its imperative to survive. Holding water, she grasped even more power, more than she had ever held. It struggled against the too tight confines of her skin, searching for space.

Bronwyn shoved it against the tumor, channeling the excess into the silent pulsing growth. It wouldn't win because she wouldn't let it. Power, more than she could have believed possible, surged through her, power that scalded, twisted and threatened to overwhelm her. All she had to do was hold on long enough for the power to do its work.

Pain built in her, growing stronger by the second. Power forced its way into the tumor's molecular structure, tearing off fine strands of it. Magic opened a searing pathway through her. Her stomach churned as her body instinctively sought to reject the damaged and diseased cells. Honey and sage rushed to protect her womb as larger hunks of the mass ripped away and coursed through Bronwyn.

Nausea flooded her mouth with saliva, her head throbbed, and her back muscles spasmed, but she battled and kept the pathway steady. Honey and sage tore into the tumor, dismantling it, tugging its roots out of Gemma's healthy tissue. Healing magic stalked the tumor and chased down every last trace of it. And only then did Bronwyn allow it to withdraw. Exhaustion swamped her, and she almost lost control of the retreating magic.

She could sense Alexander in the room. She didn't know when he'd come in, but his quiet strength steadied her, and she slowed the magic's descent into a steady trickle, releasing the last tendril with a soft groan.

Slowly, she opened her eyes. Light seared her retinas and she shut her eyes.

Alexander touched her shoulder. "Little witch? That was a lot you drew."

"I know." Cautiously, she blinked her eyes open.

"We will have words on that. But later." He crouched to her level, his dark eyes searching her face. "Is it done?"

Beside her, Gemma was fast asleep. Healthy color filled her cheeks, and her breathing chuffed deep and restful.

Bronwyn nodded. "It's done."

"I need to get you back to Baile." He didn't look happy with her. "You need to transmute this."

She would deal with his unhappiness when they got back to Baile. "Where is Hermione?"

"Downstairs." He jerked his head toward the rest of the house. "She's not happy with either of us."

"But she will be." If she weren't so tired, she would've smiled, because it was done. That awful thing eating Gemma alive was gone. She had won.

"Right then." Alexander gave her a gentle, weary smile. "Let me take care of you now. We're in this together."

"Always."

The moment hung between them and stretched somehow into more. More in ways that Bronwyn hadn't courage to put a name to. The way Alexander made her feel took her breath away. It made her question if she'd ever really known what love truly meant.

Gemma stirred and opened her eyes. "What happened?"

"You fell asleep." Bronwyn had destroyed that awful thing, but if she said so now, they probably wouldn't believe her. Gemma might, but not Hermione. Let Hermione take Gemma for all the tests, because she would do it regardless of what Bronwyn said. "You need to get tested as soon as possible."

Gemma stared at her with big eyes. "What did you do?"

"Do the tests," Bronwyn said. She patted Gemma's hand. "But do them soon."

Gemma and Hermione shouldn't live with this awful dread for any longer than they had to.

Alexander helped her stand. "Can you walk?" he whispered. "Enough to get out of this room."

Bronwyn leaned on him heavily. "You're going to make sure I do."

"Will I see you again?" Gemma watched them.

"Not if you don't need to." Bronwyn shook her head. "But now you should sleep."

"Just one thing." Alexander paused with the door open. "If after you've taken your tests, there is any part of you or your mum that wants to thank Bronwyn, do it by never telling anyone what happened here."

20

CRÉ-WITCH CHRONICLES

Alexander bore Bronwyn's weight as they left the house. With her strength spent from magic use, and Gemma's disease lingering in her system, she could barely stay upright. It would take a trip to Goddess Pool to transmute the tumor. Goddess Pool was tucked safely behind Baile's wards, and he couldn't wait to get her there.

They let themselves out as Hermione remained in the kitchen trying to get her head around all that he'd told her, and also the stiff warning he'd given her about sharing today with anyone.

The world wasn't ready for magic, never had been really.

Warren looked around as they emerged onto the street. He frowned at Bronwyn. "Everything okay?"

"Great," she said, then ruined her attempt at jaunty with a racking cough.

"She's done in," Alexander said. Warren was getting an insta-lesson in coimhdeacht duties. "We need to get her back to Baile ASAP."

"On it." Warren caught the keys Alexander threw him and opened the Landy.

Bronwyn stopped at the open door and scowled at him. "Why did you say that to Gemma?"

"The thing about not telling anyone?" He'd been braced for her response since they'd left Gemma's bedroom. He tried to nudge her into the Landy. They'd been in Greater Littleton long enough for Rhiannon's antennae to be twitching. His proximity and all the sweet cré-magic Bronwyn had perfumed the air with would have her tweaking like an apoplectic bloodhound.

Blood. Hound? Goddess, what a bad time for his twisted sense of humor to put in an appearance.

"You damn near threatened Gemma." Bronwyn braced her hand on the door opening. Close, but not close enough to getting in the vehicle and on her way to safety. "People are suspicious enough about us as it is, without you getting all heavy handed with them."

Good thing she hadn't heard what he'd said to Hermione then. He'd more or less intimated that whatever good Bronwyn had done here today would go away if Hermione blathered.

Alexander would much rather have this conversation behind Baile's wards, but she had that mulish look to her that told him they weren't going anywhere until they hashed this out. "Think about it, Bronwyn."

Her brows shot up at his snippy tone.

She would have to get over it, because between the danger to her and how worn out she looked, he was at the end of his patience. "Word gets out on the sodding internet that you cured a kid of cancer. It goes viral."

Warren whistled. "And it would."

"Right." Alexander nodded his thanks for the backup. "Suddenly everybody who needs a miracle in their life floods to Greater Littleton."

She glared at him. "And this is a bad thing? That's what I was created and blessed to do, Alexander. Heal people."

Whoops! The full use of his name. Well, she could stuff that because she needed to get what he meant and get it good. "We could be overrun. Thousands of people."

"Hundreds of thousands," Warren said, still scanning the street and alert for trouble.

"Millions even." Alexander pressed the point home. "And one of you. Even if you could manage all of them, there would be more and more coming."

Warren stiffened and locked his attention on the end of the street. "And then there would be the haters."

"Exactly." Alexander tried to see what made Warren still, but the street remained empty. He quested for his connection to Rhiannon but found it dormant. "As fast as people are going to believe you, there are going to be those yelling you're a fraud."

Bronwyn considered that. "But I'm not."

"It doesn't matter. You know as well as I do in trial by social media, the truth is irrelevant."

"But word is going to get out eventually." She finally heaved herself into the Landy. "And then we'll have to deal with the fallout."

"Yes." He had no idea how they were going to navigate the desperation and cynicism of introducing Goddess and cré-magic into this time. "But we should try to control how and when that happens. You can still heal people." Like he would ever be able to stop her. "But we need to find a way for you to heal that doesn't endanger you, the coven, or our credibility."

Bronwyn chewed on her bottom lip. "How?"

"That I don't fucking know yet." And all of them needed to get real about that eventuality and start planning. "But keeping things on the down low until we have a plan is in all our best interests."

After a moment, she nodded.

"Heads up," Warren said, his voice clipped. He reached for

the gun in the back of his jeans waistband and gripped it. Ready for trouble.

Alexander looked up and froze.

Down the street, a filmy summer dress caressing her perfect curves, sauntered Edana.

Bronwyn stared at Edana, even paler than she had been. "Oh no. No, no, no."

Her stark terror galvanized him. Last time Bronwyn had seen Edana, Edana had aided her kidnaping and shot Roderick. "Stay in the Landy."

"I know her," Warren said.

Alexander palmed his firearm as well. "That is not a fucking good thing." He raised his pistol and pointed it at Edana. "Don't move. Nothing would make me happier than to end you."

"Darling." Edana stopped, looked at Warren and laughed. "Nice to see you too. Why so hostile?" She smirked. "You were a lot friendlier last time we met."

Alexander glanced at Warren. They needed to chat about how friendly Warren had gotten with Edana, but not now. "Get in and start her up."

Warren hustled into the Landy and the engine wheezed and banged into life. Alannah needed to do more fine-tuning on her fuel of the future.

"We thought it might be you when we felt all that magic being used." Edana stared through the windows at Bronwyn. "I see our little healer is stretching her muscles."

As much as he'd love to, Alexander couldn't shoot her in broad daylight on a village street. Keeping the gun on Edana, he opened his door.

"Your mother has a message for you," Edana said. "She's very angry with you, you know."

As if he couldn't have put that together. Done with Edana, he climbed into the Landy.

"She wants you to know she has something extra special

planned for you and your little witch." Edana laughed. Suddenly, she stopped and cocked her head. She took a deep sniff. "Oh my!" She grinned. "Our lady will be pleased."

"Go." Alexander slammed his door.

Warren wasted no time in getting out of there.

Edana leaped onto the pavement as Warren floored the Landy.

"What did she mean?" Bronwyn spoke from the back, her voice growing weaker as the disease attacked her body. "About Rhiannon being pleased."

Only guessing, but still sure he had it right, he said, "Edana could probably sense you were pregnant."

"Fuck." Bronwyn screwed her eyes shut.

Alexander watched in the rearview until Edana was out of sight. "Precisely."

RHIANNON WOULD LIKE to face her betrayer, see if he dared meet her gaze, but she'd sent Edana instead. The curious ache inside her chest when she thought of him infuriated her, but she had stayed because she had another to meet with. Even clever, perceptive Fiona only knew a fraction of what Rhiannon set in motion. Edana had loose lips and would be quick to run back to Fiona with whatever information she could glean.

Rhiannon used them all, but she trusted none of them.

The cottage door opened, and Edana sidled in. She looked smug and pleased with herself. "I saw them."

"And?" Christ, she'd enjoy torturing that one.

"He was there, along with her and the new coimhdeacht." Edana strolled closer, sunlight making her dress transparent. Stupid and a whore. Well, she could use and had used Edana being a willing whore. "It was her using the magic."

"I thought so." She might not be able to wield the cré-magic without blood anymore, but she could still sense water being pulled. Earth had been her element, and a pang of regret surprised her. It had been so long since she'd felt the touch of her birth element in a way that wasn't torturously painful. Mint and thyme had been the scent of her magic. To this day, she would have neither herb near her. They served as a stark reminder of all she'd lost, all Goddess had cost her.

Goddess! What a fucking joke! The bitch had allowed her witches to be mowed down like ripe hay. She'd let it happen and let her magic disappear from the world to the point it was all but extinct. Nearly, not entirely gone, but enough magic left to waken that little healer and bring her to Baile.

Rhiannon knew not why Goddess had allowed herself to be depleted. Why would any being with that much power let it be stripped away. Of course, Goddess could never take life, not even to defend her own. But still, what a pernicious waste. If— no, when—Rhiannon wrested power from her, you could bet she wouldn't allow any other being to wreak the same kind of damage. No, when she held the power, she would keep it at whatever cost.

Edana still stood there, smirking.

"What?"

Edana started. "There is more, my lady. And you will be pleased."

"Oh?" Edana wouldn't look so pretty with her face diced and dissected.

"Yes, my lady." With the preservation instinct of a rat, Edana bowed low. "The healer witch is with child."

"She is with child?" Rhiannon went numb inside. She had waited for this for hundreds of years. The first time she had read that prophecy in Baile's great library, a kernel of an idea had formed. At that time, she had only had fleeting thoughts of leaving the coven. Yet, even then, that prophecy had struck the core of her.

"My lady?" Edana looked concerned.

"Get out."

The door shut behind Edana. Rhiannon's knees buckled, and she sat.

Rhiannon couldn't share this moment with anyone. She might have shared it with the betrayer, but that wasn't possible now.

Hundreds of years in the making. Thousands of days. Untold hours and minutes. And now it had come to fruition. His children would be hers by blood. Some emotion perilously close to regret tightened her chest. If he had still been hers, they would have raised his children together. Her sentimentality sickened her. The only reason she had given birth to a male child had been to bring the prophecy to fruition for her use. She desired power, not mewling mawkishness.

The son of death shall bear the torch that lights the path. And the daughter of life shall bring forth water nascent and call it onto the path of light. Then they will bear fruit. And this fruit will be the magick. The greatest of magick and the final magick.

It had been clear to her that she could create the son of death, the torch bearer. For a moment she had considered creating the daughter of life as well, but that had proven impossible. Despite her efforts she had only borne one child.

Incest didn't bother her. Nothing was forbidden to the magic.

"She is with child," she whispered, half afraid if she said the words aloud, she would wake and find it a dream. She'd foreseen the twins when she'd scried, but this was too important to trust to portents, and now she had confirmation. Not just one child, but two.

To have command of those twins was everything. She had come so far, sacrificed so much for the children of magic, and she would continue to do so. There was nothing she couldn't or wouldn't do to take her rightful place in the world.

He had done it. The boy child she had stolen from his father's loins, carried, birthed and raised, only to be betrayed by, had still accomplished the purpose she had created him for.

She was surprised to see her hands were shaking. The enormity of that one piece of news would ricochet through her for days, weeks even.

She had done it. She had succeeded, and now all she had to do was get her hands on the children.

Baile, Roderick, impotent Goddess, and those feeble baby witches would all try to stop her. Even the betrayer would try to foil her, but she had planned all of their paths meticulously.

Everything was proceeding perfectly.

21

CRÉ-WITCH CHRONICLES

A mild day bathed Baile's gray stone in soft, mellow light as the lure of pack had Niamh heading out to clear her head. Head-gumming hours spent in the library had left her feeling restless and frustrated. Yesterday, Bronwyn had accomplished a miracle. All the coven had asked of Niamh was that she locate fire, and she continued to fail. A gentle onshore breeze carried sea scent and kept the morning cool.

"Off somewhere?" Thomas appeared beside her.

Not feeling like company, she gave him a cool, "Just a walk."

"Hmm." Thomas turned his face toward the sun. "It's a nice day for it."

"Yup." He looked all set to drop into step beside her.

"Your menagerie is missing." Thomas looked about them. "Are you going somewhere they shouldn't come?"

Oh, he was too convinced of his own subtlety and cleverness. "I think you know exactly where I'm going."

"And you'd be right." He grinned. "It's been a while since I've seen them."

"Meaning you knew them from before." She'd been reluctant to ask him about pack. Hugged close to her chest, it had stayed her special secret.

Thomas gave her a long look. "Each Blessing has its secrets and pack was one of the guardians'. Initially because people, even witches, are fearful of wolves, and then to make sure there would always be a pack on Baile land."

"I see." She kind of did, but right now she represented a blessing group of one—technically two, but she couldn't count Roz—and the only people sharing her secret were her, herself and she. And a ghost. Lest she forget the bloody mouthy spirit. "Maybe in future you could let me in on any other secrets?"

Thomas pulled a face. "You're right, of course. Keeping things to myself has become a habit, because...I was by myself."

"Fair enough." Now she felt guilty for bitching out a being who'd spent hundreds of years isolated from his brothers and his witch. She quested for Alpha and found him. Pack moved toward her. "They're coming."

"Good." Thomas grinned at her and stuck his hands in his pockets. "You know, pack only responds to the strongest of the guardians. They mostly ignored Lavina."

"Really?" She had trouble believing that. Lavina had been a fully trained witch with her full power at her disposal. Niamh could manage a mental ride along and sometimes get animals to understand what their humans wanted of them.

"You're strong in your power, Niamh." Thomas nodded. "The animals a guardian draws are directly related to the strength of her Blessing. The apex predators only respond to the strongest of the guardian witches."

That cheered her up, and also reminded her how imperative it was they find fire and activate it.

Leaving the castle road, they slipped into the forest on the far side of the moat. The air stayed cool beneath the canopy and smelled of damp moss and rain-soaked tree trunks. Animal life teemed about them, wary and curious, brushing briefly across her awareness before going about their day.

"This forest has grown." Thomas peered up at the tangling oaks, alders, birches and hazel surrounding them. "I remember when these trees were but saplings."

"Is it odd?" She tried to see the forest as it would have been in Thomas's human lifetime. "Coming back to this time?"

He shrugged. "Not so much for me, because I've always been about. I couldn't make you see me until Roderick returned." He bunched his hands in his pockets. "I drifted along in a sort of half-light world, here but not here."

Niamh tried to imagine what that would be like and couldn't. "I'm glad you're back."

"Me too." He winked, then glanced behind them. "Warren is following us."

She had a brief, childish impulse to run away and pay Warren back for going to Greater Littleton yesterday without saying anything. Given that the need for silence had probably originated with Roderick, she suppressed the impulse and stopped and waited.

Warren entered the forest at a jog, his head tracking left and right. He saw her and quickened his pace. "Niamh." He stopped beside her and glared down at her. "This thing between us will work a whole lot better if you let me know where you're going."

"Witches." Thomas rolled his eyes. "I'm convinced Goddess created the bond for the sole purpose of letting us keep track of them."

Niamh rounded on the traitorous turd. "I beg your pardon?"

"Witches resent limits on their freedom." Thomas shrugged. "And coimhdeacht are driven to need to know where they are at all times."

"Does it work the other way then?" She turned her question

on Warren. "Like, say, when a coimhdeacht goes off with another witch to help guard her?"

"She's got you there." Thomas chuckled.

Bloody ghost had his wooden spoon out and was stirring things up. She sent him a quelling glance. "Do you mind?"

Thomas winked at her.

"I'm sorry," Warren said and spread his hands wide. "I honestly didn't think to tell you I was going, and I should have."

Well, it was too much effort to stay peeved with a man who produced an instant apology. And gave her a shy, sweet smile that reached his eyes. "It's okay. We're both new to this, and we could both learn how to communicate better."

"You should bond," Thomas said, flicking his fingers between them. "Then Warren will always know where you are and what you're up to."

Fortunately, Warren looked as wary as she felt. For sure she wanted the connection Roderick and Maeve had—granted not the way they'd been spitting and hissing at each other the last few days. She wanted that sense of belonging and being some-one's priority, but not because that person had no choice.

Now that Warren was here, in Baile, and about ready to respond to Goddess's call, the reality of being bonded intruded on her fantasy. Having lived twenty-six years as a single, inde-pendent woman, answerable to nobody, and for the most part, living her life on her terms, she suspected the bond with a coimhdeacht would put a serious crimp in her freedom.

"I don't think Warren is ready for that yet," she said.

Warren's smile widened. "Warren is getting there."

"Niamh is glad." She returned his smile. The connection between them sparked and flared into life. "And she's also getting there."

"Warren is relieved to hear that." His deep, resonant voice chased sensation up her spine.

Thomas snickered. "So adorable. I'm getting all the feels."

Warren blushed and cleared his throat. "Where are we going."

"To run with the wolves," Thomas said.

Raising his brows, Warren looked at her. "Why do I get the feeling he's not joking?"

WARREN LIKED to think of himself as fairly hard to scare. He'd hidden in a tree, behind enemy lines for ten hours and waited for his target to wander into his trap. On his last tour, he'd hot swapped for an entire day to convince the enemy their numbers were larger than they were. On the same tour, he'd taken heavy gunfire, pinning him and his squad down for three days.

The pack of wolves currently slinking their way toward him made him want to piss himself. Head below its shoulders, lips drawn back from impressive dentistry, the huge gray wolf in the lead locked gazes with him.

"Look at you," Thomas whispered, goddamn tears in his eyes. "Fucking magnificent."

That was one way to describe the wolf. Sodding terrifying was another.

Niamh shifted in front of him. "Alpha."

The wolf stopped and perked his ears at Niamh.

"Hello," she whispered. "This is Warren. You told me he was coming. He's pack."

It occurred to him that Niamh spoke aloud for his benefit.

Alpha stopped and stared at him, cunning, cold intelligence in his yellow eyes. Warren faced the gaze of a predator and it stroked something primal in him. He raised his chin and squared his shoulders.

He held Alpha's gaze, one dangerous animal to another.

Niamh laughed. "Alpha sees you as my mate."

Warren liked that idea a lot more than was good for him. He liked Niamh, and she'd never been anything but straight with him, but he'd heard the warnings in the village. She was one of those women who could tie a man up like an oven ready chicken. Now if he could only master his desire to be trussed up by her. "As long as he doesn't see me as lunch."

Alpha looked at him and Warren could almost believe the wolf was laughing.

The wolf sauntered closer to Niamh.

Warren moved to intercept him.

"He'd never hurt her," Thomas murmured and then grinned at Warren. "But that won't stop you from getting between them. Just in case."

Of course, Thomas got it. He'd been in Warren's boots. "You said it."

Niamh stilled, stared at Alpha and then looked at Thomas. "Alpha is asking if we would like to run."

Thomas fist pumped. "Yes! Tell him we most certainly would."

"How does that work?" Niamh glanced at him and Thomas. "Is that even possible? I know I can do it, but..."

"Let me introduce you to one of the hugest advantages to being coimhdeacht to a guardian. The job comes with a couple of perks." Thomas grinned. "Niamh, take his hand."

Her hand slid into Warren's, small and strong and warm.

"What now?" Niamh looked at Thomas.

"Form the bond with Alpha." Thomas moved closer to a large black wolf and touched it.

Warren couldn't quite credit his eyes. As corporeal as he appeared, Thomas was still a ghost and couldn't touch the physical world.

Catching Warren staring at his hand moving through the

wolf's fur, Thomas said, "For some reason I'm able to touch animals. Just animals."

"Like the kestrel," Niamh said. "That time in the kitchen."

"Exactly," Thomas said. "Some of Lavina's leftover power still affects me." He looked down at the black wolf. "I can still reach him through my bond to Lavina."

Warren was getting far too comfortable standing here holding Niamh's hand. Before he did something embarrassing, he said, "I'm not sure what we're doing."

"Are you linked to Alpha." Thomas kept his attention on Niamh.

She nodded.

"If you were bonded, Warren would be able to join the link, but you're going to have to use your power." Thomas waited.

The smell of basil and...something sweet...strawberries filled the air between him and Niamh.

"That's it," Thomas said. "Now reach for Warren and bring him into the link."

Niamh frowned and the smell of strawberries and basil grew stronger. "How?"

"Like a pipe," Thomas said. "Or an electrical cord. Connect one with the other."

Closing her eyes, Niamh's frown deepened. "I don't know—oh!"

The world skewed around Warren. His eyesight blurred, colors bleeding into grays and earth tones. His heartbeat pounded loudly in time with Niamh's and then a third heartbeat. Alpha's.

And his sense of smell. Dear Jesus! The ants crawling across the ground were a spicy undertone to the pungent earth and the tangy grass. He could smell not only the sea, but the thousands of components that comprised the smell of the ocean.

Alpha's heartbeat grew stronger, his blood surged through all three of them.

We run.

The wolf didn't speak so much as share its intention with him. Pack pressed all around him, his safety, his responsibility and his to nurture and protect. His mate's tiny hand in his made his blood run thick and fierce. He would die for her. Simple.

Strength and vitality surged through his muscle and sinew. They started to lope, nose to the ground to catch scent all around them. A thousand images fit themselves into the nasal overload, and they knew there was nothing out of the ordinary.

The lope widened into a run.

Pack streamed after them, paws thumping into the earth around them, wind streaming through their fur, over their nostrils.

The wind was them and they lengthened their stride to do it proud.

Grass whipped past them. They wove through the trees, around the boulders, leaping over obstacles—heart-stoppingly airborne for a moment before crashing back to the earth, their muscles adjusting to cushion their landing.

They were wild, they were free, and they ran. They ran for the joy of their powerful body. They ran as a celebration of wolf. They ran because they could, and they ran because they had to. They ran on and on because they had no reason to stop. Time had no place here.

Warren almost wept when they finally slowed to a trot and then a walk. Flanks heaving, they dropped belly first to the earth.

His vision lurched and his stomach twisted. His human eyesight returned, and he had to blink against the onslaught of color again. His depth perception improved.

He and Niamh still stood where they had been. Pack lay around them, tongues hanging out.

"Thank you," he whispered. He had no words to translate his experience.

Alpha met his stare, and Warren knew they understood each other.

Niamh squeezed his hand. "That was incredible."

And Warren nodded because he might just bawl like a baby if he tried to speak.

Pack. Alpha's yellow gaze locked on him. *Always.*

22

The other witches and Alexander had joined Niamh's search in the library. Roderick had been there briefly but had turned out to be more of a liability than an asset. After the fourth time one of the witches threw a death glare at a pacing and fulminating Roderick, Warren had gotten him out of there.

Unfortunately, the lure he'd used bit him in the arse.

"Watch out for the—" Warren leaned to the right, as if he could influence the trajectory of the Landy away from a large boulder at the side of the road.

Roderick jerked the steering wheel to the right and overcorrected. They headed for the opposite shoulder.

"Brake." Warren kept it a hair short of a bellow. "Stop."

Stamping the brake like he could push it through the floorboards, Roderick brought the Landy to a lurching stop.

Warren breathed in and out and sent a quick prayer of thanks for his life to whoever might be listening.

"Okay." He reached for more patience. "Take her out of gear."

The Landy shrieked.

"Clutch!"

Roderick winced and stamped on the clutch. "Bollocks."

"Right." Warren sent an apology to the Landy. The old girl deserved so much better treatment than she was currently receiving. "First you engage the clutch and then you change the gears."

Glaring at the dashboard, Roderick said, "This beast has a will of its own."

"Again, not a beast." Warren wanted to pound his forehead on the dash. "It's a machine and can only do as you instruct it."

Roderick scoffed. "It defies me."

"Not even possible." Warren had never met someone who had less of a feel for a vehicle than Roderick, and he'd taught Mum Betty to drive when she was already in her sixties. "Clutch." He waited for Roderick to comply. "First gear."

With more force than finesse, Roderick jammed the Landy into gear.

"Now we release the clutch at the same time we engage the accelerator." The Landy's engine raced. "Gently. Easy."

They juddered into motion.

"Return to the correct side of the road." It took everything in Warren not to yell. Sweat slid down his flank as Roderick weaved from one side of the road to the other and managed a marginally better change into second gear.

Unfortunately, he couldn't locate third, took his eyes off the road at the same time he pressed the accelerator and sent them shooting for a hedgerow.

"Watch out!"

The Landy went headfirst into the hedgerow, branches scratching her sides, and jerked to a halt.

"Sodding thing." Sweat slid down Roderick's face. His frustration at not being able to get the hang of driving made him an even worse learner.

"Everyone's fine." Warren owed the Landy a paint touch-up

and a thorough detailing when they got safely back to Baile. If they got safely back to Baile. "Now we're going to have to reverse back onto the road."

"Reverse?" Roderick looked at him in pure horror. "As in go backwards."

It took everything in Warren not to panic as well. "Yup. Same principle as first gear, only you're going backwards now, and you need to keep your eyes in the direction you're going."

Staring down at the gear lever, Roderick studied it for a long moment before engaging the clutch and reverse.

Surprisingly he did better in reverse, and they shot straight back onto the road, just as a compact sedan rounded the bend.

Warren may have yelled. He was fairly sure Roderick screamed like a horror-movie virgin.

The sedan swerved, narrowly missing their left back bumper and screeched to a halt a few meters up the road. Black skid marks covered the road and gave off the acrid stink of burned rubber.

"Fuck!" Warren opened his door and hopped down.

The sedan door opened, and a tall, slim man stepped out. He pushed his glasses up his nose and with a shaking hand, shoved his dark brown hair out of his eyes. "What the hell do you think you're playing at?"

"Sorry." The man posed a fair question. One didn't expect to find a Landy breakneck reversing out of a hedgerow on a quiet country road. "My friend is learning to drive."

Warren winced and hoped the other man didn't think the excuse as flaccid as he did.

"On a public road." The man had deep blue eyes that shot death glares at Warren and Roderick. His face reddened with temper. "Who the bloody hell teaches someone to drive on a public road?"

Again, a fair question. "It was quiet?"

"Clearly not." The man huffed and looked at him and

Roderick. He was of a similar height but a slimmer build and that seemed to register with him as he looked them over. "It could have been a lot worse."

"The fault is mine." Roderick placed a hand on his chest and bowed.

The man stared at him for a moment and then said, "You're right, it was."

"But there was no harm done." Warren tried to jolly the scene along. "Nobody's hurt and both cars are fine."

"A circumstance for which you are fortunate," the man said. He pointed at the Landy. "I suggest you get that hunk of metal out the middle of the road."

Warren took exception on the old girl's behalf. "She's a classic."

"She's a beast," Roderick said. "And I have no further use for her."

Thank God for small mercies. "I'll move her."

"Right!" The man nodded, turned around and then spun back again. "Actually, perhaps you can help me."

Roderick folded his arms and eyed the man like something in a petri dish. "Perhaps."

The man shot Roderick a nervous glance and sidled away from him. "I was trying to get to Baile castle."

"You're on the right road then." All things considered, the other driver had been fair about their near miss. "If you'd like to follow—"

"Why do you seek Baile?" Roderick stepped between them.

Roderick could be brusque, short tempered, abrupt and arrogant, all of the above currently rolling off him.

The man flushed. "I don't see how that's any of your concern."

"Then I don't see how assisting you is any of my concern either." Roderick turned and stalked toward the passenger side of the Landy.

The other driver sputtered and went redder in the face. "Well, you'll see what my concern is soon enough." He drew himself up. "I am from the Valuation Office Agency." He smirked and then said as if Warren hadn't gotten it the first time, "The VOA."

"What's that?" Roderick glanced at Warren.

"Everybody knows who we are." Eyes goggling, VOA man drew himself up to his full height.

"Property taxes," Warren said to Roderick. "They value how much your land and house are worth and how much you owe the government."

Roderick gaped at him. "That is my land, my castle, and I owe nobody a damn penny for it."

"Now see here—"

"It's not as simple as that anymore." Warren cut sputtering VOA off. The last thing he needed was a brawl on a public road between Roderick and the tax man. He kept his tone neutral as he turned to VOA. "Is that why you need to get to Baile?"

"This really is none of your business," he said and sniffed. "This is a conversation I must have with the property owner."

"Then you're in luck." Warren indicated Roderick. "This is the owner of Baile."

"Roderick Cray?" VOA squinted at Roderick. "Do you have any identification to prove that?"

"Identification?" Roderick glared at him.

"Umm...no." Warren forced a laugh. "Clearly he doesn't have a driver's license, and he left his wallet at the castle."

VOA compressed his lips. "I'm afraid I cannot take your word as to this man's identity on a public road. I will need to verify that he is, indeed, one Roderick Cray before I can have the discussion as to the value of Baile and her lands."

"I told you that I am who I am." Roderick stuck his chin out. "Do you imply that I lie?"

VOA gulped and Warren didn't blame him. Roderick was

an intimidating bastard when he chose to remind you of how big and mean he could be.

"It's not a question of lying." VOA sucked in a deep breath. "I am merely protecting the confidentiality of the individual, Roderick Cray."

"But that's me!" Roderick stepped closer to VOA.

"But I have no proof of that." VOA held his ground. "Now, if you will kindly direct me to Baile castle, I can be on my way." He straightened his shirt cuffs. "If you are Mr. Cray, I feel certain you can provide some evidence as to your identity and we can proceed from there."

"Why don't you follow us? We're going to Baile now," Warren said.

"No, we are not." Roderick whirled and marched for the Landy. "Follow the road and you will reach Baile."

VOA frowned and scowled at Roderick's retreating back. "I have been following the road. The one and only road to Baile castle. All bloody morning." He snatched his fraying temper back with a calming breath. "I can see the castle, only I cannot seem to get to it."

"Keep trying." Roderick climbed in and slammed the passenger door behind him. Sticking his head through the open window, he called, "There's only one road to the castle and you're on it."

"Right." VOA nodded and went back to his car.

Warren didn't need Mags's psychic powers to twig Roderick was up to something. He climbed into the driver's seat and fired up the Landy. "What was that about?"

"He is on the road to the castle." Roderick smirked.

Now Warren knew something was up. "Tell me."

"But he and his internal jabbering about identification and taxes will never reach Baile." Roderick let out a belly laugh. "Because the wards will not allow him to."

"Eh?" Like a great many occasions in very recent history,

Warren must have missed something vital in their conversation. "How come?"

"Because that is how they work." Looking unbearably smug, Roderick waved as VOA man drove away. "Nobody gets into Baile without an invitation, and I rescinded his."

Interesting. Warren put the Landy in gear and got them under way. The stench of Alannah's latest fossil fuel attempt had him winding up his window. "But that can only work for a short time."

"It's kept people out of Baile since those wards were first raised." Roderick shrugged.

That might have worked in Ye Olde Days, but Warren had his doubts how the wards would stack up against GPS and other modern technology. Relying on people getting tired of trying and giving up seemed a flawed strategy. He motioned VOA's car as it beetled up the hill. "Regardless, you are going to have to talk to him."

"Nay, I do not."

It had only taken a few days at Baile to realize Roderick got medieval in speech when he was about to be a stubborn horse's arse. "Yes, you do." He made a slicing motion to stop Roderick's next denial. "The fact that he's here means you are on the radar —they know about you. With computers and the way they gather our information, there is nowhere to hide anymore." He predicted Roderick's come back. "Magical hiding in plain sight wards or not."

"Hmph!" Roderick shook his head. "Why is it that one of the few things remaining from my time to this is that the king —or in this modern world, the government—is as eager as a horny tavern wench to get their fingers on a man's coin?"

"Death and taxes." Warren felt Roderick on that one. "The only things that are certain in any time."

Roderick grunted and flung his arm over the seat back. "Thomas said you ran with the wolves yesterday?"

"I did." Warren couldn't stop the grin from eating up his face if he tried. "It was fucking fantastic."

"Aye." Roderick chuckled. "My first witch, Tahra." His voice softened on the name. "She was a guardian, and a powerful one like Niamh. She would take me running with the wolves." He shook his head and smiled mistily. "Once she even allowed me to hunt with a bear."

"What was that like?" Warren liked the way Roderick allowed him more and more insights into who he was. It made him feel connected to the other man in a way he hadn't experienced since meeting Jack. He missed Jack and owed his friend a call. It was hard to know what to say, however, and lying to Jack sat shit with him.

Roderick's smile widened into a grin. "Fucking fantastic."

They drove in silence for a while.

"Tell me about Edana," Roderick said.

Warren had half been expecting a Q&A since his trip with Alexander and Bronwyn to the village. He may as well get the truth over with. "I hooked up with her."

"Hooked up?" Roderick stared at him blankly.

Damn, he needed to remember Roderick didn't speak modern idiom. His face heated as he clarified. "I slept with her. As in had sex with her. As in fu—"

"Got it." Roderick grunted. "That was a mistake."

"Tell me about it."

"That was a mistake."

Warren almost laughed. "She picked me up." Someday he would get the hang of Roderick-speak. "Meaning, she propositioned me, and I accepted."

"Hmm." Roderick frowned through the windscreen. "I doubt that was coincidental." He threw Warren an apologetic glance. "Not to infer a woman wouldn't proposition you for any other reason than your...er..." He waved a hand in Warren's general direction.

Warren couldn't resist winding him up. "My stunning good looks? My manly assets?"

Shaking his head, Roderick chuckled. "It could mean she knows who and what you are, which means Rhiannon knows as well." He frowned in thought. "If that is the case, then there is something deeper at play than merely sex."

"Rhiannon would have sent her to seduce me?" Now he felt used. He wished the sex had been better.

"She did with me." Roderick flushed.

The admission surprised Warren. "You and Edana?"

"Aye. It was a long time ago." Roderick grunted and then said, "But with me, it was mostly because of my stunning good looks and manly assets."

"Keep telling yourself that, big man."

"But with me, it was mostly because—"

"Yeah, yeah, yeah." Warren had caught the gleam of leg pulling in Roderick's eye. "Any idea why she would have targeted me?"

"No, but I will think on it." Roderick took a careful breath. "But if I were you, I might not mention it to the witches." He ended on a barely audible mutter. "Especially not Maeve."

Warren sensed a story, but he knew better than to entangle himself in Roderick and Maeve's business.

VOA's sedan wound down the hill below them, heading back to the village. Warren spared a moment's pity for the man's frustration.

As they drove back toward her, Baile slumbered in the mild afternoon and caused a warm glow in Warren's chest. Already, the castle felt more like home than anywhere he'd ever lived. "She's beautiful," he said, only realizing he'd spoken aloud when Roderick grunted his agreement.

"I was not born to land," Roderick said. "I was a younger son of a younger son and won my place through fighting for the king." He stared out the window, lost in the past. "I came here, crowing like a cock on a dung heap, bursting with my own conceit that I had been gifted this land."

Warren had heard versions of the story, but not from Roderick. He kept his mouth shut and drove.

"I was not pleased to find my land already occupied by a cave full of strange women." Roderick snorted. "I postured and threatened, waving my sword about and trying to get them to leave."

Warren didn't need to have been there to know how that had gone. He'd met the modern cré-witches and could only imagine what their ancestors had been like.

"When Goddess called me, I was outraged," Roderick said. "Here was this pagan creature calling me to serve the women who had usurped my rightful land." He clapped Warren on the shoulder. "But you become accustomed to the calling, and in time you come to see it as the honor and privilege that it really is."

One run with wolves, however fucking fantastic, wasn't going to do all that, but Warren had an inkling his new reality might not completely suck. And thank inkling went by the name of Niamh.

23

A big golden moon floated in the sky above Baile. Waxing almost full, it painted the stone walls pewter. A night made for romance, which had a snowball's chance in hell of happening. More's the pity.

The man beside Niamh tromped on silently, not a good possibility for her romantic lead. He certainly looked the part, with his strong, arresting bone structure and the width of his shoulders, but she bet if she grafted on him, he'd run a mile. The mental image of his long legs pumping away from her as fast as he could manage almost made her grin.

"What?" Eyebrow raised, he looked at her.

Niamh would take her last thought to her grave. "Nothing. Just thinking it was a lovely night."

He grunted and glanced up at the moon. "Almost romantic."

"Almost." Niamh nearly snickered.

With a shy grin, he opened the door to the cavern stairwell. "Ladies first."

"Not sure you'll find many of those around here." Niamh went ahead of him. "Nor any aspirants for the title."

Warren chuckled. "Fair enough. Always thought being a lady sounded a bit lifeless."

"There you are then." She led the way down the stairs.

Moonlight lit the way, as below them the surf pounded against the cliffs that completely obscured the beach. Sulphur undercut the smell of brine.

"What was it like, always knowing you were a witch?" Warren's heavy footsteps hit the stair treads behind her.

"I've never really thought about it." It wasn't the easiest question to answer. "I've never been anything else."

"And the hiding it from others? Was that difficult?"

"Yes and no." Growing up at Baile wasn't your average childhood. "We were homeschooled, and Mags, the twins and I kept each other company. Plus, there has always been this love-hate relationship with the villagers. We grew up knowing we had to be careful about what we said to who."

By tacit agreement, they stopped at the entrance to the caverns. Warren needed to be here. He was looking for answers, and the best place to get them was Goddess.

Warren peered into the beckoning gloom. "What if I can't get used to this calling thing? What happens then?"

She really didn't know. Being Blessed and a cré-witch hadn't been a choice for her. Like her red hair, her magic was fused into her DNA. "I would think you will go back to your life. Goddess has always been big on free will."

"Huh?" He motioned the entrance. "Shall we?"

"Seems a shame not to. Now that we're here and all." Niamh walked beside him into the darkness.

Sigils chimed a melodious welcome and bathed the caverns in blue light. The dry peace of the caverns settled around her. She tried to imagine what it would look like once all the sigils relating to elements were active and lit.

"The patterns are sigils," she said, and pointed about them. "Maeve is our spirit walker, so it's her job to put the shells and crystals and stuff on the walls and form them into a pattern. I believe the patterns relate to witches and their lives and their use of magic." She shrugged. "I'm not that precisely sure how it works, but Maeve can tell you. Apparently, they work for her as a sort of portal, and she can walk amongst the dead witches."

Warren gaped at her. "Really?"

"So she says." Niamh had heard stories about spirit walkers when she was a child. "We thought they were legends when we were growing up. There is only ever one per coven, and nobody I knew had ever seen one. Of course, that was because Maeve was here all along, not dead at all but being a statue."

He grunted and raised his eyebrows. The whole suspension of disbelief factor was still missing.

They walked from one cavern into another, and Warren's head swiveled this way and that. "There are so many of them."

"Yes." Her sigh came from the deepest part of her. "The coven used to be full of witches. Hundreds, even. As many as Baile could hold. The night of the massacre nearly obliterated all of us. We're not really sure how the witches who led to us modern witches survived." Loss welled inside her and she wanted to cry for all the lost lives, all the lost magic, and all the lost potential. "A couple of witches must have gotten away that night. If Hermione's family actually did save a healer, there might have been others who made it to safety."

"Right." He walked beside her until they reached the central cavern.

In the center, Goddess Pool glowed silver tonight. Niamh had come as far as she could with him, and she motioned Warren closer to Goddess Pool. "This part, you should do alone," she said. Standing on her toes, she kissed his cheek. "I'll see you back at Baile when you're done."

WARREN'S CHEEK STILL tingled from her kiss as she left. He didn't know how he felt about being left alone in the eerily silent caverns full of crystals and seashells. The patterns were beautiful, but the sense of other shit at play—magical-type crap—definitely hung about the place. Of course, the odd silvery light coming from the pool and creating dappled patterns added mystery.

Not sure what to do, he turned his back on the pool and stared about him. Coming here had been Mags's idea, strongly endorsed by Roderick and then Thomas. Niamh had said those patterns—sigils—pertained to a once-living witch. Even freakier, Maeve could—

Coimhdeacht, she said from behind him, the woman from his dreams.

Paralysis crept into his muscles as the hair on his nape rose. The presence of something otherworldly triggered his flight reflex, but a stronger sense of inevitability kept him where he stood.

"Er...hello." His voice echoed through the caverns.

Amusement rippled over him, as if she was laughing at a subliminal level. *You have come.*

"I did." Not that he'd had much choice between her in his dreams all night long, night after night, and Roderick, Thomas, and Mags shoving him forward.

There is always a choice, Beloved. And it is always yours to make.

"You can hear my thoughts.?"

Her amusement stroked over him again. *Concerning, is it not?*

"Mildly." Like a crap ton.

You doubt your purpose here.

She said it like she didn't mind. "It's a lot to take in, you know?" The magic. You. Me being this warrior guardian type deal.

You have long been a warrior, Warren Masters.

He'd been a soldier for most of his adult life. "Of a sort."

What sort was it?

She had him there. "Okay, I've long been a...warrior. But this feels different to that."

Because it is different. You fought for your country before, for nameless and faceless souls who needed your strength. Now you fight for Niamh, for Roderick, for Maeve, for the coven. And for me.

"I suppose." But she was wrong about one thing. "I fought for Taylor, my daughter." Taylor's birth had built the foundation of his resolve. "I fought to make sure she had a good place to grow up in. I fought for her chance to have the life she deserved."

Ah! The little one. All will be well there, Warren Masters. The little one will be well.

The comfort those words brought made his eyes sting. "For real?"

I will never lie to you, Beloved. I have no need.

When she put it that way, he could almost put his faith in her.

She is truly your child, in ways you have yet to realize, and she will be with you again.

God, he fucking wanted to believe that so bad it made him want to bawl. Debra had been using Taylor as a stick to beat him almost since she'd conceived.

He'd never been the soul-searching type, so his lack of insight on this point shouldn't come as a massive reveal, but it did. His hesitation had less to do with the magic, and Niamh, even older-than-lava Roderick. It was about Taylor. His little girl, his reason for hanging in there through the night terrors and the temper surges. The reason he'd pitched up for group every week and listened to some of the shit the others spouted. All of it was for his baby girl, and she was so fucking worth it. But if being at Baile had fallout that effected Taylor, he couldn't stay. "Are you suggesting I won't lose my daughter if I stay here and do this coimhdeacht thing."

I suggest nothing. I tell you without equivocation. You will not lose your child when you gain my purpose.

Well, hell! "You're not pulling my leg?"

I'm without form. Leg pulling is beyond my powers at the present time. The amusement vanished. *I do more than say it, Warren. I vow to you. Your child will be with you again.*

And he believed her, in a way a cynical bastard like him shouldn't, or couldn't. "All right then. I'm in."

Not yet, you are not.

Had he missed some sort of weird initiation ritual?

There is one of those, and Roderick would be devastated if I denied him, but there is more you must do to ready yourself.

"What?"

You know.

And bugger it all, but he did. He couldn't move forward with his past baggage dragging him back.

When Warren returned to the bailey, Roderick was loitering and doing his best to look as if he hadn't been waiting for Warren.

"Hi." Warren had no idea how, but he'd developed a fondness for the big guy. It couldn't be easy switching centuries and being security for a coven. Try putting that on the old CV.

Roderick raised a hand. "Everything well?"

Ah, didn't that touch the heart. The big softie had been worried about him. "Much better."

"Good." Roderick nodded and tucked his chin to his chest. "Goddess spoke with you?"

He nodded. "She actually gave me some answers I was looking for."

"You are indeed fortunate."

And for the first time since his dreams had started, he swallowed the hook. "I need to take care of some stuff."

Roderick nodded. "Thus is often the way. How long will you be gone?"

"A few days, a week at most. I need to tie up a couple of loose ends."

"I will keep an eye on Niamh for you."

"Thank you." Warren had to grin. "Good luck with that."

Roderick chuckled. "Even after all these years, it never gets easier."

"Yet you're still here."

"I'm still here." Roderick smiled and shook his head. "Possibly suffered too many blows to the head."

"Maybe." Warren fell into step with him as they headed for the barracks. He didn't need much, and he would take his bike. "Will you let Niamh know?"

"Coward." Roderick chuckled. "I will let her know, and you will owe me."

"My thanks...brother." The word fit comfortably into the growing relationship between them.

Roderick smirked. "You are most welcome, brother. And when you return, you can teach me how to ride your iron horse."

"Not a fucking ch—" But hang about. Roderick had grown up riding horses, spent hundreds of years on the back of one, and Goddess knew he wasn't taking the man through another driving lesson. "Done."

Niamh stared at the phalanx of men in front of her and reminded herself that witches did not use their magic for harm. Roderick, Alexander and Thomas had closed ranks on her.

You know who hadn't closed ranks on her?

Warren

And why?

Because Warren wasn't bloody well there, that's why. And these three Charlies had no intention of telling her where he'd gone. Her imaginary journey into why that was wasn't enjoyable either.

"But I need to know." She gave Alexander her most winning smile. And she had a winning smile. More specifically, she definitely had a winning something when it came to getting people to see things her way. Most of the time, she bemoaned her way. People had a propensity for becoming obsessed with her. Maeve assured her most Guardians had it, to lesser and greater degrees.

Alexander shrugged. "No, you don't, my darling, and your gorgeousness is undeniable, but it doesn't work on me."

Or Roderick, apparently, because he studied her and folded his arms.

Thomas was kind enough to give her a sympathetic grimace. "Sorry. Me neither. Spent my corporeal years around Guardians."

She switched tacks to firm and logical. "He is my coimhdeacht, and he cannot leave me without telling me where."

"Not yet, he isn't," Roderick said. "He has yet to choose you before Goddess, and you are yet to bond. Before that day, he is free to do as he pleases."

Bugger! He had her there. "But he could be in danger." She widened her eyes and bit her bottom lip. Dennis in Greater Littleton had climbed an oak to rescue a stuck cat when she had pulled that move on him.

"He's not." Roderick raised an eyebrow as if he was onto her. Smug shithead probably was. "We would not allow him to be in danger."

So much for that tack. And she was officially out of tacks, so she gave in to the urge and stamped her foot. "He never even told me he was going."

"It's a personal thing." Thomas, at least, attempted to look conciliatory.

The other two didn't bother.

"A woman?"

Aaand blank faces coming back at her.

"So, it is a woman?"

Freeze out.

The idea of Warren and another woman made her tummy clench. "Is he in love with this woman? Is that why he had to go and wouldn't tell me?"

"He went to set his affairs in order." Roderick unbent enough to soften his tone. "What those matters are is not ours to tell. On his return, and if he chooses, he will tell you himself."

She jumped on the one tiny glimmer of hope. "But he is coming back?"

"For you, Niamh?" Alexander winked at her and grinned. "A man would climb every mountain, swim every sea—"

"Shuddup." And with those piddling crumbs she would have to be content.

24

CRÉ-WITCH CHRONICLES

D awn came, and Warren rubbed his gritty eyes as he sat astride his bike in the weak sunlight. His thighs ached, and his leathers were soaked from an enthusiastic downpour as he had skirted Birmingham.

He also needed to pee, and he knew of a toilet close by, but being chickenshit held him back. All he had to do was walk into Betty's tearoom. They wouldn't even demand he buy a cup of their stronger than sin builder's tea. Of course, tea always came with an egg and bacon butty or a sticky bun. His stomach growled its endorsement, but he couldn't get moving.

Growing up motherless didn't leave many happy childhood memories. Nestled in amongst the shit, however, was Betty and the five years he'd spent in her chaotic, messy, always a little dusty home. What she lacked in housekeeping skills, Betty made up for in loving the unlovable. She'd forever robbed him of being able to claim nobody had ever given a shit about him.

Betty had given a shit, and he'd broken her huge, fucking precious heart.

He'd been one of the older boys, and Mum Betty had always bent his ear about setting an example for the youngsters. He'd done that all right. Led the way straight into the forces for him and two years later, another of Mum Betty's kids had followed after him. The best of the pair of them had never made it home again. Coward that he was, he'd hidden in a copse and watched the funeral from a distance. He couldn't stand to see the heartbreak in Mum Betty's eyes. Goddess save her, but she had loved every worthless one of them and mourned Rudy's death as if he'd been her own.

The tearoom hadn't changed at all. Sandwiched between the newsagent and a Sharky's Dry Cleaners, it sat on a small strip of grubby road abutting the train station.

How many times had he told Mum Betty to get the faded orange lettering on the front window repainted? It now read etty's Teas a d Eats.

Betty got up every morning at four o'clock to catch the early commuters into Manchester and stayed well past the late train in the evenings. As he'd grown older, he'd used to sit with her through the long evenings and helped out.

Even years after the nonsmoking laws had been enacted, he remembered the tearoom still smelling of stale smoke and chip grease.

The tearoom door opened, and there she stood.

Warren's pulse drummed like the clappers in his ears.

Arms folded across her chest, Betty stopped on the pavement and stared at him. Her gray hair was scraped back into a familiar straggly ponytail. She'd lost weight. Her faded jeans hung loose on her. And she still wore that sodding crappy cardigan of hers.

Wading through glue, Warren stepped onto the pavement beside his bike. Station Street separated them. A red car drove past, and then an electrician's van before he gathered enough courage to raise his hand in greeting. "Heya."

"Heya?" Betty raised both eyebrows and hunched her shoulders. "That's it, is it?"

She reduced him to thirteen again, packed with hormones, riding a wave of impotent teenage rage against life, and dying a little inside with each rejection. "I..." He ran out of words, shrugged and shoved his hands into his pockets. "I dunno what else to say."

A silver sedan crept past, slowing down enough for the driver to rubberneck from him to Betty and back again.

Enough! Warren waited for it to pass before crossing the street.

A couple more lines creased her long face, courtesy of kids like him. Her bright blue eyes were as he remembered, alert, keen and endlessly patient. Not tolerant or prepared to put up with any crap, but patient in the way of knowing the best way to handle broken children.

"Sally Holmes told me you left the forces," Betty said. Her gaze searched his face. She used to do that often. On his return from school, when he had lied through his bloody teeth to her, when he had taken some girl out. Bloody MI6 needed those eyes as a secret weapon.

She deserved better than a bunch of lies. "I got out a while back. I didn't know how to face you. What to say."

"Huh!" She nodded slowly. "Then I suppose 'heya' isn't a bad start. You look good." She made it sound like an accusation.

"I am," he said. "I've been..." Nope, not a chance he was going to tell her about the last couple of weeks. "I've been staying out of trouble."

"You were always good at that," she said.

One of her customers left the tearoom behind her and called a goodbye.

"Take care, love," Betty called after him.

Good at staying out of trouble? Warren nearly laughed. "Other than when I managed to scare my wife into taking my kid away and getting my arse slammed into anger management."

"Ah!" Betty's eyebrows hit her hairline again. "So that's what's gotten you all in a mither." She huffed and shook her head. "I'm guessing, you're also thinking I blame you for what happened to Rudy."

"I got him killed." Even now, Warren hated saying the words out loud. Taking a life stained your soul. "I came to the funeral."

"That you did." Betty sighed and looked down. "Making like a tree, you were." She looked up again, face fierce and eyes glistening. "You were a good lad, Warren Masters. A little rough around the edges and bashed about by life, but you were one of my best." She cleared her throat. "One of those I wouldn't ever forget. And I'd put my head on a block you're a good man."

His throat tightened around unshed tears and his voice came out gummy. "I should have stopped him from joining up. He asked me, and I said it was grand."

"Well, it was grand for you. At first. And then it changed." Like she had when he was a kid, she gripped both sides of his face and made him look at her. "I see those shadows in your eyes, lad, and Rudy dying weren't the only reason they're there."

"I might lose Taylor." How had he forgotten how Betty never judged? "I lost my temper one night with Debra. I didn't touch her, but I scared her. Scared her enough to make the courts think I'm a danger to Taylor."

"That one." She snorted and squeezed his arm. "I didn't like her when you first started sniffing around her. I've got a nose for that sort of trouble, my lad." After a quick tap on the cheek, she let his face go. "You should have come and seen me, Warren. After you got out. You should have come."

"I know." Mum Betty saw him true, always had. Not only the bad, but the good as well. People seeing the bad and judging, that he knew, was accustomed to. Strangely, her seeing the good terrified him more.

He let her hug him. Typically Betty, it didn't last long, and she shoved him away. "Fancy a cup of tea?"

"Got an egg and bacon butty with that?"

She shoved his shoulder. "Get on with you. When didn't I have a butty for one of my lads?"

"You still taking kids?" He followed her into the teashop. Only one or two tables were occupied now that the morning rush had finished.

"Not anymore." She dug in her sleeve, pulled out a bunched-up tissue and blew her nose. "Rudy and Finn were my last. Getting too old for it."

"You." His laughter was genuine. "You'll outlive the lot of us."

She gave him a jaunty wink. "Well, the devil doesn't want me, and God's done his best to forget my name."

DEBRA STOOD in the doorway of her semi-detached with her arms folded. "What do you want, Warren?"

She'd been a pretty, vivacious girl with honey blond hair and wicked hazel eyes. Traces of her younger self hung about in her shoulder-length hair, which was now more platinum, and her big, bright eyes. Lines of dissatisfaction had carved brackets on either side of her mouth, and she wore thick, matt foundation over her once peachy skin. She'd always liked her clothes short, tight and minimal, and today's animal print mini and fierce pink belly shirt were no exception.

"I thought we might have a chat." Antagonism whispered beneath his skin, but he shoved it down. Getting Debra's back up would result in nothing more productive than the cheap thrill of a vicious skirmish and the long-term loss of the war.

She studied him through narrowed eyes. The same eyes

that had once looked at him as if he'd handed her the world. "You know you can't be here."

"I can't be here unless you say I can, and I only want to talk to you, maybe see Taylor." He tucked his hands in his pockets, trying to look as nonthreatening as he could.

"That's not a good idea." She stiffened and pursed her bright pink mouth into angry lines. "If you want to speak to me, do it through your attorney."

She closed the door.

Warren stepped forward and grabbed the closing door. "Come on, Deb, five minutes."

Bitterness twisted her features at his use of her pet name, and he mentally slapped himself.

"Debbie?" A man's voice came from the house interior.

Debra's eyes widened and she blushed. She shot Warren a guilty glance through her thick, furry false lashes.

He knew Debra had other men in her life, but coming face to face with one punched him in the gut.

"It's my—" She cleared her throat and called over her shoulder, "My ex is here."

Her ex. All that remained of them now.

A tall, sandy-haired man stepped into the narrow, dim hallway behind Debra. He had pleasant features, clean cut and trustworthy, and wore a Polo shirt tucked into his ironed pants. Debra had traded up.

He eyed Warren with curiosity and a touch of wariness. If he'd heard Debra's side of the story, Warren couldn't blame him. "Hi." He held out his hand. "Adam Harris."

"Warren Masters." He shook Adam's hand. "But I'm guessing you knew that already."

Adam chuckled and put a possessive arm around Debra's shoulders.

He needn't have bothered. Warren had no interest in Debra, and his concern with Adam being there was more about Taylor.

"What can we do for you, mate?" Adam gave him a conciliatory smile.

Warren detected an accent. "You're Australian?"

"Yeah." Adam grinned. "What gave it away?"

Warren managed an amiable chuckle in response. "I was in the area." Not even close, considering Baile had become his new home. "And I wondered if I could see Taylor."

"He can't show up like this." Debra turned to Adam, looking for his support.

"I know that." Warren stepped in before Adam had to. "And I really am sorry, but I'm only here for a day or two, and I haven't seen her in weeks."

Debra stuck her chin out. "You could have called first."

"You're right." But if he'd called, she would have turned him down. "And I will next time."

Adam and Debra exchanged a look before Adam said, "You really should have called. Taylor's not here."

"Bugger." Disappointment twisted through him. "When will she be back?"

"Not until next week." Debra looked a touch smug as she told him that. "She's on a trip."

"Isn't she on summer holidays?"

"Congratulations." Debra sneered. "You remembered her schedule."

How he'd like to argue back, but he resisted the bait. "What trip?"

"I called to tell you." Debra flipped her hair over her shoulder. "But you didn't answer your phone, and the man at your flat didn't know where you'd gone." She glanced at Adam before she said, "Really, Warren, you should carry a mobile."

"I've got one." He dug the abused and battered Android out of his jeans pocket. The dead screen glared up at him accusingly. "Right." He hated these fucking things. They were like planting a tracking device under your skin and letting the powers that be have at watching you. "I must have forgotten to charge it."

"Then you only have yourself to blame," Debra snapped. "An opportunity came up for her to go to Spain with a school friend, and we decided it would be good for her."

"We?" His question came out silky smooth with menace. Decisions around Taylor were his and Debra's to make. No other we was in that picture.

Debra stiffened and sucked in an outraged breath.

"Regardless, it's a good thing you're here." Adam cut in before Debra could wind herself up. "We need to have a chat with you."

Warren really didn't like the sound of that, any more than he liked the long look exchanged between Adam and Debra.

"I really don't think now is a good time." Debra chewed on her bottom lip.

"Why not now?" Adam stepped back, taking Debra with him. "Come on in, Warren, we need to tell you something."

THE CHURCH HALL was as Warren remembered it, which shouldn't have been a surprise because it had only been a few weeks since he'd seen it last. The same brown and dirty white checked floor, the same caged clock hanging on the wall above the doors, and the same band of misfits with their arses sticking to the plastic chairs.

Astonishingly—not—Patrick had the talking stick and was on about his missus again.

Gary had been delighted to see him and given him a tentative hug when Warren had first arrived. The hug had been an unfortunately awkward affair of Gary's desire to appear welcoming warring with his Britishness and had ended with Gary going bright red and clearing his throat convulsively.

Jack hadn't even bothered with a hug and settled for, "Look what the fucking cat dragged in."

He hadn't told Jack he was coming. Warren hadn't known himself that he was coming to group until after his disastrous meeting with Debra and Adam.

Australia. That fucking woman was going to Australia and thought she was going to take his daughter with her. Never going to happen. The only thing keeping his head from exploding was the promise Goddess had given him. Goddess had assured him all would be well, and he believed her, despite that morning's evidence to the contrary.

Still, Australia was a long, long way away, and he'd never be able to afford the airfare. Even the remote possibility of losing Taylor rode him hard, and that was part of the reason he'd come to group.

Patrick had reached the level of whine that made Warren itch to smack him about.

"You doing good?" Jack leaned over and whispered.

Gary's glance cut their way, and he made a moue of disapproval.

Nodding, Warren tried to pay attention to Patrick.

"But she don't sodding listen to me." Patrick let his glance search the group for support. Not getting what he needed, he upped his whine. "She don't."

"Christ." Jack had reached enough. The rest of the group let out a collective sigh of relief. "You don't sodding listen, you whiney little shit."

Gary's spin shot straight. "Loving space, Jack. Neutral. Safe."

"Two years I've been listening to his crap." Jack turned his ire on Gary. "Two fucking years, and he's still saying the same thing. The only point to group is so we can learn something. That little fucker is pig stupid."

"Well..." Gary knew better than to argue with Jack. Especially when Jack had called it right. He looked at Patrick. "Perhaps Jack would like to talk." Inspiration struck and he beamed a smile at Warren. "Or Warren? We haven't heard from Warren in a while."

About to turn it down, Warren held his hand out for the talking stick. "Why not."

"Lovely." Gary squirmed in his chair. "We've missed you."

"I've been good." Better than he had before finding Baile. "I've got a new job." Technically not a lie. "And it comes with accommodation." And a drop-dead gorgeous witch attached. "And a great health plan." It stood to reason if Bronwyn could cure Hermione's lass of a brain tumor, anything he cooked up for her would be a doddle.

Patrick sniffed. "I got a new job. Three weeks back."

"Sounds perfect for you." Gary looked like he might spontaneously combust with happiness.

"It does, doesn't it." Jack got that look in his eye that meant he was on the hunt.

Warren stared back, keeping it bland. "The best I've managed so far."

Jack shifted in his chair to look at him. "Yeah?"

"Yeah." Even stretching the truth seemed wrong with Jack, but the truth-truth would be too hard to explain. "I'm happy where I am."

"Which is where?" Jack, always quick to catch a hint of prevarication, narrowed his gaze.

"Down South." And as there didn't seem much harm in it. "Small village called Greater Littleton."

"Ooh!" Fergus still stank of stale booze, and he blinked his bloodshot eyes. "The place with the castle?"

Uh-oh! He'd not seen that coming. "Baile, yup."

"Castle?" Jack turned those searchlight eyes on Fergus. "What kind of castle?"

"Medieval." Fergus flushed, and his gaze brightened. "Motte and bailey. Completely intact, down to the smallest detail.

People say it's well worth the trip to see it. Better than Windsor, apparently." Fergus shrugged. "I like castles. I'm Scottish."

"You never said anything about a castle." Jack turned back to him.

Warren went for the gap. "No, but then I'm not Scottish."

25

CRÉ-WITCH CHRONICLES

Niamh didn't think about Warren. At all. Not when Alannah served a fry up for breakfast, coincidentally his favorite. Not when she went to bed the second night after he had left, and not that morning either when she was back in the library, hard at work researching cardinal points.

That bloody map above the mantel stared at her. Actually, the map hung there. It was the pair of pigeons perched beneath it doing the staring. She stroked the cat on her lap as she studied the map. It looked ancient with its yellowed parchment and decorative swirls and squiggles. Despite that, it was an accurate depiction of the modern world.

Instead of focusing on the fire point, she'd widened her search today, hoping for one knowledge domino to set off a chain reaction. She'd gone through historical volumes, bird books, geographical texts, even philosophy tomes, and still nothing.

Her struggle to concentrate hampered her further. She didn't like not knowing where Warren was, or what he was doing. Curiosity battled with concern. Despite Roderick's assurance, Warren could be hurt. Rhiannon could have found him and decided to reduce the coimhdeacht pool by one.

Or he could be with a girlfriend, a wife even. They'd never had that kind of conversation. She and Warren didn't have a romantic relationship, and she ignored the twinge that thought caused, but another woman would bog up the works. Niamh had never had to compete for a man's attention before.

She'd also never felt possessive about someone in her life. People tried to get territorial with her. They told her about it all the time. Villagers who grew attached to her, men she messed around with, they all told her how much they wanted her when she wasn't around—which, given her dislike for entanglements, was pretty much always—but she'd never had the faintest idea what they were on about.

Now, she could safely say the feeling sucked. Zero out of five, she did not recommend.

Alannah toed open the library door and came in bearing a tray. "Hello, loveliness." She held up the tray. "I thought you could use some sustenance."

"Thank you." Peering at the tray, Niamh prayed sustenance came in the chocolate form. Alannah had made her a cup of coffee and included a few lumpy biscuits.

And yes! Chocolate cupcakes, with sprinkles no less.

She put the tray on the table next to Niamh and perched on the corner. "Any luck yet?"

"Not much." Niamh peeled the paper off a cupcake and took a huge bite. Goddess but Alannah had gifts in the kitchen. "We know the cardinal points are scattered across the world, but any of the known sacred sites or mysteries come up empty."

Alannah peered over her shoulder. "Well, that stands to reason. You wouldn't hide something where people would go looking."

"Right." Niamh mopped up a couple of cupcake crumbs.

"But we had to start with the obvious—Stonehenge, Angkor Wat, Machu Picchu and that lot— and eliminate them."

"Did you eliminate all of them?" Alannah cocked her head and studied the map over the mantel. "I don't mean to be a pain in the neck, but how could you eliminate any of those places without going to them?"

"We can't." Niamh bit into another cupcake and let chocolate work its magic on her frustration. They didn't have time to visit every sacred site in the world or chase up every rumor of places of power. "I've pored over pictures and articles until I'm cross-eyed, but they don't feel right."

The cat glared at her and gave the cupcake a meaningful look.

"Here." Alannah broke off one of the misshapen cookies and snapped off a bit. She offered it to the cat. "I made these for you."

The cat sniffed it and delicately nibbled it out of her hand.

"Don't worry." She smiled at Niamh. "Strictly animal safe."

"You would think"—Niamh waved a hand around the library—"that there would be a hint somewhere in here."

"Hmm." Alannah broke off another bit of cookie for the fox that had popped out from beneath the sofa. "It's probably staring us right in the face."

"Great." Niamh considered a third cupcake. Then grabbed one. Chocolate was good for the soul. "Now if only it would stand up and do a dance for me, I could find it." The sheer impossibility of the task pressed down on her. "If Maeve had her power, she could ask the old witches, but..." And they were right back to her having to find fire.

"I'm not sure even they knew," Alannah said. "It seems like nobody thought about where the cardinal points were, because they were working."

Niamh nodded. "Right. Roderick tried asking Goddess, but she couldn't tell us. Wouldn't tell us is more like it."

"I don't understand that." Alannah took a cupcake and bit into it. "She can't have forgotten something that important."

"Roderick believes it's tied into her power. The less magic is used, the weaker she becomes, and nobody has used any significant amount of magic for so long, she's just a shadow of what she ought to be. He thinks it has compromised her memory."

"So much thinking and supposing." Alannah frowned. "And not nearly enough knowing."

Alpha brushed Niamh's mind. He stood on a ridge above the roadway, and he showed her the road.

A lone motorcycle wound toward Baile.

Niamh's heart thumped, and excitement trickled through her. He was back.

Alannah laughed. "I take it by that smile, our missing Warren is on his way back."

"What smile?" Niamh didn't bother to bite back her grin.

Alpha surged through the connection. *Pack.*

"Do you think Roderick knows already?" Alannah stood.

"Probably." Some weird and wonderful coimhdeacht mojo at work, no doubt, but she hurried after Alannah to the bailey.

BAILE GREW BIGGER and bigger as he rode toward her. Bollocks, but he'd missed the place. How that was possible after such a short time stymied him, but he didn't really care.

Wards prickled across his skin as he crossed them. To his left, and high on a ridge, the pack stood and watched him. Warren raised his hand to them as he passed.

Pack.

Pack meant Niamh as well and his pulse jerked. She could be incensed with him for skulking away like he had. It hadn't been his best move, but if he'd told her before he went, he might not have been able to go. If Niamh had looked even the tiniest bit upset about him going, he'd have stayed to make that look go away.

A sense of homecoming crept over him, and tension lifted off his shoulders. He'd spoken to Mum Betty and Jack and settled those scores. Jack had been keeping some of his stuff for him, and he'd made arrangements for it to be sent on to Baile. The situation with Debra remained unresolved. Adam and Debra thought they would scarper off to Australia with his daughter. Warren strongly disagreed and would talk to Alexander about it. Alexander seemed like the sort to know a lawyer or two.

His ride got bumpier as road gave way to the cobblestones of Baile's entrance. The gatehouse blocked the sun from his view momentarily, and then he rode through and into the bailey.

Outside the kitchen, all long legs and curves, stood Niamh. His sense of home narrowed in on her. It was about more than Baile. Home was the gorgeous woman waiting for him.

Her full mouth split into a wide grin that crinkled up her eyes as she caught sight of him, and she waved.

He waved back and brought his bike to a stop a couple of feet in front of her.

Taking off his helmet, he let the gut punch of her roll over him. He'd never met another woman, Debra included, who could make him want so many things. It was more than sex, although Niamh was a walking wet dream, it was the real intimacy he craved. He wanted to do sappy shit with her like hold her hand, for fuck's sake, and listen to her chatter to her menagerie.

Her companions today were the blind badger, a cat and four dogs. The dogs scampered up to him and surrounded his bike with writhing furry bodies and wagging tails.

"Hi." Niamh's husky voice stroked his nape like a velvet glove. "You're back."

In a perfect world, he'd climb off his bike and kiss her with all the pent-up emotion of the last three days. "I'm back."

"You okay?" She studied him with her dark eyes.

He nodded. "I am. Better now."

"Then your trip was a success." She twined her fingers together.

"It was."

"Good."

"Yeah."

Warren stared at her beautiful face, unable to break away. Words he wanted to say but knew he shouldn't crowded into his mind. It was too soon. There was too much going on right now. He took her hand and tugged her closer . "I'm sorry I left without telling you."

"Right." She laughed and thread her fingers through his. "It's a good thing you gave me three days to cool off."

She knew exactly how long he'd been away. That made him happier than it should. Warmth radiated up his arm from their joined hands. "I told Roderick to let you know I'd be away for a bit."

"He told me." She pulled a face. "And then established a male cone of silence."

A male cone of silence sounded exactly like a thing Roderick would establish. "It wasn't a big secret." He stepped off his bike and nudged dogs away from him so he could move. "I had some things back home I needed to settle."

"And now they're settled?"

"Yup."

Her smile dulled the sun. "So, you're here to stay?"

Like there was ever a chance he would leave. He pressed his mouth to hers in a quick kiss. It was over too fast. "Was that even a question?"

26

W arren went in search of Roderick. He'd bet his left bollock Roderick already knew what he was about to say, but some things needed saying anyway.

He found Roderick and Alexander trying to dice each other into tiny pieces in the practice yards. He needed to get them to teach him how to sword fight. The little boy in him demanded he know.

"Hey." He took a seat and waited for the hacking to end.

Thomas popped up beside him. "Brother, you have returned."

"Looks that way." He folded his arms and tried not to wince as sharp blades came perilously close to living tissue.

Thomas took the seat beside him. "How did you fare?"

"Good." Better than that, other than Debra and not seeing Taylor. "I got most of what I needed to do done."

Nodding, Thomas said, "That is good. This life is not one to be lived halfheartedly."

"They been at that for long?" Warren indicated Alexander

and Roderick, currently circling and looking for an opening in each other's guard.

Thomas rolled his eyes. "You know how they are. This is not a war that will be over quickly."

Alexander launched an attack, his blade moving so fast it blurred.

"Have you ever noticed how similar they look sometimes?" Warren couldn't be the only one who saw it. It was more in the way they moved, and their mannerisms than their looks, but there was something there.

"Indeed." Thomas chuckled. "But that is not a notion either of them will willingly entertain."

"Brother." Roderick strode his away, mopping up sweat as he did. "You're back."

Warren stood and shook his hand. "Good to see you."

And it was.

"Warren." Alexander motioned his sweat drenched torso. "I'd hug you, but that would be gross."

"Right." Warren laughed. Being at Baile and amongst his new brothers made him feel lighter, hopeful in a way he hadn't felt since Rudy's death. Considering how long he'd known these men, it didn't make any sense, but then it could join the queue of stuff that baffled him. "I'm back for good."

Roderick nodded. "Good. We can proceed with your bonding ceremony."

"Does that entail dead cats and dancing naked under a full moon?"

Alexander winced.

Thomas vanished.

And Roderick said, "No cats, and the moon is extraneous."

∼

Warren couldn't get the scene from *Night at The Museum 2* out of his mind. He kept wanting to say, "It's not a dwess; it's called a tunic. It was the latest fashion three thousand years ago."

Only the disturbing news that he would be going stark bollock naked kept his sense of humor in check. "I don't see how that's at all necessary."

"It's tradition." Roderick stuck his chin out and refused to budge. "It symbolizes how you come unarmed and free of any other encumbrances to your witch."

"It's idiotic." No fucking way he was standing with his wedding tackle out in front of Niamh and all the other witches. He was wearing boxers and Roderick would have to deal.

They were in the barracks meeting space, and Roderick was trying to thrust the dress—er, tunic—at him.

"It's a tradition that goes back hundreds of years." Roderick glowered, beginning to lose patience with him. Not that Roderick had a lot of patience hanging around at the best of times. "You are coimhdeacht, and each and every brother before you has done the same."

"When was the last one?"

Grinning like he'd won the lottery, Alexander slouched against the table. "Wasn't that you, Roderick?"

"Aye." Roderick growled. "When I bonded Maeve."

"And you went bare arsed in front of her?"

Alexander smirked. "And the rest of the coven."

"Shut your mouth." Roderick scowled at him. "You have no right to comment on coven business."

Alexander lost his smirk. "Being here with Bronwyn gives me that right."

They would end up trying to kill each other if Warren let them. "Back to me and this bonding thingy."

"Ceremony, brother." Thomas popped into being. "And

Roderick is correct. All the brothers hold it dear and sacred. If you cannot do it for that reason, then do it for them."

Thomas's arm-twisting, Warren had to hear. "Eh?"

"They have lost so much. Their bonded witches, their lives. A ceremony like this, they cannot take part in, but they are able to observe. Do it the ancient way in their honor."

Warren gave it his best, he really did, but when sodding Thomas brought honoring the courageous dead into the argument, it wasn't fair. Not a soldier alive who could turn his back on that argument. He nearly broke a tooth spitting out the word. "Fine."

"Right." Roderick tossed the white dress at him. "Bathe and put that on. I will tell Maeve to call the witches."

"Now." Thomas followed him into the bathing chamber. They even had him calling it that now, but with natural heated springs and waterfalls, it could hardly be called a bathroom. "As you bathe, I will impart the most important thing a coimhdeacht needs to know."

Now they chose to inform him. "What is it?"

"First we must swear you to silence." Thomas perched on a rocky ledge.

"Is this where you show me the secret handshake and give me my decoder ring?"

Nothing, zip, zero, nought from Thomas. Predictably, Roderick glared.

Warren nodded. "No blabbing. Got it."

"Right then. The most important lesson a coimhdeacht need learn is how to block his witch when he does not want her in his mind."

Warren missed the step beneath the water and went face first into a hot spring bath. He came up spluttering and spitting water. "Say what now?"

"Do you need me to explain how that would be useful?"

Alexander lounged near Thomas and grinned at him. Nudity was no big deal amongst them.

"There are times when you will need to keep your witch out of your head," Thomas said.

"I'm missing something." Warren looked from Thomas to Alexander and back again.

"Once you're bonded, you will have access to all that Niamh thinks, feels and experiences." Thomas stretched his legs out in front of him. "And she will have the same of you. Think about that for a moment."

Warren gave it a moment and didn't have to take a giant mental leap to realize there would be times he didn't want Niamh in his head. Not because of other women though. The idea of another woman made him feel gross. But there would be stuff he didn't want Niamh to know. Times when he thought of her, things that he thought about her, that could get awkward. "Okay."

"Now." Thomas nodded. "Find the bond within you and simply turn your side of the connection down."

"Eh?"

"Like a volume button." Alexander mimed the action. "Just turn yourself right down, but always make sure you can read her."

"That's it?" Warren had been expecting something more complicated.

Thomas nodded. "Just like that. Of course, it will make more sense to you when the bond between you and Niamh is forged. But with a bit of practice, it becomes second nature." He grimaced. "We do not tell the witches how to do it, because firstly, we always need to know where they are and how they are, and secondly, they'd lose their collective senses of humor about it."

"But what about when we don't want to be in their minds?" Warren hoped they didn't make him spell it out for them. He also didn't want to consider why the idea of Niamh doing things he didn't want to witness with someone else made him want to punch something.

Roderick and Thomas grimaced.

"Similar idea," Roderick said, "but not as effective."

Alexander smirked. "I believe the best advice is grin and bear it."

Not if he had any fucking thing to say about it.

EVEN THOUGH WARREN spent more and more time in the arena, the place held a weighted, expectant quality to it that evening, as if the air itself paused and waited.

Witches stood on the perimeter of the practice ring with lit candles sending light and shadow dancing across their faces.

Roderick gave him a brief nod and strode to the center of the arena. Shapes flickered into life about him, Thomas in the foreground. The ghostly men wore a variety of dress from different eras in history and looked real enough for him to touch. Their voices rang out with Roderick's as he said, "Brother, you are called."

"I hear the call." Roderick had told him what to say beforehand, but the words came out of him without him having to think them first. He came to stand in front of Roderick.

Once again, the spirit brothers spoke with Roderick. "Brother, do you accept the call?"

"I accept the call of my free will." Warmth spread through his chest, a sense of peace and belonging. He stood amongst the true brothers of his soul.

Roderick raised his sword. "Bonded witches, bring forth your sister."

"Come, Sister." Maeve took Niamh by the hand and led her to him and Roderick.

The atmosphere thickened and time slowed. In the flickering candlelight, Niamh's eyes were almost black. The connection between them hummed and snapped like a dog on a leash.

"Blessed." Roderick's tone gentled. "Are you ready?"

Niamh scrunched up her face and whispered, "I think so."

"Coimhdeacht?" Roderick turned to him.

The moment hung between him and Roderick and Niamh, and Warren knew that he'd reached the cliff's edge. If he planned to walk away from the new version of his future, he needed to go now. "Let's do it."

Roderick sheathed his sword in his belt. He stepped behind Warren and grabbed the neck of the tunic. With one sharp jerk, he ripped the robe in two and dropped the pieces to the arena floor.

Naked in front of all the witches.

Niamh's eyes widened and her mouth popped open.

"Up here." Warren jabbed his fore and middle fingers at his eyes. "My eyes are up here."

Barely stifling a giggle, Niamh winked at him. "Just a little peek?"

"You won't find anything little down there."

They both giggled like naughty kids in church.

Roderick raised his voice. "Naked and unarmed, you stand before your witch."

"Naked and unarmed, I am before her." The words came naturally.

Ghostly coimhdeacht thrummed with energy and Warren forgot he was naked, forgot the strangeness that had invaded his life, forgot everything except the witch before him.

Her power surrounded her in a softly glowing nimbus of red.

As one, the coimhdeacht raised their swords.

Roderick raised his. "Answer with care, brother." He looked at Warren. "Your word is your bond."

Again, a sense of rightness vibrated through Warren. "My word is my bond."

"Arm yourself, brother." Roderick handed Warren his sword.

"I stand armed before her."

In a spectral sort of dance, Warren faced north with the other coimhdeacht as they said, "Under a new moon, through the long death of winter, do you raise your sword in the power of earth to serve?"

Warren's voice thickened in his throat. His muscles and sinews heated. "My spirit joined with hers. My life for hers. From this day forth."

The coimhdeacht shifted to face east and raised their swords. "Under a waxing moon, in the glorious rebirth of spring, do you raise your sword in the power of air to serve?"

The heat grew, the bond with Niamh sparked through his core. "My spirit joined with hers. My life for hers. From this day forth."

Facing south, they asked, "Under a full moon, through the deep fecundity of summer, do you raise your sword in the power of fire to serve?"

"My spirit joined with hers. My life for hers. From this day forth." Warren's words dropped like a boulder through mud inside him and settled.

Prickles broke along his left arm, almost maddening him with the need to itch.

With a final turn to the west, the coimdeacht asked, "Under a waning moon, through the wondrous bounty of autumn, do you raise your sword in the power of water to serve?"

Warren said, "My spirit joined with hers. My life for hers. From this day forth."

An unseen weight pressed his forehead to the flat of his blade. Swirls and patterns scrolled across his forearm, marking his skin with a sharp burning.

Warren turned and faced Niamh.

Roderick took the sword from him. "Join your hands."

Sparks shot up Niamh's arm—red, yellow, blue and green, all four elements at work—and colored the power nimbus around her.

Along Warren's forearm the new coimhdeacht marks rippled and flared.

"This is going to hurt some." Roderick glanced from Warren to Niamh. "Hold on to each other and don't let go."

Nobody had said anything about Niamh getting hurt and Warren wasn't down with that. "What do—"

Power slammed into him like a runaway truck. Huge hands crushed his chest, and he couldn't breathe.

Niamh cried out and he gripped her hands tighter. He wanted to take the pain from her.

Heat and light seared through his nerve endings.

Niamh's hair floated around her head, caught in two magic streams, his and hers. Their magic wrapped around each other in a frenzied dance.

Images flashed through his mind, faster than he could follow them. Her childhood, her memories, her thoughts and her impressions. He saw the practice arena with two sets of eyes, smelled what she smelled and what he smelled. Her heart beat through his chest and his through her chest. He understood the suppler, lither strength of her body.

Light shone from Niamh's eyes, brighter than the sun and painful to look at. His eyes felt as if they were melting within their sockets.

Niamh clung to him, her face caught in a rictus of pain.

His magic reached for her and dragged the pain into himself. It pulsed within him, growing fatter and stronger, stretched his skin to its limit. He planted his feet firmly, balancing his weight and anchoring her.

The relentless onslaught pounded them both and Warren lost all sense of time. He could not let go of Niamh.

It stopped so suddenly that Niamh sagged against his chest.

"Breathe." Roderick's voice rumbled from nearby. "It is done."

Sweet fuckery, but Warren wanted to collapse in a heap and bawl.

Niamh caught her breath and looked at him with huge, shining eyes. She put her fingers to her sternum. "It's you."

Caught in the wonder in her expression, it took Warren a moment to register her within him, an energetic, strong energy both alien and familiar. Her essence reminded him of honey, sweet and rich and the basil-strawberry combo of her magic nestled in his chest.

He could more than see the wonder on her face, he could feel it inside of him. "We're bonded."

"Yes, we are." Niamh leaned in and whispered, "I think you can put your trousers on now."

27

CRÉ-WITCH CHRONICLES

L ong after the coven had fallen quiet for the night, Alexander stood in the great hall. Moonlight streamed through the majestic stained-glass window at one end.

The window called to him, depicting now only three of the first four. Empty space, the space Rhiannon must have occupied, gave it a strange, unbalanced aspect. Scars from his life with her ran through his soul. So many hideous sins stained your being. He could only find a handful of actions to jot down in his redemption column, and he kept those to himself. His new life was at Baile now, and it was good. Much better than he deserved.

Warren and Niamh had bonded today, and he was glad for them, but he was marginally jealous. Whatever he and Bronwyn shared, and whatever the thing they both refused to define between them was, it wasn't the same as the bond Warren and Niamh now had.

He sensed Bronwyn before he heard her. As always, she brought him serenity.

"You're brooding," she said.

"A bit." He gently tugged her in front of him and nestled her back to his chest. She was so tiny he could rest his chin on her head. He placed his hands on her still flat belly. She seemed too delicate to carry twins inside her, too fragile for the heavy weight of fate. "You couldn't sleep?"

"Not without you." She covered his hands with hers. "You've corrupted me. I used to sleep fine without you."

He pressed his nose into her neck and inhaled the lingering honey and sage of her magic. He'd barely slept at all until he'd found her. "Give me half a chance and I'll corrupt you some more. I have a special trick or two after having lived this long."

"I bet you do." She giggled and stared at the window. "It's weird, you know, without her."

"Mmm." They may not have the bond, but she often spoke his thoughts. "The wicked womb is conspicuous by her absence."

"What was she like?" Bronwyn snuggled closer to him as if she could absorb his discomfort. "When you were a kid growing up."

"She was a wonderful mother. Loving. Caring. Nurturing."

She squinted up at him. "Really?"

"No." The mere idea of Rhiannon as a maternal goddess made him chuckle. "That was a long time ago." Longer than he cared to remember. "And I didn't see much of her. She was fairly busy hatching her evil plans to overthrow Goddess and take over the world."

Bronwyn pressed further. "And when you did see her?"

"She was...distant." Rhiannon had waited until he had grown strong and big enough to visit her special brand of pain and suffering on him. "More like a teacher than a mother."

She turned and peered up at him. "So, who raised you?"

"A series of her followers." Some better than others. All of them scared shitless to upset Rhiannon by not taking good enough care of him. "I was fine."

Bronwyn snorted. "No, you weren't, but we can stop talking about it now."

"Good." He could live without these trips down memory lane. His American darling was starting to understand he didn't like bleeding in public. It wasn't that he didn't feel or have his share of regrets and pain, but he refused to share such an intimate part of himself with just anybody.

Of course, Bronwyn was not just anybody. She was his somebody, and he wrapped her closer to him, needing to imprint her on him. He indicated the stained glass. "I never saw that with her in it."

Bronwyn studied the window. "So, we have Deidre, Tahra and Brenna. Healer, guardian and seer, respectively."

He hummed his agreement and nodded.

"And the tree? Where are they standing?"

"That's the sacred grove," he said. "Maeve can tell you more about that. It's where she meets the spirits of witches who have passed."

She pointed. "And right next to them, their elemental symbols."

"Deidre was fire. Tahra was water, and Brenna was air. Clearly mummy dearest was earth." The witches in the glass looked like they could step out of it.

"And those other marks?" Bronwyn pointed. "What are those?"

He shrugged. "Decorations."

"They look familiar." Bronwyn shifted forward and cocked her head. "But I can't seem to think—"

"What particular marks are you speaking of?" His nape prickled in a way hundreds of years of living had taught him never to ignore.

Bronwyn stepped closer. "Those little things to the left of each witch. Do you see?"

"Yes." He most certainly did see. Glyphs to the left of each witch. Etched in palest yellow glass, in strong sunlight, they would be near invisible. "Where have I seen those?"

"Library?"

He sifted through the hours he'd spent in the library. "No."

"The tapestries." Bronwyn clicked her fingers. "The ones on the wall outside the barracks."

She had it. Alexander took her hand and led her through the massive arched wooden doors into the corridor leading to the barracks.

"Here." Bronwyn stopped at the first tapestry. She touched the patterned border. "These are the sigils for water."

In the tapestry, Tahra stood by a pool. The scene was easily recognizable as Goddess Pool in the caverns beneath this castle.

"Yes." The realization of what they might have stumbled on hovered outside his conscious mind and refused to be recognized.

Alexander moved to the next tapestry.

"Air." Bronwyn touched the patterned border.

The tapestry depicted Brenna in a snowy landscape beside another pond, not dissimilar to the one in the first tapestry. A graceful stand of ghostly, white-trunked trees surrounded the pool, and a bear stood in the distance.

Bronwyn peered closer. "Do you know what kind of trees those are?"

"Birch." You picked up a thing or two when you'd been around as long as he had. "Silver birch, if I'm not mistaken." He was fairly sure he wasn't wrong about the tree.

"Fire," Bronwyn said. She had moved on to the next tapestry. "There's a gazelle in this one. It's so pretty and delicate looking" She peered closer. "We never got anything like that in Maine."

"No." He moved beside her, the sensation at his nape like fire ants now. "That only looks vaguely familiar to me."

Bronwyn stepped closer to the tapestry. "Where is this?"

"I'm not sure. It seems different." There was a pond again, only this pool was surrounded by thick savannah grass and a tree with an almost umbrella-like canopy.

"That looks like a thorn tree," Bronwyn said. "Like the ones you get in Africa."

"Africa?" He snapped his finger. "Maybe if we look up gazelles in Africa it will tell us what that one is, and maybe even where to find it."

Bronwyn looked at him with huge eyes. "And it's important we find out where, isn't it?"

It most certainly was, and the growing certainty in him made him twitchy. The pools, the elemental sigils, the specificity of the animals and the trees, it was all trying to point the way. Had these tapestries always been here? Did Rhiannon know of them? He didn't think so, or she would have acted on what they were pointing out.

"This snowy landscape, with the bear and the birch could be Russia." He spoke his thoughts aloud as he pointed to the tapestry with the thorn tree and the savannah grass. "Africa. And if the Africa element is fire, then that witch has to be Deidre. Rhiannon's element was earth."

He moved on to the next tapestry. As he'd suspected. "No witch."

"Earth." Bronwyn touched the sigils making up the border design. "Her element, and she's not in the tapestry."

A pool again. That one surrounded by a vivid autumnal scene of a forest with leaves turned orange, red and yellow. A beaver peeped out from the bank.

"Maples trees." Alexander studied the leaves on the trees. "When you think maple leaves, what do you think of?"

"Vermont?"

"No." He shook his head. "Canada." It couldn't be that simple. Could it? He went back to their first tapestry. "Here at Baile." He moved to the second. "Russia."

Bronwyn stood in front of the third. "Africa."

He joined her at the fourth tapestry. "And Canada."

Bronwyn looked at him with wide eyes. "It can't be."

"Still, those are some big places." He tamped down his excitement. "We'll need to narrow things down."

"Maps." Bronwyn turned bright, excited eyes his way. "There are maps in the library. Maybe..."

He was already moving toward the library.

Niamh snuck a look at Warren and caught him sneaking a look at her. They'd been doing that all the way through dinner of Alannah's to-die-for beef and ale stew with dumplings. After their bonding, both of them had slept through most of the day.

When she'd woken, the first thing she'd noticed had been the connection to Warren. Knowing what another person sensed, felt and thought was so weird. She kept looking at him to confirm she got the right input. Inside her solar plexus, a constant warmth tingled. If she concentrated on that spot, the sensations strengthened. Experimentally she pushed at the place that marked their connection.

Warren grinned at her and looked so much younger and less weary when he did.

She grinned back.

"Look at you two." Maeve giggled. "You're so sweet."

Warren blushed and Roderick snorted. "The bond is not sweet."

"'Course it is." Maeve wrinkled her nose at him. "It's just you who aren't sweet."

Roderick scowled. "I can be sweet."

Sinead opened her mouth, and then snapped it shut. That pretty much summed it up.

"We've found them." Bronwyn burst into the kitchen. "All of them."

They'd long since stopped asking when Alexander and Bronwyn went missing. And when they did go missing, nobody wanted to volunteer to find them. Mags would probably never recover from walking in on them in the healer's hall.

Looking smug, Alexander trailed her with a large roll of parchment tucked under his arm. "We believe we have, in any event."

All eyes turned their way expectantly.

"Found what?" Sinead's gaze sharpened.

Pushing dishes out of the way, Alexander made space for the parchment on the table.

"Oy." Roderick snatched his plate back. "I'm still eating that."

Sinead patted his shoulder. "You carry on eating, big man. Nobody's taking your dinner away from you."

"This is bigger than dinner." Flushed with excitement, Bronwyn danced on her tiptoes. "Waaay, waaay bigger."

Alexander rolled out the parchment.

"That's the map from the library." Niamh tilted her head for a better look. "The one over the mantel?"

"Alexander broke the frame." Bronwyn winced apologetically. "But you won't be mad, not when you hear what we've found."

"We'd all love to know what you've found," Sinead grumbled.

Niamh's breath caught in her throat. She'd known there was something about the bloody map.

Sensing her excitement, Warren glanced at her. "You think?"

She nodded.

An answering pulse of excitement came from Warren, like champagne bubbles in her chest.

"You've found it." Mags grinned at them like a proud mother. "You've found the cardinal points."

Alexander glanced at Bronwyn who nodded.

"What!" Roderick leaped to his feet.

Sinead rescued his plate before it hit the table and sent the contents splattering over the parchment.

Alannah helped Alexander secure the corners of the map with various tableware. "Are you sure? How?"

"The stained glass." Bronwyn waved her hand in the direction of the great hall. "We were looking at the stained glass."

"In the wee hours," Alexander said.

"Yes. It was around three a.m." Bronwyn nodded. "And we noticed—"

"You noticed." Alexander gave her a gentle smile.

Bronwyn blushed. "Well, I may have noticed at first, but you connected the symbols with the tapestries."

"It matters not," Roderick thundered.

"Right." Bronwyn cleared her throat. "Right. Well, anyway. I —we—noticed these symbols around the witches."

"Indeed." Maeve looked crestfallen. "Their elemental symbols are etched beside each witch."

"Ah ha!" Alexander raised his hand palm first. "But if you look carefully, and the light needs to be just right, you see the other symbols. The one's to the left of each witch."

Roderick frowned. "I've never noted anything to the left."

"Maybe because you've seen that window so many times, you don't really look at it." Bronwyn shrugged. "But they're there all right, and then we remembered seeing something similar in some of the tapestries in the corridor leading to the barracks."

"Aye." Roderick stilled. "There are four tapestries, each depicting one of the first witches. They were not there before Maeve and I went into stasis."

Niamh had never really looked at those tapestries, or any of the tapestries decorating Baile's walls. They had always been there, and she took them for granted.

"And each witch stands beside a pool and each tapestry is a unique setting." Alexander leaned over the map. "Each tapestry has a tree and an animal that provides the clue."

Maeve looked taken aback. "They do?"

"Yes." Bronwyn nodded, her eyes sparkling. "From the tapestries, we got three general locations."

"Africa, Russia and Canada," Alexander said.

All gazes stuck on Alexander and Bronwyn.

Alannah sighed. "That's wonderful, but all of those places are huge."

The map! The final piece of the puzzle clicked into place for Niamh. The bloody map had marked the spots.

"What map?" Warren cocked his head and studied her.

"Yes, they are huge." Bronwyn nodded and grinned. "So, Alexander had this idea—"

"I'm sure it was your idea." Alexander beamed at her.

"Oh no—"

"The map." Niamh would leap out of her skin if they didn't get on with it.

Warren laid a strong, calloused hand over hers

"The map." Alexander tapped the one on the table. "We didn't see it at first. The library is full of maps, and we spent all day going through one after the other."

Bronwyn tapped the map on the table. "And then we saw it."

"Right on the mantel." Alexander grinned at Bronwyn. "It was staring us in the face all along."

"Look." Alexander pointed to Canada. "Right here."

They all craned forward.

A small symbol, only two or three shades browner than the parchment it was drawn on. If you didn't know what you were looking at, you would assume it was a decorative detail.

Dammit! She'd assumed it was a pretty swirl. How many times had she stared at the damn map and not seen what had been glaring back at her?

"The same symbols we saw in the stained glass, and then repeated around the borders of the tapestries." Bronwyn clapped her hands.

Niamh barely dared breathe. She leaned over the map and stared closer. She pointed to one on the southern end of Africa. "Is this the fire one?"

"It is." Alexander nodded and grinned at her. "It looks like you're going to South Africa."

"We're going." Warren stood beside her. "We're going to South Africa."

28

CRÉ-WITCH CHRONICLES

F our exhausting, manic and infuriating days later, Warren sat beside Niamh on his way to a place he'd always wanted to visit, but never thought he would.

He'd managed to call Taylor before they left. A gut-wrenching ten-minute call filled with Taylor's complaints about Adam. Another five-minute harangue from Debra about how difficult Taylor was being, and a demand he smooth the way and not make matters worse had left him wanting to smash shit. Roderick had taken him into the barracks to work off the worst of his fury and frustration.

From his top-secret stash of contacts and what-the-fuck-not, Alexander had gotten them on a flight—first class, as it turned out. Alexander bemoaned the fact that his mother—of course Alexander had a more colorful description of her—now had control of most of his wealth and his former assets, but for a pauper, he managed to pull some fat rabbits out the hat when needed.

"Can I bring you anything else?" The attractive forty-something flight attendant whispered as she cast a sleeping Niamh an indulgent smile. "Is she warm enough?"

Considering Niamh had the benefit of two duvets as she snuggled in her little airline fully reclining bed, he rather thought she was as comfortable as she could be.

"She's fine." He smiled at the woman. "A drop more of that single malt wouldn't go amiss though."

She smiled and produced the bottle from her cart. "Of course." Motioning Niamh, she said, "If she wakes up and should need anything, you give me a little whistle, all right?"

"Will do." Warren sipped his single malt and had to chuckle to himself. Thomas had warned him how guardians affected the mundane—a term for those without magic, which he rather thought they'd object to if more of them knew about it. Seeing the Niamh effect in action, however, had been eye opening.

People flocked to her, went out of their way to speak to her, fell over themselves to help her. And the straight men were the worst. Warren had never seen so many men make absolute pillocks of themselves over a woman. They tripped over their feet when she passed them in the airport. One even walked straight into a huge airport advertising display. If he left her alone for more than five minutes, he'd come back and find his seat taken.

"It's the same way animals are drawn to me," Niamh had explained it to him. "It's not real and has nothing to do with me as a person. It's this thing I have."

"Animal magnetism?" He had teased back, but there was a wistfulness to her even as she gamely managed a titter for his stupid joke.

Niamh moved in her sleep, and he turned to check on her. His coimhdeacht self wouldn't allow it otherwise. He was alert, tensed and ready for danger. He scanned constantly for threats, mapped out the nearest escape route, and he was aware of her needs and comfort down to his core. To be honest, he might have hovered around her had he not been her coimhdeacht.

Niamh was burying beneath his skin, and as much as it scared him, he kind of liked it.

Her deep red hair covered the small airline pillow and spilled over the central console between them. His fingers twitched to bury themselves in the shining mass.

When they had checked in and he'd discovered they had been seated across the aisle from each other, his coimhdeacht had risen up in protest.

Niamh had smiled at the ground crew and that's all it took to have their seats reassigned to a central pair.

Her skin was the purest milk of a true redhead, and with her lively, sparkling brown eyes closed in sleep, her beauty was of a more serene kind.

Not classically beautiful—her mouth was too wide, and her eyes tilted up like a cat—he still rather thought she undersold herself if she believed the only reason people gravitated toward her was her gift. She was straight-up temptation, and he had to keep reminding himself that now was not the time.

Reaching through their bond, he touched her sleeping mind. Even though she slept deeply, there lingered the awareness of the danger they were in, relying as they were on Rhiannon being none the wiser.

As Niamh had been the only witch with a coimhdeacht, she'd been the logical witch to awake her cardinal point. How they were going to get the other witches safely to theirs had been stuffed into the already bulging sack of tomorrow's problems.

Roderick had been loudly and verbosely unhappy about the two of them venturing out alone.

Rhiannon lurked somewhere outside Baile, everywhere outside Baile, waiting for an opportunity to strike. The two of them would make themselves a target. They only had Alexander's assurance that she didn't know where the cardinal points were, or she would have destroyed them already.

Still, despite Roderick's thunderous objections, they had been out of choices. Alexander and Bronwyn couldn't leave Baile. Not with Bronwyn carrying the children Rhiannon wanted so badly, and Alexander still sure Rhiannon could sense him when he left Baile's wards. The connection had weakened since his defection, but nobody wanted to test its remaining efficacy.

Mags, Alannah and Sinead needed to stay put because Warren needed to concentrate on keeping Niamh safe. Four of them would have been a strain even Roderick hadn't wanted to consider. Thomas couldn't leave Baile, and even if he could, other than being able to touch animals, all he could contribute was floating around and booing people.

He'd also spoken to Alexander and Roderick about his Taylor. If he didn't make it back, he wanted them to make sure she got whatever he could give her. He didn't need their vows to know his new brothers in arms would do their best by his girl.

He needed Taylor in his life, and not stuck on the periphery. When he got back—and it would be when and not if—from South Africa, he was going to do something about Debra, Adam, and Taylor.

He got Debra's resentment. He hadn't been around as much as he could have been, should have been, when she had been pregnant, and in Taylor's early years, had spent more time deployed than at home. But he couldn't build a time machine and fix the past, and he'd been busting his balls to make up for his mistakes.

In Alexander's bag of what-the-fuck-not, there had to be a handy lawyer. As soon as they got back.

He hoped Niamh and Taylor would get along.

As if sensing his emotions, a still sleeping Niamh reached out and put her hand on his forearm.

Warren allowed her touch and her presence to comfort him. Of course, she would get along with Taylor because she would know how much Taylor meant to him. Sure, Niamh had that magic thingy, but he wanted Taylor to like her for more than that.

He didn't know how he was going to explain his relationship with Niamh to Taylor. Lying to his girl went against the grain, but the truth could put her in danger. He could put her in danger if Rhiannon ever dug into his past. Rhiannon could find Taylor and use her against him. That had made him not want to leave, but letting Niamh go alone or with one of the other witches was equally impossible.

For all their sakes, he and Niamh needed to find this cardinal point, wake it up, and get home as soon as possible.

"You're not sleeping," Niamh murmured. She quested through the bond. "Ah. You're worried about your daughter. Alexander promised he'd watch out for her. If he has to step in, he will."

There was no point putting on a brave face when she could slip behind it. "Yeah. I wish him luck dealing with my ex."

"He'll do fine." Niamh laughed. "Alexander can wile his way around most women. He doesn't do it anymore because of Bronwyn, but the man's got moves."

A flash of irrational jealousy shot through him. If Alexander had touched—

"No." Niamh grinned at him. "He and I were never a thing. He's one of the few people I don't affect, and I enjoyed that too much to ever jeopardize it. Plus." She wrinkled her nose. "I never liked him like that."

"Go back to sleep." Heat washed over his face.

She giggled but closed her eyes and snuggled down again. "Okay."

He'd also learned that despite his constant need to command everyone and everything in Baile, Roderick didn't mess with a witch and her coimhdeacht. Saying it was a matter between them was a get-out-of-jail-free card he intended to play whenever he needed it. Roderick's objections to them going to South Africa had ended when Warren had pointed out he was called to take care of Niamh and that's what he intended to do.

They'd snuck out of Baile in the small hours of the morning. The intention had been to borrow Hermione's car, and have it sent back, but in the end, she'd driven them all the way to Heathrow, deaf to the possible dangers and determined to pay back, in whatever way she could, what Bronwyn had done for her.

Warren looked around the first-class cabin. Any one of these people could be Rhiannon's, or anyone back in Business or Economy. Even now they could be watching him and Niamh and finding a way to use them to Rhiannon's advantage.

Across the cabin, a man was listening to his AirPods with the dim night light illuminating a book. Alexander had stressed Rhiannon had her tentacles spread across the globe, embedded in all stratums of power and influence.

For Niamh's sake, he couldn't afford to let the paranoia get away from him. He had to stay vigilant and always alert, but he needed a clear head and calm center.

Soon he would need to sleep, but not until he got them somewhere safe. His bond had come with useful modifications. Nothing like suddenly being able to climb walls or leap buildings in a single bound, but more strength and stamina, greater endurance and keener senses. He was still him, only supercharged.

Back at Baile, the coven waited, relying on him and Niamh being able to wake the fire point. Much depended on them. As a fire witch, Maeve would gain access to all her knowledge and power. A fully charged Maeve would bring the coven up to three powerful witches, and with her ability to walk with witches past, Maeve could help the coven learn all it needed to know.

He activated his movie screen and watched the tiny little plane cross the massive expanse of the Atlantic Ocean. They'd been flying for six hours; another five would see them landing in Johannesburg. Some cross-referencing and studying before they had left Baile had him and Niamh knowing exactly where they were heading.

The Cradle of Humankind.

29

Niamh understood the danger, she got how important her mission was, but she was still excited. She'd never been out of Greater Littleton, let alone halfway around the world and in Africa, nonetheless.

She'd expected it to be hot. Africa, right? Of course, she knew the southern hemisphere always operated in the opposite season, she'd even packed for that eventuality, but stepping outside the airport into a cold, sharp, bright July morning, she shivered.

Warren found the car rental and got them a car. As she stood in the concrete parking lot and he loaded their baggage, she could have been anywhere in the world.

"You okay?" He slammed the boot shut and glanced at her.

She shrugged. "Yup."

"Not what you expected?" Like he'd read her mind, which he had.

"It's silly." She climbed into the passenger side. "I get that Johannesburg is a big city, but we could be back home."

"Wait." He smiled at her. "Airports all look more or less the same."

The drive to the hotel looked like they could be approaching any large city. Tall buildings, wide highways and billboards along the way. She even recognized a number of the advertised products.

Soon though, the sense of being somewhere other started to permeate. Grass bordering the buildings and roads looked tinder dry, bare red earth showing through the low, scrubby vegetation. Bright sun ruled from a pale blue sky over a palette of browns and sages and yellows. Her skin felt tight in response to the dryness. Traffic grew heavier as they traveled. Large trucks carried goods, and smaller, older vehicles were loaded with odds and ends. Bright colored minivans whipped across lanes and wove at breakneck speed in and around the other vehicles. Expensive SUVs and sedans shared the road with ancient-looking rust buckets that belched black smoke from their exhausts.

"How long until we reach the hotel?" She'd ceded all organization and control to Warren as if it were the most natural thing in the world.

For his part, he seemed more than capable of running with the responsibility.

He consulted the dash clock. "About forty minutes." He glanced at her. "Tired?"

"Not really. I slept on the plane." Safe in the knowledge that he was watching. "But you must be."

"Not really." He shrugged. Stubble dusted his strong jaw and gave him a rakish, adventurer air. "Goddess gave me a little extra something-something." He raised his marked forearm.

The swirls and whorls of the umber markings seemed alive to her. She traced one of the swishes. "Oh!" She snatched back her hand and giggled. "It reacts."

"It's aliiive!" Warren widened his eyes and added a creepy voice. Then he winked. "But only for you. It won't do that for all the girls."

She snorted and gave him a look.

He grinned.

Since the bond, he was more approachable, easier to be with, and more inclined to kid around. For the first time since he'd appeared in Greater Littleton, it was only the two of them.

Against ridiculous odds.

She should be terrified, but the strong sense of competence and surety emanating from Warren through their bond calmed her. It was also the first time she'd been without her sister witches.

The passing scenery held more trees than she'd imagined.

"I read somewhere that Johannesburg has so many trees, it's actually an inhabited forest," Warren said.

Niamh could believe it. Some of them winter bare, and others evergreen, but huge trees shaded the streets beneath them.

The next thing that struck her was all the high walls and fences. Electric wires topped many of the walls, jarring and reminding her Johannesburg could be dangerous all on its own.

When a minibus carrying passengers came to a sudden halt, Warren swore and narrowly missed plowing into the back of it.

"They're a transport system." Warren checked his mirrors before pulling back into the traffic. "They've sprung up in response to there not being a more comprehensive public transit system."

Two people stumbled out of the minibus, and another four piled in. "You seem to know an awful lot about Johannesburg."

"I made good use of the flight." He flashed her a grin. "Goddess knows I couldn't sleep through your snoring."

He was just begging for a fat lip. "I preferred you when you were all broody and sulky."

She missed her animals as well. From this distance, she had

no sense of them. Inside, she felt empty without their near constant presence.

As promised, about forty minutes later, Warren drove under the porticoed entrance of a tower block hotel. A uniformed attendant opened the door for her and welcomed her to the hotel.

Although cool beneath the portico, the chill of early morning had already dissipated into a mild day. A cloudless azure sky stretched from horizon to horizon. If this was winter, she'd take it.

Warren took over checking them in and seeing to the baggage. They took a glass elevator from the central atrium up to their room.

"I put us in one room," Warren said as he opened the door.

Subtle African tribal prints decorated the sofa and bedspread, marrying itself to the wood furniture.

Niamh looked around her. "It's certainly big enough for both of us."

He stopped at a king-size bed. "I can take the couch if you're—"

"We're all grown up." She flapped a hand at him. "As long as you promise not to let your jammies touch mine, we can share the bed."

And didn't that cause all manner of mental meanderings. She stomped on them before Warren got a load of the x-rated movie in her head.

She wandered into the bathroom, all gleaming chrome and warm, honey colored marble. The glass shower stall beckoned her, but the large bath shouted it down. A basket of soaps and lotions sealed the deal.

"If you want a shower, do it now," she called to Warren. "Because I'm getting in that bath as soon as you're done."

❧

AFTER LUNCH, they headed out. Highways gave way to smaller, dusty rural roads. Trees ceded dominance to long stretches of arid flat savannah. People approached their car at traffic lights selling everything from carved animals to cell phone covers. They drove past larger markets conducted under dilapidated tin rooves and sun parasols. Bright piles of oranges threatened to spill over the edge of temporary tables. Large plastic containers of cooking oil, big plastic bags of crisps and peanuts, brightly wrapped sweets, all on offer. People walked alongside the road, their footsteps kicking up small puffs of dust. Women balancing huge bundles on their heads amazed Niamh as they swayed gracefully beneath the weight. The air smelled like wood smoke, earth and the aromatic sage of unknown vegetation.

Any doubt they were in the right place dissipated the moment Niamh and Warren parked outside the Sterkfontein caves.

She shivered. "Do you feel that?"

"Yup." Warren's tension coiled in her chest like a small fist. His head moved from side to side as he catalogued the tourists heading into the caves with them.

The unmistakable touch of cré-magic hummed through her, beckoned her. Excitement quickened Niamh's blood. An animal presence, large and definitely predatory, tapped at her awareness, and she opened to it. Its curiosity suffused her. The animal sensed her, recognized the call of her Blessing, but wanted to know who she was.

"What is it?" Warren stopped and stared about them.

"A local," she said.

A few tourists lingered outside the ticket office, discussing a map of the caves. Beyond them, a wizened woman stared at Niamh. She frowned, turned her back and scurried away.

Warren watched the woman. "Could it have been her?"

"No. My visitor was definitely four legged." Niamh opened the bond to Warren. "Feel."

Head cocked like a dog, he sensed what she did. "It feels... different. Like the wolves, but different."

"Definitely an apex predator." Niamh pressed against its mind, and it vanished like a popped soap bubble. "It felt feline."

"Well." Warrens shrugged and spread his arms. "You are in Africa. Big cat country."

Excitement fizzled through her, and she grinned at Warren.

Her enthusiasm reached him down the bond and he grinned back. "Just warn me if any of your new cat friends are planning to pop over and say hi."

Magic senses tingling, Niamh followed the tour guide through the limestone caves. Ever vigilant, Warren walked beside her. The tour meandered through the caves, in places cramped and difficult to squeeze through, and in others massive chambers filled with stalactites and stalagmites. Giant underground water pools reminded her of the tapestry at Baile. Despite her purpose, Niamh found it fascinating, like stepping into a subterranean world of wonder.

The caves had come to prominence because of the discovery of hominid remains, the most famous of which was Mrs. Ples, and more recently, Little Foot, believed to have lived two-point-one and three million years ago, respectively. Multiple tools, animal remains, and other evidence of hominids had been discovered in the caves and surrounding areas, all leading to the claim of it being the Cradle of Humankind. Australopithecus remains had been a major source of information, and they were believed to be a precursor to homo sapiens, which in turn led to modern man.

Warren kept her on plan by whispering, "Anything yet?"

"No." Niamh shook her head. "I can feel it here somewhere, but..." She shrugged.

At the end of the tour, they were forced to return to the car tired, footsore, dirty and hungry.

The animal from earlier brushed her awareness and Niamh stopped.

Alert to her every emotion, Warren stopped and scanned the nearly empty parking lot. "What is it?"

"The big cat." She searched the dusk for any sign of the animal. The temperature dropped fast as the sun set in a gaudy splash of red, orange and pink. A hunched figure leaned heavily on a cane and limped across the far end of the parking lot.

The woman looked up and stared at her. She took a step closer, stopped and then hurried away in the opposite direction.

Halfway through the hour or so drive back to the hotel, Niamh realized the woman from the parking lot was the same woman from near the ticket office, the one who had been staring at her.

The old woman might work at the caves. Or—

"What is it?" Warren glanced at her.

"I'm not sure." If the woman worked at the caves, there could be an easy explanation as to why Niamh has seen her twice. But her instinct prickled of something, not quite danger, but something big. Still, they couldn't take chances. "I saw that woman again. I think she was looking at me."

"The old woman." Warren nodded, his attention on the road. "You feel anything off about her?"

"No." Niamh hadn't seen the woman for long enough to get a positive fix. "But she didn't carry that blood magic thing. Sometimes you can smell it."

Warren pursed his lips. "Let's keep sharp."

"Roger that!" She saluted him.

Back at the hotel, they ordered room service and found something on television they wanted to watch.

Sprawled on the bed, Niamh half watched the movie. Doubts assailed her. The library maps might be hundreds of years old. Maybe they hadn't put the clues together right. When you wanted to see something badly enough, you could twist reality and make it into the pattern you sought. "What if—"

"Don't." Warren topped up her wineglass and put the bottle on the side table. "We'll go back tomorrow, and the next day if we have to. We know it's there; all we have to do is find it."

"We've taken an awful lot for granted." Niamh couldn't shut the door on her whispering what-ifs. "We've come a long way on gut feel and a few hints."

Warren climbed on the bed beside her. "Niamh." He rearranged her until her head rested on his chest. "You're a Guardian. You, more than any other witch, know the value of instinct. You feel this is the right place, don't you?" His arm tightened around her. "Don't you?"

"I suppose so." She'd lived most of her life trusting her gut. "But there's so much riding on this."

"We can't focus on that." His heart beat strong and sure beneath her ear. "We have our mission, and we will complete it."

His assurance ghosted through the bond and lifted her spirits. His big form beside her made her want to snuggle closer. And she did. "We'll go back tomorrow." His stomach was hard beneath her palm. "We should slip away from the tour and do a bit of exploring on our own."

"Right." Warren's gravelly voice rumbled through his broad chest. "I also thought we could do a bit of discreet asking about."

He was *cradling* her. Cradling. Her. "What are we asking for?"

"Anything unusual." Warren put a finger under her chin and tipped her head up. His warm gaze caressed her face as his voice deepened. "There's magic in those caves, and we both felt it. Wherever magic lives, strange shit happens. There must be whisperings of stuff going on."

What had they been talking about?

"Right." Niamh pulled it together. Tales around Baile had been circulating longer than either of them had been alive. There had never been any concrete evidence, yet rumors of mystery and supernatural happenings hung about the castle. "But we'll have to be careful."

"Very careful," he whispered. His gaze drifted to her mouth.

The two inches between their mouths sparked and tingled with possibility. He was going to kiss her, and she very much wanted him to.

Warren shook his head. Color on his cheeks, he cleared his throat and disentangled them.

Niamh wanted to punch something as he stood and put their dinner tray outside the door. "For now, though, let's get some rest and start fresh in the morning."

He stood at the hotel door and watched her.

She got nothing through his side of the bond, and she shivered, cold in the wake of their heated moment.

"Okay." Niamh took the bathroom first and slipped into her pajamas, a gift from Alannah with cartoon animals cavorting all over them. The mirror reflected her flushed face back at her. "Be cool, Niamh," she told herself. "Remember what happened last time you got all over eager with that man."

She took her time brushing her teeth and washing her face. Time she used to reinforce her mental pep talk. With everything going on, neither she nor Warren needed the complication of runaway hormones.

Warren smirked when he saw her pjs and disappeared into the bathroom. The shower went on and she refused to succumb to tempting mental images lurking in her brain.

Niamh turned off her light and crawled into one side of the

bed. It had seemed much bigger when sharing it with Warren was more of a theory.

The bathroom door opened, and he came out in a pair of sweats and nothing else. Broad, muscular shoulders tapered into a slim waist. A fine trail of body hair disappeared inside a waistband that hung perilously low on his narrow hips.

Niamh appreciated the view way too much. She turned her back and pushed her pillow into a comfortable position.

What was wrong with her? She'd seen him shirtless around Baile, and of course he'd been wearing even less at the bonding ceremony, but in the dark with him getting into bed with her, she suddenly felt jumpy.

The heat of him on the other side of the bed reached out to her. The memory of his face, so close to hers, flashed behind her eyes. She was hot and uncomfortable. She wanted to fidget but forced herself to lie still.

The bed moved as Warren turned out the light.

Heavy darkness settled over the room broken only by the muted sound of a door closing somewhere close by and the low hum of traffic.

Warren chuckled suddenly. "Well, this is awkward."

"Yes." She flopped to her back and tentatively touched their bond. His amusement glowed warm within her and something darker and hotter. It vanished before she could identify the fleeting emotion.

He leaned over and kissed her cheek. His lips lingered and his breath warmed her ear. "Good night, Niamh. Sleep well and try to keep your snoring to a minimum."

30

CRÉ·WITCH CHRONICLES

fter breakfast, Alexander and Roderick slipped away from Baile to make a supply run. The coven sisters had grown vocally unhappy about being confined to Baile, which was why he and Roderick didn't hang about and discuss the matter.

With Warren and Niamh away, even Thomas was tense. None of them liked the separation and none of them would breathe easy until everyone was safe in the nest again.

Making sure he drove, Alexander shivered as they crossed the wards.

They drove to the local supermarket and loaded up.

"Let us stop for a pint." Roderick motioned the Hag's Head.

Alexander had trouble believing his ears. "You want to stop and have a pint?"

"Pubs are good places for information." Roderick smirked at him. "Our enemy is too quiet."

"You know who owns that pub, right?" Even though his name was on the lease, he wouldn't get a how-are-you from Rhiannon's pets who ran it now.

Roderick's grin turned feral. "My idea gets better by the moment."

"Right, then." Alexander backed into a parking space three down from the pub door. "Let's go and poke the bear."

As he followed Roderick through the throng, he tried to catch glimpses of the staff. Except for Bonnie, he didn't recognize anyone. Bonnie had worked there for years and still remained blissfully unaware of what happened all about her. But Rhiannon, Edana and Fiona scared the pants off her, and Bonnie was a single mum, so she always made nice.

"Well, hello," Bonnie purred as Roderick reached the bar. Propping her elbows on the bar she gave Roderick a come-hither smile and an eyeful of cleavage. When she caught sight of Alexander, concern flickered across her face. "And...Lord Donn—Alexander. Long time, no see."

"Right." He gave her his best reassuring smile. "You look well, Bonnie."

"Lord Donn?" A short man dressed in tie-dyed hemp trotted up to them and stared at Roderick and then him.

Roderick jerked his thumb in Alexander's direction. "He's Lord Donn. I work for a living."

"Ha, ha." The little man sidled around Roderick and shoved his hand at Alexander. "Gresby Carmichael, aka Torrell Tree-brother, Chief Ovate of the Bristol Grove, and founder of Lore Above."

Studying him like an insect in a glass jar, Roderick said, "What is Lore Above?"

"I'm glad you asked." Gresby aka Torrell swung toward him. "It's a little podcast I began a few years back." He gave a self-depre-catory snicker. "If you consider four thousand subscribers little."

"I hear the words." Roderick turned to Alexander with a pained grimace. "But they make no sense."

"A podcast is—never mind." It would take too long. "I'll

explain later." Alexander turned back to Gresby aka Torrell. "Congratulations on the success of your venture." He really couldn't think of anything else to say.

"It seems busy today." Roderick leaned closer to Bonnie.

Bonnie almost spontaneously combusted in delight. "It's been like this for the last couple of weeks. I mean." She gave Roderick a conspiratorial wink. "We're always busier in summer, but between you, me and the deep blue sea, this year is busier than normal."

"Huh." Roderick put his head closer to hers. "Why would that be?"

"I have a theory." Bonnie looked at him expectantly.

Roderick gave her a smile that made Alexander double take. Looks like the big man had a little lady killer in him. It shouldn't surprise him; they hadn't dubbed him Roderick the Marauder for nothing.

"I'd love to hear that theory," Roderick said.

Bonnie preened and giggled. "Let me get you a drink first, love. You look thirsty." She eyed Roderick's arm like it was a prime ham. "Big man like you must have a powerful thirst."

Roderick winked. "I bet you know all about men like me."

Alexander nearly gagged.

"Um...Lord Donn...my lord...er..." Gresby aka Torrell bobbed. "Might I have a word?"

"Indeed." Alexander dragged his horrified gaze from where Bonnie caressed a beer pump handle as she gave Roderick a suggestive leer.

"As I explained, Lore Above is my podcast." Gresby aka Torrell fluttered his hands. "And I flatter myself—"

"What should I call you?" Alexander couldn't watch the natural disaster of Roderick and Bonnie anymore. "If we're going to have a conversation, I can't keep calling you Gresby aka Torrell."

"Either is fine." Gresby aka Torrell aka either is fine went pink. "Actually, I prefer to go by Ovate Treebrother."

He'd had to ask, hadn't he? "All right, Ovate Treebrother, what can I do for you?"

"I'd like to think we can do for each other." OT looked arch. "I flatter myself that I have some influence in the pagan community."

"And this concerns me how?" Alexander locked his gaze on OT and refused to stare at what had made Bonnie giggle like someone had shoved a hand somewhere she dearly wanted them to.

"There have been rumors, Brother Donn." OT paused and gave him a weighty look. "Rumors of happenings that might be of supreme, might I say imperative, interest to my listeners."

Now that he was paying attention to the crafty little man, Alexander didn't like the way their conversation was going. "Again." He gave his most disarming smile. "I fail to see how any of this concerns me."

"Your name has been linked." OT lowered his voice and glanced about him. "To magic."

"I see."

Roderick handed him a pint before going back to making Bonnie's year.

"I really don't mean to be obtuse, Ovate Treebrother." Had that epithet just left Alexander's mouth? "But I'm not much of one for rumors and gossip. I mean no offense, but I have never given the existence of magic much credence."

"No! No!" A woman shoved her way through a group of three smartly dressed women chatting over G&Ts.

OT stiffened and grabbed Alexander's arm. "Don't listen to her. She's insane! Certifiable! Pay no attention."

"Worm!" The woman wore head to toe black and barely reached his chin. A plethora of necklaces with large crystal and silver pendants hung about her neck. Eyes thickly lined in black echoed her black lipstick. She grabbed for OT's arm with slender hands, the chewed nails painted black. "You despicable, conniving little worm."

"Back, witch, back!" OT raised a palm.

The woman batted it away. "He's mine, and you know it. I saw him first."

"He is not a thing, Cressida." OT swelled with outrage.

Alexander appreciated his approbation. "Actually, I—"

"You had no idea who he was until I pointed him out." Cressida got right up in OT's face.

"Get off me." OT tried to yank his arm free. "Stop touching me."

"I went to pee." Cressida paid no attention to his demand to let him go and wagged her other finger in his face. "I couldn't have been gone five minutes and yet here you are, scurrying across the bar and trying to get to him first."

Alexander cast a longing glance at Bonnie and suddenly coveted Roderick's conversation.

He and Bonnie had their heads together. Cheeks flushed, Bonnie whispered in Roderick's ear.

"You're mine." Cressida grabbed his arm and turned feverish espresso dark eyes on him.

She might really be certifiable. "I'm afraid, flattered as I am, I must decline."

"Oh." Cressida's mouth dropped open and her eyes widened. Her delicate face had piercings through her eyebrows, dimples and nose. "You're beautiful." She sighed. "Nobody told me you were beautiful."

Strangely, he was changing his mind and liking Cressida much more than what's his name. "You'll make me blush."

Roderick snorted but continued to bewitch Bonnie.

If Alexander despised Roderick and lived to create mischief for him, he could always share this with Maeve. And sit back and enjoy the fireworks. Unfortunately, he adored Maeve, and as much as he'd relish watching Roderick squirm, he'd hate seeing Maeve hurt.

Bollocksing hell. Back to Cressida gazing at him like he was the second coming. "If you're done with my arm, I'm going to need it back."

"Oh." She blinked at her hand on his arm.

OT shoved his way forward. "I'd like to interview you for my podcast," he bellowed.

"No," shrieked Cressida. "I want you for my YouTube channel."

All this interest, flattering though it was, made him twitchy. "Why?"

They both gaped at him.

Cressida recovered first. "Why? Because of the magic."

"What magic?" He played it cool. Hundreds of years hiding in plain sight made that easy. "No need to fight, children, and as much as it pains me to break it to you, there is no such thing as magic."

He sensed Roderick paying more attention to their conversation as soon as magic was mentioned.

"Of course, there's such a thing as magic." OT gave him a look of such pitying scorn it made his balls want to disappear. "I have experienced it PERS-AN-O-LY." He jabbed a thumb into his chest, winced and rubbed the spot. "I'm a practicing warlock."

"Ha!" Cressida stuck her face in OT's. "That proves you're a charlatan. There is no such thing as warlocks. It's a made-up term by—"

"Oh, yes?" OT swelled with indignation. "If there's no such thing as warlocks, then explain how I am standing right here, right this minute, my magic rising within me."

Something was rising in OT, and Alexander was equally certain he had no interest in knowing what. "Indulge me for a moment." He cut in before Cressida could. "Why all this interest in magic and me?"

"We know who you are," OT whispered.

Cressida shuffled even closer, pressing herself against his side in a waft of dragon's blood and sage. "We worship Goddess."

"Goddess?" he drawled. *Shit, shit, shit.* That was uncomfortably close to the truth. As if indulging them, he lowered his voice. "Goddess of what?"

"Goddess," Cressida hissed. "There's only one true Goddess."

Roderick had gone deathly still.

"Right." He chuckled and sipped his beer. "And that has to do with me how?"

"You need pretend no longer." OT winked at him. "We know you serve." He tapped the side of his nose. "We know to keep it quiet."

"Now, and forgive my obtuseness here, how are you intending to keep it quiet if you put it on your podcast and YouTube channel?"

Cressida laughed and nudged him. "Well, of course, we're not going to talk about that part. I would like to interview you about the magic swirling around the castle." She indicated a similarly dressed bunch of women all leaning across their table watching him like hungry crows. "We can all feel it."

"I can also feel it," OT said. "And I'd like to speak to your wife. The healer."

"Ah." Alexander adopted a regretful expression. "I would love to oblige, but I'm not married, and I don't think I'd fancy a doctor much." He leaned forward and said conspiratorially, "I demand a lot of attention."

Looking unsure, Cressida said, "We meant healer, not doctor."

"As in?" He chuckled. "Like a shaman or a medicine woman?"

OT's jaw tightened. "We don't use those terms, but yes."

"Right." He made a show of halting his laughter. "I hate to tell you this, but you have the wrong man. Also, I don't know of any healer in Greater Littleton." He shrugged. "But then I'm not into that sort of thing."

"Right." OT looked crestfallen now. "But you are from Baile, right?"

"I am from Baile." He clapped Roderick's shoulder. "As is my brawny friend over here." Pulling a face, he leaned closer to Cressida as he said, "He might know a healer. He's a total cross fit fanatic."

"That's okay." Eyeing Roderick as if he had the plague, she tugged on OT's arm. "Sorry to have bothered you."

They slunk away with Cressida whispering furiously in OT's ear.

"What's cross fit?" Roderick joined him.

"The holy temple of Vegans the world over." They'd averted attention for now, but Cressida glanced at him as she took her seat amongst her crow murder.

"I know we speak the same tongue," Roderick said. "But there are times when I doubt your sanity."

"You and me both." His nape tingled in an unpleasant way. "We've got trouble."

Roderick grunted. "I am aware."

"What did Bonnie say?" He dragged his attention away from Cressida.

"More and more people have come to Greater Littleton." Roderick stared about them at the faces in the pub. "They ask many questions about Baile and witchcraft."

"Right." Alexander nodded. Then he mentioned the other thing bothering him. "The place is full of pagans, but you know who's conspicuously absent?"

Roderick raised a brow.

"Rhiannon's minions." They were always there, spying and lurking about the place. He hadn't seen one of them since he'd come in.

Folding his arms, Roderick grunted. "That can't augur well."

"No." He put his nearly full pint back on the bar. "Bonnie was never one of them, and fortunately for her, she never notices much around her." OT covertly stared at them. "But we need to get back to Baile and discuss how we're going to deal with all the attention we're getting."

"Ignore it." Roderick shrugged. "The less credence we give it, the less importance it will gain."

"I agree. For now, that's the best way to handle this, but we need a plan in case the situation gets worse."

Roderick shook his head. "This time is a pain in the arse."

"It also has indoor plumbing and the internal combustion engine."

"There is that."

They reached the door and a dark-haired man, tall and slim stepped into their path. "Mr. Cray, we meet again?"

Roderick stiffened. "You may call me—"

"Roderick." Alexander slid in before Roderick could go medieval on them. He held his hand out to the man. "I'm Mr. Cray's...er...cousin." Of a sort. "Lord Donn."

"Right. I've done my research on Mr. Cray. He's something of a man of mystery in official channels. But I have a job to do, and I intend to do it." The man narrowed blue eyes at Alexander's hand before dropping a large white envelope in it. "You can give this to your...er...cousin. It's our assessment of the worth of Baile castle and its attached land. You will notice that the property taxes on the property have not been paid." The man pushed his glasses up his nose. "Ever."

Alexander restrained Roderick from going after the man and tugged him toward the Landy.

Leaning his back against the Landy, a huge bastard with a shaved head was watching people entering and leaving the pub. His gaze locked on them, and he straightened as they drew nearer, bracing his weight, ready to fight if he needed to. In a strong northern accent, he asked, "You from Baile?"

Roderick squared up to him. "What of it?"

"What the fuck have you done with Warren Masters?"

Yes, indeed. The world had decided to turn its collective gaze on Baile.

31

Niamh woke to find Warren on his phone, and that he'd ordered breakfast from room service. She wasn't sure if he'd slept, but his hair was damp, and his towel barely clung to his hips, ready to throw itself into the fray of getting him naked if she demanded it. She very nearly demanded it.

A trickle of water snaked down the long line of his spine as he spoke. "Yes." He nodded. "He's a good mate of mine." He clicked his tongue. "He could get ugly if he doesn't get the answers he wants."

Warren parted the curtains and peered outside. Bright morning sunlight burnished his short, blond hair and tanned torso. He'd been putting in the shirtless hours sparring with Roderick and Alexander.

She rolled to her back before her thoughts got her into trouble again.

He turned and lifted his chin, then said into the phone, "Involuntary manslaughter, but there were extenuating circumstances, and he's a solid bloke. I'd trust my Taylor with him." At the room service trolley, he poured a cup of tea, added milk and sugar and brought it to her. "I couldn't say how he'd react to any of this. The conversation never came up."

There were definite advantages to sharing a room with her coimhdeacht, and she smiled her thanks at him.

Back at the trolley he put eggs and bacon on a plate, added a croissant, a ramekin of butter, and those cute honey jars hotels always had.

She really hoped that was for her and couldn't stop her grin when he smiled and handed the plate to her along with cutlery and a napkin.

His face got serious as she spread her napkin over her lap.

"Nothing," he said into the phone. "Yes. It's fucking quiet as the grave, and that makes me twitchy."

The man, she rather thought Roderick, said something on the other side that made him scowl.

"Thanks for that." Warren dripped sarcasm. "Because I thought my time would be better spent taking a fucking nap."

Roderick said something else, and Warren simmered down.

"I'm just a bit on edge."

More soothing followed, judging by how Warren's shoulders relaxed.

"There was an old woman yesterday."

Niamh stopped midchew, wanting to hear the next part.

"I don't think so." Warren nodded. "I didn't get anything like that from her, but I'll stay sharp."

That didn't mean the old woman was harmless. According to Alexander, Rhiannon had tricks they knew nothing about yet, and she and her lackeys could be anywhere.

"Yup." Warren nodded and said yup a couple more times before hanging up.

He turned to her with a gentle smile. "Good morning."

"Good morning." Her cheeks heated for no good reason, and she ducked her head to her breakfast. "Thanks for breakfast."

"You're welcome." Warren sat beside her on the bed. His towel gaped over his thigh. A strong, tanned, muscular thigh. The sort of thigh that demanded a woman sink her nails and then her teeth—

"Sorry?" She'd missed what he was saying. "I didn't catch that."

"I said we can get going as soon as you're dressed." He gave her a quizzical look and then grinned. "Just as long as you don't bite too hard."

Now she outright blushed as he laughed and stood.

Goddess, but she needed to remember he could get inside her head. Either that or lose all ability to be embarrassed by her thoughts about him.

She touched the bond but didn't seem to have the same access to his mind.

His tone was all business again as he said, "I thought we'd go back to the caves, but drive around the area a bit more. See what we can pick up."

She nodded and finished her breakfast.

After a shower, she dressed in jeans and a sweater, and they were off again.

On the drive to the caves, she quested for animal life around her. Myriad beasties rushed into her awareness, and she had to take a deep breath and center herself.

Warren glanced at her, and she waved him off. She was fine.

She sorted through the different species, trying to identify them in human terms. South Africa was a land of big apex predators. She could also sense the awareness of the apex predators on the prey animals.

Many species of antelope touched her mind, but she moved on quickly, not wanting to distract them by her presence, or have them draw false comfort from her being around.

Smaller predators also crossed her mental pathways. Small cats like servals and caracals emitted a similar energy to the big cat she'd caught yesterday. She also located distinctly canine predators, wild dogs and jackals, and then a strong female energy, definitely predatory, that took her a while to identify as hyena.

Life teemed at her from all directions, and she surrendered herself to it. The first time she felt the mental touch of an elephant, she squealed and sat up straighter in her seat. The intelligence was undeniable and possessed the sedate confidence of a large mammal who had no natural predators.

"Having fun?" Warren smiled at her.

Of course, he would know what she was doing. "You have no idea. It's...wonderful." There really wasn't a superlative good enough for the way it felt to connect with the wide diversity of species.

"I always wanted to see the mass migration on the Masai Mara," Warren said.

That sounded like heaven to her. "When this is all over, we should make a plan to do that."

"Consider it a date." He nodded and continued staring at the road ahead of them.

The area around the caves was full of tourist attractions. Private game reserves, a museum dedicated to the Cradle of Humankind, and the Sterkfontein caves themselves.

Warren circled the area slowly as Niamh quested.

The tingle of cré-magic persisted, but they couldn't seem to zero in on it. At times, they got so close she would have put her head on a block that around the next bend they'd stumble on to whatever was emitting that magic signature. Only to find another bend, or another hill, or another stretch of long, unbroken road.

When she recognized the same road for the fifth time, Niamh growled her frustration. "It's like it's teasing us."

Warren pulled over and frowned in the direction of the

power signature. He could feel it as well and was getting as frustrated. "Could it be warded?"

"Eh?" Such a simple and obvious deduction but the ramifications crowded her brain.

"Baile works like this, right?" Warren waved a hand. "People can see the castle and drive toward it, but they never quite get there."

"But it takes witches to set a ward." Niamh blinked at him as her brain whirled.

He shrugged. "Does it say anywhere there are no other covens?"

"Nooo." At least nothing she'd ever read. "But we've never heard of any others, so we assumed..." She ended on a shrug.

Warren stared at her intently. "Would Maeve know?"

"I don't know." The familiar impotence pressed at her. "I don't think even Maeve knows how much there is to know."

"I mean." Warren drummed his long fingers on the steering wheel. "It would make sense that Goddess existed in more than one place. I don't mean to be rude, but what sort of goddess would she be if she was confined to one small village on the English coast?"

Niamh had never thought like that. Maybe because even having been raised as a cré-witch, steeped in Goddess lore, she hadn't really thought of Goddess as a real-life goddess. She'd been remote and largely theoretical, a distant, mythical figure who in some unknown and inexplicable way led them toward a mystery-enshrouded, indistinct future.

And none of them had ever questioned further. They'd gone along like sheep. Until Bronwyn had arrived and events had fast-tracked to now. She mimed an explosion against her temples with her fingertips. "Mind. Blown."

"But it's possible, isn't it?" Warren looked around them as if he expected to find witches hiding behind every sparse, desiccated bush.

She joined him in peering about. "It's totally possible."

"Now what?" He sat back in his seat and frowned. "If there are witches nearby, wouldn't they be near the source of power?"

"I would think so. I mean we built a castle over ours."

He looked left and right. "Fairly certain there are no castles about."

"But there are caves." Excitement bubbled within her. "And those caves have pools in them. When we went before, we were looking for a power signature. Now we're looking for witches."

"Right." Warren put the car in gear. "Let the witch hunt begin."

They had a delicious lunch at a rather smart restaurant in a private game reserve. Through huge glass walls, they watched the dry savannah. Around them, diners and even the staff marveled at the amount of game that had wandered into view —a white rhino and her calf, zebra, giraffes, multiple antelope species—Niamh could have told them about all the other game lingering out of sight.

In a more optimistic mood, they headed back to the caves. Still not sure what or who they were looking for, they relied heavily on instinct tipping them off when they happened upon it.

The same old woman sat in a folding chair beneath an umbrella at the entrance to the parking lot. A younger woman stood beside her, and they both openly stared as Warren parked the car and he and Niamh climbed out.

"What do you think?" Niamh sidled closer to Warren. "They aren't hiding their interest in us."

Warren sniffed the air. "Do you get any blood magic stench?"

Niamh sniffed but got nothing more than bush and dust. "No blood stench." She quested further and connected with a small rodent. "The creatures aren't afraid of them either."

"Good." Warren tensed beside her. "Because they're headed our way."

The older woman walked with a pronounced stoop, her skin dark and wrinkled. She was wrapped in a large blanket with bold patterns covering it. The younger woman wore a combination of western and traditional dress and hovered over the elder solicitously.

Niamh walked toward them.

The women stopped when they were about eight feet away and stared at her and then Warren.

The older woman spoke in her language.

The younger translated. "The mother asks what you seek here?"

"Perhaps we seek nothing." Warren's expression remained inscrutable.

Niamh continued to quest around them, looking for any more information. Lack of blood magic stench didn't mean these women were harmless.

The older spoke in English this time, "You have come from far?"

"Yes." Niamh thought their accents would give that away in any case.

"Mother said you were here yesterday," the younger said. "She was sure you would return today, and we have been waiting since early morning."

Niamh almost apologized for their tardiness but caught herself in time.

Warren bristled beside her. "Why are you waiting for us?"

"Uh-uh." The older woman glared at him and shook her head. "I will ask the questions."

The younger woman looked slightly embarrassed and said, "The mother is a sangoma of great power. She has served the ancestors well for most of her life."

Sangoma. The term rang a vague bell with Niamh.

Warren near vibrated with tension as he said, "We saw you yesterday."

The sangoma made a noise like steam hissing out of a kettle, and her face imploded into its cavernous wrinkles.

It took Niamh a moment to realize the old sangoma was laughing.

"And I saw you." She chortled. Then she cocked her head like a dog listening. "And I heard you. The ancestors whispered to me." She clapped her hands. "I'll call them to the *indumba* to hear what they say."

"I don't understand." Niamh felt stupid to be standing here blinking at the two women. Magic seeped from them, more from the older than the younger, but there nonetheless. The magic felt both familiar and alien, like a different flavor of the same food—unexpected and novel, but not unpalatable. "What do you hope to hear?"

The old woman hiss-cackled again. "That you are the one for whom we have been waiting."

32

E xhaustion dragged at Mags, but she dared not go back to bed. Possible futures filled her nights, some of them so horrifying she sat up and watched the light grow outside her window rather than experience them again.

Moments before she caught their soft murmuring to each other, she sensed Alexander and Bronwyn on their way to the kitchen. The love between the couple was palpable, despite their refusal to acknowledge it aloud to the coven. Some of her disturbing visions centered around them. The future of the entire coven remained stubbornly murky. All she could offer was possible outcomes, and the chains of events leading to each outcome snarled together in a way that prevented her from offering any guidance.

Mags needed an outcome she could control and went searching for flour in the pantry. Alannah kept the staples in neatly labeled glass canisters. Rows of white powder in glass dared her to make the right choice. Goddess, she could hardly have been expected to know there were so many kinds of flour.

"Alannah?" Bronwyn called from the kitchen.

"It's me," Mags called back. "Alannah is out in the kitchen garden with Sinead."

One thing she did know. Alexander and Bronwyn would need all their love in the months to come. Their twins remained dark in her foresight. Almost as if fate held its breath or refused to commit one way or the other.

Goddess, but Mags ached with the need to put down her burden, the ancient burden of the seer. Being able to see the future was more of a curse than a blessing. It would be so much easier not to know and to live with hope, however misplaced that hope might be.

She selected a jar labeled All Purpose and went back to the kitchen. How Alannah did this, she had no idea. Not only did Alannah put meal after meal on the table, but she did so with the sort of effortless grace that made it look dirt simple.

"Mags?" Bronwyn stood in the doorway and frowned at the mess on the table. Four mixing bowls, a pint of milk—most of it on the table and a pile of eggshells bore testament to Mags's effort. "Are you baking?"

"No." Mags held up one batter-encrusted palm. "I am trying to bake, which is an entirely different thing."

Alexander gave her his slow, charming smile. "How intriguing."

He really was too handsome for his own good. Rhiannon had created a physically perfect specimen to sire the children she wanted. Why would she create anything less? Alexander had never shown any curiosity about who had sired him, but he must wonder. If he ever discovered the truth, they'd all feel the shockwaves rolling through Baile. She certainly wasn't going to spill the beans.

Bronwyn peered into one of the mixing bowls. "Um...not to be rude, but why are you doing this?"

"Alannah says it's good for stress." Mags stared over Bronwyn's shoulder. "So far it's only making me feel worse."

"Why don't you have a seat." Alexander guided her into a chair and scooped eggshells into one of her attempted bowls. "Let's have a cup of tea and you can tell us what's on your mind."

Mags glared as he tossed the contents of her bowls into the rubbish. "You're humoring me."

"You're right." He chuckled. "I'm frightened for the rest of us by what I saw in those bowls."

"It wasn't that bad." Bronwyn put the kettle on. "But then again, I'm totally useless in a kitchen."

Not offended, Mags sighed. "Alannah makes it look so easy."

"I can blend a poultice, no worries" Bronwyn snapped her fingers. "Make up a remedy, a concoction or a tisane. No problem. But ask me to boil an egg..." She shook her head.

"You have other talents, little witch." Alexander winked at her.

Bronwyn giggled and blushed.

Ack! Goddess, Mags wished they wouldn't. The coven thought her a prude. They might be on to something.

Alexander sat down opposite Mags, leaned across the table and studied her face. "You've not been sleeping."

"My mind is...busy." She pulled a face because she didn't really have words to express the mess that swirled through her brain. Some days separating past, present and future was nearly impossible. "The passage of events is quickening."

"Is it Niamh and Warren?" Bronwyn sat beside Alexander, and he put his arm around her.

Mags shook her head. "No." Heat climbed her cheeks. Today's stress had nothing to do with Alexander and Bronwyn. "It's not to do with anyone else. It's to do with me."

Not able to keep sitting there as they looked at her quizzically, she got up and got on with cleaning her baking mess away. Her cheeks heated as they kept watching her, waiting for her to fill them in. "I don't often see things clearly for myself. But I do get a sort of heads up when something, or someone, is arriving that I need to take note of."

Thomas popped into the kitchen. "Who's arriving?"

Mags jumped and glared at him.

"Goodness." Alannah slipped into the kitchen with a basket of fresh veggies and stared at the kitchen table while she put the veggies beside the sink to be washed. "What were you making?"

"Um..." Mags had to laugh. "Well, it started as biscuits and then I thought maybe bread would be good, or scones. And somehow I mixed up all the bowls and got this."

"Right." Alannah took a breath. "Scones sounds like a great idea. I see someone already put the kettle on."

Mags got out of her way. Alannah didn't like people helping her.

"Jesus!" Sinead stared at the mess and then Mags. "You even got it in your hair."

It was true. The ends of her hair were encrusted with dried white gloop.

"Mags is stressed," Bronwyn said. "I'm going to mix you something to help you sleep."

Now Sinead, Alannah and Thomas also stared at her, waiting for an explanation.

"It's not Niamh and Warren." Alexander reassured them. "Mags says it's got to do with her."

She shouldn't have said anything, and Mags gave an airy wave. "It really is nothing."

"Doesn't look like nothing." Sinead waded in to help Alannah. The only other person Alannah would tolerate in her space. Although Alannah seemed to have no problem with Thomas leaning against the counter near her.

Mags sensed Maeve approaching, and right behind her, Roderick. She blurted out before they could arrive and increase her embarrassing audience. "There's a man. You need to invite him to Baile."

Silence blanketed the kitchen.

Alexander recovered first. "A man, Magsie? Is this man... special to you?"

"Yes!" Bugger, willy, boobs. "He's important to all of us." True as well. "And he has a part to play in our future. I—" She caught her slip. "We cannot do this without him."

"A new coimhdeacht?" Alexander looked at Thomas.

After a brief pause, Thomas shook his head. "No. We would have sensed him near if he was."

"Maybe it is a new coimhdeacht and he's not here yet." Bronwyn also looked at Thomas.

"No." Thomas looked sure. "We felt Warren coming weeks before he arrived. It's like a ripple in a pond when a new one is called."

Sinead pinned Mags with a stare. "When you say a man, are you talking about your man?"

Damn Sinead and her dogged perceptiveness.

All eyes snapped her way.

"What's this about a new man?" Roderick swaggered into the kitchen like he was about to pee up the legs of everyone in it and rub his scent all over them.

Maeve giggled and nudged him.

"Settle down, big man." Sinead snorted a laugh. "I'm sure you've still got the biggest—"

"Jack." Mags yelled the name before Sinead could get graphic. "It's that Jack person who is here looking for Warren. We need him here...in the castle." If the floor could open right now and suck her in, that would be super helpful. "Now."

Sinead frowned. "Is it a good idea to be inviting strange men into Baile right now?" She waved a hand. "With everything going on, we might want to be extra cautious."

"Are you sure, Seer?" Roderick studied her, and Mags's face

grew hotter. She really didn't want to divulge the details, especially not those pertaining to her and Jack.

"Yes." So sure, she was stress baking. What did one say to one's future life partner anyway? Hello, how are you didn't seem to cover it. Of course, coming right out with the fact that they would have four children didn't seem the right approach either.

She swallowed and held Roderick's gaze. "He's important, Roderick. We need him."

"Right then." Alexander stood. "Let's go and invite the man to tea."

Roderick scowled at him. "That is not your decision to make."

"Right." Alexander clenched his jaw and made an exaggerated flourish with his arm. "By all means make the decision to invite the man here."

"I already have." Roderick strode from the kitchen with a smirk. He tossed the keys over his shoulder at Alexander. "Come along then."

Alexander barely caught them in time. He looked over his shoulder at Maeve. "How much would you really miss him? Hypothetically speaking."

33

Bronwyn ground dried valerian root for Mags's sleep aid. Roderick and Alexander hadn't found Mag's mystery man and had returned from Greater Littleton arguing about the best way to track him down. She allowed herself a giggle at the memory of Mags's red face. Sinead liked to mess with Mags, who seemed to pretzel herself to avoid any subject matter that was in any way racy or suggestive. How this new man would mesh with vestal Mags remained to be seen.

Movement in the doorway to the patient recovery section of the healer's hall gave her a start.

"Hi, Roz." It seemed wrong not to greet the woman, even though she never showed any signs of hearing or responding.

Roz clambered onto the large table and perched. Cocking her head, she studied Bronwyn, her eyes fixed and clear.

"I worry about them too." Bronwyn shrugged. "Maybe it's because of the babies coming, and I'm extra hormonal, but I hate Warren and Niamh being out there and so vulnerable."

Whhhrrr.

It almost sounded like Roz sympathized.

"I know. They're both big and bad enough to take care of

themselves." She flapped a hand in Roz's direction, wishing she could swish away the anxious niggle that would persist until everyone was safe and sound behind the wards again. "But you-know-who is bat-shit crazy and she's going to want to stop them from getting to the fire point first."

Click. Whirr. Click. Click. Roz waddled to the edge of the table and peered at Bronwyn. She bobbed her head a couple of times.

A strange sensation fluttered through Bronwyn's belly, and her hand went to the gentle swell that she could barely notice. It was way too early for her to be able to feel the twins.

Another flutter through her abdomen made her gasp.

With only Roz here to share it with her, she laughed and said, "I think I just felt my babies move."

Roz cocked her head and stared at her belly.

"I know. It's too soon. All the books say so." She waited, hoping it would happen again.

It did.

"Hello, babies." She peered down at her abdomen. "Then again, what do any of those books know about magical babies?"

Whoo-ho-ho-hoo

"Woohoo indeed, Roz." Bronwyn couldn't stop her huge grin. "Alexander is going to be so excited when I tell him."

Roz shuffled her weight from one foot to the other and settled her arms like wings against her. She went back to mad-dog eyeballing Bronwyn.

Bronwyn looked away, but she could feel that stare on her.

It must be her day for weird because she found herself asking, "Did you want something, Roz?"

Roz jerked upright, craned her neck and flung her head back with her mouth open.

Not really believing she was doing this, Bronwyn moved closer. "Are you in pain, or something?" She wasn't even an animal healer. Niamh should be dealing with this. "Is there something you need from me?"

Hopping off the table, Roz came close enough and pressed her shoulder against her.

Bronwyn moved out of her way, but Roz closed the gap again and pressed an elbow against her. She stared at Bronwyn, eyes fever bright.

"I don't know what you want." Bronwyn held out her hand anyway. Despite being lost in an owl's consciousness, Roz was still human.

Roz shuffled closer to her hand. She pecked at it with her nose.

"Okay." Bronwyn moved slowly as she reached for Roz's hand and held it in her own. "I'm going to hold your hand for a bit. Maybe have a look inside?"

Roz settled her shoulders.

Her hand felt dry and cold in Bronwyn's, the skin papery. Bronwyn opened to her blessing. Honey and sage perfumed the air and water responded in a joyful wave.

This, water seemed to whisper, *this is our purpose, and it is good.*

Unlike Gemma's tumor, Roz's bond with the owl felt ephemeral. More of a breadcrumb trail of energy than a line. Bronwyn traced the bond into Roz's pineal gland. It looked fragile and stretched to breaking point. Bronwyn nudged closer. The bond was deteriorating, almost as she quested around it.

With breath held, she let her gift brush gossamer light across the bond.

Age and weariness resonated through Bronwyn, a soul-deep fatigue that made her want to weep.

The animal energy of the owl was alien to her gift, but she could sense it through Roz. The bird was old and sick. The owl wanted to die. Only it's connection to Roz kept it alive, but even that faded with each hour.

Bronwyn could sense the slow, labored draw of its breathing, the reluctant thump of its heart.

And Bronwyn hesitated. She didn't know what to do. If she severed the bond, the bird would die, but she had no idea what would happen to Roz if she did.

Goddess, she was not equipped to make this decision, and she withdrew gently.

Mags had entered the healer's hall at some point and stood on the far side of the table, tears snaking down her face. "The owl must go, and it can't because Roz is holding it here."

"No." Bronwyn shook her head, hating what she read in Mags's expression. "I can't take the chance—"

A soft touch on her arm drew Bronwyn's attention to her side.

"I'm here for him," Maeve said. "He's ready."

Bronwyn's every healer's instinct recoiled from her. "What do you mean?"

"The owl's spirit called to me. I don't usually get animals, but this one is so intertwined with Roz..." Maeve shrugged and looked resigned to what came next. "It's ready to enter the vale."

But Bronwyn couldn't blindly separate Roz and the owl. "I need more time to research this." She pointed to the shelves of heavy tomes above her plants. "The answer is in there. I just haven't found it yet."

"Bronwyn." Sinead and Alannah came in together.

Sinead had the owl cradled against her chest.

The bird looked ancient, scrawny, and missing most of its feathers. A white film covered its eyes.

"Mags told us." Sinead swallowed hard. "And we found him in the kitchen garden. He's old and sick and suffering."

Bronwyn shook her head, needing to deny what they were saying. "I can't do that. This is not right. Niamh should be here."

"I think that's why this is happening now," Alannah said. Her lovely face filled with tenderness. "I don't think Roz could ask for this if Niamh was around. Niamh's spirit is strong, and she wouldn't take a chance on losing Roz."

"Neither will I." Bronwyn shook her head, trying to shake the truth of Alannah's statement away. "If I do this, I could kill Roz as well."

"Break the bond, Healer." The words came from Roz, and they all turned to stare at her.

Roz's mouth moved awkwardly, as if she struggled to force it to conform to words.

"Aunt Roz?" Alannah approached her slowly. "Did you speak?"

Nodding, Roz screwed her eyes shut and tried again. "Healer must break the bond."

"The owl is tired," Maeve touched the center of her chest. A lone tear swelled and snaked down her pale cheek. "I can feel it calling to me."

Roderick and Alexander entered the healer's hall.

Putting an arm around Maeve's waist, Roderick whispered in her ear.

Maeve drew her shoulders back again, seeming to draw strength from what he said.

"I don't have my magic." Maeve shrugged. "Not enough to transpose the bird, but I can hold its memories until such time as I can put them in the cave. I can keep it with me until Roz is ready to join it."

Roderick frowned at her. "Is that safe?"

"It won't kill me."

"Which is a non-answer," he said.

"And the only one I can give you." Maeve gentled her tone and touched his arm. "The two souls are so connected I can't separate them. The bird is part of Roz now, and she is part of it."

Bronwyn had heard enough to know breaking the bond was not an option. "Then there's an excellent chance this will kill Roz if I do it." She looked to Alexander for support. "I can't do that."

Shrugging, he reached her and twined his fingers with hers. "You're a healer, little witch. It goes against everything in you to make this decision."

"Must be now." Roz's voice was raspy from lack of speech. "No Niamh. Mother is strong within you." She took the limp bird from Sinead and tenderly rubbed her cheek against its head as she crooned to it.

Many relatives and loved ones in the moment of death would want to go with the departed. In the moment, and given the choice, would they not also make a rash decision around not being able to deal with the pain and the loss? She couldn't risk Roz following the owl into the vale. Her voice a raw whisper, she looked at Alexander, trying to reach him and let him take this terrible responsibility away. "I can't."

"Little witch." Alexander cradled her face. "We don't know what will happen if you break the bond, but it also concerns me greatly what might happen if you don't. Roz will be linked to a dying creature."

The decision felt too heavy. "I wish Niamh were here."

"No." Roz shook her head. "No Niamh."

"Niamh would try and stop her." Alannah stepped closer to Bronwyn. "You know she always hoped you would find a way to break this bond for them."

True enough. She and Niamh had spoken of her trying to break the bond.

"Please," Roz rasped. "My brother suffers."

Bronwyn's will buckled under the weight of their combined arguments. "I'll try, but if there is any danger to Roz, I'm going to pull back."

"Perfect." Alexander kissed her forehead. "The burden of

these decisions is a heavy one to carry, but your shoulders are strong."

Bronwyn really couldn't do this without him. Even after the short time she'd had him in her life, she couldn't conceive of a time when she had struggled through without him.

"Okay." She stepped out of the safety of Alexander's hold and took Roz's hand. Leading her over to the bench, she sat them both down.

"Right." Honey and sage surrounded her as water provided a trickle of power. She wanted to do this slowly and carefully.

Ever so slowly, she reached for the bond.

Snip.

It disintegrated at the lightest touch. Shit! She hadn't meant to do it that fast, but the thing had been brittle as a cobweb.

The owl made a strangely human sigh and went limp on Roz's lap.

Roz stroked it's feathers reverently. "Empty." She touched her mind and then her heart. "Empty."

"May I?" Alannah crouched down and held her hands out for the owl. "He was old and ready to return to the earth."

Maeve touched Roz's shoulder and pressed a palm to her chest. "I have him now. All that matters of him is within me, and it will stay there until I can place him amongst the sisters past." She glanced at the dead bird. "What you hold, however precious to you, is only an empty vessel."

"Gone." Roz looked at Alannah like a lost child. "The flying is gone."

Alannah waited quietly, her open palms resting on Roz's knees.

"Not gone." Sinead stood behind Alannah. "His memories are still yours, and Maeve will hold him until he can join us forever."

Roz stared from one twin to the other for a long, long

moment, and then she nodded. She stood, swaying unsteadily on her feet.

Bronwyn had kept her magic within Roz, closely monitoring, and she eased away the pain from muscles spent too long in not entirely human positions. The strength she commanded even now, only a few weeks from curing Gemma was so much stronger. How Deidre would have reveled in all they could have done, all the pain and suffering they could have alleviated.

"Are you hungry?" Alannah had the owl in her hands now. "After we return him to the earth, I can get you something to eat."

Sinead gave Alannah a fond smile. "You're such a feeder."

"It's my way." Alannah shrugged.

"Yes, it is." Sinead squeezed her shoulder. "And all our lives would be a lot worse without your way."

"Come." Maeve led the way out the healer's hall. "Let's put our friend to his final bodily rest."

Bronwyn hung back as the others left the hall. She let out the breath she hadn't realized she was holding. That bond had disappeared so quickly she would have not been prepared to save Roz had things gone south. She glanced at Alexander. "I need to use my gift, practice with it. I can't keep getting into situations where I'm working blind."

"I know." He rubbed his nape. "It's finding a way for you to do that safely and without being inundated by the world's sick and desperate that is going to be a challenge."

"It's my purpose." She held his gaze. As much as she understood the need for her safety, she hadn't been blessed merely to hide away in Baile and deprive people of what she could offer.

Alexander gave a rueful chuckle. "Don't blast me with your eyes, little witch. I'm on your side. But first, I need to take care of you and our wee ones."

Fluttering happened in her belly again, but it brushed her

mind at the same time, and she held her breath, willing it to happen again.

Alexander stilled and glanced at her belly. "Did you...sense anything?"

"You felt that too?" The wonder on his face answered her question.

He nodded and put his large hand over her belly. "Has it happened before?"

"It started this morning."

Alexander gave a short, amazed bark of laughter. "I can sense our children."

Again, the belly flutter and the soft mind brush, and Bronwyn laughed with him. "And, apparently, they can sense you too."

34

"Maeve?" Roderick stood in the kitchen doorway, the shadows of deep night playing over his naked chest. If she lived another thousand years, her heart would continue to beat faster at the sight of him. "You're not sleeping."

"No." She had known he would find her when he realized she was awake and uneasy.

Hair mussed, he wore those pants for sweat covering his lower half. He had been in bed.

Yawning, he took a seat on the bench beside her. His warmth enticed her to shift closer. His concern purred through her innards.

Reaching down, he picked up her cold feet and put them on his lap. The motion turned her sideways to him as his big hands stroked warmth into her feet. "Roz and the owl."

"Yes." She nodded. They'd started to have the sort of abridged conversations she'd witnessed between bonded couples in the old life. Entire conversations would be conducted in two or three spoken words. Arguments, even, that raged between eyes and tightened jaws. "The owl is not a heavy burden to bear."

"But you should be able to release him." Roderick massaged her instep with his thumbs.

She shrugged. He understood the problem and sensed her frustration that her blessing sat within her as if swaddled in thick blankets. "Niamh must find the fire point."

"She will." He gentled her toes between his thumb and forefinger, almost making her giggle. "And then your power will be yours to command again."

The surety in his statement comforted her, and his ministrations to her feet were most enjoyable. "You've never done that before."

"I'm learning." He gave her a rakish grin. "I have been reading online blogs."

"I've heard about those."

"Aye." He chaffed her instep. "Alexander and Warren showed me them when we were in the village. Apparently, and I'm not entirely sure what all these words mean, we can't get good internet at the castle."

Maeve knew the answer to that one, and she laughed. "Baile blocks the internet here. She will not allow it."

"Hmm." He studied her feet. "You have pretty toes. I never noticed before." He tapped her bright red polished toenails. "I like this color."

"Sinead did it for me." She peered down at her toes. "She gave me a pedicure."

"I'm not sure I would trust Sinead near my feet with implements." He commenced the massaging.

"Neither am I sure you should. You and Sinead have a novel relationship." Maeve giggled. Sinead and Roderick lived for their thrust and parry interactions.

He gave her the lopsided smile that belonged to her alone.

"She hates it, but that witch understands me well. And I her. She would make an excellent coven leader."

Maeve nodded. The need for coven leadership amongst six witches had never arisen. It had been the four Baile witches for so long, and then her and Bronwyn. For the most part they were all of one mind, but Maeve and Roderick had lived the old coven life. More witches would mean more opinions and perhaps, in the future, they would need a leader.

Roderick's face grew grave. "How many others?"

"That I sense?" He was asking about the spirits of witches clinging to Baile, the ones she could not yet transpose.

He nodded and draped her legs over his thighs. His hands covered her shins, his touch warm and distracting.

The days between his declaration and when she would need to make a decision stretched before her. For both their sake, she would give her decision full consideration.

"I cannot say exactly, but many witches died here that day." He didn't need her to tell him which day. "Their souls flutter like linens on a drying line. I cannot get a full sense of them, but they are not at rest. All the witches who have ended this part of their journey here in the intervening years." She swallowed past the thump in her throat. "And those who..."

The full casting circle who had given their lives so that she and Roderick would survive and wake in this time. Those witches could not have known the outcome of their sacrifice, that she and Roderick would end up so many hundreds of years later in a critical battle to defeat Rhiannon. They had known, however, that by sacrificing their lives and bleeding into the earth to create the power they had needed to generate, they would be forever condemning themselves to never returning to Goddess. Their souls were now lost in their moment of death, untethered from the life and death circle.

Roderick squeezed her leg. "Once your full power is restored, we can see what can be done."

"You will intercede for them?"

He glanced at her. "There is naught I would not do for you, sweeting, and yes I will speak with Goddess."

"She always did like you best." The first part of his statement left her oddly breathless.

Roderick smirked. "It's my innate charm and staggering good looks."

"It's something." She snorted; the intimate moment passed.

He'd done it deliberately. That day when he had kissed her, he had promised he would not press her in any way, and he stayed true to that.

Looking at his brutally beautiful face, so strong and almost harsh in the shadowy kitchen, a girl could wish a man might press his suit a little.

Eyebrow raised, Roderick gave her a look that brought heat to her cheeks. Aye, he had read her right.

Heart hammering, Maeve held his gaze.

Slowly, so terribly slowly, he slid a hand about her hip and edged her closer along the bench. Her knees raised between them, but he brought her within reach of the intent on his face. Then, even slower still, he tilted his head and leaned in.

Maeve's eyelids fluttered closed. Her breath came harsher and quicker. When he kissed her this time, she might not want him to stop. She might not let him stop.

"Maeve?" he whispered, a quiet request.

She shrank the space between them until his breath caressed her lips.

Bang! Bang! Bang!

Maeve squeaked and only Roderick's quick reflexes prevented her from tumbling off the bench.

"What in God's name?" Roderick glared at the kitchen door.

Maeve staggered to her feet and straightened her night rail. "Who is that?"

"I know not." Roderick stalked for the door. "But Baile did not warn me of their approach."

Mags hovered in the doorway from the main part of the castle. "I was going to say something." She bit her lip. "But you and Maeve were having a moment, and that was more important."

The banging on the door started up again. "I can see someone is in there," a man yelled.

"It's Jack." Mags made a nervous face. "You better let him in."

"Jesus." Alexander staggered into the kitchen. "Big bastard is going to break the door down if he keeps that up."

Roderick yanked open the door. "Explain yourself."

On the other side, Jack stood, legs braced, arm raised to bang again. "I think the boot's on the other foot, mate." He sneered at Roderick and shoved his way into the kitchen. "And I'm not fucking going anywhere until you tell me what you've done with Warren." He glanced at Maeve and blushed. "Pardon the obscenity, miss."

"I'd better put the kettle on." Alannah drifted into the kitchen in a pair of lounging pants and a tank that ended short of her waistband.

Sometimes Maeve forgot how beautiful Alannah was. The dumbstruck look on Jack's face was enough of a reminder to make her want to giggle.

Alannah smiled at him. "I'm Alannah, by the way."

"J...er...Jack Langham."

"Sit." Roderick jerked his head at the table. "We were looking for you today." He gave Jack a pointed look. "We didn't find you."

"A likely story." Jack sneered and folded beefy arms over his chest.

Maeve had never seen arms quite that size. They resembled tree trunks.

"We did go to Greater Littleton to find you." Alexander scrubbed his palms over his face, his bristles rasping. "It wasn't...advisable to leave a message."

Mags drifted closer, her wide-eyed gaze locked on Jack. "You're bigger than I thought you'd be."

Jack looked at her, and his gaze stuck. He frowned. "Do I know you?"

"Not yet." Mags shook her head. Her unbound hair swished over her back. She studied him like she was looking to buy. "You're taller." She raised one hand above her head. "And broader." She puffed out her elbows. "And your smile is much nicer."

"I haven't smiled." Jack's gaze smoldered.

Mags blushed. "But you will."

"Right." He dragged his gaze away from her. "Tell me where Warren is."

WARREN SNAGGED Niamh by the elbow and edged her away from the three women. It was after midnight, and these three had arrived at their hotel fifteen minutes earlier and wouldn't leave until he and Niamh met them at the bar. It was the old woman from the parking lot, and she'd brought the younger woman they'd seen before and another, even younger, woman.

Fortunately, or unfortunately, depending on your view, the hotel was hosting a tech conference, and the bar was jammed with computer geeks desperately making up for their lack of a misspent youth.

"I know what you're going to say." Niamh held up her hand to stop him from speaking.

Warren folded his arms over his chest and glared at a geek who eyed Niamh like she was his choice of chaser to his lite beer. "Good, then that saves me from having to say it."

"But we have to go." Niamh gripped his forearm with both her hands and stood on her tiptoes. She still stopped well short of meeting him eye to eye.

A slim, tall man dressed in a suit appeared beside them. "Excuse me." He swallowed and stared at Niamh. "Perhaps I could buy you a drink?"

Was Warren invisible to this prat? He gave the stranger a look loaded with *you might die soon*. "No, you can't."

"Oh." The man eyed Warren and took a step back. Still that Niamh sorcery kept him from turning tail and running. He flapped a slim, pale hand between Niamh and Warren. "Are you together?"

"Yes." Warren really didn't want to get physical with the twat. Actually, he might want to get a bit physical. Maybe a little spraining and bruising, no blood or broken bones.

"Thank you." Niamh let the twat down easy. "But this is my...er...man."

Something visceral shot through Warren when she called him her man. The sort of something that made him want to chest thump. He kept his gaze on the idiot. "Got it?"

"Yup." He swallowed and nodded, then melted into the crowd.

The sangoma and her younger sidekicks stood to one side of the bar clearly impatient and waiting for them. Well, they'd have an even longer wait if he had anything to say about their idea. And he did.

"We go with them. In the middle of the fucking night." Saying it out loud only pissed him off further. "To a cave and go poking around after a power point we've never seen." He motioned the three women. "With three total strangers in a foreign country. No, you're right." Her eyes narrowed at his sarcasm. "It's a brilliant fucking idea."

Niamh took a careful breath like she was trying not to smack him. "We need to find the cardinal point."

"Thus far, we're on the same page." He gave her a what else you got finger curl.

Her glare got fiercer. "And we've tried twice already, and we are now certain it's being warded."

"Certain?" He wouldn't go that far. "We suspect it's warded."

"They approached us." Niamh waved at the women.

The sangoma scowled and raised her brow.

"There's not a trace of blood magic on them." She inched closer to him. "One of us would have caught it, surely. It's not exactly subtle."

She had him there. "Maybe they have a way of disguising it?"

"Alexander says they don't."

"Alexander has never been to Africa. He can't answer for everyone." At least Warren didn't believe so. Alexander would likely disagree with him.

Niamh stamped her foot and pinched his forearm. Given her level of frustration he felt through the bond, he had to admire her restraint.

"Don't you think if there was a foolproof way to mask blood magic, Rhiannon would have found it by now, and used it?" She took a deep breath. "Look. They came to find us. They say we're who they've been waiting for, and they must take us to where we need to go."

"Come." The sangoma had made it across the bar faster than Warren could have anticipated. "Come to see the umlilo." She made an impatient gesture outside. "In the day, we cannot."

"Umlilo?" Niamh stumbled over the unfamiliar word.

"Fire." The youngest women stood behind the crone. "It's the Zulu word, and it means fire. The ancestors have spoken, and we have to take you to the fire."

35

T he three women had been dropped at the hotel by a relative, and now they all piled into the back of the hired car. Niamh knew Warren was seriously unhappy, but she was equally certain they were doing the right thing.

"I am Lerato," said the younger woman they had seen yesterday. "And this is my mother, Ulwazi, and my first born, Nofoto. My mother and I are sangoma. Nofoto is training."

"Sangoma?" Niamh turned in her seat to speak with them.

"Witch doctor." Lerato smiled. "We are traditional healers."

Niamh wanted to glance at Warren, but she settled for sending her excitement down the bond.

From his side, she could perceive only wariness as he eased the car onto the nearly silent roads.

"You say the ancestors sent you?" Niamh kept her tone neutral and polite. Warren might think she blindly trusted these women, but she'd been there when Rhiannon had kidnapped Bronwyn, and she'd also been inside poor Rat's brain when Rhiannon had killed him. She didn't underestimate their foe, but time was of the essence, and they needed whatever help they could get. Picturing Roderick's face if he'd been with them almost had her giggling.

Warren threw her a wry smile as he read her thought.

"My mother has been sangoma since she was younger than Nofoto. She hears the ancestors clearly. They do not favor me as much." Lerato gave a deferential shrug. "But even I heard how much they wanted us to show you the fire."

If the cardinal point was warded, then someone had to have set that ward, which meant there was power in South Africa. It had never come up before, but the arrogance in assuming that their magic was limited to the United Kingdom was staggering.

Worldwide legends of witches and healers abounded. Almost all cultures had their own version of things that went bump in the night, and strange people able to do inexplicable things.

A few short months ago, she, Sinead, Alannah, and Mags had been living their lives at Baile assuming they were the only people who could do the limited amount of magic they could muster. Then Bronwyn had come along and proved different, followed by Maeve and Roderick.

If people could have been frozen in time for hundreds of years, and one accepted that as truth, other cultures around the world sharing a version of Goddess or somehow linked with cré-magic, wasn't such a difficult leap to make.

Of course, if one made that leap, the converse held true. Around the world, there could be people in Rhiannon's camp.

"You're taking the long way," Ulwazi groused from behind Warren. "It will be next year before we get there."

Lerato clucked her tongue. "No, he isn't. If he takes the other way, we'll get caught in traffic."

"At this time?" Ulwazi shook her head.

"It doesn't matter anyway." Lerato glared at her mother. "We are on this road now."

"GPS." Warren's jaw clenched. "We are following the GPS."

Ulwazi huffed. "Does that thing know this land? Does it live on this land and draw from this land? Did its ancestors walk these paths before the white man put his roads here?"

There was no arguing with that, and Niamh tried to smooth the waters. "No, but it got us there the first time."

Ulwazi crossed her arms and stared out the window. "There is much danger."

"Danger is probably taking the fast road." Nofoto giggled and winked at Niamh.

The cave site was deserted when they arrived. Arc lights lit up the empty parking lot and a chained gate barred their way.

Ulwazi hopped out of the back, spryer than they'd seen her thus far. "Park over there." She motioned imperiously to the dusty roadside. "We go this way."

Above them, millions of pinprick stars littered the dark cloudless night, different from the northern hemisphere skies.

Niamh tucked her hands into the pouch of her hoodie. It was colder than she'd expected Africa to be. At this altitude, the winters were marked by clear, dry days. When the sun went down, any warmth from the day disappeared.

A high-pitched yowl broke the night. Warren tensed and Niamh quested for it.

"Impungushe," Lerato murmured. "He stands guard this night."

"Canine," Niamh said to Warren. "Probably a jackal."

Ulwazi followed the eight-foot chain-link fence until she stopped with a grunt of satisfaction.

"Here." She motioned Warren forward. "I cut it earlier."

With a glance at Niamh, he stepped forward and gingerly tugged on the fence. Two jagged edges parted, and he pulled harder. When the gap was wide enough for a body, she followed Lerato through.

Nofoto came next, and then Ulwazi held out her hand for Nofoto to help her.

Warren edged the fence closed behind him and stood as if scenting the night for trouble.

"Come." Ulwazi scuttled forward undeterred by the dark or the uneven ground.

Jackal called again, a warning, and Niamh tensed.

Lerato stilled beside her.

Niamh found the jackal and slipped into his mind. The night was alive with scent and sound, one of those made him nervous. She got the impression of a large cat, sliding through the night on silent feet.

"Ingwe," Lerato said. "He warns us that ingwe draws close."

"Ingwe?" Niamh tried to sort through the jackal's awareness to identify the danger.

"A leopard." Nofoto smiled. She cocked her head at Niamh. "You hear them, the animals?"

"Yes." Niamh nodded.

Nofoto's smile grew. "It is the same with my family. Some have the gift."

"Do you?" Niamh had never met another guardian.

"No." Nofoto motioned Lerato. "But my mother does."

The urge to compare notes, to talk to another guardian about how she perceived the world, nearly overwhelmed Niamh. Here where there were so many different species, it must be a constant delight.

"Later." Warren took her hand in his. "For now, let's stay focused."

He was right, and swallowing her disappointment, Niamh dropped in behind Lerato.

Lerato winked at her over her shoulder. Later they would be chatting it up.

They reached the cave entrance. A gate barred their way.

No problem for Ulwazi who drew the keys from her pocket and opened the gates enough to admit them. She closed them behind her and locked them in.

Warren's dislike of that pulsed through the bond, and Niamh squeezed his hand.

Nofoto pulled a small penlight torch out of her pocket and lit their way. The eerie dark of the caves pressed in on them, and the briny smell of the underground water clung to her skin. Their feet made soft chuffs on the sandy floor.

Ulwazi squeezed through a jagged crevice and opened another, smaller gate. A sign warned people to keep out of a restricted area. Clearly, that didn't apply to Ulwazi.

As they stepped into the inky cavern, Niamh felt it, like a pulse beneath her skin. Excitement drummed in her blood. "It's here," she whispered.

"I feel it," Warren whispered back. "Not sure if it's through you or not, but I feel it."

"Yes," Ulwazi said with a triumphant look at Lerato. "It is you for whom we wait."

Their plan hadn't gone beyond finding the place, and Niamh stood stuck to the ground and feeling useless.

Nofoto vanished into the darkness. They heard scuffling sounds and then the strike of a match. "Fire." Nofoto blew on the collected twigs and dried grasses until the flame caught. "We had this ready for you."

Of course, Bronwyn had used water to awaken the point. It stood to reason she would need fire. Confidence surged through Niamh, and she glanced at Nofoto. "Can you make it bigger."

"Of course," Nofoto grinned. She fed larger pieces of wood into the fire.

Ghostly tendrils of light braved the dark, flickering over the cavern walls. The fire burned brighter.

Niamh drew on the fire. Her gift responded. Basil and strawberry scents perfumed the air.

Two figures stepped out of the darkness.

"Oh good, you started the fire." Edana said.

Fiona gave a feral grin. "How very considerate of you."

Warren lunged for them. He stopped as if he'd hit a brick wall, his limbs frozen. His frantic gaze flit from Edana to her, and then behind her.

Shadows danced and lurched, and the cavern filled with bodies. They surrounded Warren. Niamh lost sight of him behind so many people.

Rhiannon stepped into the cavern. She pulsed with power, her blood magic making Niamh gag with its fetid stench. So much for not being able to disguise it, because until now Niamh had scented nothing.

"Hello, Niamh." Rhiannon smiled. "How lovely to see you here."

Niamh reached for her magic, but found a sickening vacuum. Blood magic stench choked her.

"No." Rhiannon snapped her fingers. "We'll have none of that."

Niamh tried to move, but her limbs were frozen, her feet rooted to the earth.

Rhiannon turned her attention to Ulwazi, Lerato and Nofoto. Snapping her fingers at each in turn, she froze them. She turned back to Niamh with a smile. "You always underestimate me. It's the curse of the cré-witches." She wrinkled her nose in a way that might have been cute coming from anyone else. "But it works in my favor, so there's that."

Fiona gave Edana a shove. "Build that fire."

"Sod off," Edana hissed, but moved to comply.

The cluster of men around Warren parted and Niamh wanted to scream.

Blood streaming down his face, Warren crumpled to the floor.

"I don't like to take any chances with coimhdeacht," Rhiannon said as she cocked her head and studied Warren. "I never make the mistake of underestimating my enemy."

Niamh strained against Rhiannon's hold on her, the need to get to Warren screaming inside her.

"What's taking so long?" Fiona glowered at Edana.

Edana glared back as she threw an armful of dried wood on the fire. "You do it then."

It didn't make any sense to Niamh. She tried to slow her brain enough to think. Why were they building the fire? That was her element, the source of her strength.

Warren groaned and one of the men kicked him in the head.

Niamh screamed silently.

"He's fucking strong. Thought we had him out for the count." The man toed Warren's ribs. "He'll stay down now."

Niamh tried to reach Warren through their bond. The same nauseating nothingness blanketed their connection.

"Now, Niamh." Rhiannon strolled closer to her. "You're going to wake that cardinal point for me, like a good little witch."

Niamh's voice didn't work, and she couldn't shake her head in denial. At the same time, she didn't understand why Rhiannon wanted her to activate fire.

Rhiannon flipped her hair over her shoulder and shrugged. "I'd do it myself, but it won't respond to me."

Niamh's mind whirled. Rhiannon wanted to destroy the cardinal points. No way she was waking fire for the bitch, regardless.

Edana sashayed over to Warren. "I really must thank you for leading us right here." She crouched beside him and put a gun to his head. "We had fun, Warren, but I'd be just as happy to put a bullet in your brain." She threw Niamh a look vicious with triumph. "Unless pretty Niamh over there behaves herself."

Niamh reached through the bond, but the stifling darkness

made her want to vomit. He couldn't be dead. Edana wouldn't threaten to shoot a dead man, would she?

Blood seeped into the sand around him.

"Did he tell you what a naughty boy he's been?" Edana stared at Niamh with a gloating smile. "It was my pleasure to set a little tracking spell inside him." She winked. "And I can assure you it was his pleasure too."

"Christ!" Fiona drew her lips back in a snarl. "You're such a fucking stupid whore."

"She is a stupid whore." Rhiannon stepped closer to Niamh. Blood magic stench clawed at Niamh's nostrils, suffocating her. "But she has her uses. Your mighty coimhdeacht led us right to you. All we had to do was wait for you, and him right by your side, to find this place for us."

Niamh screamed down the bond for Warren.

Nothing.

Rhiannon leaned close enough to whisper in her ear, "He can't hear you." She drew away. "But it won't matter for much longer." She snapped her fingers at Fiona. "Bring her."

Fiona dragged Ulwazi forward.

Ulwazi's gaze blazed silent defiance. She met Niamh's stare, trying to tell her something.

"Now, Niamh." Rhiannon glanced over her shoulder. "I'm going to release you long enough for you to draw fire." She motioned Warren. "But I need to remind you what will happen if you try anything."

Edana grabbed a hank of Warren's hair and yanked his head back. She tapped his temple with the gun barrel. "Bang, bang. No more Warren."

She had no choice. Power pulsed around Niamh. Basil and strawberries clashed with blood magic stink. Everything in her shrieking against the action, she drew fire.

Flames leaped higher, painting eerie shadows on the cave walls.

"Good." Rhiannon beamed and stepped closer to Ulwazi. "More! I can sense how strong you are, Niamh. Give me more."

Goddess, forgive her! Stare on Warren, Niamh drew more. If she didn't do this, all of the could die. They might all die anyway, but as long as she had her power...

Fire coursed through her. Goddess, help them all.

Flames grew, leaping eight feet in the air.

"Delicious." Rhiannon closed on Ulwazi and drew in a deep, languorous breath. "I am going to need a bit more thrust." She pointed to Lerato and then Ulwazi. "Eenie, meenie—"

Niamh tried to reach Ulwazi, but she couldn't move.

Rhiannon laughed. "Just a little humor." She shrugged and pulled a knife from her pocket. "I was always going to go for the biggest charge."

She slit Ulwazi's throat.

Horror coursed through Niamh. She lost her connection with fire. Voicelessly, she bellowed her horror and her defiance.

Lerato's eyes widened as if she were screaming inside.

Throwing one hard look at Niamh, Ulwazi crumpled. Blood streamed from her neck, sinking into the arid, hungry dust.

"Give me fire, Niamh. Now!" Rhiannon sank her hands into Ulwazi's blood, drawing her putrid power into her like a macabre, bloated tick.

Warren's lids flickered.

Edana cocked her gun.

Niamh couldn't think. Panic and terror clouded her mind.

"I will have her kill him!" Rhiannon pointed at Edana. "And then we'll kill the women. One by one."

She didn't know what to do. Ulwazi had died for nothing, her faith in Niamh misplaced.

Warren couldn't die as well, nor Lerato or Nofoto.

Lerato's desperate gaze locked on Niamh, steadying her.

Niamh drew fire.

A shadow flickered in the darkness behind Warren.

Rhiannon pulsed with power as she stood.

A great wrenching scored through Niamh.

Rhiannon was dragging fire from her, using Ulwazi's blood to fuel her power.

Fire fought Rhiannon, but she was mastering it.

Rhiannon screamed, her face a grotesque rictus of agony and delight. "I will have fire."

The shadow lunged for Edana, slashing razor-sharp claws across her face.

Edana screamed, her hands flying to her face. Blood streamed down her neck, staining her shirt.

Fiona spun, eyes wide as the leopard leaped, taking her to the ground.

"No." Rhiannon whirled.

Fire snatched its freedom and flung itself back at Niamh and she snatched it.

The leopard snarled.

A gun fired, the blast deafening in the cave. Then more shots as the leopard closed on the group around Warren.

More gunfire, bursts of flame flickered from barrels.

Another cat entered the cavern. Its ear-shattering roar thundered against the rock.

Lions streamed through the dark.

Rhiannon spun on Niamh. Her power surged for fire, grappling for control of it.

She was so strong, stronger than anything Niamh could have imagined.

Niamh held on, finding some wellspring of strength in her. For all their sakes, for the sake of the Baile coven, for their lives, she needed to hang on.

Lerato's gaze screamed at Niamh. Do it! Do it now!

Niamh abandoned herself to fire. Fire raged through her. The blaze soared ten feet in the air, twenty feet. Screams and animal snarls and growls echoed off the rock.

And Niamh pulled more power. It spat and strained and snapped beneath her skin, growing hotter and hotter, roiling through her muscles.

Rhiannon's eyes grew huge, her face frozen in horror. "You'll kill us all."

And still Niamh drew more.

Her head throbbed. Her bones bellowed their protest.

Niamh used her fear, her fury, her desperation, and her need and hauled on fire.

An inferno swallowed Niamh, she couldn't control it, couldn't hold it. Her spine bowed, her body pulsed, strained to its limits as she bellowed aloud and through her mind, "Get down!"

Flame engulfed the cavern.

36

M aeve screamed as the power hit her. It yanked her out of sleep and left her panting in the aftermath. Lily and orange perfumed the air of her bedroom. So sweet, so long missed, she reached for her power.

The door flew open, and Roderick barreled through. He stopped short and blinked at her. "It's back?"

She nodded, crying now. "It's back."

"They did it." Looking shaken, Roderick walked to the bed and perched on the edge. "They fucking did it."

Yes, they had, and Maeve looked around her bedchamber. So many lost souls, so many witches drifting in the ether, waiting for her to send them from this plane. They crowded around her, their sadness and their need battering her.

"Maeve?" Roderick drew her into his lap, sheltering her. "Breathe."

"So many," she whispered.

"I know, love." He rocked her. "And you will grant them all their deserved rest."

And there, amongst the many faces, one who had never

lived at Baile but would enter the sacred grove with all the other witches. "Can you get Bronwyn for me?"

"Bronwyn?" Roderick drew back and met her gaze.

Maeve nodded. "There is one here who would speak to her before she goes."

"Roderick!" A wide-eyed Sinead stumbled through the door. "You better come. The kitchen is full of wolves."

SANDPAPER RASPED HIS CHEEK, and Warren pushed it away. His fingers met fur as a low growl penetrated his confusion. He blinked his eyes open.

Jade green eyes stared at him, unblinking and penetrating. He was face to face with a leopard.

Smoke filled his lungs and he coughed.

Fear lanced through him. "Niamh!"

"Over here." She sounded muffled, her voice weak.

The leopard blinked at him, then turned and loped toward Niamh.

From the other side of the charred, smoking remains of the fire, she pushed to all fours and then dropped to her bottom. She was untouched, dusty, but seemed well.

"Are you okay?" He stumbled toward her, his ears still ringing. He had to be sure she was unscathed.

She nodded and waved a hand in front of her face. "The fire didn't touch me."

"The others?" He scanned the cavern.

Lerato sat in the dust, her arms around a sobbing Nofoto. Beside them, Ulwazi's sightless eyes stared at the ceiling of the cavern. She looked oddly peaceful.

"I'm so sorry." Niamh crawled toward them. Tears streaked her dusty face. She gently closed Ulwazi's eyes. "I'm so, so sorry."

"She has joined the ancestors." Lerato's voice caught on a sob. "Her job here was done."

Niamh put her arms around both women, her head resting against Lerato's.

The leopard snarled and lowered its body as it neared the pack of lions.

A male lion growled back, drawing his lips from his massive canines.

The leopard slid around the pack and disappeared in the night.

The other cats joined their male and slunk away.

There was no sign of Rhiannon or those who had come with her.

Warren didn't need Niamh to confirm fire was active; he could sense it pulse through her. A huge pale pink stalactite striated by lines of red glistened from the center of the ceiling, seeming to pulse as it reached for its matching stalagmite beneath it.

The scientists who worked these caves would have questions in the morning, but that wasn't his problem. He had to get his witch safely home.

IN THE CAVERNS BENEATH BAILE, the soft chime of the fire crystals welcomed Maeve back. Alongside the awake blue of water crystals, they glowed and winked down at the gathered witches.

"Deidre's happy for you," Maeve told a softly weeping Bronwyn. "She's glad you're here, and she believes you'll be a wonderful mother."

Bronwyn burrowed closer to Alexander. "Tell her I miss her."

"She knows." Maeve smiled as she added the sigils to the cavern walls that would mark the life of the cré-witch Deidre.

Deidre had never even seen Baile, had lived her entire life not knowing an entire coven of women like her existed. Now she would enter the sacred grove with her sister witches and be amongst them for eternity. It would take Maeve months to scribe all her lost sisters to the cavern walls, and there would be little rest for her before she completed the task. Spirits of witches who had died in the years she'd been in stasis followed her day and night.

Maeve drew on fire, orange and lily rose up to meet her. Cavern walls shimmered into a blur, and she entered the grove.

Beneath her feet the ferns of before had disappeared to hard packed earth. Bare tree branches surrounded her where once a dense forest had loomed all around her. Gentle mist wove in dove gray tendrils about her feet.

A transparent figure floated toward her, as insubstantial as smoke. "Sister, you are come at last."

Bronwyn pressed her palms together and inclined her head. "Blessed be."

"Blessed be." The witch spirit copied her bow.

Maeve looked about her. "The sacred grove is much altered."

"Goddess has been gone from this place for so long." The figure flickered and almost disappeared but then grew more corporeal. "But she returns."

"There is much to be done," Maeve said. "I have countless questions that need answering."

The wraith gave a wan smile. "We will do what we can, but our power has grown so weak." She waned. "The danger is growing, sister, ever growing."

Alone once more in the sacred grove, Maeve looked around her. There, on one of the bare branches, a tiny bud provided the only sign of life. Where there was life, there was hope, though, and there was much work to be done.

Releasing her magic, Maeve stepped back into the real

world of the cavern and her new time. "Right." She clapped her hands. "Let's get to work."

The clock had chimed two in the morning when a new spirit joined the throng around her bedside and beckoned to Maeve.

Heart in her throat, she climbed out of bed and followed the spirit.

Mags stood beside the bed of ripped up paper and odd bits of fabric that Roz had gathered.

In the center, Roz lay in a fetal position, her breathing shallow, clinging to life by a tendril.

"It's her time." Tears streaked Mags's cheeks as she crouched beside Roz. She took Roz's hand in hers and gently chafed it.

"Niamh," Roz whispered. A wistful smile made her face beautiful. "Say goodbye for me."

Maeve bent beside Mags. "Of course, sister. You are ready?"

"I am ready." Roz nodded. "This world is not for me. I choose to fly with my brother in the sacred grove."

The owl's form flickered into Maeve's sight. "He's waiting for you."

"Tell Niamh I wanted it this way." Roz took her hand from Mags and reached for Maeve.

Mags gave a soft sob. "We'll tell her. She loved you so much."

"She has a huge heart." Roz squeezed Maeve's fingers. "And she has more strength and power than she knows. She will be the greatest of all of us."

"We'll miss you." Mags swiped at her wet cheeks.

"No." Roz shook her head. "I haven't been here for years, not really. Tell Niamh I wanted to stay in the bond with my brother." She looked at Maeve and nodded. "Now."

Maeve took Roz's life essence within her. Memories of Roz filled her mind, and she understood. Bonded with the owl, Roz had lived in a world so much kinder and simpler than the one they now faced. Roz had been free in a way none of them had understood. She had craved to stay free.

"Rest, sister." Maeve closed Roz's eyes. Roz's spirit joined the owl's and inside Maeve, they merged into one. "Their part in this circle is done."

37

Niamh stared around the kitchen at Baile, feeling strangely dislocated from the scene. Even knowing Roz was gone, Niamh still expected her to come flapping and hissing around the corner at any moment. She'd cried for hours when they'd told her Roz had passed, and her sisters and Warren had stayed with her until she grew calm.

Beside the stove, the heavily pregnant female wolf studied her with calm, amber eyes. According to Sinead, she had arrived the night Niamh had woken fire and the pregnant female had taken up residence in the kitchen.

Niamh's menagerie still kept well clear of the wolf, which meant the kitchen had become off limits for them.

Pack. The wolf blinked and laid her head on her paws. She had come to the castle to whelp, knowing her pups would be safer here.

"I don't get it." Alexander shook his head.

Roderick snorted. "What else is new."

"What Niamh is telling us doesn't make any sense." Alexander turned to Niamh. "She tried to force you to activate fire?"

"Yes." Niamh closed her eyes and breathed. The horror of that night lingered. The fear, and nearly losing Warren, and worst of all, Ulwazi's murder. The sangoma had waited her entire life for Niamh to wake fire and died before she had seen her purpose manifest.

As he took her hand and said, "It's over," Warren's caring warmed her from within

"No." Niamh shook her head. The power she'd sensed from Rhiannon terrified her. "If the leopard hadn't distracted her—"

"But it did." Warren squeezed her hand and pushed reassurance through the bond. "And we're here to tell the tale, and fire is active."

"Only one battle is over," Roderick said with an apologetic wince. "It looks like the war is getting bigger. Alexander is right—"

"Say what now?" Sinead gaped at him. "Did those words just come out of your mouth?"

Roderick forged on without a flicker of reaction. "If Rhiannon seeks to destroy the cardinal points, why would she risk Niamh activating one?"

"Unless we're making the wrong assumption." Bronwyn rested her chin on her hand. "We've assumed she wants to find them to destroy them."

Alexander frowned and sat back in his chair. "Her single greatest weakness is needing blood magic to draw magic from the elements. From that point of view, it makes sense that she tried to drag fire from Niamh. But the rest..."

"Any good campaigner would try first to strengthen their weakest point." Roderick also sat back with a frown. "Is there any way she could do that by activating the points?"

"I don't know." Alexander looked grim. "But she's been around long enough to discover a way to get it done if it exists."

Niamh tuned them out. They'd been discussing what had

happened since her return, chewing possible ramifications over again and again.

Not much had changed at Baile, and yet everything had. Able to access her full blessing, Niamh's connection with living creatures was a constantly humming cord. She had only to focus on one of the thousands of strands woven together into that cord to find an animal's awareness. Along with a greater connection had also come her growing awareness that her blessing had a higher purpose. Living creatures were hers to protect and guard. She would be their voice.

"Sinead," Alannah called from the stove. "Can you help me get dinner on the table?"

With a meaningful look at Roderick, Sinead stood and went to help her. "The big guy's getting hangry."

Thomas lingered beside Alannah. He whispered something in her ear that made her smile sweetly at him.

Sinead's jaw tightened as she watched them, but she picked up the cast iron dish and brought it to the table.

Vegetable curry. Niamh took an appreciative sniff. Alannah had made her favorite.

Roderick peered into the pot. "Where's the meat?"

"Here." Alannah put a platter of steak down in front of him. "Would I forget you?"

"Could we try?" Sinead swatted Roderick over the ear.

He grinned at her and winked. "You wouldn't want to."

The wolf's head came up and Warren took the largest steak and put it on a dish in front of her. She sniffed delicately and began eating.

Jack sat beside Warren, looking from one to the other of them, his quiet dark eyes taking everything in. He didn't ask many questions, but Niamh got the feeling he didn't need to. Those dark eyes of his didn't miss much.

Mags sat as far from Jack as possible, sneaking glances at him when she thought nobody was watching. He was a big man, bigger even than Roderick, with dark hair cropped so short he was almost bald. Not strictly handsome, but with a raw, craggy masculinity to his face that was dead sexy. Mags was a lucky girl. If she could ever get over herself enough to actually speak to the person she'd identified as her man.

Jack had joined them, but Roz was gone.

Warren met Niamh's gaze across the table and smiled. His empathy warmed her like a small flame in her chest. The bond was always there, a low-key presence that assured her she would never be alone.

Niamh had wanted to stay in Johannesburg for Ulwazi's funeral, but Lerato had joined Warren's objections and they'd flown home the next day. They'd left Lerato with an open invitation to Baile if she should ever need it. She didn't think Lerato would ever take them up on the offer, but Nofoto was another issue altogether. The girl's eyes had gleamed with the possibilities, and Goddess knew they could all benefit from learning from each other.

AFTER GIVING THE WOLF A PORTION, Warren helped himself and handed the steak to Jack on his right. It surprised him how comfortable Jack was at Baile already. It had taken Warren a trip to Africa and a near death encounter to finally get how much he belonged here, belonged here amongst his new brothers.

Something was going on with Roderick and Maeve. As ever, Roderick was tight as a vault about it, but the man was hair-trigger tense. Warren strongly suspected it had everything to do with the stifling sexual tension between them.

Alexander had an arm around Bronwyn, alternating between whispering in her ear and eating. Outwardly he looked relaxed, but he was worried, like they all were.

The new development with Rhiannon trying to get Niamh to awaken fire, the safety of Bronwyn's unborn babies, and even the tracking spell Edana had placed in Warren kept them on edge and restless. Bronwyn had checked Warren for Edana's tracking spell and found nothing, but that didn't mean it wasn't still there.

Mags cocked her head, and then grinned. "Oh lovely! She's here."

Roderick tensed moments before tires scrunched over the courtyard gravel. Alexander and Roderick called it the bailey, but the word wouldn't stick with him.

Warren got to his feet with the other two men. Baile grew stingier about who she would allow within her wards. The line of cars driving up and down the road as they tried to reach the castle carried on through most of the day. If Baile had let this person in, then they needed to take notice.

A battered Prius that he recognized well stopped beside the kitchen wall, and Debra climbed out. She looked around her before locating him in the doorway.

She stiffened, and her face tightened. "Warren."

"Debra." He added in a murmur to Roderick. "My ex-wife."

He had tried for three hours to explain divorce to Roderick and then given up. Roderick had kept insisting that once a woman was his, she was his and nothing would compel him to give that woman up. Then again, Roderick had chosen Maeve as his woman.

"What's she doing here?" Alexander brought him back to the moment.

Warren would like to know that himself.

The passenger door opened, and Taylor flung herself out. "Dad!"

She hurtled toward him, and Debra became white noise as Warren locked eyes on his little girl. Not so little anymore. She must have grown a foot since he'd last seen her, and her blond hair was longer. That was all he got to see before she leaped into his arms.

Warren caught Taylor to his chest and clamped his arms around her. His child. Goddess, how he'd missed her, and now she was here, squirming against his chest, trying to hug him and barrage him with questions all at the same time.

Where had he been? What was he doing here? Whose castle was this? Was there a dungeon?

Debra stood by her car, twisting her hands. "I need to talk to you." She glanced at the crowd around him. "Alone."

"Woman." Roderick folded his arms. "Speak your piece. There are no secrets amongst those of us at Baile."

Probably not the most subtle response, and not welcome, judging by the sour look on Debra's face.

He'd loved her once, and for that reason, he said to the others, "Can you take Taylor inside?"

Roderick didn't look inclined to agree, but Maeve touched his arm.

"We're having dinner." Niamh held her hand out to Taylor. "Do you like curry?"

"I love curry," Taylor lied, and blinked, dumbstruck by the kick in the teeth that was Niamh. He'd almost kissed her that night in the South African hotel. More and more, he wished he had. Next time, he wouldn't hesitate.

When they were alone, Debra lifted her chin and said, "It's about Adam and me."

"You're going to Australia." He walked closer to her. Since his return, he'd seen a lawyer, who had assured him she could help.

Debra took a step back. "Well, he is Australian."

"I worked that much out for myself." Warren's gut tightened. If she'd come here to tell him she was taking his daughter halfway across the world, then she needed to learn he would fight her. Warren deserved the right to be part of his girl's life. And he would be.

"The tickets are all booked." Debra raised her chin like a fighter expecting a hit.

Warren braced.

"Adam and me." Debra sniffed. "We're new, and we want the chance to grow things between us." She glared at him defiantly. "We deserve to grow things between us."

Warren didn't know that anyone deserved that much, but if they wanted their chance, it was fine with him. He cut line. "You're not taking Taylor with you to Australia. I'll fight you if you try."

"I have custody," she snapped.

He'd said what needed saying. "Is that why you're here?"

"No." She twisted her fingers. "I've been little more than a single mother for most of Taylor's life. You know it's true. You were never there."

Old ground, and he'd tried to make up for his past failures. He was no longer prepared to be punished for them.

"And now I have this chance for something for me." She glared at him as if daring him to disagree. "I deserve to be happy too."

"What are you saying?" Warren had done his share of rubber stamping Debra's statements. Not anymore.

"I'm saying that Adam and I want a chance to be together. Alone. Taylor doesn't like him, and they argue. A lot. Plus, he has children from a previous marriage and it's...complicated."

"How does that affect Taylor?" Concern for his girl tightened in his gut.

Debra made a face. "She's not happy. She doesn't want to come with us."

"Then she's not going with you."

Debra's eyes flashed angrily. "Bloody hell, Warren. Why do you always have to make things so difficult?"

Niamh reached through the bond, her concern like a beam of sunlight through the clouds. "She's my daughter, Debra. I love her, and I want what's best for her. I believe part of that is having me in her life."

"Pity you didn't think that before."

How many times could they do this dance? He resisted the bait and waited.

"Anyway, she's on school holiday now. For the next six weeks, actually." Debra took a deep breath. "We were wondering, Adam and I, if Taylor could stay here with you. Just until we—"

"Yes."

"We get settled." Debra's mouth kept moving, but he'd heard all he wanted to hear. "Only for the next six weeks and then—"

"Yes."

"I'll fly back and fetch her."

He had six weeks. Considering what had happened in the last six weeks of his life, he knew how much could change. "When?"

Debra motioned to the boot. "I have her things."

Joy buckled his knees and almost sent them driving into the dust. The missing puzzle piece of home clicked into place. "Taylor is okay with this?"

Debra gave a bitter chuckle. "It was her idea."

Home.

The rest of his conversation with Debra went by in a blur. He was almost too scared to believe as he watched as if from a distance as Taylor cried through saying goodbye to her mother.

As Debra drove out of Baile, he stood with his daughter pressed against his side, and they watched her leave.

He looked down at her and took her hand. "You all right?"

"Yes." Taylor sniffled and wiped her nose with her forearm. "I'll miss her, but I can call and FaceTime."

"Yes, you can." Roderick would have to speak to Baile about the no internet thing.

Taylor stared up at him. "Niamh is really pretty. Is she your girlfriend? You can tell me you know."

Niamh was more than pretty. She was beautiful, compelling, sexy, earthy, and addictive. "When I know, I'll let you know."

EPILOGUE

CRÉ-WITCH CHRONICLES

Taylor stared out the library window at the sea, which must be like a thousand feet below them. The castle perched like a big bird on the cliff edge, letting her see right to where the sea ended in the straight line of the horizon. Everyone knew the world was round, but seeing it like this, you could understand how olden days people thought it was flat.

So far, the library was her favorite place in Baile. She loved books, any kind of book, as long as it had more words than pictures.

The people who lived here were different in a way she couldn't explain but really wanted to know more about. Maeve was sweet and funny and looked like a Disney princess. Mags gave good hugs and Alannah cooked even better than her friend Brittany's mum. Bronwyn, with her American accent, knew all about the trendiest looks. Even Sinead, who had scared Taylor at first, could be huge fun, especially when she was getting in Roderick's face.

Roderick was kind, but in an offhand way, like he didn't

really know she was there. For an old guy, Alexander was hot, and Jack told the lamest dad jokes that made her laugh anyway.

She liked Niamh best. Niamh had this way of making you like her, and Taylor could tell Dad really liked her. He didn't say anything about it, but he did a lot of looking at Niamh and followed her around a lot.

She missed her mum, but Adam sucked. He did this thing like he was trying too hard and it bugged her.

Dad was happy here. He laughed more and smiled all the time. He'd even been teaching her how to use a bow and arrow. He'd gotten all tense when she'd asked about the swords, but she'd work on that. She rather liked the idea of swinging one of those huge swords around. Brittany would lose her mind when Taylor told her.

The wolf pushed the door open and slunk into the room. Along with all the other animals, they had a real-life wolf here.

The wolf stared at her, and Taylor got the feeling she wanted her to follow.

Standing, she walked closer to the wolf.

The wolf trotted out the door, stopped and glanced at her over her shoulder.

"Okay then," Taylor said as she followed.

The wolf went through the kitchen and into the bailey. Taylor had learned about castles in history, but she'd never thought she'd actually get to live in one. Baile was big, bigger than she could've imagined. Not big like a shopping center, where you got scared you might lose your way and not be able to find your mum again. That had happened to Taylor once when she was young. They had gone Christmas shopping, and one minute they were together, then Taylor had stopped to look at a pink sparkly skirt, and when she looked back Mum was gone. Mum had found her, but she still remembered that choking feeling.

The wolf went to an arched doorway in a stone wall and stopped and looked at her.

"I'm not allowed to go there." Dad had dropped that rule like a hammer.

The wolf blinked at her.

Wind gusted across the bailey, whipping her ponytail around her head. The door in the wall creaked and swung open.

The wolf loped through the doorway.

Taylor looked around her. The door had just opened. She hadn't done anything, and it was like the door had invited her to step through. True story.

On the other side of the door, a stone staircase twisted along the rock face and ended in a cave. There was no railing on the stairs, and she really didn't like the look of that, but a cave...

The wolf kept trotting down the stairs.

She could peep inside and then go back to the castle. Dad didn't need to know.

Heart thumping, she kept one hand on the rock as she made her way down. Rubber legs made her go much slower, and it seemed like forever before she reached the cave.

Taylor peeped inside the dark opening of the cave.

Like the walls were filled with millions of diamonds, the inside of the cave glowed.

"It's beautiful," she whispered, her hand finding the wolf's ruff.

And so much bigger than she would have guessed looking at the small opening in the rock from above. Should she maybe be scared? She wasn't, though, and she walked through the first cave and into another one.

"We must be deep under the mountain," Taylor said, trailing her fingers over the sparkling walls.

A ripple of light followed Taylor's fingers, like the stones reacted to her touch. The walls glowed. They really glowed. And it wasn't cold or wet like you would expect in a cave.

Amongst the shiny stones, bits of shell and duller stones made up beautiful patterns of swirls and spirals. "Do you think my dad knows about this?"

The wolf walked into yet another cave

"He must." Taylor stood in the center of the latest cave they had found, head back as she turned in a slow circle. "How could he live here and not know about this?"

That was a good question. If Dad hadn't told her about this place, was that because he didn't want her to know? Why wouldn't he want her to know? Unless it was dangerous. But even as she looked around for a source of potential danger, she knew there wasn't one. Like the castle, the cave knew her, welcomed her and wouldn't hurt her.

She entered another cave, the coolest cave by far. Light shone in there, because as fancy as the patterns on the wall were in other parts, in there, they were the fanciest. Patterns covered every inch of the walls and ceiling and gave off soft blue and red light. Taylor traced one of the patterns with her finger. A tingle shot up her arm. It nearly made her giggle.

A weird glow came from the coolest part of the cave, a pool of water right in the center formed by an underground stream that dribbled out of the rock at one end. Bigger than the local pool Mum took her to in the summer, the water twinkled green, like magic.

Except magic didn't exist.

Or did it? It wasn't so difficult to believe in magic in a place like this.

Once the idea was in her head, she couldn't shake it loose. So much about this place seemed strange, and she didn't have words for the persistent humming through her body. Like when you listened to music really loud, and it made your bones jangle.

If this place really was magic, then magic had made that stream and that pool.

Mum didn't like it when she went near water without her. She could swim, but Mum didn't think she swam well enough to be left alone. Maybe the pool was why Dad had told her not to come here.

Taylor crouched and trailed her fingertips through the water. "It's warm."

The wolf made a chuffing noise.

"I think it's a natural spring." She'd read that phrase on the back of a plastic water bottle Mum kept in the fridge. *Bottled at source. Natural Spring.* Perhaps they could bottle the water here. She put her finger to her lips. It tasted like any other kind of water.

Taylor shucked off her flip-flops and dipped a toe in the water. "I'm not going in," she said to the wolf. "Just my toe, and that doesn't count." She giggled and pushed her whole foot in. "It's lovely and it tickles."

The pool changed color from a bright green to a silvery green. Lightest in the center where she could see right down to the bottom.

Before she could talk herself out of it, she stood and walked into the pool.

Walked into the pool!

Mum would be so cross. Dad would lose it. She might well be grounded for the rest of her life.

She should get out, but she didn't want to. Water lapped against her thighs, warm and gentle.

"*Blessed.*" A woman's voice, so soft that she didn't seem to hear the sound with her ears. Taylor didn't know how or why, but she knew she could trust that voice. "*I have been waiting for you.*"

"I'm here," she said.

The lady's voice had a laugh in it, like she held it back. "*As am I.*"

It made her laugh without really knowing why.

"*In water are you offered to me, and in water, I accept you,*" said the lady.

Without having any idea why, and not having heard those words before, Taylor said, "In water do I offer myself, and in water do I serve."

❧

And there's more to come from
the Cré-Witches of Baile in Raised In Air,
#3 Cré-Witch Chronicles

❧

A COVEN DIVIDED.

As enemies gather in and around Baile castle, the cré-witches and their warrior guardians fight amongst themselves to tackle their uncertain future. Desperate and smarting from her failures, blood witch Rhiannon has a deadly new weapon at her disposal.

Coven seer, Mags, is caught in the maelstrom of her own mind, her grasp of past, present, and future blurring into a living nightmare. With Mags the only witch capable of activating air, can she hold onto her sanity long enough to activate her element and save herself and air magic?

A newcomer to Baile, Jack Langham has stumbled behind Baile's wards but with no clear understanding of his purpose there. A loner with a dark past, Jack may be the only fixed point in Mags's shifting reality.

The stakes have never been higher, and time is running out

for Mags and air magic, in this the third volume of the Cré-Witch Chronicles.

Chapter 1

Drip!

The cave opened in front of Mags. A cave she knew well in the landscape of her mind. The air smelled musty and damp. A strange, almost sweet aroma: earth, wood, and musk hovered at the stiletto edge of her ability to identify it.

Drip!

Dark flattened the rock to variegated shades of gray. She strained her eyes into the gloom to identify features, mentally check-boxing the familiar shapes. To the left, the sharper outcropping rising nearly twenty feet to midway up the wall. On her right, a haphazard scattering of fallen boulders like crumbs at a giant picnic. They meant something, those boulders.

Drip! Drip!

The something escaped her, and the more she peered at the strewn rocks, the more they remained merely lead-hued riddles. She knew this cave.

Drip! Drip! Plonk!

Mags braced for what came next, what always came next. Not water dripping, but blood. Spreading like charcoal stains over the dusty floor. Sweating from the rocks in bubbles that swelled full quivered a moment and then seeped down the rock.

Blood became obscenely, brilliantly red against all the monochrome around her. Blood snaked in rivulets down the rockface and crawled toward her bare feet.

Every instinct in her willed her feet to step back from the

encroaching scarlet, but she couldn't move. The blood was inescapable, tepid and tacky between her toes.

The earth-wood-musk-scented breeze ruffled her hair, pressing her linen skirt and blouse to her body. Blood licked at her ankles. Claggy wind against her skin, the smell now so strong it etched into her sense memory.

Then. Absolute stillness. Not even the beat of her heart.

Springing for all around her, skeins of gray and red silk wove through the cave. Like crazed worms, the silk threads wound over and through the rock, the blood, even the darkness itself. They worked faster, speeding to a frenzy of squirming, wriggling strands. Propelled by an unseen hand, the threads were woven into a static image, forcing her outside of it. Now she was standing beside a giant tapestry and watching it.

In the sharper ledge to her left, a figure appeared in the weave.

Alexander.

He blinked at her, and then as fast as the threads had created him, they unraveled him and the rockface reformed.

In a sickening twist, the vision imploded and vanished in a pop that left Mags blinking as reality reasserted itself in front of her.

She was standing beside her window in her bedroom. The land surrounding Baile spread beneath her in a gentle, verdant blanket, blurring into a powder blue sky littered with puffy clouds.

∾

Order Raised In Air

∾

For first dibs on news, deals, and giveaways, and so much more, join the @Home Collective

Or if Facebook is more your thing, join the Sarah Hegger Collective

Anything and everything you need to know on my website http://sarahhegger.com

ABOUT THE AUTHOR

Born British and raised in South Africa, Sarah Hegger suffers from an incurable case of wanderlust. Her match? A hot Canadian engineer, whose marriage proposal she accepted six short weeks after they first met. Together they've made homes in seven different cities across three different continents (and back again once or twice). If only it made her multilingual, but the best she can manage is idiosyncratic English, fluent Afrikaans, conversant Russian, pigeon Portuguese, even worse Zulu and enough French to get herself into trouble. Mimicking her globe trotting adventures, Sarah's career path began as a gainfully employed actress, drifted into public relations, settled a moment in advertising, and eventually took root in the fertile soil of her first love, writing. She also moonlights as a wife and mother. She currently lives in Ottawa, Canada, filling her empty nest with fur babies. Part footloose buccaneer, part quixotic observer of life, Sarah's restless heart is most content when reading or writing books.

PRAISE FOR SARAH HEGGER

Drove All Night

"The classic romance plot is elevated to a modern-day, wholly accessible real-life fairy tale with an excellent mix of romantic elements and spicy sensuality." Booklife Prize, Critic's Report

Positively Pippa

"This is the type of romance that makes readers fall in love not just with characters, but with authors as well." Kirkus Review (Starred Review)

"What begins as a simple second-chance romance quickly transforms into a beautiful, frank examination of love, family dynamics, and following one's dreams. Hegger's unflinching, candid portrayal of interpersonal and generational communication elevates the story to the sublime. Shunning clichés and contrived circumstances, she uses realistic, relatable situations to create a world that readers will want to visit time and again." Publisher's Weekly, Starred Review

"Hegger's utterly delightful first Ghost Falls contemporary is what other romance novels want to grow up to be." – Publisher's Weekly, Best Books of 2017

"The very talented Hegger kicks off an enjoyable new series set in the small Utah town of Ghost Falls. This charming and fun-filled book has everything from passion and humor to betrayal

and revenue." – Jill M Smith, RT Books Reviews 2017 –
Contemporary Love and Laughter Nominee

Becoming Bella
"Hegger excels at depicting familial relationships and
friendships of all kinds, including purely platonic friendships
between women and men. Tears, laughter, and a dollop of
suspense make a memorable story that readers will want to
revisit time and again." Publisher's Weekly, Starred Review

"...you have a terrific new romance that Hegger fans are going
to love. Don't miss out!" Jill M. Smith – RT Book Reviews

Blatantly Blythe
"Ms. Hegger has delivered another captivating read for this
series in this book that was packed with emotion..." Bec,
Bookmagic Review, Harlequin Junkie, HJ Recommends.

Nobody's Fool
"Hegger offers a breath of fresh air in the romance genre." –
Terri Dukes, RT Book Reviews

Nobody's Princess
"Hegger continues to live up to her rapidly growing reputation
for breathing fresh air into the romance genre." – Terri Dukes,
RT Book Reviews

"I have read the entire Willow Park Series. I have loved each of
the books ... Nobody's Princess is my favorite of all time."
Harlequin Junkie, Top Pick

ALSO BY SARAH HEGGER

Printed in Great Britain
by Amazon

82647168R00208